Novels of
The Dark Apostle
from E. C. Ambrose

ELISHA BARBER

ELISHA MAGUS

ELISHA REX

ELISHA REX

BOOK THREE OF

The Dark Apostle

E. C. AMBROSE

DAW BOOKS, INC.

DONALD A. WOLLHEIM, FOUNDER

375 Hudson Street, New York, NY 10014

ELIZABETH R. WOLLHEIM

SHEILA E. GILBERT

PUBLISHERS

www.dawbooks.com

First Printing, July 2015
1 2 3 4 5 6 7 8 9

DAW TRADEMARK REGISTERED
U.S. PAT. AND TM. OFF. AND FOREIGN COUNTRIES
—MARCA REGISTRADA
HECHO EN U.S.A.

PRINTED IN THE U.S.A.

ELISHA REX

"Lest perhaps by gazing at his face thou receive a seed of desire sown by the enemy and reap sheaves of corruption and ruin."

—St. Basil, *Renunciation of the Secular World*

Chapter 1

⬩

In the manor house on the Isle of Wight, where he had been exiled for too bloody long, Elisha sat hunched at a dining table cluttered with books, practicing skills that most of his friends learned when they were children. He carved a few painstaking letters, then cursed under his breath. He smoothed out his wax tablet and started over, squinting at the page his teacher prepared with questions he was to answer in the wax. That "o" should have been an "e." Elisha rubbed his temple. He was not meant for such labor.

Mordecai pushed back his chair, went to a chest, and pulled out a slim codex. "Here, try this instead." He slid it across the table.

Grateful, he dropped the stylus, stretched his hands, and opened the book. The pages held dense blocks of words alongside grotesque illustrations of people being tortured—tongues pulled by tongs, burns applied, racks of instruments not so different from his own medical tools, a woman bound to a stake, flames licking up around her. Elisha shuddered. "What is this thing?"

"An inquisitorial manual," Mordecai said drily. "Not merely to remind you of the consequences of our being discovered. There may be references among the testimony that would be of use in future confrontations with the necromancers."

"Do I really need to know this?"

"You tell me, Elisha. What will it take to survive the next time?"

Elisha thought of Morag, the least of his enemies, who had nearly slain him more than once, and Elisha's stomach curled. When Morag's master came, what then? When Elisha met another magus, or two, or three who knew death so much better than he? He had been eager to get out of here, to find his enemies, and do what—die more quickly this time?

Elisha's eyes fell upon a passage, and he painstakingly worked through the Latin. *"The Devil grants to witches a great influx of power upon dying, and thus the witch must either be dispatched quickly and without foreknowledge, or in such a manner that the flesh is ex—excoriated,"* he sounded out the word aloud, *"thus preventing the witch from mastering his diabolical aspect."*

"That is why witches are dunked—drowned—because the body's need to survive distracts the witch from any magic he or she might prepare," Mordecai said with a meaningful glance.

"When he asked me to leave his lodge and come here, Thomas told me a story about an old blind woman who lived in the chapel at the back—she was there when his wife and daughter were killed. When the townsfolk came, this woman was raving, covered in blood and holding a bloody bit of Alfleda's hair. They dunked her for a witch, but she got away."

"A magus, do you think?"

"Or a mancer, taking a talisman from the dead princess. Thomas said Alfleda had been so mutilated she could be identified only by her nightgown." He should never have pressed for information about a crime two years gone. Even the pursuit of the mancers should allow his friend, his king, to grieve in peace.

Elisha flipped a few pages of the text, through one appalling image after another, then he shoved the book away, recalling the discussion of how to kill him in order to secure Thomas's crown, and how narrowly he had avoided the stake. "This is what Brigit's always railing about; the laws about torture don't apply to witches."

"She is not always wrong." Mordecai regarded him evenly. "Still, it's a good thing she's not with the mancers."

"What makes you say that?"

"Still has the hanging rope, doesn't she? And maybe your hair from when the hangman cut it. If your enemies had those, only the ocean would stop them finding you."

Which was why they had come to Wight to begin with: the watery border that prevented Elisha from searching for his enemies prevented them from finding him as well. Elisha slumped into his seat. "Morag met her. At the grave. She came to mourn over me." He scrubbed his hands over his face, feeling the tendrils of Mordecai's concern.

"You did not mention this."

"It didn't seem important."

"Everything is important," said Mordecai carefully. "You still want to believe she would not hurt you."

"She won't—unless I get in her way. She wants justice for our people; it's hard to argue against that."

"Most of those people would not count a Jew among their number."

"They don't know any better."

Mordecai's presence felt infinitely deep and sad. "We have been trying to tell them a thousand years and more, Elisha." For a moment, it seemed the shades of his slaughtered family hovered near. "Does she fight for freedom, or for the chance to be the new oppressor?"

A knock at the door gave Elisha the excuse to break

away. If Morag had communicated about Brigit to any of the others; if they learned what she was capable of, how could Elisha stop them?

Mordecai conversed with the woman in the passage beyond, and returned unrolling a cloth bundle with a couple of books and a folded parchment.

"A letter for you." Mordecai offered the parchment, dangling a ribbon with a red wax seal bearing the stamp of the king's ring, Elisha's false name written out in Thomas's clear, careful hand.

With the back of his Damascene knife, Elisha broke the seal and opened it. His lips moved along with his finger as he found the letters, the words, the spaces which showed where one thing ended and another began.

My dear Elisha,

I hardly know how to address you. How long should my greeting be? In comparative rank, my titles should cover the page. We are not companions of rank or kinship, except in the kinship of battle.

Allow me to apologize for my anger on the day we parted. You sought only the knowledge of our enemies, the better to fight them, but the death of a child, especially in such a brutal manner, can drive a man near to madness. When I came to the lodge to confront you, I felt you had betrayed me in turning your funeral into a circus, then took this mockery yet further in opening up the past. Of course, you needed to know about the princesses, the better to pursue our enemies, and I hope that you can forgive my reaction. With all you have done for me, I should have more trust. Trust is not an easy thing for either of us, I warrant.

While I should have liked for you to remain close by, being reminded of the terrible events at the lodge has made me ever more determined to keep those I care for far from the perils of the crown.

In happier news, I believe that Rosie is already with child.

Though she does not wish me to suspect until the pregnancy is well along, I have seen the signs before. Also, she manifests the skills of the magi now, because of it. I wish that you could be here for the birth. She has her mother and a flock of ladies more flattering than useful, I fear.

There has been no further incident regarding our enemies. I wonder now if they spoke so broadly about their conquests merely to impress my brother with their power when, in fact, they have little. In any case, their absence is a relief. The Londoners remain restless in spite of my lifting my father's poll tax. There have been riots in London over your death, and, when the priests raised your coffin to find it empty—well, it has made the rumors fly. The clergy are hunting for you, while the peasants are making of you a new saint. Why did they not support you in your life, I want to ask. Some of the barons urge action against them and I must intercede for patience and mercy. Truly, if I were to take up again the Scottish cause or to make war in France, I think that Gloucester and a few others would take arms against our own people in my absence. Over my protest, the bishop of London has summoned a papal legate to investigate the rumors surrounding your death, and the mayor fears outright revolt. It is hard to know how I shall gather all these forces once more beneath the crown. I pray that distance shall keep you safe— and keep me from your condemnation. A king cannot always afford to be merciful.

In the hopes of placating his allies, I have held a funeral for my brother. I think there is no need for his treachery to be broadcast, though Dunbury has had some misgivings.

I trust your own work goes well, and I am sorry I have no better for you. I would I could be there to feel the breeze off of the ocean, for London is a very nest of vipers. This is a land in need of healers, and I have exiled my best.

Yours,
Thomas

And after that, the word, "Rex" with a line drawn through it, as if the writer had thought better of it.

It took Elisha a long time to puzzle through the words, even with all the care that Thomas had taken in forming his letters. Alaric buried, Rosalynn pregnant, Thomas trapped in a nest of vipers, and Elisha far away and helpless. He shoved back from the table. "I'm leaving."

Mordecai's head snapped up from his new books, his eyes flaring. "What news?"

With a calming gesture, Elisha said, "For a walk, that's all."

He stalked down the passage and out into the twilight. Most times, he crossed the manor's dry moat and headed for town, to market or to listen to a passing bard. Today, he turned away from people and moved steadily upward, crossing a stile. His attunement was instant after the last several weeks of practice: He knew these trees and stones and sheep. He cast his deflection, using the Law of Opposites to project a sense of his own absence, thick and complete, and the sheep did not even stir as he passed nor the crows fly from their trees to keep an eye on him. Lucky the mancers didn't know about the crow woman, either—her searching messengers were not blocked by water. Mist rolled along the rills and valleys, enveloping him, and letting him pass to the other side.

It had not been the king's intent to make him restless. Thomas fell prey to the assumptions of the rich: the princes' boyhood would have been taken up with tutors, their manhood with writs and courts and training. Either Thomas imagined Elisha would enjoy that life, or merely that it would make for a pleasant change from battle. Instead, his eyes felt dry, his head ached, his shoulders hunched from too long at the table. Even the lessons in sorcery became rote with repetition, and there was no hint of threat, in spite of their fears. He might live for decades here without ever meeting another mancer.

But he did not believe the mancers had abandoned their fight for the throne—they had spent too long in search of it. To Elisha, it seemed only a piece of an even larger plan. Elisha slipped his hand into his pouch and touched the lock of Thomas's hair he always carried, but it held no warmth and gave him no sense of the man as it used to do. The water, perhaps, or the distance between them, prevented his awareness.

He came beneath the trees, to the great elm where crows congregated, cackling with unpleasant glee. The sensation caused Elisha a moment's pause. Nothing made crows happy but a corpse-strewn battlefield, or the promise of it. Focusing his awareness, he reached up toward the birds. A few of them fluttered and ruffled their feathers. Something fell, tinkling as it tapped the branches on the way down until it landed a few feet away.

Elisha picked it up: a low-relief lead badge, like the ones given out to pilgrims at the shrine of St. Thomas in Canterbury. He made out the image of a man on horseback, an unkempt man reaching up toward him. The horseman had his sword in hand, using it to sever his rich cloak: St. Martin of Tours, one of the patrons of France. The image made him think of the French magus who had died in his arms—and it also decorated the sign that hung over Martin Draper's shop in London. Martin, another friend he could not see again. Elisha tried to shake off his melancholia, rubbing his fingers over the medal. A French saint, on English soil. Interesting.

A few crows hopped lower, peering at him from the branches and from other nearby trees.

"What do you want?" he asked them aloud, their black eyes and sharp beaks reminding him of his burial day.

They tipped their heads, bobbed and croaked, then one of them swooped at him. "Shit!" he yelped, dodging the blow. He covered his head, cloaking himself in an instinctive deflection, but the crows already knew he was there and could not be deflected.

They swooped down, diving at him, and more of their treasures pinged his arms and head. St. Martin of Tours rained to the ground around him, along with a few others. So many? A handful of French medals, he could imagine, would be found around here, but a hundred? He scooped up a few and ran.

Thankfully, the crows did not want to fly far at night, and contented themselves with shrieking bird insults at his back and collecting their stolen trinkets from the ground.

Torches burned before the manor house, awaiting his return, but three horses stood in the yard, and Elisha hesitated. They'd never before had visitors, yet he sensed no great distress from Mordecai—and found a familiar presence along with him. He stepped up to the door and ducked inside. Three armed men stood in the dining hall, with Mordecai still seated before them.

"Good Lord, you are alive!" said Lord Robert, one of Duke Randall of Dunbury's companions. Robert's expression moved from dismay, to delight, to anger—a frown that looked out of place on his pleasant, oval face.

"Sorry, my lord, I'm sure you know why it had to be secret."

"Absolutely." Robert thrust out his hand and clasped Elisha's. "Hate to be the last to know—but I'm certainly glad of the truth! By the Cross, that funeral was dreadful to see."

"If you've come to berate me for my death, the king's done that a month ago."

"The king—that's what I've come to you about." Robert took a breath. "The king's vanished, Elisha, and Queen Rosalynn with him. They're gone."

Chapter 2

⬧

The air left the room. Then Elisha said softly what he already felt. "I know."

"What? How?"

He darted a glance at Mordecai. "I have a talisman of the king. It gives me a sense of him, though lately it gives me nothing. I thought it might be the distance, or the water." He dropped the handful of badges on the table where they chinked together and dully gleamed.

Robert nodded quickly, but his lips set, and his eyes looked haunted.

Prodding the badges with his finger, Elisha steeled himself to ask the next question. "Do you have reason to think they are dead?"

"It's hard to say." Robert made a motion with his hand that brought a man-at-arms to refill the mug at his elbow. He took a long swallow before he spoke again. "They were summoned by a messenger to a private meeting at a house outside the city. Their men waited by the door, but they didn't return. There was some blood, but not much of it, and no signs of struggle. We found a concealed tunnel, but it emerges near a busy market—seems unlikely anyone could've been smuggled through there, but somebody's done it. This was nine days ago."

Mordecai carefully closed his book, his dark, watery gaze meeting Elisha's. If they were right, the mancers had no need for smuggling and certainly not through public places: they had another, much darker means of travel.

"The Duchess says none of the blood is her daughter's. But there's plenty of ways to . . . to die." Robert sighed, then said, "There's more."

More? Nine days gone, and Elisha only now found out. When had Thomas sent his letter? He wanted a chair, but forced his legs to support him.

"Gloucester and the mayor took things a bit far. The duke and duchess were up in Lincoln and had to race back when they heard. Meantime, Gloucester started making arrests, thinking your supporters have taken them as retribution for your execution."

Elisha's fists clenched. "I'm sorry," he whispered to no one.

"More likely it was one of the barons with French connections, taking advantage of the recent fighting, thinking to place one of Edward Longshank's French bastards on the throne."

"I think the French are massing boats." Elisha gestured at the pile of badges, sifting out Saints Brendan and Nicholas, both protectors of sailors. "The crows have been collecting these. There's a woman who speaks to crows; I think she sent them to warn us."

"Damnation." Robert slammed down his mug, then took a deep breath, shaking his head.

The threat from France was all Elisha could ask Robert to bear. He would not mention sorcery until he could speak with the duke and duchess, preferably behind closed doors.

After a moment, Robert composed himself and went on, "Nobody's asked for ransom or come to claim the throne. It's as if whoever's got them only wants to see the kingdom in flames. God knows London will be—if it's not already." Robert scrubbed a hand over his chin. "The citizens expelled Gloucester and the mayor both and barred the gates. The duke's convinced that his daughter and the king are inside the city." He took a gulp of air. "Buried there. He's gone half-mad with grief, Elisha. I pray you can help him."

The words stung, but Elisha steeled himself to take his part. "Does he want me to arrive as a man or as a miracle?"

"The inquisitor's already there, Elisha. Bishop of London is playing host."

Elisha's shoulders tightened at the thought of facing the church's investigation, but his king, his friend, needed him. "Then we'll let them sort that out."

Mordecai drew his book toward him—hiding behind the knowledge it represented. "Housekeeper's getting supper. We can leave after that," he said carefully.

In a few steps, Elisha pulled up a stool to sit beside him. "Stay here, Mordecai. At least for now."

"You will need help."

"You know what'll happen if the inquisition hears about a sorcerous abduction and finds you." A shock of fear escaped the surgeon's controlled presence, and Elisha touched his shoulder, solidifying the connection they already shared. "There will be a time for your help."

After a moment, Mordecai gave a nod. "I'll stay. For now."

The housekeeper entered, followed by the other servants carrying bowls, bread, and a steaming pot. The meal was brief and mostly silent, Elisha impatient to return across the water. Thomas and Rosalynn might be held by French agents, to be sure, or their skins might already be dangling in shreds from a mancer's belt. Elisha shoved his bowl away, anger and need swelling through him.

"Your things—?" Robert suggested.

"I have nothing but what Thomas has given me."

They rose and moved toward the door, the men-at-arms going ahead to see to the horses. Robert paused beside Elisha, dropping his voice to a whisper. "Do you know about Rosie?" he asked.

"The baby?" Elisha nodded. "I had a letter from Thomas today."

"He must have written it just before. . . Holy Rood, Elisha, what a damnable mess."

"We'll find them, one way or another."

"The duke'd want you to go for Rosie, but we need you in London, even if she's not there. He thinks the peasants'll listen to you. If the siege of London lasts, it'll be civil war, on top of the French fleet's arrival. The king and queen will have nothing to return to."

They rode hard through the night over the hump of the island to wake a captain whose boat carried them across the Solent. The next day, they kept their pace across the New Forest and out toward the city.

From a few miles outside London, they spotted smoke curling into the wind. Robert and Elisha shared a look, their horses dancing against the sudden tightening of the reins. Tents clustered on the outskirts of the city, and a column of smoke darkened the dull sky. "Good God," Elisha growled, "Do they mean to burn the city down?"

"Let's hope not!" Robert led the way down another side road and up to the crenelated grandeur of the Inns of Court, normally occupied by ranks of barristers. Today men in the colors of Dunbury stood to stiff attention at his approach. Both men slid down from their mounts and left them to the guards at the door as they went inside. Their eyes followed Elisha, the awareness of their interest shivering along his extended senses.

"—must be some way. We need those bombards, for intimidation at least, even if they're never fired."

"Yes, Your Grace, but—"

"I don't need another of your excuses, man, get the damned work done, would you?"

Elisha froze in the low corridor, listening to the thunder of Duke Randall's voice. It rang with grief and fear. Once before, this duke had gone to battle for his daughter, when she was spurned by the king's son, but he had done it with resignation and honor, never fury, and for that he had earned Elisha's loyalty. Robert had described him as half-mad—what might it take to push him the rest of the way?

"Your Grace." Robert's heels set together as he gave a brief bow.

"Robert." The duke, shorter by a head, clapped Robert's shoulder. "You've brought him, then? Tell me you've got him, or we're truly lost."

These words stabbed at Elisha. If the cause were so desperate as to depend on him, they were already lost.

"Yes, Your Grace, but he's also brought confirmation the French are massing."

"Saints preserve us," the duke sighed as he turned, then his round face flushed with relief. "Thank God, Elisha, thank God. Come in! You,"—this to the mail-clad fellow who lurked by the windows—"be off and about your business."

"Yes, Your Grace." He bobbed a slight bow, shutting the door as he went.

"Elisha," said the duke, "take a seat. Can we get you ale or wine?"

Shaking his head, Elisha said, "It's not a visit, Your Grace. Tell me what's happened—where are the fires?"

Losing his tremulous smile, Duke Randall regarded him from sunken eyes, rubbing his palm over the bald patch that topped his head like a monk's tonsure. "At least four parishes are in flames. We've got a man up the church tower. As far north as All Hallow's, East to Saint Andrews and West to Saint Mary's. South, it's nearly to Thames Street, Dyer's Hall."

"Damn it." Where the warehouses backed up to the river hung a sign with a cloak upon it—the symbol of St. Martin, the namesake of his friend. "Where's Martin Draper?"

Already shrunken in his coat of mail, the duke sagged further. "Still inside the walls."

At that, Elisha dropped into the chair, thinking of Martin, who once gave him a strip of cloth that saved his life. "What can we do?"

The duke turned away and stood before the fire. "It's all gone so terribly wrong. From the moment that thrice-cursed Alaric denounced my Rosie, I've felt as if I entered the gates of Hell."

Elisha considered the duke as a frightened father, trying to hold a kingdom together, not knowing if his daughter lived or died. "I can search for them, Your Grace."

Randall's head fell, his voice rough. "Even if you find them, Elisha, it would be too late. The French army will sweep in and find us at the ruins of a burned-out city."

"I won't countenance that sort of talk, Your Grace," said Robert, slicing the air with his hand. "If anyone can put this to rights, it'll be the two of you."

Dropping heavily back into his chair, Duke Randall began, "We need to get inside the walls, preferably without damaging them. With luck and the Lord's blessing, we can re-take the city before the French supporters can muster for their cause. We don't know if Thomas and Rosie are in there, and we've tried everything we could to find out—you don't want to see how exhausted Allyson's become with her searching."

Elisha wanted the chance to make a search of his own, but in the triage of these dread events, the fire was more urgent.

The duke drew a deep breath, and pressed his hands between his knees. "Ludgate's held by a group calling themselves the Brothers of Saint Barber. They've released the prisoners held there, and barred the gate itself. When they know who you are, Elisha, they'll let you through."

Elisha might have laughed if it weren't so deadly serious. "They think I'm dead, executed by the king; that's what set this all in motion."

"That's where the lies come in." He held up his palms to forestall argument. "I know you're not in favor of twisting the truth, but I'll wager my castle those people won't believe the truth, and we'd rather the barons didn't hear it, either. The king's cozy with the man who killed his father? No, besides, we want to lift the taint of sorcery as much as possible, or they'll likely deny you, as well."

Elisha held his tongue. The city was burning, maybe Martin along with it. Thomas was gone — it wasn't a time to stand on principles.

"Good," said the duke, shifting in his seat. "The story is this: that I, who benefited from the death of King Hugh, took exception to Thomas's justice against you and smuggled you out of the grave, hoping the new king would believe you dead. Now, wanting to placate the peasants, I produce you from hiding as a sign that I'm willing to do whatever it takes to appease them, but that canonizing you would be premature."

"But your daughter is married to the king. I'd think that changes your motives."

Randall smiled grimly. "So my family gains a royal wedding without actually giving you up. It's the kind of duplicity they expect from nobility, isn't it?"

"Aye, there is that," Elisha had to admit. "It could work, if they trust me."

"They want you for a saint, of course they trust you. Sending my best man to fetch you, plus the secrecy surrounding your arrival, will lend the proper intrigue. It should be enough to get you through the gates and find out if they've got the king. He is still God's Anointed. I don't know that they would dare to hurt him. And if they had killed him, they'd want us to know it."

Elisha breathed in the mingle of emotions along with the wood smoke. "You don't believe they have the king, do you?"

"To be true? Not anymore. For the same reason, that they would want us to know it, they'd demand a ransom or make some threats. The king is a lot more valuable than that blasted city, and they know it." The duke straightened. "I'll give you men to protect you in case the citizens get rowdy."

"If they think you're coercing me, they will get rowdy. No, I think. . ." His mind flashed back to the tents on the outskirts and the banners that flew among them. "There's a band of mercenaries who fight under a man called Madoc. Give me a few of them, if they'll come."

"As you will." Robert gave a short bow and headed for the door.

When he returned, Elisha went out to meet his guard. Poor and ragged, six men stood in the street outside, warily eying the duke's guards in their fine, matching tabards. A young man, much taller than Elisha recalled, gawked at him. "It's you! You're alive!"

Madoc, a stocky man with a full, black beard, stomped forward, sniffing at the air. At the battle of Dunbury, it was he who ordered Elisha to pretend death in order to stay back and help the wounded. Now the mercenary narrowed his eyes. "It's some new witchery, eh? That man was buried alive—some of us turned out to watch."

"No witchery, Madoc," Elisha said, striving for a reassuring tone, but Madoc put up his hands in a boxing stance, and Elisha hesitated.

"It is him," the youth insisted again, carrying a pike now instead of the banner he had guarded on the battlefield of Dunbury. "I'd know him, I tell you. And that man's the one that tried to kill him at Dunbury, when the duke's men tried a sortie. If I hadn't've guided the king's men to find him, for sure yon Robert would've had his head off! Praise God the bombardelle missed him."

"We were trying to save his neck from that charge of treason, you little fool," Robert burst in. "If you hadn't brought the soldiers, they'd never have had him hanged, would they?"

The youth went a little pale and ducked his head.

"Robert," Elisha said. "Let me handle this."

Grumbling, Robert backed away, but he did not leave the street, and Elisha sighed. Taking a few steps forward, despite Madoc's gestures against evil, Elisha set his hand on the young man's arm. The banner-bearer's eyes widened, but he stayed his ground as Elisha said, "You saved my life when the bombards fired, who else would know that but us?"

"Aye," the lad whispered.

"That's why I remembered you now, all of you," he added, turning toward Madoc.

"If it is you, Barber, by God, how'd you live through?"

"The Duke of Dunbury is in my debt as well, for my saving his friend, the Earl of Blackmere; for his castle; and for his own life. He arranged for my escape."

Crossing his arms, Madoc growled, "It was a mad execution with lightning and thunder. More sorcery, I figure."

"Figure what you like, but I am Elisha Barber, and I need your help. I'm to convince the people holding the wall to let me in and hear me out before they burn down the city, right? The Duke thinks they might listen to me, since I'm the one who started all of this."

"You're not a saint."

"I'd have to be dead for that, Madoc."

"Whatever's become of the latest king—did you do it?"

Elisha met the black eyes. "I swear by every saint ever martyred I had no part in it."

Something softened in the man's stance. "Had to ask, didn't I? After all, he put you in a box."

Elisha's jaw clenched. "He had no choice."

"Naw, I suppose not, given what happened to his Da."

"And from what I hear, he's been a good king. Lifted the poll tax, right? And he didn't take the excuse of the riots to kill everyone who came to my funeral." Elisha wet his lips. "I might even rather like him, if I got to know him."

" 'e's not bad so far, I'll grant you." Madoc tucked his thumbs into his thick belt, and gave that sudden grin like a spark into dry-brush. "We'll come along. After all, whatever else you may do, Elisha Barber, you do put on a good show."

The little party passed along Fleetstreet toward Ludgate, crossing the dank and reeking gully of the River Fleet. Shuttered court buildings and the barricades before the Whitefriar's and Blackfriar's monasteries revealed the terror of their inhabitants in spite of their strong walls. When they came in view of the gate, one of the figures atop the wall shouted down, "I'd be stopping there if I was you."

Obediently, Elisha froze, and his bodyguard shuffled to a halt around him. He took one more step to stand out from his guardians and peered up at the distant figures. A dozen arrow tips aimed at him from the rampart, ready to shoot him down. "My name's Elisha Barber, and I need to talk to whoever's in command."

"There ain't no Elisha Barber. Bloody King Thomas's had him buried to die!"

Elisha forced himself to relax. From here on, Thomas was the enemy, in spite of every instinct of his heart. "He tried," Elisha called back, "but he's failed, 'cause here I am."

"If you're having a joke with me, I'm not laughing. Elisha Barber saved a lot of lives hereabouts, and we won't settle for a sweet-tongued liar."

"There's got to be somebody inside who'd know you," Madoc pointed out. "The way that you proved it to us."

There was one. Elisha glanced north to where the spire of St. Bartholomew's pierced the billows of smoke. What was he afraid of, after all? He and his brother's widow had parted on terms as good as could be, though she blamed him for the deaths of her baby and husband both. Still, not as much as he blamed himself. Elisha swallowed the lump in his throat and shouted, "My brother's widow Helena would bear me witness."

The man leaned over the wall to get a better view. "Nathaniel Tinsmith's widow? She's down 'ere trying to convince us the barber's no saint."

"She cursed me on the day I left for war. Have her tell you the curse."

"I'm on that, I am!" the man bellowed back, then he moved away and returned in a few moments. "All right, Barber, if that's what you claim, what's the curse?"

"She cursed me to love and to lose my love."

"It's him." A woman's voice rang with wonder.

"Go to the door," hollered one of the men.

"Who's that with you?" another demanded. "King's men or the mayor's?"

Madoc yanked his broadsword from its sheath and brandished it to the heavens. "Our own men!" he roared, and his men hooted their assent, to the amusement of those above.

One hand resting on his medical pouch, Elisha walked toward the smaller door cut into the gate. A panel slid aside and suspicious eyes glanced left and right, then the door swung in, and he stepped through, followed by his personal guard. From another door in the gate tower's stone wall came a trio of men, and one woman, a large piece of cloth binding a bundle to her chest. From inside came the squeal of a contented infant.

Elisha's knees went suddenly weak, and Madoc caught his elbow. "Steady on, there."

"Aye, thank you." His brother's widow once lived as a whore in one of the brothels he tended as a barber and yet she looked more beautiful now than she ever had before, her face alight with the happiness of her faith, and her new calling.

"You needn't have come," he said. "I'm sure you'd rather not—"

Helena came to meet him, her approach revealing the happy, misshapen face of the orphan she carried. "If the Lord has forgiven you, then so have I." In spite of her words, she looked doubtful.

"Thank you," he said. "Have you heard any rumors of the king?" Elisha scanned the scene around him as he spoke, both for information, and distraction.

"Only that he's vanished, and the queen with him," she replied.

One of the men stepped up quickly. "We reckon he scarpered to avoid our wrath. If we got our hands on him, we'd serve him right! What he's done to you was just the last straw!"

Frowning, Elisha pointed out, "He's only been the king for a matter of weeks."

"Aye, but it's high time the nobs started paying us some mind. We're paying their bloody taxes, fighting their bloody wars, then there's a drought or a freeze, and we're the ones who starve for it. You've seen it, haven't you? Sure you have, tending the sick and all. We're the ones suffering, and we're asking for our say, now."

Indeed, Elisha had seen it, the way doctors and surgeons avoided hospitals full of the poor, the way even Duke Randall dismissed them out of hand. And yet he knew the other side as well, for Thomas would bury his best friend alive rather than allow his people to be plunged again into war. Elisha tried to imagine what Thomas would do. "Aye, I've seen enough of trouble to last me a while, but burning the city's no way to cure what ails us."

The breeze shifted, carrying an acrid wash of smoke, and the baby coughed then started to wail. The smoke blew hot against his skin, with a tingle that caught him unawares, then burst into a flare of agony. Elisha cried out, slapping his arm as if to put out the flames.

Bouncing the baby, Helena started at his cry. "What's the matter?"

"It's the smoke." His eyes teared as panic struck through him.

"We'll get inside, out of the wind." She reached for his elbow, but he stood fast.

"I can't, not until the fires are out." The smoke touched him again, trailing fingers of pain that encircled his ankles, then a haze that struck him blind, his skull throbbing. He knew in an instant that it wasn't his own, not his memory, nor his pain. The heat of the smoke twisted down his scarred throat and brought with it an edge of cold that he knew all too well. "Oh, God."

Flinging off the supporting hand, Elisha ran headlong into the smoke, scattering the crowd that gathered to see him, abandoning his bodyguard and his questioners. He ran for the Dyer's Hall praying under his breath that he would not be too late.

Chapter 3

❖

As Elisha sped through the streets, dodging rubble and leaping ditches, he breathed the terrible smoke. Drawing upon the strength of his talisman of King Thomas's hair, he sent his anger out before him. A thing without substance except to another witch, it still silenced the rowdy revolutionaries and sent them stumbling out of his way, crying out and crossing themselves. They shouted in his wake, caught up in the emotions. Without contact, he had only enough power to send those shivers down their backs, but it was enough—just as once, from his premature grave, he had made his howl of injustice felt: the moment that had led to all of this.

Flames danced against the far horizon, between St. Paul's and the Tower, consuming the houses of rich and poor alike. Bells rang in the church towers as priests sounded their needless alarm—the orange glow and hovering pall of smoke were enough to signal the ruin that approached them. To one side far ahead, he could hear the chant of a fire brigade, a group of desperate neighbors trying to beat back the flames from their own homes. For a moment, the voices gave him hope, then they burst into screams as the fire spread beyond them. The leaning upper stories, nearly touching across the streets, provided avenues for fire to race overhead even as those who fought it hauled up their water buckets. Other streets echoed with shouting and cheers as a fine house crackled into flame, and arsonists broke doors open to steal things that wouldn't be missed in the heap of cinders that would remain.

Heat flowed from his left-hand side as flames crept down the wood-and-plaster facades. The fire spread in a crackling march, ever closer. Right in front of them, a trio of men, hooded and armed, smashed open the panels of a shop front and leapt inside, one of them pausing to glare back at Elisha. Elisha had no time for petty burglary. A stone wall groaned ominously, its mortar cracking with the heat, and Elisha dodged further south along an alley, across a churchyard, and out the other side.

He ran down the muddy streets and around the corner into Thames Street, with its warehouses backed up to the river that brought these wealthy men their stock. Smoke billowed from the tall houses, their proud glass windows smashed while a hollering mass of citizens clogged the street. A backdrop of flames obscured the sky beyond them. Ahead, unseen among the press of people, someone screamed, and others called out to the Lord, prayers shouted over the din, recognized more by rhythm than words.

Glass ground beneath his feet, glittering shards disappearing into the muck. Here and there, torn scraps of cloth, ruined pottery, and a scatter of spices marked where the mob fought over the fine things they could not afford, taking what they could beneath the cover of chaos. The destruction choked him nearly as much as the smoke that turned his stomach.

At last, he burst through into the cleared space before the burning buildings and confirmed what he already knew. Flames licked out the windows of Martin Draper's house, blackening the plaster and warping the empty wooden frames. Houses to both sides burned as well. The blaze began blocks from here, and he had no idea how it would end aside from badly.

It was all well and good to enter the city, but what the Hell could he do now? Use the river somehow? What magic could end this inferno?

A few dozen rowdy citizens ringed the fire, some of them holding back the well-dressed women who used to live there. One of the women screamed, a long wail that fell away into sobbing only to rise again as her captors shook and caressed her. A few bodies lay on the pavement, blood pooling around them.

Extending his senses, Elisha swept his touch among the dead, each a well of awful cold that reached up to him like a dog recognizing its master. He searched for the touch of agony that swirled in the smoke and called him here. A huddled figure on the outskirts yet lived, and Elisha started forward to help where he could and find a plan to save the rest.

He had gone two steps when he noticed the rope.

From the hands of three men standing to the side, a heavy rope stretched taut up and over the wrought-iron arm that once held Martin's sign. The other end of the rope hung straight, swaying slightly, and Elisha could not see it for the crowd before him.

Barely knowing he did so, he curled his fist, summoning the death all around him, calling home that terrible hound, whipping a cold wind that frosted the blood on the hands of the rioters, warning them back. Flame was not the only temper of a man.

Gawkers whirled and screamed. A few released their captives, letting loose the terrified wives and children to struggle with the corpses of their men. Others clung tighter, shielding themselves behind the innocent. The frigid brush of death showed upon their clothes, painted with blood—the indelible mark of the murderers.

Elisha found his voice, hoarse with the remnants of his humanity. "Stand aside."

They obeyed, knocking each other over in their rush. A few thought to escape, but the crowd had grown so thick around them that they had no place to go.

From the end of the rope a man dangled head downward, his hands scraping the pavement, his ankles and legs streaked with blood. They had stripped him to his hose, golden striped cloth garish with fresh crimson. From the waist bruises blackened his flesh, showing the shapes of the boots that made them. The right side of his ribcage looked distorted as he twisted slightly in the hot wind. Blood obscured his shattered face, trailing patterns of droplets and streams onto the ground. If it had not been for the hair—that dark, lustrous hair Elisha had trimmed so many times—the barber would never have recognized his friend.

A rising fury blasted away Elisha's caution. He sprang toward the flaming buildings and caught Martin's swinging body in his arms. Cradling the broken skull and crushed ribs against his chest, he faced the men who clung to the rope. One dropped it and fled, straight into the arms of the waiting crowd. The next looked ready to join him, but stopped as their leader spoke.

"Who the devil're you?" shouted the giant of a man at the head of the trio. Blood spattered his face and boots and, for a moment, Elisha mistook him for Morag, the dead necromancer.

Elisha raised his chin and forced back the numbness of his shock. "I am your death if you do not release him."

The man laughed with the overblown vigor of a drunk or a bully. "Can't very well take me down with a corpse in your hands." His large face crinkled with laughter, his big belly shaking with his shoulders.

Behind him, his companion mustered a grin and shouted, "Yeah!"

The power of death gathered in the pit of Elisha's stomach, a black and roiling mass longing for exercise. He drew breath, and death rose within him. It spread through his body like a frost, feathering his lungs and heart and flaring down into his fingertips and toes, chilling his nose and lips. His breath puffed out in a cloud of white against the roiling smoke. So close to, the fire should have warmed him, but even such heat could not reach him.

Martin's blood seeped through to Elisha's skin, slicking his hands. It sizzled, then froze against the brand upon his chest. Through the tingling of his spread-thin self, Elisha felt that blood. Every spatter marking the boots that had battered Martin, every streak that stained someone's clothes or marked the brooms and tools and sticks they carried, every stain that rimmed the features of the laughing man—each one cried out to Elisha with the touch of his friend. He focused his power on the man with the rope.

The laughing man hiccoughed, darted a glance to Elisha's still face, and grinned to the surrounding crowd as if to show he'd gotten the best of the stranger. Someone told him to drop the rope—voices as thin and distant as clouds.

The blood sang into Elisha's heart. Madoc and Helena appeared, their lips moving, gesturing toward the fire Elisha had all but forgotten. The blood alone he remembered and the brutal man who wore it. Contact.

The man's smile froze, and he shuddered, his head twitching, trying to shake away the sensations that crept over his body. Death stroked his skin and pinched his cheeks. He jumped aside, whirling, wrapping the rope around his arm, his glance returning to Elisha's face. The grin returned, twisting, as his lips spasmed. One hand scrubbed at his face, smearing the blood. He prodded his cheek, his eyes flaring wide as the flesh shriveled beneath his touch.

Screaming, the man slapped and clawed his face. His eyes darted back again, and his hand flew open, releasing the rope, shaking it free. He backed away, waving his hands. "I've done it! Make it stop! By God, make it stop!"

Martin's full weight sagged into Elisha's arms as the rope slid free and tumbled around them. It mattered not, for the strength of eternity supported him and flowed through him—and onward, an awful, inevitable wave. Every person who wore Martin's blood stopped as they felt the frigid power pass over them, as they suddenly felt the force of what they had done. The blood froze painfully into their skin, dark stains that would mark their shame forever. Some prayed, some wept. A few came close enough to touch Elisha's arm, but they did not dare. Their leader, no longer laughing, collapsed, his body heaving with sobs.

"Elisha."

The voice came so softly, he almost missed it in the chaos that filled him.

"Elisha," sighed through his being, changing the blood song as it echoed through a hundred different contacts. *"Let them go."*

"No," he said through clenched teeth, but the ice trembled.

"Let them go, for they know not what they do."

With a snapping of his will, Elisha severed contact, shoving the ferocious swell of death back to its dark hole deep inside. He sagged to his knees, clutching Martin against him, clinging to the slender warmth that touched his flesh. Cupping Martin's battered head, Elisha gently turned his skill inward, seeking out the injuries through the knowledge in his hands. Broken ribs, he knew. That would be the easy part. The bruising and torn flesh of his ankles and hands could be healed, but Elisha shuddered at the ruin of Martin's face. As he held his friend, careful not to inflict more harm, Elisha studied the broken eye sockets and torn skin, the blood-smeared mouth that once had touched his own. Against his gentle palm, shards of bone shifted with his every measured breath. Clear fluid oozed from Martin's ears; his brain itself was wounded and that was a wound Elisha had neither knowledge nor skill to heal. Martin's presence faded in and out from Elisha's awareness, flickering as the light all around them.

"Martin!" A disheveled woman, her dress ripped open from the neck to reveal skin a few shades too pale, dropped down beside them. "Does he live?"

Elisha knew not how to answer.

"Elisha," moaned Martin's voice within. *"My house is burning."*

"The city is burning, Martin. Hundreds of houses." And Elisha could no more save them than he could re-assemble the ruin of Martin's skull.

"I'm his wife, Ysabeau. Tell me what to do. I'll do anything." She lifted her husband's arm, carefully laying it upon his chest, stroking him gently. "He thought he could reason with them."

The buildings behind gave an ominous groan.

"Bring me there," whispered Martin inside Elisha's skin. The focus drifted apart, Martin's presence dwindling again.

Elisha pursued the tortured spirit through a spiral of heat and pain and darkness, a welcoming, comfortable darkness that felt so cold. The tendrils of power he had laid through Martin's body shivered as Ysabeau worked her fine, uncalloused fingers under the rope at her husband's ankles.

Something shimmered against Elisha's awareness, and he caught at it, all of his strength trained upon this instant. Sensation blossomed under his touch. For a moment, light bathed him, and a joy in his presence, a celebration of himself that brought heat to his cheeks and tears to his eyes. That feeling swelled in his own heart, envisioning Martin's happiness, and his brief misery at parting from a lover only to revel at the pursuit of the next. If any man had known how to live, it was Martin.

Ysabeau touched his shoulder, her tone pleading and broken with tears of her own. "We need to move," she said. "The houses will fall any moment." Her voice shook against a backdrop of prayers and cries.

"Clear the street," Elisha said. "Move everyone toward Saint Paul's. The fire's moving too fast."

"Bring me there," Martin repeated. *"I can stop the fire."*

"You're not strong enough."

"Transmutation of elements," murmured Martin's voice, stronger now even as his warmth receded. *"Fire to water."*

"It can't be done."

Behind him, someone screamed. The ground shuddered as a house collapsed and splinters singed his face and arms. Elisha ducked his head, huddling over Martin, defending him the best way he knew how.

The flickering presence rallied, surging with a renewal of that curious joy, sending comfort and faith and a distant hope. *"Elisha,"* sang Martin through his blood, his bones, his heart, *"there's power enough if you let me die."*

Chapter 4

❖

Elisha hesitated a moment longer, his head bowed over his friend, then he shifted his arm under Martin's knees and slowly lifted him as he rose to his feet. "Ysabeau," he called, and the lady ran to them, her eyes bright.

Elisha wet his lips and said, "Mistress, he wants to go home."

Her hands flew to her face, holding in the panic. Her shoulders trembled, and her gaze flicked to the burning houses, tracing the frame of her home and business. Quickly, she nodded and flung herself away.

"Thank you," Martin whispered through the contact that flamed between them. He need not have spoken, even that way, for Elisha sensed the gratitude that flowed from him, a golden brilliance that warmed his hands and heart and throbbed in the brand upon his chest. Shaky, he took the first step.

The fire devoured Martin's house from the top down, catching hold of it during its spread, so that the street level had not yet been engulfed. As he ducked inside, the upper floors groaned, and flames spread through a gap from the shop next door.

"I had so much to tell you," he said aloud, his voice

ringing in the hollow place against the growing roar of
fire.

"No time. Tell me the happy things."

Elisha laid him on the long countertop, the veneer
already buckling with the heat. "There are none."

"You live; the king has failed."

"No—this was his plan, too. Thomas hated what he
had to do." Elisha pulled off his tunic and balled it into a
pillow for Martin's broken skull. The slender chest shivered with irregular breaths. Gently he settled his friend's
arms, his hand lingering on the scraped fingers, bereft of
their rings. "Thomas. . . the king is my dear friend."

"Oh, my beloved barber," Martin sighed. *"You're in
love with the king."*

"No!" Elisha protested, but he imagined the king's
face in profile, watching him from those eyes, and said
again, very softly, "No."

At that, Martin laughed. The feeble sound issued in a
series of fragile breaths, but it bubbled up through the
contact and spilled over, filling Elisha's spirit with a wave
of joy. It wounded him more deeply than the pain: none
would ever again hear Martin's laughter. The touch grew
faint, sapping Martin's waning strength and Elisha
winced, torn between the sound of joy and the knowledge of death.

"Go," sang Martin's blood. *"Go, Elisha, and find your
king."*

"I'll miss you terribly." Elisha's trembling fingers
stroked the blood from Martin's lips.

"Good," Martin chuckled, and his chest rose with a
sudden, deeper breath, a drawing in of the power all
around him, the power that gathered on the moment of
death. In the crackling flames, Elisha heard the chanting
of eternity, seeking another victim, then, too, he heard
the echo of Martin's laughter and knew he had to go.

Leaning close, Elisha kissed him.

The brief pressure sparked a storm inside. In their shared vision, Martin lay whole again, his face restored to that seductive smile, the dark curls of his hair gleaming by firelight, his whole being alight with his laughter. Just for a moment, Elisha imagined he could save him, if only he might capture that vision and set it free again into the flesh. But all flesh must die.

Martin's power leapt in the air, stirred by the kiss he had longed for. *"Go, go, go!"*

Fire snapped at Elisha's legs, and he leapt away. Martin needed contact with the fire to work his casting—a contact Elisha could not bear to witness. The blood tingled on his palms and into his chest as Martin's flesh met the flames. Ducking the door, Elisha ran into the street, screaming as fire consumed his friend, crying out to the Lord and whoever might hear. He let loose a tiny stream of death, cooling his skin until he shivered.

A black tide welled up and struck him down, a frigid blast that tumbled him into the dirt. It swept through him, howling, knocking away his reason and compassion. In the heart of the darkness, a star gleamed. It flared into fullness, the brightness of it searing at Elisha's mind as it smote back the night.

Then the contact splintered and vanished. The blood on his hands felt neither hot nor cold; all trace of Martin's presence was gone. Elisha huddled on his knees in a silence as vast and full as the ocean. His lungs failed him, but someone slammed a hand against his back, and he gasped a breath.

"Don't ye be hiring me for a bodyguard next time ye plan to go mad!" Madoc grumbled into Elisha's ear as he bent beside him.

"What happened to the fire?" called another voice.

"Shut up!" shouted Madoc. "Let the man breathe!"

"It was a miracle," someone answered. "On yer knees, ye sinners all!"

A sound of warning rumbled at the back of Madoc's throat, and Elisha raised his head. Ysabeau and Helena, with the help of Madoc's men, had managed to push back the crowd, and they all stood or knelt a little ways off, still staring at the buildings at Elisha's back. The two women clung to each other, Ysabeau weeping against Helena's shoulder, the baby wriggling between them until a pink hand waved free and caught hold of Ysabeau's bedraggled hair. Tools, weapons, and bundles of stolen goods littered the space between, like a battlefield without the bodies. Those, he knew, lay at his back.

"What did you see?" Elisha asked.

"A woof, a pop, and the fire's out," Madoc answered gruffly. "Your work?"

Elisha's head shook.

"Not a miracle, at least?"

"If I could work miracles, Martin Draper would live."

Cocking his head to one side, Madoc rolled his eyes toward the heavens. "Sometimes, God's best men have to die in order to do His work."

That kindled a fire altogether new in Elisha's breast, and he straightened, wiping his hands on his ruined undershirt. "No," he said, "they do not. Not like this." He staggered to his feet, pushing away the offered hand. He faced the crowd, his fists balled at his sides. "Hear me now!" The strident voice startled even him, and the murmuring crowd fell silent.

Elisha thrust his finger west. "I am walking back to Ludgate. When I get there, I'm throwing open that gate and the Duke of Dunbury is taking this city, do you hear me? Anyone who had a part in this—anyone, whether you bludgeoned a man to death or simply stole from him—every one of you had better get out right now, or, so help me God, I will find you. And I know how." He searched the crowd and saw the faces pale. The murderers' tainted hands traced patches of their skin, made dark by the slightest touch of death through Martin's blood.

"As for the rest of you,"—Elisha took a deep breath that stung from his lips all the way to his gut—"why did not you pick up a bucket? Why did you not raise a hand to save a man's life? Why, for God's sake—" He broke off, shaking his head. With a gesture as if he could throw them all aside, he said, "I lived for years among you. I always believed we were better than this." He turned his back to them.

Thames Street stood before him, the shops broken and empty, the houses black and gutted by fire. A dozen or so corpses lay on the ground, the bodies of private guards, a few city soldiers, a few residents so envied that they were killed for it. Little clusters of family members knelt around the dead, dazed or weeping. At the sight of them, Elisha remembered himself and spread his awareness. He moved like a ghost to the one fallen man yet living, a young guard with an even younger woman cradling his head, her hand pressed against his chest to stop the blood.

She looked up at his approach. "A surgeon, please, sir!"

He wanted to be comforting, the way he used to be, but he felt a weary bitterness as he dropped to his knees. "Let me examine him," he told her.

The girl hesitated, and Elisha reached out, slipping her hand aside and replacing it with his own. Stab-wounds pierced the young man's chest and stomach, slicing the flesh, but stopping short of most vital organs. Elisha shut his eyes and hoped his weariness did not extend too deep. He found the hovering resonance of his talisman of Thomas's hair and called it forth, using his own body as the guide to teach the young man how to heal. Working from the inside out, he sealed the flesh, joining vessel with vessel, nerve with nerve, and finally smoothed back the skin, leaving it faintly scarred, trembling beneath his touch, against the torn and bloody tunic.

The guard's eyes blinked open and he jerked upright, knocking Elisha back on his heels. Slapping at his side where a weapon should hang, he shouted, "Get off me! Get the brigade! The city's aflame!"

"Shane," the girl sobbed. "Praise the Lord, Shane, you're alive!"

At those words, he froze, wary eyes turning toward her, to the street, back to Elisha. "Are you the surgeon?"

"The barber," Elisha corrected.

Frowning, the guard searched out his wounds, finding the slash marks easily enough with his probing fingers, but finding no injuries beyond, and his eyes drew slowly back to Elisha's face. "Thank you," he whispered.

With a one-shouldered shrug, Elisha rose and walked away. The healing left him shaky, as always, as if he needed another reason to be off-balance. If he kept to his plan, he could exit the city and recover alone with Martin's memory. But the crowd still hovered, and he knew that was not to be.

"Here, Barber!" Madoc cried out, waving his arm.

Elisha managed to lift his head. "Aye?"

"This one's asking for you." He pointed down to a bulky man seated on the ground, his features warped by graying flesh and too-gaunt cheeks. His sunken eyes lit upon Elisha and he blubbered something, with a frantic gesture of his unresponsive hands.

Elisha recognized the man who'd held the rope, and his stomach clenched, repulsed as much by what the man had done as by how he, Elisha, had punished him for it. He whispered thanks to Martin for stopping him from something much more terrible, and set out toward his victim.

Squatting before the newly-ugly citizen, Elisha murmured, "I'm sorry. No matter what you've done, I had no right."

Flailing his hand toward the sky, the man said, "G-g-god thruck me dow."

"No," said Elisha. "God wasn't here today."

The crumbled hand thrashed toward him then, fastening to his arm and jerking at it so that Elisha's hand flapped. "H-h," the man started, swallowed, and tried again. "Hands of God."

Pulling away, Elisha gritted his teeth. "You're wrong."

"N-n-no!" The twisted face screwed itself up, and his other hand came up with a folded bit of parchment. Then, the lips curled into a recognizable grin. "Proof!" he announced clearly. "F-f-from t' sky!" He waved the parchment in the direction of God, who had apparently delivered it into his lap.

Elisha snatched the page from the waving hand and held it before his tired eyes. He made out his name, scrawled on the front.

Coming up quietly, her arm still draped around Martin's wife, Helena asked softly, "Would you want me to read it for you?"

"No need," he said, then sighed. "I don't mean to be sharp with you."

"You had a terrible day," she said, touching his arm. "We all have."

Elisha nodded, and slipped his finger along the opening, breaking the seal. He read the message a few times, struggling to make sense of it, despite its brevity. "Elisha Mancer," it read, "Welcome home."

Four words that chilled him, hand and heart, so that the parchment trembled, and Helena put her hand to his, steadying him with a touch and a confused glance at the page. "Mancer?" she said. "What does that mean?"

Elisha started to answer, then broke off, his throat parched in an instant when he turned over the page. There, he stared at the broken seal, a round of wax impressed by the king's signet—the ring that must have been taken from Thomas's own hand.

Chapter 5

❖

Elisha traced the seal first with his eyes, then with one finger, the rough wax of the pattern catching on his calloused skin. He thought of Martin's final claim, that Elisha was in love with the king, and his chest felt unbearably tight.

"What is it, Elisha?" Helena asked. "I don't understand."

His head jerked up. "Who gave you this?"

The injured man gave a few twitches of his head. "G-g-g—"

"Horseshit! More like to be the Devil." He started to crumple the thing in his hand, then froze and kept it clenched, focusing his senses on the seal, trying to gain some knowledge of who had made it, and how they had come by Thomas's ring. It showed him nothing but the same fearsome void Elisha felt when he had touched Morag, the mancer's presence negated by the skin he wore, his very life denied by his intimacy with death. "Damn it!"

"Elisha, please," Helena scolded, her hand reaching to cover the infant's ear.

Ysabeau, tucked against Helena's side, whispered, "It's the king's seal, is it?"

Pierced through his numbness, Elisha darted a glance toward Martin's widow. Light-brown hair straggled about her shoulders, framing a face not as lovely as Helena's, but open. Her eyes, though red from smoke and tears, watched him keenly.

"I have to go to the duke," Elisha told them. "You should rest. Both of you."

Helena turned to her companion. "Let me bring you to church, mistress, or to my house, if you'd rather. It's full of children, but all are welcome."

Ysabeau's lips compressed, and she shook her head sharply. "My house was empty; Martin sent the boys to his sister's estate in the country a few weeks ago. As if he expected something." Again, she eyed Elisha. "I will be praying about this, you can be sure. First, I'd like to be there when the duke's men ride through and when the murderers go out." She pulled together the torn front of her gown and crossed her arms tightly.

"Come then, if you will, mistress, but we move quickly," Elisha said, already setting out.

"Aye," grumbled Madoc, "so quickly we sometimes outstrip our own bodyguard."

Elisha took long strides, and Martin's wife, slightly taller than Elisha, and a good deal taller than her husband, easily kept pace at his side. He needed no magic to part the crowd this time, they fell away from him, those who had been marked by blood hiding their faces. The silence behind him dissolved, filling with the babble of a thousand witnesses who did not know what they had seen.

"You were his barber?" Ysabeau asked after another turning.

"Aye," he answered. "Five years or more."

She snorted with amusement. "I wondered why he had his hair tended so often. I need wonder no longer."

"It wasn't like that, mistress."

"It was for him." She smiled a little. "We met at the assizes while he was studying mercantile law, and I attended the lectures disguised as a man, since women are not allowed to enroll." Her smile broke into the laughter of remembrance. "He claimed he loved me right away, and he was dreadfully disappointed I turned out to be a woman. Then we both realized what a good match we might be. I think he still wishes—" The laughter faded as she took a sharp breath. "I mean, wished . . ." Her voice fell away.

Tucking his cold hands under his arms, Elisha said, "I am sorry for your loss." After they walked a few steps, he added, "And for mine."

"Do not say too much," she began softly, "But say, if you can, that your carrying him home," she took a breath, "that his being there somehow put out the fires?"

Quietly he answered, "It did."

"Was it a miracle, then? That's what some o' them would have us think." Madoc gave a bob of his head back over his shoulder.

"It was what was needed to save this city," Elisha said. "More than that doesn't matter."

"You've earned enough veneration today to elevate you forever in the eyes of these people," Ysabeau observed, and Madoc grunted agreement.

Clutching the letter, Elisha tried to ignore the babble of the crowd that tracked their steps. "I punished them all, and I was tempted to do worse. That's more the sinner than the saint."

"I think it was your restraint that bought their adoration," said Ysabeau.

"I don't have time for adoration." He put on a burst of speed as they neared the gate and shouted up to the guards, "Open! For God's sake, open the gate!"

"We don't answer to you, even if you have returned from the grave!" one man called back.

"Open the gate before I use your head for a battering ram!" Elisha replied.

"Do it!" cried a voice behind him.

"Aye, bring them in!"

"Listen to the barber!"

Then, with a maelstrom of shouting, the crowd broke around them, still avoiding Elisha himself, and a hundred hands were laid upon the bars and latches, a hundred more upon the chains that would draw open the gates. Madoc pushed by, shouting for attention, then counting off: "One! Two! Three! Heave!"

The gates groaned open to a subdued cheer. Along the road some distance, the duke's soldiers started up, running back to their camp with the news. The crowd lingered just inside the open space, perhaps unwilling to hand over the city they had taken, at least, not so easily.

"Where are the killers?" Ysabeau faced the crowd.

"Aye, where?" Others took up the cry and the search, catching hold of their neighbors to thrust them forward. Two dozen souls huddled before the angry crowd, and Ysabeau stalked forward. Three or four others came with her, widows and sons.

"Get out!" She pointed toward the road. "Get out, or God shall scourge the earth of you."

A party of mounted men came down the road in procession, the duke among them, with a man in the gold and miter of the archbishop at his side. The wretches forced to flee the city parted to either side and hurried off.

A few more cowering figures were dragged from the crowd, mostly men, a few women, and youths. One of these latter struggled free, sprinting toward Elisha. Two sturdy men got hold of him, but he broke away. "I would have saved him! Please, Barber!" He held out a hand stained dark as if still dripping with blood. Snarling, the larger man tripped him, but Elisha shoved the note into his belt and stepped up.

"Let him up."

"He's one o' them—you can see the marks," the man protested.

"He claims that he's not, now let him up."

The young man scrambled to his knees and crawled forward, holding out his hands like a supplicant. "I'd have saved him, sir—I tried to get him, before they strung him up, I did."

"I tell you, lad, I'm in no mood to be lied to. If you're lying and looking for mercy, it won't be just me you're facing, but all of them." Elisha gestured to the citizens, who watched with grim and angry faces, eager now to prove their fealty by following his mandates.

"It's true, sir, I swear it."

Over the tousled head, Elisha met Ysabeau's eyes, glimmering once more with tears. "I don't know," she whispered. "They dragged me away, I couldn't see. . ." her voice trailed off, and she pressed her hand over her mouth.

"Please, as God is my witness, it's true."

Elisha lowered himself to one knee, and laid his hand on the young man's back. A wave of fear passed through the contact, and he reeled with the force of it in his raw, too-open state. Nonetheless, Elisha righted himself, shaking his head to his guards who came to his aid. To the youth, he murmured, "Tell me what happened."

Trembling beneath his touch, the young man answered, "We was throwing rocks at the windows, I can't deny that. I was, too, and hoping to steal, maybe, but it went wrong. We'd got restless, not being able to leave the city, see? Somebody in the first shop tried to scare us off, and they caught him. But what they done—" he quaked, and choked back his response.

"It's over now," Elisha said, remembering the bedside tone of a healer. "Go on, tell me about the draper's."

"Somebody'd already broken in there, and a house was burning down the way. I would've got out, but I was in front and there was too many people. We were trapped. I got on my knees to see could I crawl out. That's when he came out. He acted. . . peaceful, see? Calm, as if he just came out to talk, and he started saying he'd listen, that he wanted to help, if we'd just back off. I was all for that, and you could see some o' the others were, too. They wanted to listen, but that huge man jumped up with a cudgel and knocked him down."

As the words flowed, Elisha caught glimpses of the scenes through the boy's eyes. Less focused than a true witch's sending, but still, the images held the clarity of shock, and Martin's appearance, viewed from between threshing legs, shone like a vision from God.

"He fell right in front of me, and they started kicking. That man brought out his rope. People ran to get around me, I had this break in the crowd, and I grabbed his arm and shook him. 'Come on,' I says, and he tried to, but they had his legs—" In the boy's memory, Martin's hand was torn from his. His darkened fingers grasped at the air and held nothing.

Tears stung Elisha's eyes. "Sit up," he said, supporting an elbow. "Thank you for trying to help him."

Miserably, the youth nodded. "What you said, why didn't we help and all—I should've tried harder."

Elisha gripped his shoulder. "It was only you, against all those men, you couldn't do it alone." The words blazed into his mind with a radiance as if Martin himself was reminding Elisha to take his own words to heart. "Put your hands together."

"Like praying?"

"Aye, like that. This . . . it might hurt." In faith, Elisha did not know if he could undo the damage he had caused—the body resisted change if the skin was unbroken. Likely, it would be agony, but, for Martin's sake, he must try, or condemn the youth to the life of an outcast, marked for a crime he did not commit.

Elisha pressed his hands to the boy's hands and bowed his head over them. Once more, he reached for the talisman that hummed at his side, the lock of Thomas's hair resonating and answering his need. Using the affinity of one hand for the other, he showed the body how to heal, the toughened, stained skin became clear and smooth again. The boy cried out, and Elisha gripped him tighter, sending him strength, until the rigid pain left his body. At last, Elisha released him and sat back, his weary hands falling into his lap. "You're free," he said. "Stay if you want to, you have my blessing."

Flexing his fingers as if he'd never seen them before, the young man nodded, then flashed a smile and waved his clean hand in the air.

"What is this, Elisha?" breathed the voice of Duke Randall.

Slowly, Elisha raised his head as the duke swung down from his horse, the crowd of citizens falling silent again. Putting out a hand to Elisha, the duke asked, "Can you rise?"

With a gasp that burned his insides, Elisha said, "I don't know." He knelt in the dirt, exhausted, and shrugged limply, then took the message from his belt and put it into the duke's outstretched hand. "Thomas is in terrible danger." He caught his breath and stilled, glancing about, hoping none had overheard the slip: no barber, much less himself, should be using the king's given name. "It may be too late. I can't tell."

In an instant, his eyes were dazzled as another man stood before him, an imposing figure in a high, golden hat, his shoulders draped with a matching cloak. The archbishop stared down at him, eyes keen over a sharp nose.

"It seems, Your Grace, that even you did not realize what a formidable person your foresight has brought to us."

Elisha ducked his head, wiping the glitter of gold from his gaze.

Cloth-of-gold crinkled as the man bowed. "Allow me to be the first to recognize you — Your Majesty."

Chapter 6

❖

Startled, Elisha glanced warily about again, but he knew there had been no mistake. The archbishop of Canterbury, the prelate of the entire nation and beholden to none save the pope himself, had addressed him as the king. "I beg your pardon, Your Grace?"

The archbishop lifted his hands and cried out, "Arise, Your Majesty, God's anointed! Had I not with mine own eyes witnessed the miracle, I should never have believed!" Those eyes shimmered with tears, his hands trembling as he raised them to the heavens. His voice rang, deep and stirring, rich with reverence. "Did you not see, my brothers, my children? God has granted him the holy touch, that sacred power reserved unto kings! A blessed miracle! Thank you, Lord!" Then he dropped to his knees in the dirt, hands clasped, and his voice rang out in Latin, echoing from the gate tower.

With a murmur and rustle—and an occasional cheer—Elisha's followers likewise knelt, except for the healed youth who stared in wonder at his hands, then flung himself prostrate to the ground.

"Get up," Elisha said, shaking the boy's arm. "This is madness."

"Your Grace," intoned the other priest, still mounted

on his horse, his accent lilting toward the French, "I hesitate to criticize—"

"Did you not see?" shouted the archbishop again, breaking off his prayer. "And there have been other miracles! A whole extraordinary series of them, from the moment when God's power and will entered into this humble man. As once the Lord elevated a simple shepherd to become the king of his chosen people—yea, verily, even as His only begotten son once worked as a mere carpenter, the Lord has once more granted unto these undeserving sinners a leader in our time of need!"

"It's madness," Elisha said again, but none seemed to be listening. Even Duke Randall stood gaping before him.

But the archbishop, crazed with the light of God, almost glowing in the vigor of his faith, wasn't finished. "King Hugh, a man in his prime, fell as if aged beyond measure. You yourself, Father Osbert, have travelled all the way from the Holy Father to bear witness to these events. King Hugh's younger son slain on the eve of claiming the throne—his elder son condemned this man to die, but the casket was raised and lo! For it was empty!" The archbishop sprang to his feet, arms spread, cloak flaring out, the golden cross upon it struck with sun. "And I have heard reports of the noise and violence raised up there. As if he fought to rise against a great enemy, and well he might, for surely the Devil himself would have prevented his return.

"And then even our King Thomas, whom we had accepted as our rightful lord, even he was taken from us! And we prayed in misery. All these signs and portents, all these moments, surely they show us God's disfavor! We wept, and prayed, my children."

A chorus of assent rose up at Elisha's back.

"Perhaps, indeed, we face the end of days, my lambs, but we need not face them alone, no! For the Lord's wrath was bent to this, to reveal His true servant, the one He chose to lead us through the darkness!"

The pope's inquisitor, Father Osbert, blinked down at them, then slid off his horse and stood, frowning.

"Has he not, even as our Lord Jesus Christ, healed his flock of many afflictions?"

"Yes!" roared the crowd, and "Amen!"

"No," Elisha breathed, as every moment of his last few months was twisted to have some other meaning entirely. "No!" he said again, louder, and scrambled to his feet. "Your Grace, forgive me, you can't do this. You can't simply—" But he had no words for what was happening.

Duke Randall coughed apologetically. "Your Grace, as admirable a man as I find the barber to be, he has no royal blood, nor even noble."

"It is the mark of divinity that makes a king. Blood is royal when God proclaims it so!" thundered the archbishop.

"He smothered the fire, Your Graces!" called a voice from the crowd. Elisha whirled, but could not find who had spoken.

"We felt it, Father," cried another. This time, the man limped from the crowd and grasped the legate's sleeve. "We all did, at his graveside, Father. We felt his goodness, and we felt our own shame."

Elisha's stomach churned. He wanted to laugh aloud at the absurdity of it all. He wanted to vomit at the preposterous stories of his own deeds as others testified around him. He was a sorcerer, a killer—damned to Hell for any of a dozen offences. And yet, the grains of truth at the heart of these wild stories gave him little ground for denial. Yes, he healed that young man's hands. Yes, he healed the wounds of the fallen guard and eased the ills of a thousand others. Diabolical magic or the royal touch? Thomas was king. Thomas had need of him—if he lived. How could Elisha ever do what he must if he were imprisoned by chains of gold? And how could Thomas ever forgive him usurping his throne?

"You can't do this!" He spread his hands before him, pleading. "I beg you to stop."

The archbishop turned, his face pink with excitement, then he gave a little gasp—for an instant as dumbstruck as Elisha himself—his eyes flared, the color fled his features, and he fainted to the ground, sagging in a sigh of gold and white.

At a hint of movement, Elisha thought the papal legate might come to the archbishop's aid. Indeed the man crossed himself fervently, mumbling in French and Latin, then dropped to his knees, his gaze arrested by Elisha's outstretched hands.

A scar marked the center of each palm, a short tear, healed with Thomas's help. A little of Martin's blood pooled in the left-hand mark, and Elisha pulled back his hands, horrified.

"I was branded," he protested. "You know that—you all must know that." But his voice faded as he clenched his hands, the scars just as visible at the back as on the palm. "They're not what you think."

Helena parted herself from the crowd, approaching almost timidly. She reached out and took his fist in her hand, staring at the pale mark, then peeling open his fingers. "These are no burn scars," she murmured. "How did I not notice them?"

"Helena," he said softly, urgently, "you, of all people, must know I'm not divine."

"And I," snapped another voice. Sister Lucretia pushed up close, glaring. "I was there, in the Tower, the night before his execution. Treason, and sorcery! Black Magic!"

Elisha flinched to see his old friend's face so twisted with her anger.

"Madame! Good Sister, surely you do not accuse His

Grace of blasphemy?" The black-robed inquisitor inched forward on his knees. "Or can you explain the signs that have been seen?"

"The fiend may counterfeit miracles, Father."

"And the very stigmata of our Lord? How do you explain this?"

Helena met Elisha's gaze. There had been a fiend involved, true enough, but Morag had been a devil of mortal origin, and Elisha did not know how to tell the story without drawing in Thomas, or Alaric's death.

Lucretia faltered, her veil fluttering as she turned away. "I cannot, Father. That's why you're here, isn't it? To explain false miracles?"

Gravely, the man nodded his silvered head. "Indeed, Sister, I shall seek out such truth as may be, but I have seen the healing with my own eyes and have heard these witnesses with my own ears—a hundred citizens or more who saw the inferno doused at this man's intervention. It is my task to seek for heresies, or for saints." His deep-set eyes searched Elisha's face and figure. "It is another matter to investigate God's miracles in the presence of the one who was their tool." Then he gave another nod, deeper this time. "Your Majesty."

Almost, Elisha took the lord's name in vain. Almost, he flew into a rage to let them think the madness was his own. But the claim was not so lightly set aside, not if his every gesture should be taken as a sign, his every movement as holy.

"Elisha."

He turned to Randall's voice, hoping for some wisdom to dispel this insanity, but the duke gently shook his head, placing a finger to his lips as he, too, sank to his knees, head bowed.

"No!" Elisha seized him. "No," he whispered urgently. "Not you, too."

"Look around you, Elisha," the duke whispered back,

clinging to his arms. "How can I defy this? How can I be the last man standing? Someone must take the throne."

"Thomas! And Rosie."

Randall winced, then pulled away. "When they are found." He held the crumpled note in his fist. "If they are found, Elisha. Until then, who will stand against France? Who will mediate between the peasantry and the barons?"

"But the barons will never accept me—this will only rile them more. Surely there is another more worthy. Who stands heir to the throne?"

"Thanks to the blood I share with Hugh, it's me," the duke said softly, his face a decade older since his daughter's disappearance. "I'll take it, if I must."

But it would be the death of him—his pasty skin said as much.

"Many will stand with me, if I support you. More will stand with him." Randall tipped his head toward the archbishop. "Especially when they see the army at your back." He lifted his chin in the direction of the citizens of London.

A growl of frustration or fear lodged in Elisha's throat, and he stalked over to the archbishop. Here, at least, was a problem he might affect, a small thing, well within his skill. He laid his hand at the prelate's temple, by the skewed rim of his golden miter. The man's dark eyes flew open. He smiled faintly. "Bless you, Your Majesty," he sighed. And he felt like nothing at all.

Elisha's breath caught. The hollowness of a necromancer? In the archbishop? It couldn't be. Elisha was simply exhausted, stunned by grief, by casting, by this man's declarations. Still, the words echoed in his memory, Morag's master telling Alaric, *We have made kings before and unmade them.*

"We must arrange a coronation as quickly as possible, or risk the further wrath of the Lord if we should ignore the signs He has sent us," the archbishop said. The man's manner hadn't changed. He gave away nothing, his voice warm, his face open and almost radiant.

Elisha struggled and found his breath at last, looking for an excuse to touch the archbishop again, to be sure — but in his exhaustion, would he even know? He had numbed himself with the sense of death and had yet to master the grief of Martin's passing.

The archbishop reached up for him then, taking Elisha's arm to draw them both to standing, and his touch conveyed a faith so deep it seemed fathomless.

Chapter 7

❖

"**Y**our horse, Your Majesty," said Lord Robert's voice, suddenly at his elbow, tinged with humor.

Wrong, then. He had been wrong about the archbishop. Elisha clutched the pommel with one hand, seeking balance, as Robert knelt, fingers laced, to help him into the saddle. Once Elisha was mounted, Robert checked the stirrups and handed up the reins. "Last time I escorted you to the Tower, 'twas in a cart." He grinned. "I never expected to do it again, much less like this!"

"Nor I," said Elisha faintly. "Thank you."

"Ought to at least wave, or something," Robert muttered.

Taking a deep breath, Elisha sat up straighter and gave a wave of his hand. Most of the citizens cheered. Sister Lucretia looked pale and crossed herself but spoke no more, not risking the archbishop's disapproval. Madoc kept shaking his head in disbelief, while Ysabeau retreated to Helena's side. As a few of the duke's guard came forward, the crowd opened to let them pass in procession, Elisha riding alongside the archbishop, who scattered blessings among the crowd and occasionally murmured fervently in Latin. Elisha's time with Mordecai had given him a bit of Latin, but he wasted little effort in translating prayers. Instead, he sought attunement, the familiar stride of his horse comforting him. Smoke still hung in the air, but they need not pass the place where Martin died. They rode instead down streets of charred houses where bodies still lay amid the ruins of their lives. London needed to be rebuilt, not only the buildings, but the unity of her people as well.

At his back rode the ominous presence of the black-robed inquisitor, and the stolid sense of the duke himself. Citizens dodged ahead of them or emerged from their barricaded homes to blink up at him. While many would have seen the former kings in this fashion—at a distance, on horseback—many had known Elisha for decades, personally. He rode to his new place supported by members of all three estates of life: those who worked, those who fought, and even those who prayed. What would his enemies think? What if some of these, the archbishop even, were his enemies? But why would a mancer, and one in such a position, proclaim Elisha king? Of course he had been wrong about the archbishop—perhaps only desperate to deny the crown he was offered, the crown that belonged to Thomas and his heirs. Save that all of Thomas's heirs were dead.

They came up to the barbican, the first defense of the Tower, and the yeomen stood aside, gaping. From below, in the shadowed well at the base of the gate, came a chorus of roars. Elisha's flinch made his horse snort and dance.

"The royal menagerie, Your Majesty," said the archbishop serenely. "The emblems of your kingdom welcome you home."

Rather, Elisha thought, the lions smelled blood. He shivered.

Turning down the path and over the drawbridge, they passed beneath the portcullises of the Tower and into the outer defense where Elisha slid down, shaky, and allowed himself to be escorted to the king's chambers, a range of rooms above the thick wall, painted with diamonds of red and blue, lit by huge silver crowns hung from the ceiling upon chains. Thomas's rooms. Thomas's bed. Elisha brushed his fingertips over the blankets.

"Servants shall bring up a bath for you, Your Majesty," someone was saying, "and they are preparing a feast as best they can. The stores are somewhat less since we have been besieged." An old man stood before him, tonsured head bowed, hands clasped. "John de Ufford, Your Majesty. Your Lord Chancellor, until you shall see fit to replace me."

Elisha put out his hand, and, after a moment, the old man took it, giving a little bow. In the warm grip, surprisingly firm, Elisha felt his steadfastness, his intelligence, his curiosity. Satisfied, Elisha released him. "I'm sure you'll serve me well, as you have my predecessor." His throat felt dry, his words stale. The king's presence haunted the place, as much as his first wife's death lingered in the lodge they used to share.

"Lord Richard DeVere, the Lord Chamberlain has, alas, been prematurely executed for his failure to safeguard your predecessor. If it please Your Majesty, I shall assume his duties over the household until it can be determined whether his heir is fit to rise to the position."

Executed, because his king had vanished. Elisha felt hollow.

"We'll give you a moment, then, Your Majesty." Ufford bowed himself out of Elisha's presence and shut the door, though whispering could be heard outside for a few minutes, followed by the patter of feet, all the men he now commanded hurrying about their business.

Once they were gone Elisha stalked the rooms, servants springing out of his way, darting glances as if they wondered at the sudden distance between themselves and him. Like the lodge, the bedchamber, solar, and small chapel contained little of a personal nature. A few books and writing things, crucifixes of ivory, Christ staring down at Elisha, no doubt surprised to find a barber claimed as one of his successors. Elisha rubbed at his palm, wiping away the blood that remained from the day's work, and felt a sudden kinship for God the Son, a weary, tortured man, proclaimed a king. Elisha's own mocking would come later, he had no doubt. In the meantime, he had to uphold the trust too many placed in him, and acquit Thomas's job as best he could. He slipped out the talisman, Thomas's hair, and pressed it between both hands as he returned to the chapel. If any witnessed this, let them believe that he prayed. Let him believe such a prayer might be answered. Closing his eyes, Elisha gave his being to the search.

Centering himself, drawing back the tendrils of his awareness, Elisha focused them to a single purpose, that of finding Thomas. First, he must conceive some notion of where to look; he would exhaust himself in searching every house and tree, even assuming his power could reach so far. He envisioned one prison after another, from the nearby gloom of Newgate, to the dank cell in the bowels of this very tower, where he had awaited his own execution. Even across whatever distance lay between them, he had contact through that lock of hair. A magus less sensitive could not put it to such use; so, for perhaps the first time, Elisha's accursed sensitivity served him as he probed all the places a man might be held, and all the while he whispered Thomas's name.

The shadow of his awareness flitted over landscapes of darkness and stone, in and out of every dungeon he could name and more which he only imagined. Briefly here and there, he touched the presence of other prisoners, even a few of the magi, though they did not rise to his touch, and he had no way to maintain the contact.

Elisha expanded his search to barns and stables, inns

and outhouses, and finally shed all boundaries but the presence of Thomas himself. His senses stretched thin, a tenuous web spread all around him, as if he could attune himself to the world. All that reached him were echoes of himself, as if his cry bounced off distant mountains to carry back his growing fear.

In the learning of the magi, the Law of Contagion stated that two things once a whole, would always maintain a close kinship. Even if, Heaven forbid, Thomas were dead, that lock of hair should still search out his corpse for the connection it shared. Instead, Elisha found nothing.

The web of his awareness shriveled, and his presence retreated back to the physical, his miserable body hunched on the floor in a painted chamber.

A knock echoed, followed shortly by the door swinging open. The shuffling servants stopped short at the sight of him, and Elisha pushed himself up, wiping despair from his features, as they continued past, the first pair lugging a wooden tub, others following with buckets of steaming water to fill it. Still others set themselves to work at the huge fireplace, building up the coals, and Ufford reappeared at the end of the gathering, bowing, furrowing his white brows. "Do forgive me, Your Majesty, we ought to have seen to the bath right away." He flipped open a ledger he carried under one arm. "Is there anything you require? Any special tasks, meals, persons? Have you brought a confessor of your own, or body servants?"

Elisha perched at the edge of the bed as activity swirled about him. Anything he required? He could barely conceive of what that might mean to a king. He required the true king's return. In order to do that, he needed those around him he could trust. "Personal guard," he murmured. "The men who accompanied me into the city."

Ufford raised an eyebrow. "A mercenary troop?"

"Offer them permanent employment."

"Very well, Your Majesty." The quill scraped across the page, and Ufford looked up again. "Confessor?"

"Father Michael of Dunbury."

"A village priest."

"A devout man," Elisha countered, and Ufford nodded mildly, making another note. *"New king is a fool,"* Elisha imagined him writing. *"Duke and archbishop must be God-struck to take a barber for a king."*

The quill poised, but the servants had succeeded in filling the bath and stood aside.

"My word, man, you do look a fright!" The Earl of Blackmere swept in, followed by a few servants of his own.

"By the by, Your Majesty," said Ufford, still in that mild tone, "there are some people who wish to see you."

Blackmere's servants set down a pair of chests and opened them to reveal piles of clothing in silk and velvet. "We are much the same size, you and I, and these might do until you get your own." The earl started plucking things from the chests, arranging them on the counterpane. "Take off those things."

Elisha shrugged out of his shirt, staring at the blood, then tossed it onto the fire. "Some, my lord? Who else?"

Then she stood at the door, a dark veil draping her hair and down her shoulders, clad in a gown of green like the one in which he had first seen her. "It's true then, you are alive." Brigit pressed her hands to her lips, quivering with the effort of containing herself. "And more than alive!" She shook herself, nearly smiling, nearly weeping, and Elisha remembered lying in his grave, touched by the distant fall of her tears.

"I told you you were not ready for this," murmured an older man who stepped up to take Brigit's arm. "Come with me, my darling. Forgive us, Your Majesty." He managed something like a bow, and Brigit was drawn away, looking flushed and frail.

Shaking off his surprise, Elisha realized he should have known she would be here, as soon as she learned what was happening. Likely, she was staying in town since Alaric's funeral, looking for ways to ingratiate herself with the new monarch, or to establish some standing before she gave birth to the child she carried. Again, he thought of the grave. She had been the next to last person to see Morag alive, and Elisha could not simply dismiss her from his life. In two paces, he reached the door. "Come to the feast!" he called after them, and they paused, Brigit glanced back with a dazzling smile, as her companion glowered, pulling her closer with a protective arm. He urged her on before him down the stairs, but his bright eyes lingered on Elisha's, his mouth grim. And there was something familiar in the set of his brow. Her father, the magus Rowena's husband.

"We've lit the fire for you, Majesty," said Ufford, and Elisha whirled, imagining the stake and the angel. Ufford drew back, fingers tightening around the book he carried.

"I need you all to go. Everyone. Please."

With a snap of his fingers, Ufford summoned the attention of the servants, who glanced up uncertainly then gathered their buckets, resettled the drapes, replaced the poker, and filed out past Elisha with a series of little bobs and courtesies. "We shall be on the tower steps, Your Majesty."

The earl gestured toward the clothes strewn all over the bed. "Your Majesty, I have —"

"Please, my lord," Elisha said, leaning back against the nearest wall.

The earl bowed his head and ushered his own servants, shutting the door behind them. Elisha gazed at the bed with longing, covered now with expensive clothes.

The bed was large enough to suit four patients at hospital. The bathtub steamed quietly near the fire, so Elisha shed the rest of his clothes and stepped in, his skin stinging at first with the heat.

He scrubbed the soot from his face and the ashes from his hair, letting Martin's blood slough away. Oh, if Martin could see him now. And Brigit, returned to seek the throne through him, as of course she would. But how well did she know the mancers? And had the mancers set him here?

Elisha shut his eyes, pushing back the layers of fear and confusion. He was ready for none of this, yet somehow he must be. Beneath all else, he was weary to the bone, weary from casting, weary of dying. He rubbed his hands over his face, finding that some of the blood was his own, a thin cut caused by some broken glass in Martin's house. Now he sat in Thomas's house, at the heart of a nation about to burn. He once used his own blood to conceal Thomas's presence, and he thought of the echoes of himself, as if his searching cry echoed from distant, unseen heights. Could Thomas be concealed from him again, by the same means? His heart quickened with the thought, even as his body relaxed into the warmth of the bath. He needed to make another attempt, but later, when he had regained his strength. With the last of his focus, he healed the slender cut.

Unfurling his senses to the boundaries of the rooms, Elisha let himself sleep.

Chapter 8

❖

All too soon, the clank of changing guards and the rustle of servants outside woke him. Still, the little rest was better than none. Elisha scrubbed himself dry with a cloth and tried to work out the layers of clothing the earl had laid out for him. Hose and undergarments, a fine undertunic and a tunic even finer for the top, laces at his arms and chest, and soft slippers of red. He slid the lock of Thomas's hair into a tight sleeve, taking one lace in his teeth to see if he couldn't get it right. Then a knock, and the parade of servants returned, two of them scowling at him. He lowered his arm and held it out for their expert tugging and tying. "Thank you."

"It's what we're here for, Your Majesty. We know our place," muttered one of them, twisting a final loop into the bow, then stepping back.

Ufford arrived behind them. "I trust Your Majesty has had a good bath." He eyed Elisha up and down and gave a faint nod of approval. Then he brought out a small wooden box and opened it to the body servants. They settled a heavy gold chain about Elisha's shoulders. Heavy in more ways than one: Alaric had been wearing it when Elisha killed him. Elisha swallowed, the enameled golden cross that was its pendant rested over his brand, a weight upon his heart.

They emerged from chambers into a little party of guards, including Madoc and his men clad in Tower livery, red with golden lions. It was not Elisha's livery, nor had he arms to display in such a fashion. Every step he sank deeper in deception. But he had not prevented this from happening, and someone had to keep the kingdom together long enough for Thomas's return—and defeat the mancers already in their midst. Elisha imagined Thomas in those moments he seemed most regal, squared his shoulders, and breathed in majesty.

Madoc scratched his beard speculatively and gave a nod before he stiffened to proper attention.

"The seating order, Your Majesty." Ufford kept to Elisha's elbow as they crossed the yard. "The Duke of Dunbury at your right hand, with his lady wife. The earls of Gloucester and Blackmere beyond. To the left, the Archbishop of Canterbury, the Bishop of London, Father Osbert of the Holy Office of the Inquisition, then the Earl of Surrey."

Elisha nodded. The evening grew damp, and ravens called from their crenellated perches as the party passed into the inner tower and upstairs to the hall; not large, but packed with tables, benches, gowns of every color, lords of every stature, to a man taller than Elisha himself.

"Make way!" called a yeoman, and the assembled nobles rose, bowing as Elisha passed by. A few stood straight as stone and stared at him. Mortimer—who had been close with the dead Alaric, and perhaps working against him—Elisha recognized among these. A very nest of vipers indeed. His every fiber urged him to bow, to lower his gaze from these nobles or risk a beating, but he lifted his chin and stared back. From this moment forth, for good or ill, he was the king the archbishop had claimed. Mortimer dodged the gaze as Elisha swept past to the seat reserved for him. Not quite a throne, thank God. Once he sat, the others, too, resumed their places. A bell rang out, and boys and maids appeared, carrying vast platters of meat, jugs of wine, loaves baked of the finest white flour wrapped in matching linen.

One of the boys filled Elisha's plate; a mound of food rich with spices, beyond anything even the duke's table had offered. And this, when the chancellor had apologized for the sorry state of their stores.

"A blessing upon the meal." The archbishop rose, spreading his hands to encompass the hall. "We thank you, Lord, for revealing to us this day even a sliver of your great and most mysterious intention. We shall endeavor to serve your chosen monarch and to live as your Son would have us live. We honor the flesh and the blood of Our Lord, Jesus Christ, as we break bread together. Amen."

"Amen," Elisha murmured, along with the rest. Every eye, framed by the plucked brows, broad headdresses or velvet caps that marked their nobility, watched him.

He swallowed, trying to wet his throat. "At your pleasure, my lords and ladies," he said, skewering a piece of beef on the tip of his knife and biting into it. Gravy ran down his fingers, and he licked it from his lips. Platters and knives clattered around him as he finished his morsel and wiped his hands on a cloth. He followed with a swallow of wine that warmed his tongue.

"Mind your palate, Elisha, there are two more courses after this," Randall murmured at his elbow.

Two more? "The chancellor said the feast was poor because of the siege."

"For an occasion like this? It should be four."

Elisha watched the duke break off a chunk of bread and use it to sop up the gravy. "Don't stare, Your Majesty. It makes them doubt."

Fighting a flush of embarrassment, Elisha turned back

to his food, eating slowly, letting the boy change out his fingerbowl and cloth.

At his other side, the archbishop passed the time in discussing a new style of vestments his inferior church-man was considering. Arrayed before him, the nobles ate and talked, snippets of conversation rising up to him. By a judicious use of his awareness, Elisha focused here and there around the room

"—strange times, though. Have you heard about that inn at Chelmsford? Raining every day for a month! Landlord's afraid to step out." The lord chuckled, but the man to his right complained, "Here we are, hours away, and we've got drought! Maybe it is the end times coming, even the skies gone mad."

A man in dark riding clothes entered from the stair and approached, bowing, bringing a page to lead him to the duke's side.

"With permission?" Randall asked, and Elisha nod-ded, allowing his patron to slide out and have a whis-pered conversation with the fellow at the corner of the room. Elisha took the opportunity to lean across to Duchess Allyson, touching her hand.

Aloud, he said, "I do thank you, Your Grace, for your hospitality and your husband's." But to her skin, in the witches' way, he told her, *"For a moment, when he pro-claimed me, I thought the archbishop could be a mancer."*

She nearly startled away from him, but managed to form a gracious smile, despite her shadowed eyes. "You are most welcome, Your Majesty," she replied out loud, though her voice trembled. *"He's been prelate for more than a decade, and was Lord Chancellor before that, with-out a hint of scandal."*

"They've been working a long time in secret." He searched her face and said what he needed her, and all of them, to hear: "I hope you know, Your Grace, that I harbored no plans to take the place of the king, your son

by marriage. If God has placed me on this path, I hope He will direct it for the best." The words felt strange. Still, the reflex arose from years of training: to pray, to cross himself, to call out to God in a moment of need. He had been a boy the last time he placed his trust in God, before he had seen an angel die.

"And take this cup from you, Your Majesty?" boomed the archbishop.

Breaking contact with Allyson, Elisha faced the man. "I was not born, nor raised to this, but I will do the best that I'm able."

"Tell us, Your Majesty, if you would, when did the stigmata first grace your hands?" The prelate drew back, gesturing with his own hands, a flash of jewels and gold-woven cuffs. He never seemed to spill the gravy. Concern wrinkled the corners of his eyes, and wonder turned a smile at his lips—his every gesture and expression limned with longing.

A dedicated and venerable churchman, or a secret enemy? Elisha took a long draught from his goblet and set it down gently, his fingers lingering on the cool, chased silver of the base. The scar stood out pale against the sun-darkened skin of his hand—darker, he suddenly saw, than that of any noble present, who prided themselves on their pale flesh. Elisha leaned back and faced the archbishop, laying his hands upon the table, spreading his awareness in the prelate's direction. "I struggled with a devil in the darkness. He would have taken my soul, Your Grace. The devil pierced my hands—" He held them up, the room quieting outward from his table as the nobles became aware of what was happening. "I was sore beset that night, Your Grace, but slipped his blade. When next we met, it was the devil who died, atop my grave."

Breath seemed arrested in the room, though several crossed themselves. The archbishop still wore his little smile, still revealing nothing, his presence muted, but plain, a litany of Latin, a sense of grandeur, as if the man were full of his position.

Father Osbert, the inquisitor, spoke at last, "An interesting tale, Your Majesty. One I should like to hear in more detail, at some time, if you should be willing." He gave a bow of his head. A dark wing of hair, streaked with silver, slid forward. "His Holiness the Pope would be most intrigued."

"Charge your goblets, all!" Blackmere rose, holding aloft his goblet. "To his Majesty! May he vanquish every devil!" A few chuckles, a few cheers, the sloshing of wine in silver. Blackmere lifted the goblet to Elisha and cried, "Huzzah!"

To God's ears. Elisha smiled, accepting the blessing, and noticed Brigit's keen interest, the tingling sense of her presence far out among the crowd, reaching back toward him.

Chapter 9

◆

Three days later, Elisha stood straight, his arms out, as four servants hovered around him with borrowed garb while Ufford and Allyson looked on, murmuring to one another. This time, the Earl of Blackmere had fussed about in his belongings to find his absolute best, a raiment of brocades stiff with gold work and silks so fine they caught on Elisha's rough fingers as he held them up.

"Ah!" The earl rose again, a shirt of deepest blue held out before him. "Try this."

Dubiously, Elisha accepted it, once more holding a shirt in front of his chest, concealing his scars. Three days of searching the city and interrogating the leaders of the peasant revolt had revealed nothing of the proper king. The mayor, reinstated, drew up plans of the damaged areas as his men drew from the wreckage both the living and the dead. Thomas was not among them, and now Elisha stood poised to make good on the archbishop's intentions: This afternoon, they would crown him king.

"Yes, that one," Allyson declared. "It does well with your eyes."

"Good." He started to pull it on, only to have the servants pounce on him, slipping it over head and shoulders. Lacing ran from his elbows to his wrists, but the servants left it loose, loosening the neckline to be sure he would be properly anointed when the time came. With the scar over his heart thus revealed, despite his clothing, Elisha felt more vulnerable than when he had been bare-chested.

"Where's the coat? Yes, the Cathay brocade. Excellent. We shall make a king of you yet, Elisha Barber," the earl crowed.

"If we must," Elisha murmured.

The Cathay brocade hung loose around Elisha's hips, and one servant immediately set-to with needle and thread, taking in the extra fabric while Elisha tried not to sway.

Duke Randall appeared at the open door, smiling for the first time since Elisha's return, though even this looked tremulous. "Good tidings."

A momentary light filled his wife's weary face, but his smile fled; so it was not the news they awaited so eagerly. "A few more of the barons have come around. They're not with you completely, but they are at least grateful for the peasants' docility. Tomorrow, we'll meet with a few of them and start mediating the peasant disputes."

"There's work to be done re-building the damage inside the city, Your Majesty," Ufford put in, "The mayor has been asking. Shall I make arrangements for builders?"

"Aye," said Elisha, "I'll trust you."

The Lord Chancellor merely inclined his head, but he seemed more at ease, now, resuming his role even with such a peculiar king.

"The bombards have arrived from Dunbury, a bit late for the siege, of course," Randall said. "I had been thinking, given our French concerns, that we might install them at the Tower."

"I wish we could haul them to the shore and blast the French before they ever get here," Elisha said. "A lot fewer dead that way."

"We'd have to know where they are landing, and

when." With a nod, Randall stepped aside to give his wife a swift kiss on the cheek, then he gestured toward Elisha. "This looks good."

"Sufficiently regal, do you think?" the earl inquired, as he moved to join them, his head cocked to one side.

"Quite," Randall remarked. "And it's a good thing, for the procession has arrived."

Ufford raised his brows at this, then trotted back down the stairs of the earl's in-town chambers with the duke close behind.

A tremor crept up Elisha's back. Feasting and fine clothes were one thing, but coronation itself was quite another. Any man might play at king in the privacy of a few chambers, even with the archbishop's claims and the rumor of miracles spreading out from London faster than the fire that had scorched its heart. But to take the oath, in the Cathedral, before God and all the barons. . . Still, he could not persuade them to wait, not while the French lurked and there was no sign of the proper king.

Allyson drew herself up and approached, taking Elisha's hands in hers. Through the contact, she told him, *"Thank you, Elisha. I know this is not your wish, but it lifts his burden. More than that, the project gives him a new focus, rather than dwelling on our loss. It nearly shattered him."*

"Don't give up yet, my lady. The lost may still be found."

"How, Elisha, if all of our searching cannot reveal them?" Her voice within him echoed with the sadness he saw in her shadowed eyes.

"That I cannot say." No matter how he wished it different. Last night, the two of them stayed together in the king's chamber, sending their secret senses out, finding a hundred echoes of Elisha's presence, and none of Thomas or Rosalynn.

"I wake up nights imagining the things I will do to them if they hurt my daughter—and that is all that keeps me from the edge of madness."

"If they have hurt her," Elisha replied, *"I'll help you."*

They shared a brief, grim smile, then he broke the contact. "We shouldn't keep the audience waiting too long."

"I still say we ought to have undertaken the procession from Westminster—it'll be a bit of a ride from here to there," Blackmere muttered as they descended to the street. "And there are proprieties to be maintained."

Elisha took a deep breath. "I'm sure my reign, God let it be brief, will be full of impropriety. We might as well begin it that way."

The servants stepped up to drape Elisha's shoulders with a full cape of velvet and ermine. Little tails of black-tipped fur waved in Elisha's face as the duke opened the door. The man who would be king stifled a sneeze as a wayward tail tickled his nose.

A cheer rose from the street, carried in waves to either side like the fierce wind of a bombard's blast. Elisha braced himself.

The earl and the duke strode outside, joining a gauntlet of other barons, most of them unfamiliar—Mortimer, Gloucester, and the loudest of the doubters had been relegated to the back of the procession. A long red cloth pointed the way between the ranks of nobles, to Elisha's own horse, another gift from Thomas, and likely the least of the mounts in the royal stable. Nonetheless, the mare looked grand in her new finery. She was the only mount Elisha trusted to carry him, and he smiled at the sight of her.

As if the smile shot sunlight into the dour day, the cheering grew yet louder. The barons, clutching various ceremonial spears and crosses, glanced behind them to where the townsfolk and peasants gathered, while the cluster of clergy set to meet him formed a mass of dark robes and pale faces set off by the glitter of the golden things they carried. A group of former soldiers—many of them men that Elisha had tended at the battlefield—set up a holler of their own, waving their arms. Raucous laughter permeated the party of soldiers, and Elisha suspected that some of these had begun to celebrate last night—if not before.

Close by, Randall murmured, "Come, Elisha. We can't wait all day."

"Aye." Elisha squared his shoulders and descended the steps onto the broad red cloth. The omnipresent servants helped him to mount, turning to assist the rest of the barons to their horses as well. Some of the spears jingled with silver bells on the morning breeze and banners snapped to attention all around.

The abbot and his monks set out at a stately pace accompanied by chants Elisha caught intermittently. After them rode a large man, armored head to toe, and bearing a huge sword across his lap. The king's champion, who would defend against all comers, any man who dared deny the rightful king his place. Elisha guided his horse in behind, but not too close, half-afraid the fellow would turn his blade against Elisha himself. The usurper.

He managed to keep his smile most of the way to the gate, but the slow pace of the procession became grueling before they'd even passed from the shadow of the wall. To the right rose the spire of St. Bartholomew and the last of his smile fled among the graves where his brother lay. By the time they reached the cathedral, his brief excitement left him wearier than ever, and his day had only just begun. Servants guided his cape lest he become entangled in it as Elisha slid down from the horse with little grace and let his clothes be resettled for his entrance along another span of crimson wool. The solemn procession turned noisy as spears bumped pillars and boots clattered into the broad space of Westminster. When they neared the altar, the clergymen parted, leaving Elisha alone before the archbishop. His presence struck Elisha with a force nearly physical as he bowed to kiss the man's ring. The first time he touched the archbishop, he thought he sensed the strange negation of a mancer. There was no hint of that now.

"Have you made the proper observances before the Lord, my prince?" the archbishop inquired.

"I have, Your Grace."

"And is your conscience cleansed before the Lord, my prince?"

Elisha stared into the blank face above him, his throat dry. Anticipating lightning, or at least thunder, he lied, his voice falling in the hush of the Lord's house. Surely, if God had any power in this world, He would apply it now. "It is, Your Grace." But nothing happened to disrupt the ceremony, and Elisha realized he'd been half-hoping that something would.

"Then rise and take your place."

As he had been tutored, Elisha straightened and crossed to the stone pulpit, ascending to the throne placed there for him. Gilded from its feet to the peak at its back, the chair bore a painting of Edward the Confessor, there to witness the crowning of his descendants. Elisha turned his back on the stern saint and sank into the chair with a relief he prayed did not show. Under the heavy cape, he shivered.

From the packed pews, barons glared up at him—or was it the flickering light which painted their faces with such hostility? No, for Duke Randall and his lady gazed proudly at their pupil, and Brigit, standing a few rows behind, glowed in spite of her father's gloomy air.

Facing each corner of the vast church, the archbishop called out for the people's acclaim to accept this new king. In his turn, Elisha faced them as well.

He descended on cue, other hands removing his cloak and coat as he lay down before the altar. The cushions provided ample comfort against the hard stone floor, and his mind drifted with the Latin liturgy spoken above him. He shifted, staring at the distant arches, trying to stay awake if not interested, and felt a jab of pain. Biting down on any response, Elisha still drew the archbishop's glittering gaze.

When the man looked away again, his sermon carrying on, Elisha crept a hand up and found a needle still protruding from the seam of one cushion where a hasty seamstress must have forgotten it in the rush to prepare the grand event. A bit of blood damped his shirt from the needle's scratch, and he hoped it wouldn't show. Given the uses of blood he now knew, he couldn't afford to leave even a few drops lying about. He worked the needle free and stuck it into the cloth of his own sleeve, then froze, trying to assume the proper posture as the archbishop gazed down at him. He'd gotten the needle at least, though he could do nothing about the cushion itself.

At last, he rose to his knees, hands spread as the split sleeves fell back from his arms.

The archbishop towered over him, a pot of sacred oil in his hand. More Latin embroidered the air as he dipped one finger and pressed it against Elisha's inner elbow on the left, then on the right.

Elisha flinched, his flesh recalling the thin burn of a brand placed just there.

The archbishop's eyebrows sank over his dark gaze, his lips pinching off the Latin words. His finger jabbed again, smearing oil, warm from his touch, upon the brand at Elisha's chest; one eyebrow edged upward as his finger inadvertently traced the scar of Thomas's blade. How had it been for his king, kneeling here, receiving the blessings he was born to? How would Thomas react when he knew Elisha had been there after him?

With a sharp breath, Elisha glared and the hand retreated, the archbishop's lips curling slightly upward, turning his words from a blessing to a taunt as he moved in a slow circle to Elisha's back, dabbing the oil between his shoulder blades. It felt too much like blood. It dribbled and the archbishop wiped it away. Elisha's next breath caught as the archbishop completed his circle to stand before him once again.

Lips forming the endless stream of language, like a spell for his Lord, the archbishop drew the cross on Elisha's forehead with oil that oozed down along his nose, causing an unbearable flutter in his left eye.

Schooling himself to stillness, Elisha let it go, sacred oil anointing his nose and trailing down to follow the hard line of his lips until the dart of his tongue stopped its progress. Only that uneasy conscience made him so susceptible, imagining that the oil worked its way along his scars, the reminders of his sins, and seeped through his flesh to find out the truth of his heart.

The archbishop withdrew a few paces into the telling quiet of the vast cathedral. Outside someone cheered, and the sounds finally reached within, Elisha's supporters calling out their acclaim, giving the silences between all the more power. Such acclamation was a historical precedent of kingship, Ufford had explained. At the coronation of the Conqueror, the acclaim of the masses had been so loud the new king's soldiers took it for a riot and dozens were killed.

The rest of the ceremony became, in Elisha's mind, a blur, cacophony alternating with silence when it seemed nobody knew whether they should cheer or weep. At the feast which followed, Elisha ate little, and nothing that had not already been sampled by a royal taster. Finally, his companions led him back up into the Tower, the stronghold of England's kings, and the prison of her traitors. In himself, it now housed both.

Chapter 10

❦

Elisha waved off the cheers and fawning at the steps to St. Thomas's tower, where the king's quarters awaited. A few guards, including Madoc and another of his men, stood by in the shadows to escort him up, and another figure, draped in a long cloak, moved a little nearer. Brigit. From the way the soldiers stared through or in another direction, she had cast herself a deflection, but he was too sensitive to her presence to be deceived. Already, the crown weighed him down, the oil sticking his silk shirt to his chest, and all he wanted was to be free of this finery. But he needed the chance to speak to her, without her father's hovering or the new attention of the court. Elisha stared at her until she nodded in acknowledgement, then he turned away to mount the stairs. Walter and Pernel, the body servants he inherited along with the chamber, waited inside with the fire stoked high and two lanterns lit. They relieved him of the crown, the chain, the cloak—peeling away the layers of another man's life—while Brigit quietly followed and waited by the bed. The movement of the servants' hands over his clothing, deft and professional, took on a different meaning with Brigit watching. He felt her eyes upon him as the servants released the lacing at his wrists and helped him shrug out of the heavy brocade, its deeply dagged sleeves brushing the floor. Elisha palmed the blood-tipped needle and took the chance to drop it in the fire when he turned that way.

"Thank you," he told the servants when they finished. This time, they gave no reaction, though Pernel might have smiled a bit. Their indignation at being servants to a man with even less standing than themselves had somewhat relaxed over the last few days, much to Elisha's relief.

Ufford stopped in with a brief knock to take charge of the regalia. "It proceeded well from where I stood, Your Majesty."

"As well as may be," Elisha replied. "Thanks for your help."

Closing the box over the chain, Ufford said, "I understand your confessor has arrived from Dunbury. He shall be installed just beyond the gatehouse. Parliament is not in session, of course, but most of the members are not far off, and the others are returning. It may be an opportune time if you should wish to call them."

Returning? Coming to denounce him, no doubt, but he gave a weary nod. "Thank you all. You may go."

Ufford bowed himself out, but the body servants shared a look, and Walter moved toward the adjacent chamber. Elisha stopped him with a gesture. "Out for the night, please."

"If you're certain, Majesty." Walter stood with bowed head, but eyes upturned, watching. Pernel bowed his lanky form and nudged Walter into following suit. They gathered their bound pallets from the corner. "We'll be on the landing, then, Majesty."

Elisha hesitated, trying to think of an excuse to send them further, but this was the most privacy he could expect. Clad only in the white undertunic that reached his knees, Elisha watched them go, his gaze lingering on the door for a long moment before he turned to face the woman who awaited his attention.

"You realize," she said as she lowered her hood, "that you've just invited me to stay the night."

"I beg your pardon?"

"Servants on the landing." She let the cloak fall away, revealing the long line of her neck, the pale edge of her chemise framing the swell of her breasts in a tightly laced gown. The gown fell loose and fashionable just beneath her breasts, a style that could conceal her pregnancy for another two months, easily. "Even by casting a deflection, I can hardly open the door and slip by them. But perhaps that's what you wanted?" She drew her fingers along the thick coverlet of the royal bed and came to stand at its foot, the crimson bed curtains like fire and blood at her back.

His throat felt dry, and he moved away to pour a goblet from the waiting jug of wine. "You came to me, Brigit—what do you want?"

"As your look upon the stairs showed me, Elisha, I can't deceive you." She swayed forward, joining him at the trestle table, her fingers inviting him to pour another goblet. "You have what I want. I am humble enough to ask you to share it." Her green eyes focused on him over the goblet, then she raised it before her. "Elisha, Dei gratia Rex Anglie."

The floor chilled his bare feet in spite of the huge hearth at his back, and he took a swallow.

"The part about the laying on of hands, that was brilliant!" She beamed, settling onto the bench opposite, leaning a little forward. "I don't think Hugh ever supported the claim. He just gave out little trinkets meant to carry his healing. But to convince the archbishop! A masterstroke."

Elisha gave a startled laugh, and made a show of kneeling to jab at the fire. She thought he had made his elevation happen. Was it better for him if she believed it? He withdrew his emotions to the skin, and deeper—she would expect as much, if she came close enough to touch him. "A holy man is always eager to find a miracle."

"To be honest, Elisha, I wouldn't have thought you had this in you. Any of it. You never seemed eager for power."

"A man is a fool who doesn't take what he's offered."

She laughed, low and thrilling, and Elisha closed his eyes, still kneeling before the fire as at a pagan altar. Offering indeed. He let his awareness encompass her as she spoke. "My mother wanted a witch upon the throne, to change the course of England. We always imagined it would be me."

Elisha replaced the poker carefully and came to the table, sinking into the chair at its head. Firelight deepened her red-gold hair and put a blush upon her cheeks and throat, and he did not know what to say.

Brigit frowned a little. "What are your plans, Elisha?"

He laughed again, the combination of strain and wine and her nearness making him feel almost as giddy as if he had worked magic all day long. "Plans? I have none, but hopes in plenty. I hope I live to survive whatever barons come to challenge me. I hope that France takes just long enough in getting here that we can find a way to counter their attack. After that, I hope the barons don't retaliate too strongly for the peasant revolts." He ruffled his hands through his hair, wincing as his shoulder gave a hint of pain from the needle's prick, then letting his hands fall back to the table.

"Mmm." She reached out her pale fingers, their nails smoothly rounded, and stroked the back of his hand, tracing the scar, then let her hand curve gently into his with a tantalizing warmth. "There's so much to think on, love," she murmured. "I never imagined."

Caution urged him to withdraw his hand, but the contact would reveal her just as well—probably more so. "I'd prefer your honesty." If she had any.

The purr left her voice, her grip tightening. "You're not ready for this, Elisha. You don't know what to do or how to do it. I'm not criticizing you—you've never been at court, you simply don't know. You'll look to Duke Dunbury and his lady—at least she's a magus, but he's always trying too hard to please the other barons. Ufford will give you all the advice you need about stately living and politics, but he'll never understand where you've come from, what you've seen. And now you even have your own confessor?" She nearly laughed at that. "You want to live; I want that, too. I want our people to live peacefully and openly, Elisha, and your being here gives us that chance. Let me advise you, stay near you. Let us work together. I can bring the magi behind you; even without magic, we have influence in so many places. Gloucester and Mortimer are against you—we can deal with that. You need not rule in fear." Her thumb stroked over his hand, radiating comfort.

"How would you deal with it?" he asked carefully. "By killing them? That would have been Alaric's way. Or was he no more than your path to the throne?"

This time her face flushed from within—the emotions of pregnancy getting the better of her usual control. Elisha smiled inwardly, grateful for any advantage.

"Don't taunt me with his name, Elisha." Tears sparked at the corners of her eyes, and she flicked them away with her fingertips. Through their contact, she replied, *"Alaric was a schemer before I knew him. I never knew all of his plans."*

True—their altercations in the New Forest had shown him that much. Elisha wet his lips, sending his trust even as he spoke, "Would Thomas have been next for you if he hadn't remarried?"

Brigit's hand tensed in a tiny spasm, her eyes briefly hard. That question struck too close.

"You're trying to win freedom for our people," Elisha said in the witches' way, gently as with a nervous patient.

"That's right," she snapped back. *"I would do what it takes. With you declared traitor, then dead—"* She shook off that thought.

He went on carefully, *"But I'm not. I'm alive, and then some."*

"Earth and sky and fire, Elisha, you—" She shook her head again, but this time in wonder. *"Every time I think you've fallen, that you're beyond all aid, you rise. It's no wonder they stand in awe."* She took his other hand then, her thumbs covering both scars. *"Let me help you this time. You have the power, Elisha, all the power now. Let me guide you, as I did back at Dunbury."*

With a shock of heat and remembrance she showed him their kiss in the ruined church, the lessons they shared in the stream, and that moment she opened her body to his, embracing him body and soul. Or so he had believed. Her sending shot into him, a thrust of urgency and desire, and Elisha flinched. Her thumbs covered his wounds, but called up, too, the memory of the knife that stabbed his hands together. Elisha turned the memory, pulling it back before she saw too much. He broke contact, his heart thundering as he sucked down a breath.

"What happened to you?" she whispered. Her hands clutched together, pleading, but her gaze, her lips, for just a moment, hardened against him.

"You met a man at my graveside—the man who tried to kill me."

"He saved you before, from Alaric. It was the same man, wasn't it? Some sort of magus." She frowned then, concentrating, and Elisha's doubts congealed, thickening in his stomach.

"He didn't tell you what he did?" Elisha probed. "What he is?"

"Do you know?" She tried to keep her voice sympathetic, but her lust had shifted, searching now for power, the things that others knew and did not share.

"He did this." Elisha held up his hands.

"I'm sorry," she sighed.

Elisha shrugged one shoulder. "I take it you didn't talk long?"

"With the gravedigger?" She almost looked affronted. "Rather repulsive, wasn't he?"

An evasion, not an answer. "More than you know," Elisha replied. He wiped at the smear of oil by his left eye, and Brigit relaxed toward him again.

"But you need rest, my king. Come, let me sing you to sleep." She rose and held out her hand. After a moment, she spread the fingers and waved them. "Come, Elisha. You should have nothing to fear, not tonight."

He once said something similar to Thomas, before he even knew who he was, beyond the fear, the pain, the bone-weariness of hiding. Elisha, too, was hiding—especially from her. He took a deep breath, drawing back his senses, lacquering over the secrets of his heart as if he applied extra dressings to a wound, anticipating blood. Then he rose and took her hand to let her lead him. She allowed him close without moving, her breath stroking his face. "I burned the hanging rope, Elisha. It will never hurt you again."

And in her touch, he knew that was true.

Brigit's lips gave a rueful turn. "Don't be so surprised, love. Have I truly been so cruel?"

Elisha merely shook his head as they drifted toward the bed and sank into the mattress. She draped the coverlet over his shoulders and lay on top of the covers at his side, making no move to unlace her dress. Wiping away the last of the oil from his face with a soft cloth, Brigit sang softly, one of his mother's songs, one he used to sing as he stitched up the soldiers in the make-shift hospital at Dunbury. She played him like an instrument—or thought she did—knowing seduction would avail her nothing. Some part of him wanted to give in to her new modesty, accepting her at her gentle word and chaste deed. But, even as his eyes slid shut, his head buoyed by Thomas's pillow, his deeper heart knew better. If London was a nest of vipers, then tonight he lay by their queen. Or one who wished she was.

Chapter 11

❧

$\mathcal{H}$is wrists, shoulders, and hips ached, his knees
throbbed from crouching too long, and every
breath was labored. The inside of his cheek pinched with
pain, but he let the blood ooze over his lip, quietly, quietly. The tang of blood mingled with the aftertaste of
porridge. His open eyes saw darkness, the cloth that kept
him blind was snug, but not biting. Never that. And he
finally knew why. What a fool he'd been, not to realize!
He could almost feel Elisha's hand upon his brow, tracing a line of blood. How would he know if it worked?
How would he know if—

Elisha lay still a moment, bewildered by thoughts and
sensations that were not his own. A jolt of understanding
slapped the sleep from his mind, but he squeezed his
eyes shut, curling into himself, reaching back. The softness of the king's bed overlaid the damp, hard floor, the
scent of the dying fire and the woman beside him mingling at the back of his throat with the taste of blood, the
lock of hair bound inside his cuff gone suddenly warm.
Elisha flung himself into the tenuous contact, searching.
East and south—little but water. West? North? The ache
in his bent spine intensified. Elisha whimpered, stretch-

ing himself, but the impression was dark, distant, steeped with despair.

"Elisha?" Brigit's voice emerged from the darkness, her hand clutching his shoulder.

He shook her off, the contact fracturing. No!

"Are you in pain?"

"Hush! Don't touch me!" Elisha scrambled from the bed, pushing away Brigit's fallen cloak to kneel on the floor. He pressed his wrists together, anything that might strengthen the affinity he had briefly shared. He returned to the dismal place of his dream. Distantly, he heard a cry, turning his darkened eyes. "Rosie?"

"If he's done eating, get him gagged," ordered a thick voice in the dream, a rumble Elisha strained to hear.

Someone touched his face, and he flinched, but the hand gripped his chin. "Shit, he's bleeding."

"Oh, Hell—not bleeding! What'd he tell us? No fucking bleeding!"

The hand squeezed tighter, fingers digging in, promising more violence. Lower, thicker, "You'll regret that when hisself comes back."

Cloth shoved harshly in his mouth could not stop the bright sense of triumph that cut the darkness. "Wipe it up—every drop—shit—" Water dashed over his head—
—and the contact was gone. Elisha gasped, rearing back, shaking out the aches of Thomas's bondage. His eyes snapped open, and the king's chamber slowly resolved around him, made ruddy by the dim glow of the dying coals.

Brigit lay on the bed, staring down at him, brow furrowed. "Nightmare?"

"Yes," he said, but the word was a breath of exaltation. Thomas lived! Rosie, too. Somewhere to the north. They were fed, kept in darkness, bound, but alive.

Brigit's hand sank down to touch his cheek, and Elisha bestirred himself to offer the pain, the fear, the despair, rushing to conceal whose living nightmare he had suffered. It wasn't enough, but it gave him a direction, and a sense of distance, a place to start looking. Thank God, they lived.

"Majesty?" Walter's soft voice outside the door, accompanied by a gentle tapping.

Brigit's hand stilled upon his cheek, seeking the memory of the angel's touch her mother left him so long ago. Elisha leaned a little into the touch, letting her believe he was soothed by this, hiding his elation. Then the urge to smile left him. Thomas's captors knew he had bled. Even if they never knew his effort worked to reach Elisha had worked, they knew Thomas had tried, and they said he would be punished. How they would hurt him without letting him bleed, Elisha dared not imagine.

"You'd better go," he breathed to Brigit.

"Why?"

"Please, just go." He gathered her cloak to pass it up to her, and their eyes met. What would she expect? What could he give her now, to cover for the things she must not know? "Thank you," he whispered.

"You're welcome, Your Majesty." She leaned a little more and kissed him, light and swift, upon the cheek—a touch that tingled with dangerous curiosity and a hint of resentment—then swirled the cloak once more about her.

"Majesty?" The knock repeated. "Heard a bang, we did."

Elisha pushed himself to his feet. "Come," he called out.

As Walter and Pernel entered, Brigit slipped out, her deflection already in place.

"Are you well, Majesty?" Pernel inquired, while Walter moved to stoke up the fire.

"I suffered a nightmare. I'm better now. How long until day?"

"Not long, Majesty."

"Good, I've got work to do." Elisha lifted the lid on the nearest chest of clothing, then waved a hand in Pernel's direction. "Lanterns, please."

"Aye, Majesty." The servant complied, holding the light while Elisha found day clothes—something without too much cloth or lacing. Seeing what he was up to, Pernel set down the lantern and sprang to it, helping Elisha dress. "What sort of work, Majesty?"

"I need a map. We must have some."

Pernel chuffed. "Some, Your Majesty. It's to do with the French, eh?"

"That, too," Elisha said, oddly pleased by his servant's more casual question. Perhaps the darkness and the hour created an intimacy that made the man let down his guard against royal disfavor. "Attend me?"

"Course, Majesty. They'll be in the archive." Pernel and Walter shared a look as they helped Elisha on with a mantle against the night's chill. Then Pernel led the way down the stairs, a few guards joining quietly in the walk, out to the space between the walls and in again, toward the Tower itself, glowing in the last of the moonlight. Pernel's small lantern reflected that glow. A yeoman warder stamped the butt of his pike on the stair, then saw their faces revealed by the torch above his head and stepped aside with a bow. "Majesty."

Elisha still found the address a bit disconcerting, but he accepted its power tonight to pass him inside the kingdom's greatest fortress, with the freedom of all it contained. Knowledge. Mordecai stayed back on Wight, immersing himself in knowledge. Perhaps his teaching had been this effective: making Elisha realize the strength in knowledge before action. With his long strides adopting the king's urgency, Pernel took the stairs two at a time until they reached a small chamber with a high ceiling and a rack of scrolls and volumes that nearly reached that height. "Here we are, Majesty. Maps, you say?" Pernel lit two more lanterns, filling the room with their glow, as they gazed up at the shelf. "Shall I wake the archivist?"

Elisha shook his head. "Not yet—not now." The two men approached their problem, sliding out this scroll then another, until they converged on the chest.

"Francia!" crowed Pernel as he unrolled one of them onto the table. "Our lands or theirs, Your Majesty?"

"Both, for now." He unrolled a parchment and frowned at it, unsure what he was seeing. It looked like a tangle of thread with words bound in among the twisted lines. He found Londinium marked at its center and lifted it for a better look. "What do you know about the north country?"

Pernel looked up from a thin, square volume. "Meaning Yorkshire or Scotland, Your Majesty?" His face in the side-light looked troubled, and he lowered his eyes to the page.

"Either—I don't know." Elisha let his awareness spread further around him, sensing the servant's retreat. "You need not be afraid of me, Pernel," he said softly.

The answer came at a mumble that Elisha strained to hear. "I went north with his Majesty King Thomas, before, y'know?"

"When he was the prince."

Pernel bobbed a nod, his eyes showing white at the corners where he peered back at his new king. "You can have up your own servants, Majesty—"

"Peace," Elisha said, holding up his hands. "He is not my enemy."

Pernel frowned, and Elisha considered how much to say. "I did not ask for this, and I did not harm the king or queen." He drew a long breath. "If it were up to me, Pernel, they would be here, and I would not. Help me find them, please."

The frown deepened, Pernel's long face drawn down, his hands clutching the great book.

"You're not the first to think me mad. You don't like me because I've taken his place." He leaned a little closer, even as Pernel stiffened, his breath caught. "Help me find him."

Pernel swallowed hard. "God's truth, Your Majesty?"

"God's truth. His enemies and mine are the same—it's not just France I'm talking about."

"No," said the servant, after a moment, "France would've asked a ransom, wouldn't they, Majesty?" He set aside the book and took Elisha's map. "Yorkshire. Scotland?" They rose and went to the table, weighting the map with a ruler, stylus and ink stone. "Went up this way, we did." Pernel traced one of the crooked lines past a series of words. "The coast don't look much like this. This map don't go far enough," he muttered, then he dropped down back to the chest.

With the map now oriented properly, Elisha looked at the top, the coastline Pernel had indicated. He closed his eyes and focused on what he had felt in Thomas's desperate sharing, bringing every sensation back to mind. Yes—the salty taste of the sea. Elisha braced his knuckles on the table. "The coastline," he said shortly. "Anything with that coast."

"That'll be sea charts, though, Majesty—"

A knock echoed through the little room, and both men froze. Elisha wet his lips, his stomach clenched. "Come," he said, but he could not muster the right air of command as the archbishop entered.

Clad in a robe of exquisite wool—so finely woven that its simple cut belied its cost—the archbishop raised a lantern of his own, making his arched brows seem the more pointed. "I saw you cross the yard, Your Majesty, and thought perhaps you sought my own domain. The church lies below." His eyes traced the spread of maps. "What stirs you from your rest, Majesty?"

Elisha straightened, shifting his hands behind his back, fingers splayed, hoping to forestall anything Pernel might say. "France. What else keeps England's king awake?"

The archbishop tipped his head. "It is rewarding to see that a man who rose for his other gifts should also take an interest in our foreign relations. That is . . . unexpected."

Almost as if it were also *undesirable* for Elisha to concern himself with France. Elisha shuffled the maps a bit. "This one doesn't show all the coastline." He plucked out the map Pernel first located and prayed he was looking at it the right way around. "I find I don't know enough about our enemy."

"Have you then devised a plan to avoid war, Your Majesty? I know it usually falls to Dunbury to create such stratagems, but I fear that recent events have left him less fit than one might wish, poor man." He crossed himself, glancing skyward.

"You serve on the king's council as well—what can you tell me about our recent dealings with France?"

"I am not a worldly man, Your Majesty. The enemy I fight rarely shows himself for pitched battle." He radiated a holy sincerity, hands folded before him.

"But you must've been to visit the pope, yes?" Elisha rolled the map out atop the first. "What do you know of the lands between?"

"It was primarily a sea voyage, Your Majesty, and I fear that I did not suffer well the waves." He gave a pinched but rueful smile. "Here is Avignon, where the Holy Father resides, in a palace so grand that it puts the Eternal City, Rome herself, somewhat to shame, surrounded by the wealth that princes only long for." His long fingers stroked across the parchment, then pinned it down. "They say that only a Frenchman can now serve in that highest office of the Church. Perhaps Father Osbert can tell you more? I believe he is a Frenchman born and bred."

"The inquisitor? What if he's a spy?"

The archbishop reared back and crossed himself. "Your Majesty! Can you make such a claim against a priest of the holy church?"

"It is my job to be suspicious. You gave me this role for holy reasons, Your Grace. But if I am to keep it, it will be worldly deeds that earn the crown."

"As you say, Your Majesty." The archbishop inclined his tonsured head, he worked some idea around in his pursed lips and finally said, "I understand you have summoned your own confessor?"

"A priest I know."

"I am at your service, Your Majesty, for any spiritual need."

"You have other tasks to keep you, I'm sure." Elisha held out his hand. "Thank you for your insight and guidance thus far, Your Grace."

The archbishop's eyes sparkled as he reached out and took Elisha's hand, giving only the slightest inclination of his head. His hand was cool and unexpectedly strong, his presence a more subtle blend of faith, calculation, avarice, curiosity. He moved to withdraw, but Elisha clasped the hand in both of his.

"I wouldn't be here if not for you, Your Grace. Don't think I don't know that." Elisha allowed something of the peasant's subservience to seep into his stance. As he increased the contact, the archbishop's presence flickered, like a feeble flame blown by the opening of a door. A false presence—a projection. How sensitive must a magus be to project a presence not his own?

"Surely another would have recognized what I have,

Your Majesty." The archbishop returned his smile, or rather, his teeth did, though his eyes resisted. He looked down then at the scar on Elisha's upper hand. "You are a marked man, my liege. It was only a matter of time before you came to the notice of the Lord."

"All I can say is, I'll do my best to uphold the honor I've been given." Elisha released him. "Your Grace."

"I have no doubt, Your Majesty. Fare you well with France." Still smiling, he swept himself through the door.

Chapter 12

❖

Elisha whirled to Pernel, causing him to drop the arm-load of scrolls he had discovered. "He was Thomas's confessor, wasn't he? The king's confessor?"

"The archbishop, Majesty? Yes."

"How often?"

The servant stared at him, and finally said, "Weekly, just about, Your Majesty. Monthly, at least."

"Saints and martyrs," Elisha murmured, knotting his fingers into his hair as he slumped against the table. And Thomas was a pious man—he would not have held back in his confession. How much did the archbishop already know? Likely he was one of the first to know about Rosalynn's pregnancy. Thomas needed an heir, or the kingdom remained unstable—and someone who wanted that instability would need to do something about it before that heir could be born. Even if he was no necromancer himself, the archbishop could have spread the word among the mancers. Would Thomas have mentioned their friendship? Of course—he would want absolution for the lies he told to try to save Elisha from the flames. Dear God.

Pernel cut him a glance and slowly gathered up the maps.

Would they kill Thomas now? Whatever their purpose, they weren't through with him yet. They used terror, pain, and murder to generate their power—witness Morag's position as a gravedigger. War with France? Why not! Why not take that a step further and set up Elisha as king, ruling the citizenry in opposition to the barons.

By supporting Elisha's elevation, the mancers forged a civil war steeped in personal betrayal, vengeance, and injustice. All England would become their cauldron. And when the French arrived, they would find a nation already on its knees.

"How's the king's confession any of your concern, Majesty?" Pernel grumbled under his breath, so softly that only Elisha's extended senses caught the sense of it as the servant dropped his pile of scrolls on the table.

"How much did King Thomas trust you?"

The servant straightened, hands trembling, his sandy head bowed. "I am pleased to say I had his Majesty's trust in everything, Your Majesty." Pernel forced his hands to relax. "With absolute discretion. Ask anyone. Your Majesty."

"Give me your hand." Elisha held out his own, planting his feet, facing the man.

Pernel sucked a breath through his teeth, drawing his hands close. "You're not—that is, Your Majesty." He blinked fiercely. "I heard stories about what happened after the fire."

"You'll not be withered into an old man, I swear it." Elisha displayed his palms, the scar tissue smooth at their centers.

"Fought the devil, you said."

"And the devil has taken our king."

Pernel's head shot up.

"Our king," Elisha repeated softly, "and I'll be the first to admit it, to anyone I can trust." Again, he offered his hand, praying that the risk would pay off, that he wouldn't have to prevent Pernel from speaking about anything that passed in this room. He suddenly realized what Thomas had meant in wanting Elisha exiled, not only for his own safety, but to avoid his witnessing the things a king might have to do to protect his kingdom.

The servant's hand edged out and finally touched Elisha's.

"Thomas trusted you for absolute discretion," Elisha repeated, watching, keeping contact, and letting his awareness search the man.

Pernel stood proud, though his hand still trembled. "He did, Your Majesty." Conviction filled his presence. He would serve Thomas with his life.

"Would you swear an oath with me, Pernel? To serve me as you served him, as I pray you will serve him again?"

Their eyes met, a killing offense for some nobles. "You don't trust the archbishop?" Pernel asked, wavering. "Majesty?"

"I do not."

Pernel took a deep breath. "Walter's probably told him where to find you this morning. We had word to keep careful watch, that his grace was worried for your faith and thought you needed more guidance. We're to tell him . . . not private things, you understand? Things like this, or like nightmares." Pernel dropped his gaze then. "Forgive me, Your Majesty."

Elisha shook off his apology. "For the archbishop's benefit, in front of everyone, you go right on hating me for a usurping scoundrel. In the meantime, take those maps and find every stone fortress on the northeast coast, churches, too. Stone, with some kind of undercroft. It must be remote." Elisha drew back his hand to rest his chin on his fist.

"You think the king's being held there, Your Majesty?"

And for the first time, Pernel mentioned them both in the same breath without a hint of irony at Elisha's stolen title. "I hope to God they're not moving him," Elisha thought aloud.

"The nightmare!" Pernel scooped up his maps and faced Elisha, flushed. "You had a vision."

It was near enough the truth, though Elisha shuddered to think of the rumors that would be spread through the servants' halls in the next few hours.

Outside, a bell rang for Prime: the Tower's inhabitants would be rising. Pernel smothered a yawn, but nodded. "But you should be at chambers, Your Majesty, to break the fast."

Elisha nodded, taking up the best map of the Channel. "Fast indeed. We have a lot of work to do."

Pernel grinned back at him as they descended to his chambers to start the day.

By the time the bell rang at midday and urged them to supper, Elisha slumped in a rich chair, in a great room, surrounded by arguing lords and barons, the map he had brought now covered with a dozen others, each a little different. His head ached with arguing. Where would the French land? How did anyone know they were coming at all? Why not let them in, at least the throne could be taken by someone with royal blood. Any reference to "royal blood" made Elisha long to leap up and flee to the archive to pore over the maps until he found Thomas and brought him home.

"If you believed that, Kent, why didn't you challenge the coronation?" Randall shouted.

Kent blanched, lips tightening, and flicked a glance at Elisha. "And argue with a miracle?" He crossed himself elegantly. "I don't know how to do that—none of us does. Even the chroniclers and archivists who stayed up these past three days to find a legal challenge dare not throw up the love of law against the word of the Archbishop, never mind the evidence of our own eyes. Men have been healed." He rapped his knuckles on the table. "London yet stands, the peasants once more await our direction—quite nearly everything is right again." He shook his head.

"Everything except the king," Elisha said carefully.

"I'll ask you not to put words into my mouth, Your Majesty." Kent, a tall man grown thick around the stomach, crossed himself again, as if merely applying the title to Elisha made him think of doing penance.

"You won't be charged with treason for doubting me. I'd have to charge myself for that. But the doubt must end. France is coming, and we're still in here, fighting with each other. Don't let your doubts hold you back from action."

"But how do we know this, Majesty?" said Mortimer. "Rumors, only, but there are always rumors."

Sweat slicked Randall's red face. "You were there at Dunbury when the French ambassadors approached Prince Alaric. Every word and deed was a threat. That gaudy reliquary they gave him was a threat. The kingdom's been a mess since before Hugh died—God rest him. If you were King Philip, wouldn't you press the advantage?"

"Some preparation is prudent, as always, Dunbury, but I won't levy men for this phantom war." Mortimer leaned back, eyes half-closed. A murmur of assent passed the room. "Call up Parliament, Your Majesty, and let it come to debate. If the vote is for an army, then we'll raise our levies."

"That could be months," Randall snapped.

"And the season for war is nearly over," said Gloucester. "Even the French would hesitate now."

"William the Conqueror crossed the Channel in September."

While they shouted at one another, servants moved among them, silent, laying out the tables with ale, bread, cheese, steaming plates of leeks and roasted fowls. Elisha's taster was already at work, filling him a plate, and taking a few bites of each item. He finally nodded to approve Elisha's reach for the bread, a hard thing to poison. Since his accession, every moment and action seemed freighted with hazards, but he took a quiet, guilty pleasure in eating the king's bread. Finely milled flour made it soft and white, while an oven kept under the watchful gaze of an entire staff ensured the crust was perfectly crisp, never over-cooked—nothing like the hard, dark loaves of his childhood, nor the mealy bread he could afford on his earnings as a barber. Once in a while, he had been lucky enough to have a good baker as a patient and to be paid in bread.

Weighing the loaf, Elisha looked down at his hands. The scars remained in part because Thomas's own hands had not yet healed from being branded for stealing food. "My Lord Chancellor?" He gestured Ufford closer. "If I want to pass a law to say that no man can be bodily punished for the theft of food, do I need the approval of the council?"

"No, Your Majesty. You can proclaim a writ," Ufford said, but his mouth turned down.

"You don't approve."

"The Bakers', Butchers' and Mercers' guilds will not approve if the punishment is lifted for theft, Your Majesty."

Elisha envisioned rank upon rank of people standing between the throne and justice. "Labor, then. Anyone convicted of such a theft must do labor to the value of the theft."

Ufford's eyebrows ticked upward. "It would be like hiring thieves, Your Majesty. Wherefore should they not keep stealing?"

Elisha frowned. "Triple the value of the theft?"

Ufford considered this a long moment. "They might accede to this." He gave a little bow and turned away to the clerics who sat by, ink at the ready.

Washing down his bread with a swallow of ale, Elisha watched the great men of his council settle in to their meals, stabbing meat and tearing bread, glaring at each other or leaning close, muttering. The archbishop settled coolly at the opposite end of the room, delicately breaking morsels of bread to sop up his platter, disdaining the earthly fights. Elisha was king, and yet, to take any useful action, he needed them—their knights and levies, their support. Mordecai worshipped knowledge, building it into a bulwark to defend his sensitivity. But Elisha sat in knowledge now, certain the French were coming, and the knowledge availed him nothing.

Ufford returned to his side, finishing a morsel of food and delicately wiping down his fingers.

Elisha pushed back from the table, and his own stillness spread slowly across the room, men taking a few hasty bites, pushing back their plates, and gesturing for servants to take them away. They stared up the table, at him. "What will it take to convince you to prepare for war?" he asked.

"What it always does, in the absence of an actual invasion, Your Majesty: the support of parliament," Kent replied.

"Then call them," Elisha demanded. "Whatever members are not already here must be recalled. The Lord Chancellor said they had not gone far."

Kent exchanged a glance with Gloucester. "I am sure that is true, Your Majesty," he said carefully.

"What else, then? Why does the idea make you nervous?"

"I, Your Majesty? Certes, I am as happy to sit parliament as any other man." He offered a tight smile.

Elisha pushed back from the table and beckoned to the baron. "Give me your hand, my lord Kent." He held out his own.

Kent rose slowly and walked along behind the chairs, then bowed before Elisha but stiffly. "I do not see why—"

"I did not ask you to see, I asked you to give me your hand." If they wanted a miracle king, by God he would give them one.

Sinking down to one knee, Kent placed his hand lightly over Elisha's, his breath caught and mustache twitching.

"Why should I not call parliament, my lord Kent? Am I not king, by the acclaim of both church and country?"

"Of course you should, Your Majesty, I have just said you should." Kent's pale glance darted away, his touch humming with deception.

"Then why does my calling parliament make you nervous?" Elisha sent his own tension into his palm, flooding it with warmth. Lacking the affinity to make a fire or cast a glow over their hands, he focused on the gems that twinkled in his crown, the sunlight that bathed the chamber, and cast himself a dazzle that gleamed upon his head and shone from his eyes.

Kent stiffened, glancing up. "Because they are already here, Your Majesty. Not a formal summons, of course, merely a suggestion from one of their peers. Most of the barons are already installed in their London houses, or in temporary lodgings about the city." He dodged Elisha's gaze. "I have done nothing improper, Your Majesty."

"I should thank you for making my task easier, which is, after all, why I have a council to begin with." He let the light die down, and Kent snatched back his hand. Turning to Ufford, Elisha said, "My Lord Chancellor, it seems the parliament is nearer than we thought."

"Indeed, Your Majesty. Near enough that those who did not attend the coronation should already have come to pay their respects." He flipped open his book, pen poised. "Parliament shall be summoned, Your Majesty. Shall we set the date at a month from tomorrow?"

"A month? But they're already in London!"

Elisha's outburst broke the awe of his earlier manifestation of power, and Gloucester let out a soft groan while a few others drew themselves up as if girding for the fight to continue. Randall cupped his brow in his hand, leaving Elisha feeling like an unruly child.

The Lord Chancellor cleared his throat and said gently, "Many of them are, from what we have just heard, Your Majesty. First, we must determine who is present in town already and who is not. Also, even for those who have returned to London, some of their homes were lost in the recent fire, and we shall have to locate them in their new quarters. Letters must be written to summon each and every one—both those present, and those not, and, to avoid any hint of favoritism, those who are not present must be given opportunity to respond to the summons. It is not merely the lords, of course, the bishops must also be summoned, and the knights of the shires, and the burgesses, if you wish. A month is hardly enough, even to expect a reply from Lancashire, never mind Cumbria, Your Majesty."

"It ought to be at least six weeks, Your Majesty," one of the councilors offered, "and is generally more."

Kent, who had drawn back at Elisha's protest, stalked back to his place, his spine straight and head held high.

Awe would not be enough, even for a pious man like him. England was, in spite of everything, a land of laws — and it was to the law that even the king must accede. "A month tomorrow," Elisha agreed, and prayed it would not be too late.

Chapter 13

❖

The rest of the day, and half the night, all of the Tower scribes were engaged with scripting the summonses. Elisha painstakingly signed every one of them until his wrist ached and his fingers could barely hold the quill. He requested a bare room for this—bare, for a king, meaning only two pages, the Lord Chancellor, and the requisite scribes and yeomen, a dozen men to oversee his childish script and know exactly how long each signature required. Nine letters, over and over again. *Elisha Rex*, *Elisha Rex*, a chant that just might make it so.

When a herald arrived to a gentle knock and a long bow, Elisha dropped the quill with relief a little too obvious. "Yes?"

"His Honor, Geoffrey de Wichingham, Mayor of the City of London," the herald intoned, standing aside as the visitor swept in.

A stocky man clad in stiff velvets that rubbed together as he moved, Wichingham moved forward in mincing steps, gave an elegant bow, then took a few more steps and bowed again, his gold-trimmed cloak trailing after him. In a few more steps, he bowed a final time and remained so, his thick gray hair tumbling forward.

"You must command him, Your Majesty," Ufford whispered.

"Approach?" Elisha said, and Wichingham obeyed as one of the pages trotted out with a cushion for the mayor to kneel on.

"I thank your gracious majesty for the honor of addressing you, Your Majesty."

"The honor is mine," Elisha said, though Ufford's shaggy brows informed him this had been too much. He hurried on. "What brings you to court?"

"Merely to thank you again for your swift and decisive involvement in the matter of the fires." He blinked at the ground near Elisha's new slippers—slippers, because he was rarely allowed out of his chair, never mind out of the Tower, so he need have no fear of walking. "Your Majesty presented quite an impressive display on that occasion, such that many of our citizens still speak of it in wonder, and are, blessedly, more than eager to assist in the efforts to repair the destruction which, in many cases, they themselves were party to."

"I'm glad of it," Elisha replied.

The mayor plowed on, his eyelashes fluttering as he blinked too much. Symptom of an illness, or merely a nervous habit? "Yes, Your Majesty, well. I know that I speak for the Guilds and the burgesses when I say that we are all most grateful for your intervention, and that, of course, we celebrate your subsequent rise to your present lofty position."

If he had to listen to the man speak for much longer, even in praise, Elisha's eyes would glaze—or simply slide shut. "I thank you for taking the time to say so."

The man glanced up with a brief compression of lips that tried to be a smile. "You are kind to say so, Your Majesty. I am, of course, also well-pleased to be restored to my position within the city. It was, to say the least, quite distressing to be so abruptly expelled from the place I work so hard to safeguard and improve. Among the many details of your advent, which I admired, was the justice, duly tempered with mercy, which you applied to those most dangerous elements among the rioters. As I say, the citizens have been most helpful in restoring the city thus far. No doubt, given the absence of the worst miscreants, not to mention the concern over Your Majesty's justifiable wrath, they will continue on best behavior in the proceeding months."

"Are you coming to a point, your honor?" Elisha shifted on his seat, still a little uncomfortable with the idea of himself as the punisher of wrong-doing. Had he been too harsh? The mayor did not seem to think so.

"Yes. And so, Your Majesty, it is with greatest humility, that I most humbly petition that you cease to apply that justice with such . . . directness."

"I'm sorry?" Elisha puzzled through the man's words, but still found no meaning in them. "I don't know what you mean."

The mayor drew a deep breath which puffed up his laces and ribbons and chains. "The punishments, Your Majesty. While, at the outset, they served to encourage good behavior while disciplining those who had committed fell deeds, they are, at this point, making some of the citizens rather concerned."

"I have punished no one since the day of the fire, your honor."

The man's fleshy face wrinkled into a frown. He pulled out a handkerchief from his sleeve and blotted the sweat that shimmered on his brow. "I am aware, of course, Your Majesty, that there have been no formal proceedings of the court, but still, the . . ." He deflated a bit. "You really . . . have you not had a hand in this?" He glanced at Elisha's hands with a little shudder.

Elisha stretched his awareness to encompass the

kneeling figure, fidgeting in his confusion and fear. "Perhaps you can start by telling me what *this* is, and what makes you think the punishments have continued."

"Well, the bodies, Your Majesty. Four of those whom you marked upon the day of the fire and expelled from the city have since been found within the city, dead, Your Majesty. It appears, that is, when it was brought to my attention, I imagined that you were fulfilling the promise to punish them if they returned." He managed an awkward smile. "Your Majesty, it is a fine thing for a man in your position to fulfill his promises, but if you could see clear to be a little more restrained . . . ? While we surely have no objection to the king's justice, the condition of the bodies has been—discomfiting."

Elisha still had no idea what exactly had happened, but a sick weight settled in his gut. "You and your men have found four people, murdered? Mutilated?"

The mayor flinched and gave a quick nod. "Their skin, Your Majesty. The parts that had been touched by your wrath had been removed."

"Dear Lord." Elisha sat back, clenching the arms of his throne. Mancers, it had to be.

"Perhaps, Your Majesty, someone among your followers has taken it upon himself to carry out these punishments," Ufford began.

"Murders," Elisha snapped. He pushed up from the throne. "I need to know who's done this, and what's happened to the other punished men. If we can find where the others have gone, we might be able to—" He broke off, catching Ufford's lowered head, the strain in the man's shoulders evident even if Elisha could not sense his frustration. "What is it, man?"

"Certes, the crimes must be investigated, Your Majesty, but you do have people for that, including the honorable mayor himself." Ufford regarded the kneeling man. "Now that he understands Your Majesty was not a party to these acts, I am sure he shall endeavor to discover who might have been."

The mayor said something, more a breath than a word, and Elisha squatted before him, causing him to shrink back, sweating more ferociously than ever. "What was that, your honor?"

"Witches, Your Majesty." He blinked and scrubbed at his face with the kerchief. "Begging your pardon, Your Majesty, I know that once you yourself were accused of such a thing, and I expect that it may be a sensitive issue, but it has been said that perhaps the deaths were effected by sorcerous means."

A witch hunt. And Elisha's own actions had started it. For a moment, he crouched there, trapped. Should he encourage the hunt, because it was the truth? In point of fact, evil witches had everything to do with it. Or discourage it because they were more likely to discover the secret ranks of the magi than they ever were to find the lair of the mancers? He pictured Rowena, Brigit's mother, bound upon the stake, and the fire in her daughter's eyes.

Elisha covered his own fears. "It is just as likely that they were, as the Lord Chancellor suggested, punished by those who support my elevation. Before I got here, I understand that many of them wanted me for a saint?"

The mayor nodded.

"So," Elisha pushed back to his feet, his stomach churning, "it may be that mutilating the bodies gives the killer a sense of being closer to me." He shook his head as if he could dispel that notion.

"Relics." The mayor wrung his kerchief in his hands.

"Of a sort." Talismans, but Elisha would not use that word. "Pray continue your investigation and report to me whatever you find. In the meantime, I shall make sure that my wishes are known and the crimes should stop."

"Would Your Majesty wish to issue a proclamation?" Ufford inquired.

"Can you see that it's written up?"

"And that it strongly separates your royal person from these despicable crimes, Your Majesty." Ufford gave a bow and strode over to the ready scribes.

"If there is nothing else, your honor?"

"Nothing, Your Majesty. Thank you." The mayor rose to a bow, walked backward, bowing again until he finally scurried out of the hall.

With a wave of his hand, Elisha summoned a page. "Send for Duke Randall of Dunbury, would you?" The boy bowed deeply and hurried away while Elisha stalked the room. One of the scribes carried a great mound of parchments over to a broad desk and began sorting through them. "What's all of this?" Elisha picked up one of the pages and found a lengthy greeting to Thomas that briefly chilled him and reminded him of last night's contact.

"Petitions, Your Majesty. They arrive in advance of a parliament."

"But they can't have arrived yet, and these are addressed to my predecessor." Elisha replaced the page and sifted out another, this one requesting permission for a lord's daughter to marry.

"Most times, parliament can't even address the petitions, there's just too many, Your Majesty. Some can go to the king direct, of course." He gestured toward the one Elisha was holding. "As for the rest." A shrug.

"What happens to them?"

"I'm to sort and store them, Your Majesty, in the event there's time for them to be examined and answered."

Elisha eyed the mound of papers, reflecting the needs, desires, and whims of his people. "Is there?"

"Almost never, Your Majesty." He set one aside, then

another. "Marriages among the lords, yes. Land disputes involving barons, yes." He ran his hand through the papers. "Visits to little parishes for the laying on of hands? No. Disputes involving chickens, no. Ride to Chelmsford to relieve a curse? No."

"Wait a minute, Chelmsford is cursed?"

"With weeks of rain, aye, Your Majesty."

"You've not heard of this? It is the talk of the taverns." Randall came in, the herald trotting alongside, and bowed to Elisha, then straightened. "I suppose you've not been long back to the mainland, Your Majesty."

The title still sat awkwardly, the more so when it came from someone he knew so well, someone he was so used to addressing as his superior. Randall's clothes looked loose, his face haggard, but it was true that a certain light had returned to his gaze with Elisha's accession. A project, Allyson said, to take his mind off of their daughter's disappearance. So be it: Randall's aid had so far been invaluable to navigating his new role.

"What is your will, Your Majesty?"

Elisha forestalled him with a hand and read through the relevant parts of the Chelmsford petition. Raining for weeks. He should have known something was wrong with the weather—how often did London get so many sunny days? But in the New Forest, Elisha had met a magus who knew the rain. This curse was Sundrop's doing, and Elisha knew exactly why. "This is a curse I could lift."

"Surely it is not so pressing that it requires your personal attention, Your Majesty; not when we must prepare for parliament, not to mention handle Kent and Gloucester and the rest."

Elisha shook his head. "The petition states that the rain is centered upon a certain inn, but falls lightly on its orchard. I have to ride to Chelmsford, to apologize."

Randall made a soft sound that might have stifled his

sigh. "You don't ride to them, Your Majesty, they ride to you. Or you may send a letter. To whom do you need to apologize?"

Elisha considered how to explain, in front of those who did not know the ways of the magi, how to even try to reach a man who lived in the rain. "I believe that someone has placed a curse on that inn, someone the innkeeper and I have both wronged. I am not sure any other could carry this apology, and the man who placed the curse will certainly not come to me."

"You have called up Parliament to ask them to summon levies for war, Your Majesty, the barons are at a critical moment. You cannot simply ride away." Randall looked small, bald, vulnerable.

Meeting Randall's gaze, Elisha said, very carefully, "The man in question is very . . . sensitive." He placed emphasis on that last word and saw Randall's understanding nod.

"Could my wife carry the message, Your Majesty? She is well-spoken, as you know."

"It's worth a try." Allyson was a magus, and it might work, but Elisha suspected that sending an emissary in his stead would only infuriate Sundrop all the more. He smiled, for Randall's sake, but the expression felt too tight, binding him like the crown and all the weight it carried, holding him down.

"I shall have her sent to you for your message, Your Majesty. And now?" He looked expectant.

Elisha led the duke back toward the throne and had a chair brought out so they might both be seated, isolated together, before he spoke. "There's been a series of murders in London, the people I sent from the city. I believe my other enemies may be involved, but Ufford refuses to let me investigate personally."

"As well he should, Your Majesty—especially if your enemies are involved. We cannot risk losing another king." His expression hardened, burdened but determined. "But it rather sounds, in this case, as if it might well be your friends to blame."

"Is there someone you can suggest to aid in the investigation?"

"I know a man who might, if the mayor will have him. I'll see to that as well, Your Majesty." He scrubbed his hand over his balding scalp. "When the barons hear of this, Your Majesty, they will be all the more adamant against you. It is one thing to have a king declared in part by the acclaim of his people and quite another if those people begin killing in the king's name. It is precisely the sort of thing that makes the barons nervous."

"Nothing I do or say seems to make them any less so." Elisha spread his hands. "How am I supposed to calm them down?"

"Your accession was rather unusual—instigated first by the citizens, then by the church. It might do a great deal of good if you were to assume a more traditional approach to your reign. You must woo them, Your Majesty, in the way of kings."

"I don't even know what that means."

"Largess. Give them gifts, answer their petitions, take them hunting." Randall leaned forward. "That last might be a good choice. The New Forest has been closed to hunting since the princesses' deaths. It's been two years, the deer must be ready for harvest."

Elisha almost laughed. "You do know that for me, given my birth, to hunt in the New Forest would have been a death sentence a week ago."

With the first smile he'd given in a long time, Randall nodded. "It would thus be a fine symbolic gesture as well—you would not only claim your power, but also share your bounty."

"It would be better if I had any notion of how to hunt."

"How are you with a bow?"

"Hopeless." Elisha shook his head. "As a barber, I've been exempted from mandatory practice."

"Hmm. A problem, but not insurmountable. As I recall, you are good with hounds."

"Will they help me win the barons' hearts?"

"Well, Your Majesty, if they don't, they can always bite them instead! I shall issue the invitations—a small party, I think—and you issue the orders. A privileged gathering for a few days in advance of the parliament. It should suit your needs well, Your Majesty."

It would suit him better to find out who had killed those people and what became of their stolen scars, or at least to travel to Chelmsford to soothe Sundrop's temper, but Elisha set aside those concerns when he entered the kennels and found himself surrounded by eager hounds, and the most eager among them: Thomas's great dog, Cerberus, who pressed his huge head into Elisha's chest with such affection that it almost relieved the ache of the dog's absent master.

The last thing Elisha did before leaving was to take the great seal from Ufford's keeping and stamp the hot wax on his new writ about thievery, although in his own heart, he acted in Thomas's name.

Chapter 14

❖

Elisha's part in the hunt consisted of picnicking on roast pheasant with Randall's selected half-dozen lords and barons, while teams of beaters pushed the game toward an agreed location then blew a horn, at which point the lords all mounted up and took arms to form a half-circle, waiting for a good shot. The beaters loosed the hounds to drive the deer straight into them. A less sporting event Elisha could hardly imagine. Kent, Gloucester, and Mortimer, Elisha's greatest critics on the council, formed the heart of the group, along with Randall himself, Elisha's ally the earl of Blackmere, and the young Bishop of Exeter whose noble background and apparent openness to Elisha's coronation gave him a balanced view between Elisha's supporters and his detractors. Each man brought along a servant or two to attend him, plus the beaters, huntsmen, foresters, and scullions to manage the hunt itself and the feasting to follow. Rather than ride a great distance to one of the larger royal lodges, Randall deemed it a better choice, and more festive, to erect pavilions in the field not far from Beaulieu Abbey to serve as their temporary home—a home with fine carpets, richly carved furnishings, and body servants.

Mortimer's ally, Farus, lurked in the background, dodging Elisha's interest, if not avoiding him completely. His chill, metallic presence tingled at the edge of Elisha's awareness. Farus, the *indivisi* who drew all his magic from iron, had never liked him and had tried, at least once, to kill him. Elisha kept alert, his awareness spread open to any hint of danger, but doing so left him open to the memories as well. Here, he and Thomas fought bandits together, and there, he had killed a king and nearly died himself in fighting Morag. In a lodge not far away, Thomas's wife and daughter were slain. And yet, here, too, Rosalynn thrilled to her part in the secret events of Thomas's return to his birthright. And here, she had fallen in love with the displaced prince, conceiving of the plan to marry him. Where were they now?

The horn's blast interrupted his thoughts and grooms brought their horses around, each already fitted with a quiver of arrows or a sling for a spear.

"What fun, Your Majesty!" Blackmere cried as he mounted his own horse and turned about, grinning. "We should go hawking next. Have you met the falcons?"

"I have not." Elisha found a smile for the earl. The barons' enjoyment of the hunt filled their presence with a martial delight, as if they went to battle, but a battle in which only the enemy would die, and the result would be venison for supper. Even Randall looked relaxed as he argued a point of forest law with Kent. On this, the second afternoon of their hunt, the mad idea looked to be a great success.

Gloucester rode by to his position, tugging on his gloves while his tall chestnut horse lifted her feet like a lady at a dance, his slightest movement translating into her direction; an ideal partnership.

"She's a fine horse, my lord Gloucester," Elisha said, and the rider looked up, his sharp beard making it hard to judge his expression.

"Thank you, Your Majesty," Gloucester answered stiffly. "I was not aware you had an interest in horses."

"I assume you are the breeder?" This earned him a cool nod. "Anything a man puts his heart into achieving is worthy of interest."

"And what shall you, Your Majesty? What do you put your heart into achieving?"

Elisha thought of Thomas's letter, saying that his land needed healers and he had exiled his best. "Right now, I am working to save the heart of England, my lord. I hope you will join me in succeeding."

Gloucester flicked his gaze away and took up the reins to cross to the far side.

Blackmere leaned over and murmured, "On the battlefield at Dunbury, you once said you couldn't speak fair."

"I did not think you heard that, my lord." Elisha patted his own horse's neck.

"I was too injured to hear it the first time, but Lord Robert's repeated the tale a dozen times since then—half, at least, since your coronation, and it's been barely a week." The earl gave a tip of his head, adding a little salute that brushed his woolen cap. In deference to the hunt, he wore a tunic with closely fitted sleeves and an over-tunic with longer, dangling sleeves that hung well back from his elbows. A peacock, the king had once described him, his plumage barely dulled for a day in the forest.

The trees ahead of them rustled, vines trembling at the trunks of the huge oaks. A pair of deer bounded forward, the hounds and huntsman holding back, to give the lords their chance. A great, red-hued stag darted right, then swung about when Kent launched his spear. It grazed the stag's side, sending the animal on a wild course toward the middle of the circle.

Blackmere's horse startled, stamping backward and

nearly tumbling him. He held his bow, but his false sleeve tangled the quiver of arrows, spilling them to the ground as he got the horse back under control. "Damn! Your Majesty, may I borrow an arrow?"

Elisha grabbed him a few and held them out, his own mount snorting and stamping at the excitement as the stag went down to Mortimer's spear on the far side. The barons cheered and whooped, then turned their attention immediately back to the killing ground.

Something tingled his hand, as if the arrows, too, longed for death and excitement as much as the men. Never before had he such a sense from a thing neither living, nor dead. Could it be a spell for hunting? Elisha started to withdraw, but Blackmere plucked an arrow from Elisha's fist, taking aim as another, smaller stag wheeled through. The arrow sang, a shrill, sharp note through Elisha's awareness, but it arched high, Blackmere frowning after it. "Surely my aim's not—"

At the further end, Gloucester's horse turned aside, and the man cried out, a shaft feathering into his side. He managed to keep mounted, clutching the reins as he slumped back, cursing, blood coursing from the wound.

In an instant, Elisha nudged his horse and galloped behind the other hunters even as the bishop and Mortimer slid the wounded man from his horse. Cries of anger and fear took the place of cheering.

"Stay back! Get a surgeon," the bishop shouted, dropping to his knees by the fallen man.

"I am a surgeon," Elisha said, swinging down from his horse.

"Your Majesty," Randall began, but this was not a thing to be delegated, not when the chill thrust of death already struck the air.

"Don't touch me!" Gloucester shouted. "'Tis a royal arrow." He gulped for breath, trying to twist away from Elisha's approach but pinned by Mortimer's hands.

"I was the archer," Blackmere called. "My God, man, I am so sorry. My horse bucked at that last stag, and I—"

"No man makes such a shot by accident," Kent said, leaning over them.

The arrow stuck from Gloucester's chest. Bands of purple ink decorated the shaft to identify it, but the blood seeping around the wound quickly stained them dark. Elisha heard the struggle of his breath and felt the chill that rose with every moment. "My lord, I can save your life. Please let me try."

"It's the same that happened to William Rufus two hundred years ago, Your Majesty, but his killer had the good sense to flee." Kent glared at Blackmere, who blanched.

"My lord of Gloucester, do you wish to make confession?" the bishop asked.

"Stop talking as if he's already dead!" Mortimer shouted. Gloucester reached up to grip his hand.

The bishop edged back, hands pressed together, murmuring in Latin.

Elisha snatched the wool hat from Blackmere's head and wiped away the blood by the arrow's shaft then caught the shaft low down with the other hand. "My lord, do you want to live?"

Lips trembling, face pale, Gloucester stared back at him, eyes already glazing with the pain that surged in his flesh. Beneath his tunic, close to his skin, Elisha wore a few talismans, including the bit of cloth given him by Martin Draper which he once used to tend the wounded earl of Blackmere. He called upon this now, focusing his being on Gloucester's injury. The radiant warmth of Martin's affection sprang at his call. He pictured the shaft of the arrow, sending his awareness down deep along it, finding the piercing of the chest, the slice that impinged upon the baron's heart. When he worked over Blackmere, Elisha did not yet know how to use his secret skills to heal. Today, he used them all—the anatomical knowledge of his medical training, the probing of his magic, and the power of his talisman. He bound the strands together and drew the arrow forth.

"No!" Mortimer reached for his hand, trying to stop him. "That arrow is the only thing keeping him alive!"

Elisha ignored him, letting his intensity burn upon his skin so that Mortimer snapped back his hand as if singed. As he drew up the arrow, Elisha wrought his spell from the Law of Opposites: as the arrow had pierced, so now it sealed each layer, drawing them closed as it withdrew. Elisha held the image of the heart, healed, the muscle joining together and the vessels patched and whole. Letting out his breath, Elisha sat back on his heels, the arrow in his hand, still stained with Gloucester's blood. The patient blinked at him, then fumbled at his chest, shoving aside Elisha's hand and the woolen cap he used to clean the blood. Beneath his pierced clothing, a bit of knobbed flesh showed where the arrow had struck.

"It's a miracle," the bishop cried, holding up his clasped hands to the heavens.

"You allowed your friend to shoot me," Gloucester muttered. "You made this happen, just so you could heal me." He sucked in a breath, still pale. "That is no miracle, Your Majesty, that is sorcery." Shoving away from the ground, with Mortimer's help, the baron rose to his feet and lurched back. "I think we shall be going." For a moment he swayed there, lips compressed, then gave a short bow and walked away.

"Your Majesty?" Randall spread his hands.

"Go with them. See if there's anything to be done to mend this."

The duke bowed and hurried away.

Elisha snatched the arrow in both hands to break it over his knee. By God, he had saved the man's life—would it have been better to have let him die? But then

Blackmere would carry the blame. A hunting accident that could be no accident, and yet, it had been. And it wasn't Blackmere meant to use those arrows. Raising the arrow in his hands, Elisha bent his awareness to it. The purple ink, smeared now with Gloucester's blood, carried a subtle flavor of its own: the blood of another, some stranger, mingled with the paint. Sorcery, indeed, marked Gloucester for death, but it was not Elisha's doing. The man must have been marked as well, wearing something stained by the same stranger's blood. Whoever had placed the blood could then control the arrow, sending it to the heart, which was the sense of excitement and blood-lust Elisha noticed.

"Your Majesty," Blackmere began.

"Where are the rest of my arrows?" Elisha rose, the earl coming with him, as the confused huntsmen and beaters rounded up the dogs and fallen spears. One of them took charge of Mortimer's kill, pulling out a knife to begin the slaughter.

Two grooms handled the loose horses, Elisha's among them, but the arrows remaining in his quiver felt perfectly ordinary. "Did anyone touch these arrows?" The nearest groom shook his head, but the other piped up, "Someone might've done. The horses made for the field, Your Majesty, and a few from the encampment helped us to get them back."

"What's happened here, Your Majesty?" Blackmere whispered.

Elisha rested his head against the horse's neck. The casting, on top of the strain of entertaining the barons, settled into his bones. "Someone's trying to ruin me, to break whatever alliances we might make. The arrow was marked to fly to him, no matter who shot it. I'm sorry it had to be you, my lord." He thought of the murders in London, carried out by villains who seemed to be on Elisha's side, killing those who angered him. If the barons caught word of that, their suspicions would be confirmed.

"Your Majesty." Randall walked up, his weariness returning. "We shall see them at parliament, but likely nowhere else. They seem convinced this whole occasion has been a setting for you to show off your powers. And so it was intended, but not that power." He shook his head. "If the barons won't come around to your support, Your Majesty, the parliament may work against us. It gives your detractors a chance to convince the rest. I don't know what might happen."

"Can we muster enough men to guard against the French, Your Grace?"

Randall and Blackmere exchanged a look. "A full-scale invasion, Your Majesty? Doubtful," said the duke. "Unless we know where and when to expect them."

"Can we make a good guess?"

"They'll be looking to land where they already have an ally, Your Majesty, somebody to cover their presence until they're ready to march inland, but we don't know who might be working with them."

Kent, who argued for the return of royal blood, even from France? Too obvious. Then Elisha thought of Mortimer, who covered up the assassination of a French magus who had come seeking safety outside Elisha's door. Mortimer claimed it was an attempt on Elisha, but he lied. What if it truly were as the victim had feared, a part of the French king's campaign against his own magi, with Mortimer's help? "Mortimer," Elisha said. "He may not be the only one, but he's one."

"He's one of the marcher lords, from Wales. He hardly has strong ties with France." Randall's fingers rubbed over his bald spot. "Of course, that means he might be amenable to bribery with French lands in trade. What makes you name him?"

"He's been hiding things, even from Alaric. If he's got

access to a good port on the east or south coast, look there."

Nodding, Randall said, "I'll have the rolls searched. We may come up with something. In the meantime, I'll order the men to strike camp. We might as well return to the Tower and be ready for whatever we can."

In a few hours, Elisha rode for London, the air of celebration overtaken by a miasma of worry, the barons dividing into factions rather than ride together as they had on the way to the New Forest. Gloucester wore fresh clothing, and Elisha's inquiry about the ruined tunic was met with dismay and a gesture against evil, so there would be no touching the garment to confirm the taint. No matter, the damage was done. Whether the earl had lived or died, Elisha's enemies won that moment. What else were they planning?

On the road outside of London, they met Lord Robert, flanked by a pair of soldiers, and riding hard. He reined in sharply when he saw them, his horse circling at his tightened reins. Randall and Elisha spurred on to meet him, and he bowed his head, water running from his dark hair and dripping from his clothes in spite of the sunny day. "Your Majesty, Your Grace—it's the duchess."

"What? What about her?" Randall's face drained of color, his face slick with sweat.

"Peace, Your Grace, she lives, she's only shaken." Staving off panic with one hand, Robert said, "We rode out to Chelmsford, to the rains, and she insisted on riding into the water. She said that's how she must carry her message." His dark eyes sought Elisha for confirmation. "Seemed like the clouds gathered up over her, like the rains could see her or care she'd come. She bowed her head, like praying, and, well, the sky opened. We saw a flash so bright for a moment, I could hardly see, and when I could, I saw her on the ground. The lightning still hovered in my eye." He held his hand before him as if he could see it still. "I rode in for her and got her on my horse, Your Grace, and she stirred. It did not hit her, but you could see the mark on the ground, black as anything, and little bits of glass. Her horse bolted at the strike. Likely that's what felled her. I brought her back to the Tower to recover."

Robert's broad shoulders hunched a little. "She bid me keep quiet, Your Grace, but, well, I knew you'd hear of it, and I thought it best be from a friend."

Randall sat a moment as if thunderstruck himself. "My wife's been struck by lightning."

Wincing, Robert said, "Nearly so, Your Grace. She'll be all right."

"She rode as your messenger, Your Majesty." Randall's glance raked Elisha's face. "Apology refused." The duke spurred his horse and burst ahead of them on the road to London and Allyson.

Chapter 15

❖

Riding the final measure, Elisha told Robert of his suspicion of Mortimer and asked for his aid. Given the expression on Randall's face, he doubted the duke would be much help to him, for a few days, at least. Allyson could likely have healed herself—certainly, Elisha could have done it, but too many people knew what had happened and expected to see some sign of the trauma. Thank God Allyson's injuries were minor, or it might have sent her husband straight over the edge unto madness. Even Randall's aid might not be enough to compensate for the barons' growing hostility, and Elisha's friendship with Blackmere became another black mark against him. He still had weeks before the parliament, and his hopes of being heard looked increasingly bleak.

The next day, Elisha discovered that law and procedure were not the only impediments to action: religion, too, must take its toll, for it was Sunday. The long mass included a sermon by the inquisitor, Father Osbert, who spoke with spirit about the crusade against heresy and false miracles put up by the Devil to snare the unwary. He even found a hunting metaphor to slide into his speech.

In the gallery provided for royal use, Elisha kept still

and tried to think it was not directed at him. The inquisitor had, so far, been observant, but not judgmental. If it
weren't for the dozen others gathered in the king's gallery with him, Elisha might have quietly excused himself
from the service. But when he looked away from the altar, Elisha found Brigit gazing at him with warmth,
Blackmere with contrition. Randall and Allyson sat
close together just beyond Brigit. The duke's attention
focused solely on his wife, who wore a bandage over her
eye and another at her wrist. She spoke to the rain, to
Sundrop, its master, and he answered her with fire. So let
Chelmsford drown—Elisha had his hands full with the
growing tension over the upcoming parliament.

With Ufford in attendance as ever, Elisha gratefully
fled after the service had finished. Outside, a steady
stream of citizens tramped past the large arch of the inner wall. A few slowed, then stopped, staring in his direction. Before long, a crowd had gathered there, not close
enough to disturb the guards, but large enough that they
stood at the ready.

"What's all that?" Elisha asked.

"The parishioners at St. John ad Vincula, Your Majesty," Ufford replied. "A larger crowd than usual. I have
heard that all the churches have been crowded since
your advent at the fire." He tapped his fingers on the
cover of his large book, then raised his wild eyebrows.
"They want to see you, Your Majesty, though many of
them are afraid, given the murders in town, and this latest incident in Chelmsford."

The crowd wavered with uncertainty, fear and hope in
conflict among them. A few of the citizens used crutches
or wore conspicuous bandages. "And the others wish to
get their own miracles," Elisha murmured. "Have I any
other duties today?"

"'Tis the Sabbath, Your Majesty. The day of rest."

Beyond the arch, some people knelt in prayer, others

crossed themselves as they stood, a hundred pairs of eyes fixed upon him, even when they pretended to be looking away. Elisha found he was rubbing his palm, his thumb and fingers stroking over the scar. The archbishop had given them a miracle-working king—for what? The archbishop wanted to make him a holy man, then stand by and watch him fall, while the web of mancers killed citizens and tainted arrows, aiming their malevolent intent at Elisha's supporters. Elisha considered dodging the eyes, the prayers, the hope; they reminded him of the men who gathered outside the hospital at Dunbury, desperate for his help, because he was the only one who would help them.

Elisha started walking.

"Your Majesty?" Ufford called from behind him, but he was already past the inner rank of buildings, waving aside the guards.

The citizens edged back from him, but more fell to their knees, hands clasped at his approach. "Mercy, Your Majesty!" someone called.

The rest dropped into deep bows and curtsies, a sea of bowed heads. He could not heal them all, not without a week of attunement and knowledge of their every condition, but he called upon his cloth talisman, the one most associated with healing, letting it echo his desire and build into a warmth of healing at his fingertips. One of the guards edged into his path, and Elisha shot him a glare, stepping past to an old woman who knelt, mumbling over her hands. He touched her head, and she sighed, her eyes rising to his as he sent her the strength for healing, for her body to use as it would.

"Bless you, Your Majesty," she said, and tears sprang to her eyes. Elisha turned away, to a young man with a bandaged arm. His own arm twinged as they touched and, at least for the moment, he took away the pain. As the young man called out his blessings, those who had backed off, who crossed themselves in fear, now surged ahead, and he moved on to the next, and the next. At last he sank into a chair Walter carried out to him, a steady stream of people coming to kneel at his feet, touch his scarred hands, murmur their blessings. He expected to feel drained, exhausted from healing, as he had every night at Dunbury, but every smile, prayer, and whispered thanks sustained the healing warmth. And it was not until the last of them moved away, the last of the fear converted to wonder, that Elisha leaned back and yawned.

The archbishop stood in the shadowed arch, the inquisitor by his side, both watching, neither saying a word, though Father Osbert's quill moved carefully over an open page, as if he noted everything he saw.

Rising wearily, Elisha gave them a nod and returned to his chambers, full of worries. It was well enough for the king to heal his people, but it was still weeks before the parliament, and the barons were even less likely than before to support him. He paced while Walter prepared the fire and went for food to appease the king's growling stomach. Then Elisha stopped by the chantry, where a small desk stood with its inkpot and quill, where Thomas might have sat to write his letter.

After a moment, Elisha, too, sat down and took a bit of parchment, the texture still unfamiliar in his hands. He hesitated so long over how to spell Mordecai's name that the quill dried out and had to be inked again. Even then, he started badly, with a scratch across the page and a few blots that he quickly sprinkled with sand. His hand tired of the labor before he had done much more than list his troubles: the murders in the city, the incident while hunting that only inflamed the barons more, the question of how to handle France if they could not raise an army. By the time he sealed the letter and rose, his servants moved quietly about, re-warming his meat, frowning as they poured water over his ink-blackened fingers.

Walter hurried off with the letter in search of a messenger heading for Wight, while Pernel and a couple of squires laid out his supper. Just as he was finishing, a solid knock brought Lord Robert to his door, eyes alight. "The answer's Hythe, Your Majesty. It's above Hastings, in Kent."

"Kent?" Elisha rose from his table.

"Don't get excited now, we don't think that Kent himself knows anything. The town's been held by the Archbishop of Canterbury, but he owns all sorts of things. Mortimer's sister's husband is castellan there, at Saltwood. Same bloody place they planned the murder of St. Thomas á Becket." Robert crossed himself, looking slightly dazed.

Before he could ask, Pernel brought out the map and showed him the town of Hythe, on a perfect cove just across the channel. For a moment, Elisha's hopes returned. Still, he had no army and had only the parliament to wait on in the hopes of getting one.

"How fares the duchess?"

"Very well, Your Majesty, and that's put the duke back to rights, leastways as much as he can be without Rosalynn home. Still can't get over that lightning." He shook his head. "Like the bombards, only straight down from the heavens."

Lightning and bombards. Elisha caught Robert's arm. "We can do it! We don't need the barons, just the bombards. We know they're massing—the French—they might come any day now."

"They're likely just waiting calm seas."

"Yes. If we can ensure a good crossing, we can bring them when we want them, where we want them. We could even steer them into the bombards' range."

"The bombards are here, Your Majesty, outside London," said Robert uncertainly.

"Then get them moving toward Hythe."

"I'll talk with the duke."

"Good man! In the meantime, I'll ride for Chelmsford and see if I can't end the rain."

"If you think that's wise, Your Majesty. Yon cursed storm nearly killed the duchess."

"It's a chance I must take to save the kingdom."

Still mystified, Robert bowed and departed.

"Good news, Your Majesty?" Pernel asked.

"The best." Elisha grinned, then glanced down at the map in his hand. Better would be finding the king. A weighty guilt settled over him like the ermine cloak of office that should have been reserved for Thomas alone. "Or nearly so," he murmured.

The ride would have been accomplished much faster if he didn't need to wait for a retinue to be gathered, riders to be sent ahead for lodging, routes planned and checked—a thousand things that bothered no one but a king. The archbishop looked speculative, and the inquisitor asked to ride along, the better to document the strange storm. Elisha felt Brigit's presence often as she moved so quietly in the background of these preparations that he wondered if she were casting another deflection. Since her visit to his chamber, she watched him with gentle eyes and soft smiles, and he did his best not to show his revulsion.

They rode through an ominously dry landscape, sheep munching despondently on tufts of browning grass, nosing the runnels of failing streams. Ahead, dark clouds crowded the horizon. A group of townsfolk, friars, and nuns clustered over the near hill, praying. A girl on the outskirts started shouting, pointing, and a few of the better-dressed folk arose, hurrying to bow and curtsy.

"Oh, Your Majesty! Thank you for coming!" A well-dressed woman blinked back tears.

At her side, a stout fellow with a twisted bow of a

mouth looked over Elisha's horse and resumed staring. "Started down there, at the Lamb," the man said at last. "Landlord's not come out for weeks. Ain't answered his door for three days now."

Hope and doubt stood side by side. Elisha chose to reply to the former. "Thank you, Goodwife. We'll see what might be done."

"If prayer avails little, Your Majesty, there might be more to this," Father Osbert began but stopped himself with a gracious nod. "But yes, let us see what might be done."

In the town below, the line of rain carved deep grooves into the grass before running down into the river. The steeple could barely be seen through the downpour and thick mud delineated the streets.

Father Osbert crossed himself, and said faintly, "I have heard of such wonders, but until now, I have not been witness to them."

"You need not ride on with me, Father."

The priest swept his gaze over the townsfolk then back to the rain. "If there be demons at work here, you shall have need of me, Your Majesty."

No demon but himself, and the man who lived in the rain. Elisha reined his horse about, to come close to Father Osbert, and said softly, "I'll return if there's any sign of demons, Father. If that's the case, it is these good people who will need your protection."

The priest gravely inclined his head.

To the others, Elisha said, "None of you are beholden to come with me into the rain."

"We are, yer Majesty," Madoc announced, urging his pony forward along with a few of the other men-at-arms.

"Very well." They rode forward, Madoc taking the lead, each man putting up his hood as they crossed the boundary into the pounding rain. Mud sucked at the horses' hooves, their ears drooping back, heads lowered. They rode only as far as the bridge before Elisha reined in, shaking back the folds of cloth that defended his hands, and caught the rain in his palm as he sent out his presence. *"Sundrop,"* he began. Overhead, thunder rolled, and the sky darkened. His mount shivered and snorted.

"Hear me out—"

A sound like a bombard's blast at close range smote the sky along with a brilliant flash. Madoc's pony reared, and he fought it back to a standstill, mist swirling from its nostrils. Elisha's horse danced in spite of his calming hand upon its neck. He tossed the reins to a guard and slid down, stumbling as his boots struck the watery surface and sank into the ooze. A short distance ahead, a black smear marked the ground with a twinkle as of glass: the place where Allyson might have died. He slogged forward, his sodden cloak dragging at his throat, until he yanked it off, handing it to Madoc as he passed. The rain beat upon his head, dragging the black locks of his hair to loop over his ears.

"Go on, then!" Elisha cried into the storm. "Do your worst! Only don't kill my horse, or my men—don't let more innocents be lost." To the rain alone, he said, *"The fields of Essex are dying for this, Sundrop. Did Chanterelle want you to crumble her beloved earth into dust?"*

Thunder smacked at his skull with a jolt he could feel. His skin thrummed with it, his bones ached, and Elisha flinched. Imagine God's chosen king finished by a stroke of lightning from an unnatural storm. A fitting end. He swallowed, struggling to master his breathing as the oppressive sound tremored around him. Then it dissipated, and the blow did not fall.

The clouds roiled and a man emerged from the slanting rain. Elisha took a deep breath and approached, his boots squelching in the mud while the other man made no sound at all. The young man's features slowly resolved, solidifying from the drops, although the rain still streaked through him, his face formed of streaming water.

"You." Sundrop's lips curled, and Elisha wondered suddenly how old he was. The gray of his face and the ruffling of his colorless hair against the rain made him ancient, while the anguish of his eyes made him a child, helpless with grief.

Elisha took another step. He wanted to reach out but only spread his hands and spread his patience to the falling rain. "You loved her," Elisha breathed.

"You are with Death," the clouds spat against his ears. *"What do you know of love?"*

"Do you think that love never dies?" The answer seemed flippant, even tempered with his memories of Brigit, and he was not surprised when the rain slapped his face.

"She died for you!" it howled, stinging his skin with sudden ice.

"God knows I would have saved her."

The sky grew less gloomy as they spoke, as if the clouds lessened, although the patch of darkness lingered on the right-hand side, just past the bridge, soaking into the thatch and pounding on the sign that marked the accursed inn. The sign of the Lamb. That irony stung at the back of Elisha's eyes, and he bowed his head. He recognized the place from Chanterelle's sending, her father's establishment, where she learned to love the earth because it could hide her from the groping hands of the customers her father sold her to. Chanterelle helped Elisha to understand his affinity with death, and she came to his aid when he struggled against Morag in the New Forest. Then Morag had hunted her down, slew her, and used her ashes to lay a trap for Elisha in turn. Elisha's fists clenched.

"I'm doing it—sending the rain back to Essex, for the

earth. Are you through now?" Sundrop's touch was a lash of pain. The rain felt raw, seared by screams and weeping.

Elisha winced, his healing instincts drawn and helpless.

"I won't harm you," Sundrop's voice cracked, his presence rippling uneasily through the rain. *"She would not want you hurt."*

Elisha radiated calm and comfort. *"You knew her before she was a magus."*

Sundrop's gaze snapped back to him. *"She loved the gardens, always. Those trees—she planted them."*

A row of apple trees impossibly dense with fruit stood along the riverside, nurtured by one who loved the earth and all that it could give. The rain fell more gently there, a patter on the rich, green leaves. Elisha's chest felt tight. *"Who were you, back then?"*

The rain wavered in patterns on the ground, then a shaft opened in the rain, drawing Elisha's eye to the opposite bank, to the millwheel churning in the running stream. *"Jerome, the miller's boy."* And a whisper so faint it barely reached his skin, *"She would never let me touch her. Even to dry her tears."*

Elisha watched the rain caress the apple trees. The earth and the rain and the things that grew between. It was the kind of tale they told after feasting at the Tower: a tragic maid and her true love. Elisha thought back to when he'd first met Sundrop. Had she known that he had made himself for her?

"I'm sorry," Elisha murmured.

"So what?" Rain lashed back at him. *"You regret befriending her? Making her a target for your enemies?"*

Elisha let himself grow numb to the cold. How long had it been raining here? Sundrop must be exhausted. *"They already wanted her, Sundrop. She had been listening, and they knew."* Even such an able spy was no harm without a master to report to, or at least, an accomplice to spread the word. *"Who did she tell?"*

Stalking into the rain, nearly vanishing, Sundrop paced then returned, his face clearer this time. *"Rye. Who is with crows."*

But the crow woman clung to her own. She wouldn't reveal her friend to the mancers. *"That doesn't—"*

"Parsley is Rye's brother. Parsley is for hire—for anyone's hire. I had not known how hard he was."

Parsley, the iron magus. Whom Mortimer called "Farus." Who killed a man at Elisha's door, on behalf of the French. *"Did Parsley sell her to the mancers?"*

"How can I know!" Sundrop howled, and the storm clouds blew up overhead. Elisha's hair tingled. *"He's the one person I cannot reach, who flees the threat of rain."*

And so he besieged the enemy he knew. The sign of the lamb rattled dangerously overhead. *"I can help you find him."*

"Why? We cannot even trust each other, we who should stand together!" Sundrop flung wide his arms and thunder rolled. Elisha could feel him reaching through the air. *"What do you want from me?"*

"Your power could be more than this, Sundrop. Your grief is better spent against the men who killed her, and the cause they work for." He steadied his emotions and let his presence shine with his urgency. *"I want your help against the French. With your kinship, you can herd them where we want them to be. We can break their invasion before it begins."*

Sundrop wheeled to face him. *"And you can force the iron mage out of hiding. He will not come if he senses me near."*

"Then you must let this go, Sundrop, and join me as a man and not a magus."

"Like great Cnut, oh mighty king, you think you can command the tide." The rain warmed to a summer's shower. *"It just might work, oh mighty king, if I am at your side."*

Elisha smiled at the return of Sundrop's poetry. Then a rumble gathered over them, and Elisha retreated, his retainers falling in around him as his boots struck the muddy street. A tremendous crack smote the sky, with a sizzle that stood up the hairs at the back of his neck. Lightning struck the inn, its glow casting their shadows hard upon the rain as the thunder shook the sky. Elisha whirled back. Too wet to catch fire, the thatching collapsed inward, puffing smoke from the gout of flame that took hold in the heart of the inn.

Sundrop staggered away from the smoldering ruin, laughing. "May God have mercy on the lamb!" he cried, then pointed at Elisha. "Lead on, oh mighty king." He swayed, and Elisha caught him, the rain solidifying in his arms to a pale young man. With its master's collapse, the rain dispersed, leaving an echoing silence and the scent of burning.

Chapter 16

On their return, with Sundrop installed in a fine room in the Tower's guest quarters, not far from Duchess Allyson, Elisha summoned Mortimer. The man entered with a cautious step, darting his glance about as if fearful of the king's wrath, but his presence hummed with a suppressed energy that reminded Elisha of the battle-hungry crows.

He offered a perfunctory bow and knelt stiffly. "What is your will, Your Majesty?"

"I don't believe we've had a chance to talk, Mortimer, since I took the throne."

The lord's posture stiffened. "No, Majesty, I don't suppose we have. And as much as I appreciate your attention to my humble self—"

"You and Alaric always seemed to have lots to talk about."

Mortimer raised his chin to meet Elisha's gaze. "Indeed. God rest his soul."

"Amen," Elisha replied, matching Mortimer's blank expression. "For one thing, I need to speak with you about your choice of . . . friends? Rather, Farus isn't anyone's friend. More of a tool. Or maybe a weapon."

They regarded each other coolly, Mortimer's presence

revealing the humming nervousness beneath his guise. Then Mortimer said, "Have you seen the royal menagerie? It's really quite interesting, especially for those who are not widely travelled. It's rather noisy, I admit. One must speak carefully to be heard. Perhaps I can show it to you this evening?"

"I'll look forward to that," Elisha said, dismissing him and watching him stride out the door, a pair of his servants coming to meet him. Elisha's entourage—Ufford, and a couple of guards and pages—lingered nearby, but not close enough to give the appearance of listening. No wonder Mortimer suggested they go to hear the lions roar.

During a long day spent reviewing and responding to petitions of various sorts, Elisha contemplated his position with the barons and the inquisitor's homily about heresy. "Ufford? What can we do about the exceptions to the law against torture?"

"Exceptions, Your Majesty?" The wild eyebrows formed a ridge.

Elisha leaned forward. "Witches, heretics. If the archbishop had not spoken up when he did, I might have been taken for a witch myself. If he were not as powerful as he is, he might have been claimed a heretic."

"Such crimes fall under church jurisdiction, and the law is confusing regarding their prosecution."

"Then I think it is high time we sorted that out."

"Very well, Your Majesty. I shall have the clerks begin compiling the law for your examination." He gave a short bow and went to do the king's bidding.

Elisha gathered a few companions for dinner to introduce Sundrop, although the rain-magus had little to say and looked ill-at-ease through the meal, even after apologizing to Allyson. He glanced often to the windows, perhaps hoping for a storm.

Randall allowed his wife to sit between them, she dividing her attention between Elisha, and her husband. She appeared fully recovered, while the duke's round face looked haggard. "The bombards should be there in another day and a half, though I warrant the local population will be a bit concerned about the number of men descending upon them. We'll make use of the higher ground toward Dover, if we can get the fleet aimed in that direction." Randall raised his eyebrows at Sundrop, who merely dipped his head.

"He's still weary from the last few weeks," Elisha sent to Allyson, with a touch on her hand.

"Will he be capable of what you want?"

"I think so," Elisha replied, but watching the young man toy with his goblet, he wasn't sure. Sundrop was, quite literally, out of his element. Randall and Allyson looked alert, present, but their clothes began to hang a little loose, their eyes always haunted. He, who was with death, must seem the most lively of the bunch. Aloud, he said, "I wish we could have this over already."

Sundrop spoke up. "If need be, across the narrows of the Channel, I can just reach the coast of France. I can sweep the clouds away. I'll need a place to send them, of course." He wafted his hand above the table as if drawing up the rain. To their startled faces, he said, "I am not feeble or infirm." His long fingers stroked down the grain of the wood. "It's just that she was my purpose. She is the reason that I am this."

Allyson's eyes brimmed over with tears. She pushed back from the table, her chair clattering to the floor as she turned away. Giving a little bow, Randall hurried after her, leaving Elisha and Sundrop at the table. The rain magus blinked at him then leaned back and popped a grape in his mouth, his gaze once more drifting toward the window.

A knock resounded through the room. Elisha pushed back as Pernel bowed into his presence, followed by a man in Mortimer's livery. "If your majesty is prepared," the stranger said, bowing as well.

"Yes, thank you." Elisha rose. "See you all on the morrow, then."

Sundrop, too, stood up, that light returning to his eyes. "Remember Daniel and the lion's den," he said, trailing after Elisha and his guide as they went down. Pernel and two soldiers fell in with the king. Once outside, the rain magus turned to a different path, but Elisha could feel him fading as the air grew moist, until he would be once more cloaked in mist as if he, too, rose up off the river.

Elisha paced the stones between the walls, the guards above giving slight bows if they noticed him. For tonight, the men at the outer barbican—including the menagerie's keepers—would be Randall's, watching out for him, witnessing whatever Mortimer might reveal. Eerie calls and soft growls filled the air as they emerged from the inner gate, along with an odor of animals, something between a barnyard and a slaughterhouse. Crossing the moat, they descended the stone staircase that circled the base of the outer gate, to an open iron grate where Mortimer's man bowed again. Lord Mortimer waited there, glancing at Elisha's trio of followers, arching a brow as he faced Elisha.

"Wait here, would you? I shall escort his Majesty," Mortimer announced.

Mortimer's servant gave him another bow, and Elisha nodded to his men to stay as well: he would get nothing from Mortimer without privacy. Rather than lurk on the narrow stairs, the servants retreated a little to the top of the stair and settled on the embattled bridge overlooking the moat. Above, the guards leaned down, watching. Good.

With a broad grin, Mortimer, too, bowed. "Come, Your Majesty, see a most unusual part of your wealth."

"Thank you." Elisha extended his senses as he stepped

through the arched door into the half-round well at the base of the tower, and the smell of unfamiliar animals grew stronger. Elisha searched for signs of deflection, for Farus, the mancer's spy, but cold iron lingered all around them, making it hard to look for the man who devoted himself to the metal. Another drawbridge loomed overhead, a dark stripe through the sky over the higher rank of animal cages, now empty for the evening. In the city above, first one, then another, and finally the entire bristling forest of church spires began tolling the hour. With a rattle and groan, the drawbridge rose ponderously up, sealing the tower for the night and lifting the darkness of the menagerie below. Elisha blinked, his eyes adjusting to another change in light. A white shape loomed at him from the back of a dark cage—a huge, white bear that ambled forward and sniffed.

Elisha drew back from the big, black nose, catching his breath, his heart drumming a little harder. Bear skins adorned a few of the duke's chambers, but the bear alive and in the flesh filled most of its stone enclosure, the bars allowing its muzzle to protrude. After a moment of sniffing, it returned to the back and dropped its great bulk down onto its belly, its stubby tail touching one side of the cage while thick, black claws scraped the other.

"A gift from the King of Norway, a noble tradition that began almost a hundred years ago," Mortimer said. "They have white bears often in their lands, perhaps because of the snow."

"I see," said Elisha faintly.

"You should come hunting more often, Your Majesty, to get used to the great beasts." Mortimer flashed him a hard stare, then gestured grandly to the next cage where a pair of sleek, spotted cats as big as Thomas's dog lounged and licked their paws. "Leopards. For King Henry, of course. These two are female. The male is here—" He backed up as he spoke, leading Elisha on-ward, then flinched a little. As Elisha came around the buttress, he, too, stopped short. The great leopard sat just inside, rubbing his huge spotted head up and down against a pair of iron bars, ears flattened to either side.

Mortimer laughed, but the sound echoed, brittle and high. "There was an elephant, I understand, as big as a house, and they built a special stable for it, but the beast died and had to be buried there instead." They moved around the curve, out of sight of the entrance, with the bulk of the gate tower between them and the moat. A troop of monkeys bounded about their enclosure, whooping and screeching. "So," Mortimer began, "you wished to speak to me."

"Alaric thought he could trust you, my lord. I think he was wrong."

"I am wounded." Mortimer pressed a hand to his heart. "Not as you were wounded, of course, Your Majesty,"—a smile—"but, unless you were much closer to his highness than I imagined, I don't see what basis you have to say such a thing about me."

"You lied to him about the attempts against me."

With a tip of his head and a little frown, Mortimer said, "I can see that you would not trust me. In fact, I am surprised you wished to speak to me at all, and under such circumstances." Close by, at Mortimer's back, some-thing roared, and they both paused.

"You took a shot at me with a crossbow. I suspect that was a lucky thing—you saw me and took the chance. And everyone was meant to believe the Frenchman who died at Dunbury was killed instead of me."

"I've admitted that as well." Mortimer spread his hands. "At the time, you did not seem to me a person of great consequence. Circumstances have changed, of course, and they may yet change again."

Elisha stayed his words with a turn of his hands, his scarred palms outward, drawing Mortimer's gaze, the lord frowning, then his face clearing with a little catch in his throat.

"Farus did what he meant to do." One of the leopards gave a breathy growl that settled into harsh panting. Elisha took a step closer to the tower wall. "You wanted him to kill me as well, but he killed the Frenchman, and you concealed that fact from Alaric. You'd rather have your prince believe you responsible for a mistake than to think the Frenchman was important. Why?"

"You are right about something." Mortimer tipped his head in invitation and started walking again, leaving Elisha to catch up. "The crossbow was a lucky moment, and I couldn't pass up the chance." He glanced back. "But the Frenchman's death was an unfortunate accident. Do you plan to punish me now that you are king?"

The monkeys hooted as they passed by.

"Tell me about the Frenchman," Elisha snapped as he caught up.

"But you should still see the lion, Your Majesty. It's quite the finest specimen here."

"I don't care." Elisha caught his arm forcing Mortimer to look at him, forcing contact. He wanted to feel the lie. "Your henchman killed a member of the French ambassador's staff, a member of the French king's household. You knew it, and you covered it up. Why?"

"Why not ask me?" A figure pushed away from the last cage and straightened, a cold presence, until now indistinguishable from the metal bars of the cage itself.

"Farus! Thank you for joining us." Mortimer shook off Elisha's hand. "Yes, it does seem as if you could answer the king's questions better than I."

"Seems to me he already knows enough, my lord." Farus tossed something back between the bars and the roar echoed again. The lion pounced forward, dense, black mane swirling about its tawny face, claw-spiked paws the size of maces pressed against the bars. Bars of iron.

Elisha swallowed. "Farus doesn't work for the French, Mortimer, he works for darker forces."

"We shall be rewarded in Heaven for the restoration of a godly monarchy," said Mortimer.

"No. His true masters are using you to steer this kingdom into madness. The French already a part of it."

Farus glared down at them from the stone lip that held the bars. "The time for talk is over."

"I am sure you are correct, Farus." Mortimer took a few steps closer, then swung to the side, just at Farus's shoulder.

The iron-magus placed his hand up, measuring it against the lion's paw, then he raked the pads with his cold, hard fingers, spattering blood.

The lion roared again, its gaping mouth fronted by teeth as sharp as swords. When Farus casually turned the nearest bar, bending it aside like a chandler shaping wax, Elisha ran.

The lion gave a different cry when its wounded paw touched ground; it would attack Farus first, wouldn't it? Elisha skidded to a halt at the other side of the curve. Men shouted overhead, but the gate under the stone arch stood closed—along with the other grate at the top, from the furious shouting. Elisha shook it, but the gate didn't move. Taking a step back, he glanced up at the top of the stone wall overhead. Too high for an easy escape. The bars, then. Elisha set his hand to the grate, forcing himself to breathe more carefully, to focus. A bit of rust, a hint of death, and the bars would fall before him.

"And me inside—Farus, you said—" Mortimer's voice broke into a shriek.

With Mortimer between him and the lion, Elisha had time. Walk away and let him die, taking his knowledge with him.

Elisha whirled. Once again, Farus deceived him, deceived them both. Elisha was not the target. He ran back, shouting, stumbling. The lion surged around the bent bars, slapping at Farus, but the claws tore through his sleeve only to clang off his skin. At his back, Mortimer gave a high-pitched giggle, clinging to Farus as his shield. Farus slipped sideways along the bars as the lion lunged again, and Mortimer floundered to stay with him. Stepping through the gap, Farus shoved Mortimer aside. Farus drew back his hand, bloody, as Mortimer cried out.

Farus stepped calmly inside the cage and drew the bars straight behind him. As Elisha watched, the blood on his fingers turned from red to clear, then he wiped from his hand what looked like water.

Clutching his arm, blood seeping from parallel slashes, Mortimer scrambled up. The lion snarled, its breath shivering Mortimer's hair. Mortimer dodged, thrusting up a little dagger, but the beast knocked him back, and the dagger spun away.

Tripping over the bones left from some animal's supper, Elisha reached for death, and found it—dogs and pigs devoured, ghostly lions and leopards, a keeper torn to shreds, even the dank residue of quartered traitors who once hung upon the gate above. The black power swirled up at his call, twining through his skin, echoing inside his chilling flesh. His breath turned to mist. Overhead, something clattered as Farus worked his way up to the second rank of cages, sliding out, staying back against the iron.

"Your Majesty!" came a voice high up. "Jump for the ladder!" A rope ladder dangled down, but still several feet off the ground. Another man held a bow, pointed down, but shifted his aim this way and that as men and beast moved.

Black mane lashing, the lion crept closer, his paws straddling Mortimer's legs as the lord pushed himself backward, only to rap his head against stone. The great muzzle lunged forward.

Elisha lunged as well. His fingers sank into the lion's pelt, its flank shivering as if he were a fly. For a moment, Elisha felt the thrum of animal thoughts—hunger, pain, anger—and under it all, the terrible beating of an alien heart. Sending his power into his hands, Elisha shocked it with cold. With a breath of ice, the lion toppled.

Mortimer took the impact with a grunt, then a sob, muffled by the beast that covered him.

Drawing back his power, Elisha jumped for the rope, seized it and scrambled up, to the encouragement of the guards. They cried out in dismay as he leapt off onto the top of the arch, level with the second rank of cages. Farus must have seen him, too, for the shadow of iron burst into movement, dashing by the last of the cages and coming to the narrow wall that separated the enclosure from the moat. "There!" Elisha shouted, pointing. "Catch him!" But no one else was close.

Launching himself to the wall from his end, Elisha ran after, his men howling behind him. He slipped but caught himself, wincing, his palms were bruised and his foot splashed into the moat. Ahead, Farus froze, then started again, his trembling arms outstretched for balance. With a burst of speed, he could have escaped. What had spooked him? The sound of a splash? He was still too far ahead for Elisha to catch up.

Elisha dropped down and swung his hand into the murky water, his flesh once more crackling with the chill of death. Before the forming ice trapped his hand, he yanked it free, rose, and threw.

The slushy ball caught Farus in the center of his back. He stumbled, arms flailing, righted himself, and kept going.

Elisha scooped himself a second handful of ice, flinging it ahead. Farus howled even before it reached him and slapped at his back. Then he struggled with his wet tunic, so the second ball struck bare skin over his left kidney. A red welt spread from the contact, and Farus screamed, twisting like a cat as Elisha ran and reached for him.

Farus freed one arm, ripping his shirt. Rust pitted his back and side, spread over him like a flesh-eating disease. He pivoted, bringing his weapon-like hand to bear against Elisha, but his heel slipped and he teetered.

With a lunge, his fingers still wet with ice, Elisha snagged his arm.

Farus's right arm slicked and crumpled under Elisha's steadying grip as the water ate into him. He sliced at Elisha's hand with his left hand, the fingers once more hard and sharp as knives.

Conjuring his healing power to seal these fresh wounds, Elisha kept hold. *"Tell me about the mancers, Parsley,"* he said into the iron-mage's withered flesh.

"Tell you? You are one—or you should've been. Thinks he'll be rewarded in heaven, but they'll make of this place a hell on earth and them the masters. Serve them, and be free." He rammed Elisha's chest with his head, knocking the breath out of him.

Elisha staggered back, losing his balance, dragging Farus with him. Struggling to free himself from Elisha's grip, Farus twisted further. His eyes flared as both men plunged headlong into the moat below.

When they splashed into the murky water, Farus shrieked as if demons clawed him down. Spirals of red swirled out like blood into the water. The iron-magus rusted.

His fingers dug in like hooks, trying to haul himself up as Elisha fought for the surface, arms wild. Farus's grip trembled as the rush of decay overwhelmed him. His other hand snared the back of Elisha's neck, sinking fast, dragging him down. As a child, Elisha had nearly drowned, a memory so black he smothered it at the back of his heart. He remembered it now as the water mounted over him and the grip of iron pulled him under.

Marshaling his strength, Elisha kicked away. Brittle iron, riddled with rust, cracked at the blow. Elisha's head broke the surface, and he flailed to keep himself up, his fingers scraping against stone. He gasped as the water sucked him down again. From his hands, ice crackled outward. Already, the water thickened, his clothes dragging at him.

Fighting the pull, kicking upward, Elisha released his power, shaking off the ice, his hand breaking through to the air. Water surged down his throat as he struggled. He gagged, then the water thinned, the sky rippling overhead. Then a hand seized his arm, hauling. His rescuer grappled with him, Elisha's face breaking the surface again, then the hand clutched under his shoulder, holding him.

Coughing and spitting water, Elisha stared up into Pernel's face. The manservant lay atop the narrow wall, his legs dangling over the drop on the other side, one of the guards on top of him, weighting Pernel and keeping them both safe. Another soldier knelt more carefully, and, between the three of them, they brought Elisha back onto the wall, their hands lifting and pulling. Once safe, he seized Pernel's hand before it could be withdrawn and sat, panting, dripping.

"Thank you," he breathed at last. "By God I thought I'd drown."

Pernel gave a nod as he broke the grip, staring at his own shivering hand, then the lump of Elisha's scar. At last, he drew his hand close to his chest. "Majesty, are you injured?"

Elisha shook his head and, for a few minutes, they

waited while he caught his breath, the gate guards hollering from their end of the wall, more men filling up the bridge.

"The other man, Majesty? You fought with someone?" The guard glanced down toward the moat, frowning.

"He sank." Elisha gulped and wiped back the wet hair from his face. "Mortimer?"

They blinked back at him. "Didn't the lion take him, Your Majesty?" Pernel asked.

Shaking his head made Elisha's whole body shiver. "He was alive when I left him."

The standing guard swiveled expertly on the wall and cupped his hands to his mouth. "Lord Mortimer may live!"

At the far end, the men turned from shouting after the king's well-being, to solving the problem of the sealed gates. In a few moments, a terrible crash resounded down the wall, followed by a second crash as a party thundered down the steps to the cacophony of the animals below.

By the time Elisha rose and walked unsteadily with his companions back to the drawbridge at the gate, they met a similar group emerging, Mortimer in their midst cradling his arm. Blood, dirt, and fur stained the lord's dark clothes and smeared his face, framed by unkempt hair and beard. He held himself with dignity, squaring his shoulders and drawing a deep breath before he folded himself into a bow. Holding the posture a long moment, Mortimer dripped blood that swirled into the water pooling around Elisha's feet.

Finally, he met Elisha's gaze. "Perhaps we should speak again, Your Majesty." He tipped his head. "Under more favorable circumstances."

Elisha searched his tired face. "Join me with some friends to break the fast."

Mortimer nodded.

To the gate guards plus the dozen others that surrounded them, Elisha said, "No one from Mortimer's household is to pass from the tower, understood?"

Mortimer's shoulders drooped, and he drew his wounded arm closer. "Am I under arrest?"

"Not yet." Elisha stepped closer and the lord caught his breath as Elisha took his elbow, examining the wound.

"Lion swiped him good, eh?" one of the guard's asked as Elisha moved aside the shreds of cloth.

Indeed, it resembled claw marks, but Mortimer's furtive glance caught Elisha's eye. "It's not deep," Elisha murmured, "but stitches would be wise."

"But how'd you kill the lion, my lord?" his waiting servant asked Mortimer.

Again, their eyes met, and Mortimer said, "It was the king who felled the beast." He leaned on his man as a party of guards escorted him back to his chambers.

The crowd accompanied Elisha with a buoyancy, as if they'd heard joyous news or witnessed a moment of greatness.

Back at the royal chambers, a flurry of servants stoked the fire and fetched him dry clothes of warm wool. As Pernel and Walter assisted, removing his wet tunic and undershirt, a few of the others whispered about his scarred back—scourged! The murmurs of legend wove about him, and Elisha felt helpless to prevent it. After a time, the servants subsided, leaving him by the fire with a mug of warmed wine and a fur throw across his lap. Dozing, Elisha imagined the Christ of the royal chapel coming down off the cross, berating him for his arrogance, saying, "Verily, pride goeth before a fall," and Elisha shivered awake to the creak of the door.

"If I might disturb you, Majesty." Pernel closed the door behind him.

"Please." Elisha waved him closer, and the young man nearly danced across the room, a roll of parchment in his hand.

"The map, Your Majesty, of the coast." He flourished the scroll, then spread it upon the table, placing a pitcher on one corner and spoons on the others. Elisha put off his weariness to join him, running his hand over the coastline with its lumps and its spidery black writing wriggling inland or sometimes out to sea at the mouths of rivers. "I'm sorry it took so long, and still it's not complete. If you need to search south, below the Humber, or above Edinburgh, you'll need another, Your Majesty."

"Tell me about it. Everything you know."

"Been as far as Carlisle, with his royal highness." With his finger, he drew an invisible line most of the way up, going off the page. "Must be over hereabouts, Your Majesty. King Edward had to shut down some coal mines outside Newcastle during my da's time, but we caught wind they were back to mining again, so we did a tramp over there. Royal castles are already marked, and I've added a thing or two so far. I'd have more, but . . ."

Elisha waved away his regret. "It's a good start; I don't want to delay the search any longer—he's already been gone too long." The map's pattern of lines writhed and stilled before his tired eyes, so many worms in a rich garden, but which might point him in the right direction? "Everything you know."

"The sea up there is gray and rough, mostly, with tall headlands, but the land smooths out a bit here."

A knock sounded on the door, then Walter's voice followed, "Your Majesty, I've got some stew to warm you."

"Enter!" Then, to Pernel, Elisha said, "What's this?" He pointed to a protrusion near the Scottish border, marked with an elaborate cross.

"The Holy Isle." He crossed himself. "I thought of that, Majesty."

Walter held the door while a pair of servers entered, carrying a tray with a steaming crock and more of the pure-white bread. The odor of beef stock wafted in with them, as did a slender figure, cloaked and silent, whose presence warmed Elisha's skin and tingled in his chest. Brigit, employing her deflection. What did she want this time? And how could he get her out without revealing her for a witch?

"It's been rebuilt since the Northmen, of course," Pernel continued. "Lots of monks but still a number of ruins where—"

He stopped short as Elisha caught his arm, then released him. "Later." He smiled and straightened. "We'll need to clear the table, in any event."

Walter paused in the act of carrying a second trestle table while one of the servers fetched the legs, and the cloaked Brigit silently walked by, around Elisha's back. He could feel the bright spike of her interest.

"We've got another, Majesty." Walter propped the tabletop on one foot. "Sorry to interrupt."

"This is fine." Elisha lifted the spoons that weighted his map and it curled with a rustle. "We'll come back to it later."

Brigit's hand slid along the back of his neck, ruffling his hair as they set the table. Walter and Pernel were visibly confused, even hurt by his tone. *"What's that?"* asked Brigit against his warming skin. *"It did not look like France."*

When the servers had finished, Walter gave a short bow and exited. Pernel frowned after him until Elisha said, "Go on. I'll ring if I need you."

Pernel's bow was longer than usual, then he shut the door behind him.

"Buggers, aren't they? Earth and sky, could they be more obvious? I don't see how you can abide their presence, never mind letting them dress you." Brigit shuddered as she slipped back her hood. She lifted the lid of the crock and inhaled deeply, her disgust turning to pleasure. "Mmm. May I join you?"

"I don't seem able to stop you," he snapped.

Her green eyes flashed back up to his, her lips pressed together. The lid of the crock clattered back from her pale fingers. "Do you want me to go? Truly, you seemed so lonely the last time. Then that nightmare. You need someone. Someone close, who can truly understand what you're going through."

"I have a confessor."

"What, Father Michael? He's hardly worthy of your new status."

"Do you know the best part of my new status, Brigit? I decide who is worthy. I choose." He tapped a finger against his chest.

"Is that why you took the lords a-hunting? Is that why you've issued a writ about petty theft? For goodness sake, Elisha, either one of us could burn at any moment, and you are off hunting and worrying over bread!" She snatched up the loaf and tossed it into the fire where it sent a puff of smoke and ash.

"You have no idea what worries me."

"Scotland, apparently—but not even Scotland. Do you think the Northumbrians will rise up in arms?"

"The royal clerks are already researching changes to the laws against torture, Brigit, I am trying—"

"Clerks and knowledge will not be enough to defend the magi. Haven't you seen enough by now to know the barons will never support you? Your laws will never get past the parliament."

"We are a nation of laws, Brigit, this is how it's done."

"But you're frustrated with how long it takes, even I

can see that. You still bow to the barons when they should be bowing to you. Every *desolati* in the nation should be—"

Someone banged on the door, and a man's voice shouted, "Brigit! I know you're in there! For the love of God, you brazen whore!"

Chapter 17

❖

$\mathcal{B}$rigit's cheeks flared pink, her mouth open, but no sound emerged.

"Sir! You can't just—" someone protested outside.

Elisha pushed back and crossed to the door, letting her father in with a bow, waving back the startled servants on the landing. He worried over what she might do if he didn't have an eye on her—but the risks of her eying him back had grown too much. What if she found out about his search for Thomas, that her hope of influencing the throne would be dashed if Elisha succeeded?

"Sir," he told the man who swept by him, "I think you should take her."

The man turned, even more red than his daughter as he gave a hasty bow. "Forgive me, Your Majesty—really, that was—I'm sorry. Unforgivably rude." With his graying ginger hair and round belly, he bore only a slight resemblance to Brigit. Once the apology was done, he swung back to his child, puffing up his chest. In their reddened faces and curt gestures, the resemblance manifested.

"Come then, child. It's clear you're not wanted here."

Brigit's voice fell low, her gaze swinging from one to the other. "You don't understand what's at stake, neither of you."

"Aside from what little reputation remains to you?" Spreading his hands, the fellow inclined his head. "Your Majesty has not yet been. . . blessed with children. There was a time I should have wished for more of them."

Elisha nodded vaguely, but his gaze stayed with Brigit; golden and glowing, the fury rippling from her like the lion's mane as the creature moved to pounce—and he wondered if opening the door to her father might not have been a terrible mistake.

"If you haven't a care for me or for our people, Father, the very least you might do is stay out of it!"

"I do care," he protested, "Of course I do, but it does not give license for this kind of behavior. Sneaking to a man's bedchamber? Whisking off to visit your husband on the battlefield, yes, but this? And he not two months in the grave!"

The gathering inferno of Brigit's presence took on a tremor as her eyes widened, shifting toward Elisha and away. "You do not know of what you speak, Father," she said, with a gesture pushing down her anger. "If you wish to berate me like a child, you might've chosen a better time and place."

"You chose the place!" He pounded forward, bracing his hands upon the table. "You chose it. Don't forget why your mother died. Forgive me, Majesty, if forgiveness there might be for such unseemliness."

Outside, a couple of page boys gaped. Elisha clicked the door shut between his chamber and the audience, and walked forward in her father's wake, a single word capturing his attention. "Husband?" he echoed. "Brigit?"

She took a step away to keep them both in view. "My mother died because she tried to show Prince Thomas how much better his land could be, if witches could work openly. We have a chance now, Elisha, you and I together. There is a way we can put the barons in their place and protect our people—"

"Brigit," Elisha said sharply. "You never mentioned you were married."

"Married to Prince Alaric she was, Your Majesty. And she's bearing his child, though that's still not widely known." When he shook his head, his hair fluffed out, a nimbus of fatherly confusion. "After so long being outside of court, we came here to take her rightful place, to be acknowledged—then he died—God rest him." Looking heavenward, he crossed himself with the precision of a marksman.

"It was Alaric who betrayed your mother, Brigit," Elisha said, anger, hurt, and confusion interwoven. "Because he envied her attention to Thomas. When were you married?"

"Where did you hear that?" she asked, her attention keen, but her father cut his hand through the air between them, glowering.

"They married the end of April, Your Majesty." At this, he ducked his head and toyed with the fat buckle of his belt. "It was a small ceremony, you understand. It was hard to know how the prince's father would take it, you see?"

Frowning, Elisha counted back in his head. "The night of the church fire." His party moved toward the battle that night, stopping to help at the fire where he smothered the flames from Brigit's hair and helped the prince escape, not knowing who he was. The first night he had met either of them and had unwittingly become entangled in the affairs of the crown. Alaric's boyish face grinned in Elisha's memory. Trysting in the church the prince had said. Even when Elisha did not know who he was, and they had no expectation of meeting again, Alaric kept this secret. When Brigit had seduced Elisha to get pregnant, she was already married. And here she stood, trying to do it again.

Her father's face twisted, but when he lifted a knuckle to rub his eye, Elisha realized he was close to weeping.

"The marriage was her mother's dream, you see?" he whispered. "And she not there to see it. Lord knows I never asked so much as for her to marry a prince." His hand fell, slowly curling, fiddling with his buckle once more. "And then the fire broke out. Accidental, I'm told, although I shouldn't wonder if some envious acquaintance had a hand in that."

"I thought you said it was a secret," Elisha murmured.

"It was meant to be," Brigit returned, folding her arms, "but Father couldn't help telling a few people, could he? 'We'll be back at court soon, our expulsion was all a terrible mistake, you see?'" She put on her father's manner, then flung it aside. "Mother wanted to help our people, to craft a better nation by being close to the crown. But you undermined her every attempt."

Dropping his hands from his belt, the old man growled, "She should have been more careful. It was the death of her once they knew the truth."

She lifted her chin, that bare sweep of pale throat. "Elisha Rex is hardly likely to be the death of me." For a long moment, she stood that way, then her brow arched a little, one eye glancing toward him again, but he said nothing.

"You're angry about Alaric," she said with a brittle smile. "Of course you are. How many times must I tell you"—her next words echoed through his skin, as if she touched him, though she stood yards away—*"I should have met you first."*

From the first day they met, it was deception. Did that explain why her deflections worked so well? All he ever saw were her lies. "It's time for you to go."

"You want to be a just king, Elisha, and I want to help you."

"You cannot work for justice if there is vengeance in your heart."

Her pose wavered, her face for a moment almost vulnerable, and he remembered she wept at his graveside, tears of genuine grief. She loved him in her way. A selfish love that watched him hang, that watched him buried, that would not hesitate to let him burn. "My mother's death is only part of this. Think of the old women who are dunked and drowned. Think of yourself: you healed a hundred people in the yard on Sunday, Elisha, how many more could be healed if you could openly share and teach what you know?" Her hands clasped together, her presence wavering between desperation, hope, and fear. But of what?

"How can I trust you?" He asked, but not aloud. The child they shared, like the healing he shared with Mordecai, formed a bridge between them.

"If you don't, if you turn me away, you will face your enemies alone."

"Are you threatening me?"

Brigit shook her head fiercely. *"You face dangers beyond the French, beyond the barons."*

"What makes you say that?" He spread his awareness as carefully as he could but touched only the barest edges of her emotions, as if they seeped out past her careful wards.

"The nightmares," she said simply, but the question discomfited her. *"And the inquisition. Even if you defend the magi here, you cannot protect them from the Church. You really think the barons will approve a law to protect us? If you ally with me, we can both prosper."*

"With you as my queen."

Her eyes flared, beautiful, green, flecked with gold, as if echoing the crown she longed for. *"Yes, Elisha. What could we not be, together? For the good of our people."*

Our people. At most, one in a hundred. What of the other ninety-nine, who had no magic? What of Thomas, and Randall, and Rosie? When he found the king, he would abdicate his throne, but Brigit would not leave it so lightly. "I cannot give you what you want."

"Will not, you mean." The color fled her cheeks and throat, the tide of hope swept away from her presence. *"I am not afraid to do what must be done. I will be queen, Elisha, with you, or without you."*

The old knight, her father, reached out and opened the door, where the handful of servants lingered to either side, eyes quickly averted.

"Your Majesty." Pernel and Walter dropped into bows almost painfully low and rose without lifting their eyes. "Your Majesty, forgive us, we should have known. None should have passed us without your blessing. Please," Pernel, always the more talkative, stammered his apology.

Elisha stood still, hands folded at his back, muscles tight. "My guests are leaving."

"Come, child," the old man said again, this time taking her arm, sliding his other arm about her shoulders. "Come away. We'll go to church and pray forgiveness." His chin trembled, his eyes watery, and she suffered his touch, but turned her head as they reached the door.

"Fare you well . . . Your Majesty." All sense of hope, desire, or regret washed away with her icy stare, then she turned her gaze forward, rejected her father's arm, and stalked down the stairs into the darkness.

"I have made an enemy today," Elisha murmured.

"Just a woman, Your Majesty, and not one with many ties at court," Pernel offered.

The two servants entered, shutting the door behind them. Walter drifted toward the table and found a little broom to sweep up the drift of soot that had flown out at the loss of Elisha's bread. "Not to your liking, Your Majesty?"

"She threw my bread in the fire. I'd like more."

"Aye, Majesty." Walter bowed himself away backward toward the door.

"I'm not going to punish you—either of you. But I am going to want you to stay close. Clearly the pages aren't enough. If you need to go out, send up one of the door guards." He pictured the expression on Brigit's face. "Or two of them."

As Walter went to get bread, Pernel stared thoughtfully after him, then back to Elisha. "Your Majesty seems concerned."

"She's more powerful than you know, and now she knows I've been looking at Scotland." Brigit seemed to think the child would give her leverage if everyone believed it was Alaric's. If she had suitable witnesses to the wedding, she might convince some of the nobles that her baby was the only remaining heir of the blood. He thought of Thomas's lost daughter, slain by witches, as Brigit's mother had been slain by men.

"She is no friend of ours, Pernel. Remember that, no matter what she says or does."

The servant gave a short nod, but Elisha needed no special senses to know Pernel doubted the danger Brigit might present. Finally Elisha returned to his table, to the cooling soup. He reached to serve himself, but Pernel took up the ladle and spooned out a generous portion.

The soup caressed his lips with a hint of grease and tasted of bay leaves. When he had finished, sopping up the last of the soup with hunks broken off a fresh loaf, Elisha pushed back. "We need the map. I've wasted too much time already."

In moments, the table was clear, the map replaced. "Walter, watch the door, if you please. Pernel, I need you to tell me everything you know about each of these places, in turn and slowly. I want to. . ." but how could he say what he planned, in terms that did not make him appear mad? Madder than he already seemed, at any rate. Elisha's fingers knotted together. Thomas was lost, without a word, and the longer Elisha sat in the king's chair and lay in his bed, the more their peril grew. Staring down at his joined hands and the scars that made him holy, Elisha knew what to say, though he grit his teeth before he spoke. "I'm going to pray about it, as you speak. To listen for guidance."

Pernel's mouth made a little "o," and he swallowed a few times before he spoke, pointing to one of the castle markings. "Kingstonhus at Greater Yarmouth. It's a pace back from the sea. Stone, not too big. Stopped off there once, when his royal highness had business in Norwich."

As Pernel spoke, Elisha prepared himself, drawing the lock of Thomas's hair from his sleeve to press it between his clasped hands. He shut his eyes and remembered all that he could of that short, sharp vision he shared with Thomas. The smell of the ocean, the dank feel of the stone. He listened to the flow of Pernel's words and hoped for . . . he laughed silently to himself. He was, of course, like any visionary, looking for a sign.

Pernel's finger ticked up the coastline, describing whatever he knew or guessed about each place, and Elisha's head sank to rest upon his knuckles. He heard the names, pictured the places, sometimes using details of other places he had been, and each time, he found nothing. Surely Mordecai would applaud the effort, given how much knowledge he gained, but eventually Elisha sagged, the lock of hair pressed beneath one palm, flat to the table, his cheek pillowed on his hand. He opened his eyes, gazing sideways across the map, the indications of rivers and the names of towns swimming together in a tangle of black and red, crosses stabbing like knives so that his palms twitched in remembrance, and he wanted to weep.

Pernel coughed and took a swallow from a flagon of ale, but his voice still sounded hoarse. "That's the lot of what I know, Your Majesty. Might be, I could find you someone from the area" — another cough — "and we can get a map further north, maybe Scotland."

Elisha stared at the landscape of the table top, the

pocked texture of parchment, the looming shapes of the flagons and spoons that held down the map, the drawn features of the manservant rising over all, swaying slightly. "I don't know what to do," he whispered.

"Church?" Pernel croaked. With a shake of his head, he took another swallow. "Your Majesty?"

"Rest, I think." He sighed and shut his eyes again. "Mortimer will be here to break the fast. I need Randall as well—that's Dunbury. Tell him to bring his map. Ufford, too." He tapped his fingers on the table.

"Yes, Majesty."

"And you get some rest as well."

Pernel bowed. "Yes, Majesty."

Silent, the servant helped him to his bed.

When Elisha woke in the morning, dragging his eyes open, he found Father Michael preparing to celebrate the Mass in the chantry attached to the royal chambers. He groaned and let the servants bring out his clothes. At first, Elisha knelt resentful on the floor as Father Michael lit candles and prayed, a rapid patter of Latin filling the little room, braiding together the smoke and incense. He had no part except to witness, and since homily was reserved for feast days, his mind could wander then focus on the day ahead. By the time the priest finished, elevating the host, then packing away the golden chalice and monstrance which had held the holy wafer, Elisha felt weary, but curiously alert.

The faces of his guests mirrored his own exhaustion, all pretense and posturing abandoned, as Randall outlined their plan, the four of them at table while a half-dozen men stood guard around the room. As Mortimer listened, he chewed more slowly. Finally, he set down his knife, cradled his bandaged arm, and looked up.

"You cannot tell me all of this and let me leave the room, Your Majesty."

Randall replied, "No, we cannot."

Elisha clenched his jaw, catching the dart of Randall's warning glance.

"If you aid us now," Randall said, "you will be executed as swiftly as time allows, with your family allowed to maintain your lands and titles. We do not have patience for games, we do not have time to negotiate. Ample witnesses will state they heard you call out to the man who opened the lion's gate last night. You believed he would protect you, leaving the king at risk. You planned to kill the king, as part of a plot to enable a French invasion." Randall thumped his hands upon the table.

Elisha began, "Surely, we can offer leniency, in exchange—"

"In exchange for treachery, Your Majesty?" Randall's round face set hard. "You can't think like a doctor any more. You must think like a king."

Quietly, Mortimer asked, "And if I am silent? We still have laws against torture, do we not?"

"If you say nothing, you shall be treated like the traitor that you are: executed in the high square, in a manner befitting the severity of your crime," Randall said. "Your family will be stripped of privileges, lands, and titles. Your name will be blackened, and your quarters hung in the four corners of the realm."

At the back of his head, Elisha ran through the litany of punishments for treason, the same he himself had faced not so long ago. "How can I do this?"

"How can you not?" Randall snapped back. "Listen to me. This kingdom is at risk—have you forgotten? In a matter of days or weeks, we shall be overrun. It was you who wished to avert war. If we suffer a traitor to live, Eli—Your Majesty, we shall have no end of traitors and no end of wars. You, of all people, cannot afford to look weak."

Elisha gripped the table. He knew nothing of how to be king, of the things that kings must do. "It was you who said I could have been king by right of arms—a second conqueror. It was instead, my hands that brought me here." He lay his palms down on the table, the scars displayed. "Those who believe in me don't do so for my strength, Your Grace."

To his left across the table, Mortimer stared into his goblet, fingering a small gold cross at his throat. "Three lights," he said. "The French are to send a few scouting vessels. A lookout in the Saltwood tower will see three lights shining from the water. Then we are to light three lights in reply, at Saltwood, at St. Leonard's, and at Lympne. My steward and a few men at arms know about the lights. No one else, I swear."

His breath hitched in his throat, and Elisha wanted to lay a hand over his, to reassure him. But what comfort could there be? Mortimer, the proud companion of princes, shrank in his clothes in the face of what would be. He raised his eyes then, lined with fear, and whispered to Elisha, "You are a merciful man, Your Majesty. You returned to stop the lion. You won't punish my family, will you? I have two daughters not yet married."

"And their father is a traitor," Ufford cut in.

Mortimer flinched, and Elisha put out his hand to forestall any further attack. His presence resonated with a crackle of his guilt, his anger, as if his ribs were the too-small cage that must contain a lion. "Write out what we need to know, Mortimer—the names, any instructions your followers have—and transfer your keys to the Lord Chancellor. Ufford, see that he's given ink and quills. Let him write his family."

"Yes, Your Majesty," said Ufford, his white brows knitting together.

"We must make all haste for Hythe," said Randall. "Once the execution is carried out."

"Tomorrow?" Ufford suggested. Mortimer dropped his head to his hands, then gave a little cry, wrapping his hand to his wounded shoulder.

Elisha looked away, to the entrance of his little chantry where morning sun glowed red, green, blue, gold through the stained glass window. What he told Randall about his believers was true—and if he must choose between being a martial king, and a merciful one, then he knew what he must do. Elisha reached out, laying his hand over Mortimer's, gently, letting his touch warm with the need for healing. He laced their fingers together, making contact, reminding the flesh what it was to be whole as his own shoulder twinged with mirrored pain for a moment, so that both men gasped. Then Elisha rose and walked away from Mortimer's wonder as the soldiers came up to take him. Food held no interest for Elisha, nor did talk of war, and he missed the simplicity of the battlefield, where his only task was to live long enough to help as many wounded as he could. The country needed Thomas. It needed its king.

They spent the day in hurried preparations, gathering the relatively small force that would accompany them, sending messages by trusted hands, witnessing to Mortimer's confession: evidence, at last, that should convince the barons.

In the cold light of the following dawn, Elisha joined the procession to the field beyond the White Tower where a notched block waited for a neck to fill it. The archbishop and Father Michael both hovered near the prisoner, no doubt speaking words of comfort along with prayers for the dying. A burly, hooded man stood by with an ax, waiting his moment, and Elisha's own throat ached, the scar of his hanging feeling rough against the high, velvet collar that stroked the underside of his chin.

At last, the yeoman brought Mortimer to kneel at the

block, and he cried out, his lean face made the more pale by the white garment he wore. "Your Majesty!" he called, his face already wet with tears, and Elisha flinched. This is what he had done to Thomas, all unwitting, on the day of his own burial.

"Please, Your Majesty." Mortimer pushed back against the yeoman's hands, beard quivering.

"No need to torture yourself, Your Majesty," Randall said.

Elisha sucked in a breath, then approached and squatted before the traitor. "What is it?"

Head bowed, Mortimer whispered, "Would you do for me, Lord, as you did for the lion?"

Inwardly, Elisha reeled. For a moment, he searched the gloomy sky. One way and another, Elisha was the death of this man. "Lay down your head."

Tears streamed from Mortimer's eyes, and he stifled a sob, his mouth curling as he tried to hold back his fear, but his head lowered, jerkily to rest upon the block, his chin fitting the curve, his shoulders shaking.

The block itself, stained with old blood, curled with shades that rose to Elisha's command. Mortimer twitched when Elisha lay his hand upon the traitor's back. A tremor of gratitude cracked the dread that darkened Mortimer's presence. "Peace," Elisha whispered, and he summoned death, binding its cold with the comfort and release of Martin's passing. Between one shuddering breath and the next, Mortimer's heart failed, and his chest rose no more.

The archbishop's gold miter framed his too-still face, but Father Michael softly prayed beside him.

Elisha stepped away and motioned for the ax, though he himself was executioner. As he had sworn that he would never be.

Chapter 18

❖

Four days later, with the sound of the axe that took Mortimer's head still ringing in his dreams, the king's party reached Hythe, a small town near the seaside. Elisha dismounted alongside St. Leonard's church, a tall, gray Norman building that dominated the town from its steep slope overlooking the harbor. Lord Robert took Saltwood, with a small troop of men, while Randall rode on to Lympne, the locations where a show of force might be necessary. Sundrop, his spirits buoyed by the knowledge that Farus was dead, rode to join the bombards on their promontory. The nearer he could drive the ships, the more likely the plan would be successful. Even before they rode, the rain magus stretched out his power toward the coast of France, dissipating the clouds, and pulling them aside, creating a calm, clear passage for the French ships. The clouds hung at a distance ready to sweep in when he chose and drive the ships to their death. Perhaps the rocks alone would be enough to wreck the claims of France.

As his horse was led away, Elisha looked up at the porch before the church. Why did the death of Mortimer—traitor to his country as well as to Elisha himself—weigh so heavily, while he allowed a thousand soldiers to sail to their doom? He would never see their faces nor hear their voices; he knew them only by the badges the crows had stolen, and the ruin they would wreak upon his land.

"Key," said Madoc gruffly, holding the lantern beside him, and the local priest sighed loudly before he mounted the stair to unlock the door. When it creaked open, Madoc stomped up beside the priest while a few men lingered to guard the entrance. Beneath the peaked roof of the porch, three sundials sheltered from the lowering day. Elisha frowned up at the useless dials.

"We had the church lifted back in King Henry's day, so that we could hold the procession of St. Leonard without leaving holy ground," the priest remarked, climbing a second set of stairs. "The Mass-dials were hidden. There has been talk of locating a new Mass-dial outside, but the spirit has not moved us to do so."

Elisha came into the shadows, only to stop short again, gasping and steadying himself with a hand to the stone. A narrow passage opened to either side—the processional the priest referred to. And it was lined with bones.

A thousand deaths overlapped and undulated like a nest of eels. Their chilly touch came at him from all sides save above. The long bones of legs formed neat piles on one side, thick stacks higher than his head, with the occasional skull set in among them. Thousands of ribs curved together, the raw materials from which to build a man. Surely there were not enough skulls—but even as he formed the thought, he felt them ranked together on shelves elsewhere in the church, their dark eye sockets a pattern of black pits, regular and terrible. Ahead, Madoc crossed himself and muttered in Welsh.

The priest stared down at them. "We are justly famed for our ossuary. If you wish the tour, I shall—"

"No," they both said at once, and Elisha pushed himself up the stairs, tripping and arresting his fall upon the inner door. He had attributed the gathering gloom of his heart to Mortimer's death alone, not knowing the place they must enter. Hoping to regain his balance, Elisha reached for attunement, letting himself know the place where they must wait.

"It's unholy," Madoc rumbled, his hand fixed upon the hilt of his sword.

Elisha nodded, gathering himself to follow the priest inside. "The tower is there, Your Majesty. If there is anything else that you require, my home is across the lane."

A stained glass window showed St. Leonard before his holy hermitage. The patron saint of prisoners. Elisha's skin tingled with the presence of the dead and now with this coincidence: Did the prisoners he sought pray for St. Leonard's intercession? The power of the place seeped in through his awareness, the displaced dead woven in a thicket around the heart of the church. Madoc made a circuit of the nave, lighting a few candles that could not glow bright enough to reach the vaulted ceiling. It smelled of wax and bones and Sunday incense, and the salty thrum of the ocean a few steps away.

At last, they mounted the narrow stair into the tower, circling round and round, their shoulders brushing the wall. They came to the cramped bell chamber, where thick beams supported enormous bronze bells, and clambered along to the ladder which brought them up, at last, to the rooftop, to breathe deep of the ocean air. To their backs and to both sides, the dark crescent of the town stretched out, with a few patches of light at windows or moving through the streets. Ahead, the ocean rolled, catching highlights from the moon.

"Wish we knew how long we'd have to wait," Madoc said, setting the lantern by the narrow spire he leaned against.

"It might not even be tonight, but if they've been waiting fair weather, they'll have it now." Elisha leaned on the wall before him, gazing out to sea, the wind ruffling his hair.

"Not sure I like this witchery."

Elisha's head sank.

"Most o' the men don't know what's up, just we've got wind o' the French plan."

"If you can't reconcile yourself to this, Madoc, I'll find another guard to wait with me."

"Naw, Your Majesty." Madoc pushed off, his scabbard rapping the stone as he came to join Elisha at the overlook. "Me mum's given me a blessing against witchcraft." He glanced sidelong, his beard and eyebrows casting spiky shadows up to his face and forehead. "Dunno but that your type is a bit of a blessing in itself, eh?"

Elisha laughed. "It's a blessing that brings its own curse."

"Yon archbishop claimed you as holy." He wagged his head this way and that. "Could see my way clear to think it, seeing as you heal with a touch—a proper king, eh?"

"I need contact. To work magic, any magus needs contact."

"Certes? Not with a look, then?"

"If the magus is especially sensitive, the contact might be distant, a bit of hair, a spot of blood."

"But yon rain-master, that boy thinks he can call up the storm?"

"He loves the rain so much he can feel it in the air, even from a distance. Most aren't that sensitive."

"You are sensitive, eh? But not to rain."

The last edges of pink sunset rippled along small waves, then merged into darkness. "Aye," Elisha echoed, "but not to rain."

Madoc regarded him for a long while, apparently unwilling to press for more. At last, he gave a grunt, then one hand slid beneath his leather jerkin. Probably touching the cross, to ward off Elisha's presence. Madoc's own presence felt solid, warm, emanating a calm almost priest-like, the reason why he so appreciated the stolid captain as his guard. Madoc's dogged center, unruffled by all that happened, gave order to the uncertainties that swirled around Elisha.

"Take it in turns?" Madoc suggested. "I'll give a nudge."

Elisha nodded, settling to the floor to wait. He might have gone to Saltwood, demanding entry and a good bed, while some other stood watch in the tower, but, like Mortimer's execution, this felt too important for him to remain in comfort. For now, he was king, and these deaths belonged to him. The layered strength of the bones below him echoed within his own skeleton. Would it be possible to claim the deaths of the sailors? Could their slaughter buoy him up? But the thousand bones of the strangers in the ossuary provided less power than the immediate deaths of the crows he knew, or his subtle touch upon Mortimer's back followed by the sudden, sharpness of the ax as it struck off the traitor's head. Sickened by the rush of that moment, Elisha had turned the seductive strength aside, like a man fending off an overeager hound. It called to him as he slept, edged with the golden, shrieking horror of the mancers' passage, that mysterious place where they bent the world to their desire, as if Mortimer waited there to guide him deeper.

He shuddered and woke, the weight of Madoc's cloak kicked off as he stirred. The glow of the single candle lit Madoc's back and the square roof of the tower, just a bit wider than his own height. Good thing Robert hadn't been assigned to this post—he'd not be able to lie down from one thick wall to the other. Stone spikes rose up from each corner, pointing toward the stars.

Elisha rose and stretched, his back aching. "You did not wake me."

"Would've in a moment," Madoc told him without turning, his hands grasping the edge of the wall.

"You see something?" Elisha joined him as Madoc gave a nod.

"Boats?" The guard straightened, squinting out to sea.

Squinting with him, Elisha stretched his awareness in that direction. A strange, sharp spike of pain punched back from the water, and he recoiled but forced himself to push beyond it, to the horizon. He sensed a patch of darkness shifting with the sea, more solid than the sky—a ship, with a tiny light upon its bow that rose and fell with the waves. As they watched, a second light joined the first, then, a moment later, a third, rising and falling together. Elisha's heart hammered, his breath catching. Dear God—it came!

"The lantern," he said, turning, but Madoc had already taken it up, opening the side and nudging the candle out of the way to slide in an oil pan and wick, then another, tilting each wick to light them against the first, until the lantern's glow leapt up several times brighter. He reached to hang it upon an iron hook, their view obscured by the sudden glow.

To the north and behind them, another light flared into the night at the tower of Saltwood under Lord Robert's care, and to the other side, a third, small at first, then growing. Lympne, and Randall. Shielding his eyes from the glare of their lantern, Elisha leaned back toward the ocean. They could descend now, their work done, while the scout vessel returned to its commander, to summon the ships to die.

"Couple more hours yet, 'til dawn. But not much." Madoc's grin gleamed. "Be nice to see them bombards turned against somebody who's earned it."

Not the words Elisha would have chosen. He swallowed, again stretching his awareness, searching for the ships that hid beyond the horizon, a few thousand eager men, restless to be fighting, just like Madoc and his men back at Dunbury. It was not their battle, not really, but they knew loyalty and duty. They went where the lords directed, and they stood ever-ready to die. He sought the hearts of those distant sailors. He wanted to apologize.

Instead, that spike of pain once more cracked his awareness, like lightning in the darkness. Down below, a single small boat scraped the sand, and pain radiated from it like ripples from a sinking stone. Someone stepped out to walk up the shingle, pausing, then continuing on toward the foot of the church. A fearful voice cried out further up the road, and he heard the clatter of steps as his men went to investigate, but they moved away from the presence he sensed, as if they did not notice it at all.

Elisha sent his awareness down to the stone, down, gathering the strength of Death from the bones below, racing toward the lonely steps that moved up the street—an agonized, echoing presence, familiar, yet changed. A second, slight presence followed after in her wake. Almost, she had passed by the church before Elisha resolved the sense of what he felt: a woman he knew, shadowed by the death of someone close to her. Then he was bounding down the steps. Rosalynn! By God, his prayers were answered.

She walked by, oblivious, the thousand piled dead concealing him from her own magical senses.

"What's wrong?" Madoc cried out, then thundered down behind him. "Majesty?"

Outside, the walker froze.

Elisha threw open the first door, but Madoc caught his arm. "Majesty, wait for the guards."

The floorboards creaked, Elisha stiffened, and the heat of living flesh seared through his web of awareness. It carried the tang of fear and the wail of a hurt even he could not fathom. And more, it carried a name, a presence so distinct and familiar that Elisha would be held no longer.

Breaking Madoc's grip, Elisha flung open the outer door. "Rosie!"

"Yer Majesty! Elisha, wait," Madoc growled in the darkness, but Elisha was down the steps and half out the door. "Blast ye, Barber, something's wrong. Didn't you hear that shout?"

"Rosalynn, I'm here," Elisha cried, shrugging off the shield of Death that concealed him.

Madoc smashed into his back, tumbling them both and knocking the wind from Elisha's chest.

"Get. . . off," Elisha panted. "The queen."

"If that's the queen, then I'm the bloody bishop. Something's drawn off the guards, Majesty. Don't go out there."

Elisha fought Madoc's grappling hands. Rosalynn's pain and terror spun through his own emotions, and the echo in her presence was suddenly plain: she had lost the baby. Thomas's baby. His scalp pricked with the dread that came over her as she listened to the violent sounds of Madoc struggling with him on the ground. Through the contact, Elisha snapped a warning, flesh to flesh, encouraging Madoc to let him go.

Then something shocked through his hands, and Elisha let go with a gasp. Something defended Madoc, something deep and strong that flowed through the soldier's spirit.

With a surge of power, Elisha rolled them both, landing on top, Madoc smacking against the wall with a puff of breath that clouded the air. Madoc did not understand. He had only the senses of a *desolati*: reacting to the sight of something unfamiliar, the sound of a fearful cry—unlike the awareness of the magi who could sense the presence of another and recognize them from that alone.

"Elisha? Is that you?" cried a broken voice from the darkness. "What's happening?"

Snatching the soldier's sword from his grip, disarming his own bodyguard, Elisha scrambled up and spun, hope lighting his path toward the darkened street.

"Elisha? Oh, thank heavens!" The wounded voice rang through the darkness, her arms outstretched, then she drew back, almost flattening herself against the opposite house, fear radiating around her. "No, don't touch me, not yet." Hair tossed around her head as she shook it violently, staying his pace with her outstretched arm, her figure shrouded by the darkness.

"Rosie, why?" He halted in the porch, hurt.

The voice dropped low once more, almost unrecognizable. "I know how sensitive you are, Elisha, and I've been through so much. With everything that's happened these past months, I must feel like a whirlwind to you even at that distance. For you to touch me now, I can't imagine how it would hurt you."

Grateful for the darkness that hid them from each other, Elisha smiled, brief and sharp: even at a time like this, Rosie talked too much. Tears burned his cheeks. "Thank God you're alive, at least. Where's Thomas? Is he with you?"

Another wild shake of the head. "I had to leave him, I took the chance. Sweet Mary, it was the hardest thing I've ever had to do. I thought my father was here—but you! You're the only one who can help Thomas now. Dear Elisha." Her hand flew up, pressed to her hidden face as she quaked.

Elisha took another step, only to be stopped again by her muffled cry. Something moved behind him, and Elisha softly cursed himself for letting the man stay. Madoc had to see, even with his blind *desolati* eyes, that Rosie needed help.

"It's not a bloody woman, Barber," muttered a voice from the darkness.

Elisha half-turned, a snarl growing in his throat.

"Someone's with you! I thought I sent off all the soldiers. I couldn't bear for them to see me," she whimpered. "Oh, God, does he know who I am?"

"It's all right," Elisha snapped, then reined in his anger at the new wave of fear that touched him. "He's leaving." His hands balled into fists as Madoc rose. "Right now."

Madoc, a stocky, vague shadow, separated himself from the church door, towering upon the steps as he descended, his hand reaching for his sword and coming up short.

Elisha yanked out the blade. "Don't move."

"Ye must be made t' see!" Madoc insisted, though he held out his empty hands, his teeth flashed briefly as if bared.

"Is it one of them, those terrible cannibals?" Rosie's voice wavered.

"He's no mancer," Elisha said, then stopped, the sword wavering a moment as he recalled that mysterious protection that pulsed against his hands. "Are you, Madoc?"

"That's the one ye can't trust," Madoc howled. "Look at it, just look at it!"

"And turn my back on you? Not likely," Elisha snorted, though his glance wandered in that direction, for the figure moved behind him.

"We're strong enough, together, Elisha, you and I," Rosie said. "I'm here, if you need me. I have some power in me, in spite of everything." Indeed, the damaged voice grew stronger as he listened. Was she then a full magus? Not merely feeling the echo of her baby's power? He had to see her more clearly, to make contact and know what had happened to her, and she wouldn't come any nearer with Madoc still there.

"Don't turn yer back t'that! For the love a' God, Elisha Barber!" Madoc reached out.

"Be careful," she cried, "it wants contact—don't let it touch you. I know what they can do."

Too much distraction. Madoc lunged aside, diving for the church.

Rosalynn shrieked, and Elisha scrambled up after him, back to the sanctuary. Madoc grabbed something and thrust it into one of the candles, whirling as Elisha dashed into the low room, stolen sword at the ready.

Madoc raised his hands, lifting over his head a burning brand. By the dancing light, blood trickled from his hairline and his eyes flashed white. The flame trembled as Madoc shook, those eyes staring beyond, out the door, his lips parting his beard though he made no sound.

Sweat slicked the sword in Elisha's grasp as he froze, slightly crouched, and Rosalynn's scream broke into silence, her presence looming behind him, filling the doorway and touching him with tendrils of fear.

The sword tipped in Elisha's grip, its polished blade casting off crimson glints. Among the glints, a reflection shivered and returned, lit by fire—a man's face, surrounded by the blood-streaked locks of a woman's hair and framed by the shreds of flesh that once had been Queen Rosie's cheeks.

Chapter 19

"**W**hat's the matter with you, Madoc?" Elisha shouted. "Don't you know enough to bow to your queen?" He raised up the sword as Madoc jerked his eyes back to Elisha's face. Another magus, even Elisha, could be fooled by projections and by blood that captured another's presence, but a *desolati* like Madoc had only the evidence of his physical senses. Elisha had been so bound up in his magical awareness, his recognition of Rosalynn's pain, that he hadn't looked hard enough at the actual figure that approached.

The flaming brand trembled in Madoc's grasp.

"Don't, Elisha, I don't need that, not now," said the voice outside, and Elisha clamped his teeth together to keep from screaming. Fabric rustled against the door, and Madoc's eyes twitched to the side, toward the town.

"Goddamn it, man, you saved my life at Dunbury Ford—I expected better from you." He threw the sword at Madoc's feet. "He's no mancer, Rosie. Mancers have more backbone."

"Forgive me, yer Majesty," Madoc murmured, and dropped to his knees, the sword lying between them.

Elisha struck his hands together as if wiping away the issue, desperate to stop his shaking as Rosalynn's face flashed before his eyes—her face whole and happy in Thomas's presence—then torn in half with this stranger glaring through. Elisha turned and the mancer retreated out the door, back into the darkness where the truth could be concealed a while longer. "Rosie, wait."

"You saw his face, Elisha, you saw how he looked at me." The voice shook with tears. "You mustn't see me, not like this."

Elisha tried to slow his heart and stop the rising bile that stung his throat. Behind him, Madoc retched. The flickering light of the torch sputtered and died.

Swallowing his fear, Elisha moved slowly from the porch, his mind racing as fast as his heart. "I can help you, Rosie," he said softly. "I'm a healer, you know that."

"This is beyond healing—you saw the look on his face!" The stolen voice verged upon hysteria and Elisha shuddered. Now that he knew the truth, he could hear the falsetto, the man adopting Rosie's manner in an attempt to make his disguise more convincing.

"He's just an ignorant peasant." As his eyes adjusted, his mind filling in the details of the monster before him, Elisha said, "If you will not let me help you, then tell me what I can do, Rosie. Where's Thomas?"

The figure, swaddled in a heavy cloak, wavered. "Oh, Elisha, it's so awful." It gasped, then lurched to one side as if it would fall.

Elisha took a half-step forward, then snatched back his hand, the mancer's own words ringing in his ears. *"Don't let it touch you."*

As he stood, his knees tensed for a leap he could not bring himself to make, the air took on a sudden breath of heat and the figure raised its head.

From the muffled form emerged a chuckle, low and languorous, sliding from the high-pitched imitation of Rosie's terror to something deep and dangerous. Elisha tucked his hands under his arms, shivering, the armor of

Death long since shattered about him, leaving him exposed. Slowly, the figure rose, rolling its shoulders, tossing back the tendrils of bloody hair that snapped in the breeze around it.

Elisha reached for the chill power he had abandoned, but Rosie's presence swelled up through the ground and lashed him through the wind. Distracted, he caught snatches of her dying—the knife cutting open her belly, violating her womb, carving up along her throat to stop her stupid babbling voice. His flesh pricked as if by a thousand needles, he almost heard what she was screaming. Then the wind snatched it away, and his relief at being saved from that vision shamed him, flaming along his cheeks.

"But you are not ignorant, are you, Elisha Barber?" drawled the strong voice of the man behind the mask of murder. "Not ignorant at all, nor a peasant any longer, Your Majesty." He swept into a bow, then straightened. "But should I curtsy instead?" Again, he laughed, then sighed. "No, there's no purpose to the game. What gave me away? Was I not as absurd as the queen? I thought I captured her tones very well myself. I broke your guard with the first sound of tears and nearly had you at my side just now. I could feel the leap of your compassion through the darkness."

Elisha's jaw clenched. Without Madoc's brand to light his vision, he might not have seen until it was too late. Now, Madoc hurried around behind him. The church at his back grew brighter moment by moment, until Madoc had lit enough candles to cast the glow of stained glass out into the street, staining the mancer's robe. The mancer hoped to lure him out into the darkness, where his projection could hold a little longer.

"And your friend, what is he? Just a peasant?"

Swallowing the nausea that filled him, Elisha told the truth: "My bodyguard."

The new wave of laughter knocked him back a step with its rich appreciation. "Oh, Elisha, how you delight me! I see now why Morag worked so long to win you over and why he failed to harvest you. Even if one could possess you, yet some of the joy of you would be gone. Joy does tend to scatter during the harvest after all."

For a moment, Elisha felt the edge of Morag's knife against his throat. He reeled, catching himself upon the doorframe. His shadow danced after him, leaving a swath of golden light that cut the blackness. The voice, the manner, and the mention of Morag resonated with a sudden certainty. Here, at last, stood Morag's master, the one who cowed Prince Alaric, the one who appeared from a wound in the fabric of the world, and vanished there when he was done.

The mancer lifted his robes with a delicate touch—no longer womanish, but a gesture of long habit—and walked three steps forward into the light. He walked quickly and Elisha dodged out of arm's reach, but his enemy dismissed this with a twiddle of his fingers as he halted, his face to the light.

Rosalynn's skin showed pale with the purple-gray of bruises and the hollows where her eyes should have been. The ill-fitting skin draped awkwardly along the wrong bones beneath. Her full cheeks sagged, and one ear jutted up higher than the other, a red line of blood oozing down alongside it like another strand of the dark and tangled hair. When the mancer smiled, her lips stretched in ghastly imitation. He opened his mouth, the cut beneath the chin gaping open a little, and he stuck out his tongue, waggling it this way and that, flicking the tip into the crevice between his lips and hers, bulging the cheek and letting a trickle of blood spatter the ground.

Elisha's stomach rolled. For an instant, he shut his eyes, then snapped them open again. Madoc was right, he must not turn his back on this. He straightened and forced a smile. "Why not step inside and see each other clearly?" He mounted the steps to enter the church, bright with candles, rich with the dead.

Madoc stood to the other side of it, his back pressed against the wall and his sword drawn. He glowered and gave a twitch of his head as Elisha stepped inside.

"*Desolati* are fools, every one," said the mancer. "Let him do what he will, it might amuse us."

Lifting his chin, Elisha strode into the room and faced the door. "Do not act as if we are together, you and I. That was Morag's first mistake."

"But don't you remember how he made you feel?" The voice carried the promise of such belonging and power that it brought a rush to Elisha's loins. The sensation spread through his body with seductive golden warmth.

Elisha forced himself to meet the mancer's gaze, the eyes shadowed by Rosalynn's brows above them. Already, as he faced the reality of Rosie's murder, he calmed. The tendrils of the dead rose up, misty, and he drew them in.

"You see?" said the mancer. "We are not so different after all." He spread his hands, Rosalynn's empty fingers wrapped over his own and bound with bits of thread like poor embroidery. "Oh, yes, I can feel you reaching."

The warmth drained away as chill death seeped up to take its place. Gore edged the places where Rosie's skin wrapped the stranger's body, staining the cloak that concealed most of them both, and Elisha seized the frigid pain that washed through him. "No. I value more the life in men than what their deaths might bring me."

"Then why do you call upon these poor souls to aid you?"

"You do not know me."

"On the contrary," the mancer said, reaching up toward his face. "It was I who elevated you." With a careful curl of his wrist, he peeled back the face that hid his own. With long fingers he swept away the gore that decked his skin, and grinned. "But you guessed that, didn't you?" He drew a kerchief from his cuff, his doubled fingers wiping his brow and down along his nose as if cleaning himself were his only concern. He moved in shadows and fear and hid himself at the center of the kingdom, the king's own confessor, one man Thomas and his wife would trust beyond all others, for he was, after all, a man of God. The archbishop shrugged the skin back over his shoulder, the hair spattering blood against the wall.

Elisha flinched at the gesture. He reached inward, gathering the cloud of Death and giving it shape by his anger. "And Thomas? What have you done with the king, Your Grace? Is he, too, nothing but a pelt you torture for your own ends?" The words hurt even to say. He wounded himself with that image of Thomas, though he refused to believe it. He had to refuse, or he had nothing left.

By the door, Madoc tensed, his knuckles white on the hilt of his sword.

"When you presented yourself at the gate, stigmata on your hands, a willing army at your back, a few miracles already achieved—my God, it was a gift! What better way to play you than to set you in the center of the board and let you watch the kingdom dissolve beneath you? Such a pleasure, to snap the bonds of loyalty one by one. I thought, with you distracted, the barons might have their chance at you, and clear the way for . . . other things. I underestimated you and your little duke. And now, will you have victory over France? They should praise you to the heavens." His lips twisted sourly. "Long live the king."

"Where is he?"

"All that was his is yours, Barber, why concern yourself with him?" The mancer began to unfasten his cloak, then paused, holding his hand before him like a lady showing her new ring. He rippled his fingers, and Rosie's skin wriggled against its bindings. "Well, almost all."

Unfurling the lash of Death, Elisha snapped his knowledge like a whip about the room. Rosie's spattered blood steamed against his extended reach and his awareness leapt through it to the skin that draped the mancer's shoulders, revealed as he lowered his cloak.

In a swirl of fabric, the archbishop spun into the room.

Madoc ducked and thrust out his sword, only to be fouled by the wild cloak, flung free on a wind of no god's making. Madoc cried out, enveloped by the fabric, tumbling toward the wall and hitting hard, his sword slashing in a silver gleam from the dark that concealed him.

Still spinning like a mad dancer, the archbishop flicked his hands, and Rosie's hands flew free even as Elisha seized control through his knowledge of the murdered woman. Her fingers writhed into the air, making for the mancer's throat.

Elisha's fury gave strength to the skin as he urged the flesh to remember what it had been. The empty hands curled and flexed, but reached only to brush against the mancer's throat, a gesture almost loving.

The archbishop fell silent, his eyes darting. He spun to a halt, clasping the hands in his.

The heat of that grasp knocked back Elisha's power, a blast of arctic air as Death howled its frustration. Elisha's own fists knotted, urging on the hands that he had claimed.

"You will not catch me that way, Barber."

"Shed your skin, you serpent—I will have you." Elisha half-crouched, the rush of his control fusing inside his skull with Death's proud laughter.

Dropping the dead hands, the archbishop scrabbled for the face that hovered by his own and swept the skin from his shoulders. The skin's face turned toward his, its arms reaching. With a shriek, he flung it across the room and Elisha cried his victory as he raised one hand to snatch it from the air. Rosie's breasts slid over his arm as he clasped what remained of her, the pitiful thing falling limp against him, threatening to slip away.

The archbishop lost all semblance of fear, and stood watching, as if he'd meant for this to happen.

Instinctively, Elisha drew the skin closer, then screamed as Rosalynn's last moments flashed through him. Agony burned through Elisha's power as Rosalynn's memory wailed her killer's name. Her dying voice pleaded for mercy or a miracle as the outrage of betrayal shattered into despair.

Someone raped her. Someone ripped her womb. Someone kissed her as he cut her throat. A monster who claimed Elisha's face.

Elisha staggered to his knees, clutching the skin to his chest where his brand burned anew. It could not be—it had not been! Swathed in the chill of Death, Elisha opened himself to Rosie's memory.

Stripped to her shift, Rosalynn stood bound by the wrists, her eyes swollen shut with bruises. She ducked against the stone of her prison as the salt breeze slapped at her hair. Thomas deserved better from her—she was the queen, and finally showing her magical heritage. He bore his own torment with the strength she loved so well.

"Rosie!" called a voice.

Rosalynn caught her breath, and felt the presence; strong, compassionate, the healer's strength and the magus's power.

"Rosie, thank Heaven I've found you."

He touched her then, the sudden heat of contact making her flinch.

"Oh, God, I'm sorry; I didn't mean to frighten you, not that way."

But he did not withdraw his hand, and she felt sure

she knew that touch, hope surging through her from her bare feet to her tender wrists. "Elisha, dear Mother Mary, can it be you? Truly?"

She shook back her hair, and his strong, quick fingers helped, every stroke along her skin sending that reassurance she counted on from him, the warmth that radiated through his skilled hands. Tears stung her bruised eyes, and she swallowed as if she might clear her dry throat.

"How did you find us? Have you freed Thomas? I don't know where they keep him. Sometimes they bring him up to walk—" She rambled, her voice a mumble through parched lips, and she forced herself to stop. Thomas must be as patient as a saint to endure her.

"Hush, you'll understand everything soon," his voice murmured at her ear as he reached up to loose the chain that held her. She sank into his arms, her knees unable to support her.

Though she knew how unseemly it must be, for the queen to be so embraced, neither could she stir herself to withdraw. Truth be told, she wanted little more than to curl into his strong peasant arms, her face tucked against his beating heart, and simply be held. He seemed so tall and strong. The tears flowed freely.

Elisha, caught up in the vision, stopped the rising nausea that churned in his stomach every time the imposter touched her—every notion he had of himself through her sensitive flesh. He had not been there. That fact remained despite all that he felt.

Briefly in her weakness, Rosalynn's cheek snuggled to her rescuer's chest where his heart raced almost as hers, cushioned by the softness of the dark, curly hair that peeked from the neck of his shirt. As her rescuer lifted her, she turned, giving up the comfort of him, her awareness sweeping the courtyard, her memory filling in what she knew of her surroundings as they stepped out from the roofed corner where she had been held, the corner still

reeking of horse dung. She sensed the three mancers loung-
ing by the gate, warm in the sunlight. She frowned. Had he
tricked them somehow, in order to get through? Then, with
the frayed edge of her awareness, she caught the presence
of Thomas. "Elisha, there's Thomas! Can you see him?"

Another pair of the monsters carried Thomas between them, and she could feel the strain in his bound
body. They dropped him to his knees, but he did not say
a word. Thank God he had learned that lesson. After her
last punishment, they both had.

Rosalynn's memory shied quickly away as she craned
her neck, struggling to see him with her own battered
eyes. "Tell him we're fine now, Elisha. He needs to hear
your voice."

But he wouldn't hear Elisha, not Thomas—without
the contact of one magus to another, he would believe
his senses, and he would know the truth.

"He'll know soon enough," spoke the voice through
her flesh. Her savior carried her across the yard, retreat-
ing from Thomas's presence. Where were they going? To
the table? What happened there, she could not say, for
they kept her face to her own wall, but the screams had
been enough. Once again, she turned her thoughts away.

"I don't understand. Do you need me quiet? Tell me
how to help. I haven't any talisman, or I should have
tried something," again, her voice caught, and she whispered, "No, I shouldn't. The things they've threatened,
Elisha, not against me, but him. Dear Lord, I couldn't
risk that they should hurt him. They've kept him bound,
of course, but they've not touched him. They are evil and
yet even they dare not harm the king."

They dare not, Elisha knew, because the slightest
scent of blood might bring Elisha down upon them like
the Wild Hunt of Faerie. He grit his teeth as the vision
moved, the mancer lowering Rosalynn onto the table,
and pulling her toward the center.

"Elisha?" She struggled to master her quavering voice. The cold of the stone struck her through her thin chemise, and she shivered. "I do wish you would tell me the plan," she said, softly in case she might disturb his work, whatever that might be.

He shifted her carefully, almost tenderly, into a hollow at the heart of the stone, then his warmth knelt beside her, but his touch had changed.

She winced as he took up her sore wrists, stroking them gently with his thumbs. Lightly, he kissed her wounds, and she shivered again but not from cold. Rosalynn grew very still beneath his touch. His strange, alluring touch. "Elisha?"

"Hush, now, Rosie." He lifted her arms over her head and other hands clasped them, rough hands that seared her with their mockery as they tried to conceal their laughter. They must not ruin the scene.

The scene? Quickly, she scrambled for the notion, grabbing for the hand with clumsy fingers, but the idea fled as metal once more clamped her arms. Rosalynn jerked against the bonds. "Elisha, what's going on? Elisha, talk to me!"

His strong hand wrapped her ankle, drawing her leg out straight. She kicked him, lashing out wildly now. "Don't do this! Elisha, stop it—if this is your plan, it's gone too far!"

Iron snapped shut about her ankles, her legs stretched and spread despite her struggles. No, no. What was happening?

Her savior's shadowy face again appeared over hers. His touch upon her stayed as steady as ever, the reassurance he projected warring with his actions. Something slashed through her chemise and ripped it away.

Across the yard, Thomas cried out, "Rosalynn! Rosie, where are you?" His broken voice, barely recognizable, fell into coughing.

"No!" Rosie screamed, for Thomas as much as for herself.

His hands, no longer compassionate but crazed, rubbed all over her body as she jerked at her chains.

The mouth abandoned hers to her screaming, roving down to her breast, her belly, lingering there, then further.

"Elisha, no!" she wailed, tears burning down her cheeks as he forced himself upon her.

Across the courtyard, Thomas's ragged voice cried out, "Leave her alone!"

Elisha, too, cried out, stumbling to his feet and hurling aside the skin, breaking free of the memories but knowing they would never leave him. Shame flared through him, his own wicked hands that tortured her to death. He smacked at his skin, wiping away whatever he could of her, whatever he could of himself as if that might prove his innocence—beating back the horror that assailed him. Rosie, Rosie—dear God!

He trembled and wept. Then his knees buckled and he fell to his face on the flagstones, heaps of bone towering over. The familiar chill of death embraced him, urging him to make the choice. He had one refuge yet, in the peace of the grave.

Chapter 20

$\diamond$

Elisha's left arm clutched his stomach as if he might stop the retching. Fighting off the vision hurt even more. He had lived through Rosalynn's ordeal, through her own sensations. Just then, he wished that he, too, died with the slashing blade, if only so that he might never relive that memory.

Death chanted all around him, a wild cacophony. Every one of the deaths that had ever touched him shrilled in his ears and howled through his brain. His brother's voice wove through the tumult, bewildered and angry, and somewhere nearby, a baby wailed. The shame consumed him no matter how he fought it—he didn't kill her! And yet she went to her grave believing he had. Had they even buried her? "Oh, God," he cried to the hollow church. The lock of hair he kept at his wrist pressed between his thundering heart and the unyielding stone. "Oh, Thomas, where are you?"

A hand stroked the nape of Elisha's neck and he jerked, eyes wide. The hand caught hold and lifted him to his feet. His knees shaky, Elisha fell against the archbishop's chest, only to be hauled upright again.

Elisha swayed, and something tingled at his arm, clutching the other man for support. A patch of fabric dangled on a thread from the mancer's neck. Dried blood and oil stained the cloth, familiar blood, and the thread, too, reminded him of something in its shaggy darkness.

"You should have kept to the peasants, Barber, and left the matter of France to your betters." Sticking his hand toward the back of his clerical robes, the archbishop produced a dagger and rammed it home into Elisha's chest.

Elisha shuddered in the archbishop's grip. He stared down at the gilded hilt. It winked with rubies, echoing the candle flames, as crimson blood welled up around it to darken his shirt.

A very good blow. Clean, well-aimed. Difficult to patch that wound. His heart seized.

Elisha reached for the dagger, then hesitated. A few minutes, at most. Less, if he pulled it free. Sooner or later, it must hurt. Such a blow, to kill him, it must hurt. His legs trembled, and he slumped to his knees to wait for the pain.

What did the heart do, truly? The ancients put forth many theories with which Mordecai regaled him at their studies. Elisha pictured Galen's drawings, composed by studying dissected apes, and how the tubes went this way and that, gaping open, bloodless at the front to give an illusion of wholeness. Elisha's hand strayed to the hilt. Ecclesiastical gold, surely. Only the best to murder the king.

The king. The first jolt of pain sprang through his tightened chest, and he gaped.

"What the Hell've ye done?" someone shouted, an echo in the hollow of Elisha's mind.

"He would've killed me, my son, surely you saw him reach for my throat. I shall bear the weight of all that I have done—in elevating him, and now in laying him low. Would to God I had seen his evil sooner! Still, what more fitting end for the man who slew the queen and usurped the throne, than to be slain by one of those he deceived?"

A rustle of fabric cast aside as Madoc discarded the cloak which had muffled him. "By God, he never killed her."

"We were all of us betrayed by him. You will see the truth in time." The archbishop crossed himself. "Never before have I been forced to slay a man. I find myself weak with the deed. Come, my good man, lend me your strength," the archbishop called, his sonorous voice shaky.

Killing. Death. That, too, should mean something. If only the wound did not throb so, perhaps he could work out the meaning. "I'm dying," Elisha said, with something like laughter. Already, his hands and feet grew cold, trembling, and shadows danced before his eyes.

The archbishop stepped back, wobbling, one hand outstretched to the bearded soldier beside him, whose sword was wavering. The mancer reached for contact. If he made it, the soldier would die. With a sneer, Madoc ducked the arm and marched three steps toward Elisha.

"Take heed, my son! He's a witch and a traitor!"

"Aye, yer Grace, o'course he is," Madoc answered. He hawked at the back of his throat, and spat.

The glob landed neatly on Elisha's forehead. Madoc's eyes glinted with his smile as he turned on his heel and stalked from the church.

In an instant, the archbishop discarded his projection of holy benevolence. "Bodyguard, you say? I'm sure you'll find a better one in Hell. Judas, perhaps—he's always been ready for those with ideas above their station. And I don't believe you would object to kissing a man."

Madoc's spit was warm on Elisha's forehead, another marker of the shame from which the blade had freed him. Silly to rely on a dagger at a time like this. His fingers crept toward it, growing increasingly numb. They caught on the ridge of scar upon his left breast, just a bit aside from the fresh wound. Then it had been Thomas's knife, flashing to kill the stranger who murdered his father. Elisha's lips formed the king's name. His throat ached. He should not die. He could not die. He could not remember how to save himself. He gulped in a breath around the pain and coughed blood.

A sensation like a hole bored through his head and sudden light flooded in where Madoc's spit dripped down, making contact. The howling in his ears transformed, as if the dogs that bayed to shred him barked now on his behalf. Death, Elisha named the sound; Death as familiar as his own name and as accursed.

The brilliance of Madoc's faith suffused his mind through that contact. Elisha reached again for the knife as the gift of strength unfurled within him, and he remembered all. With a careful hand, Elisha pulled free the blade, the wound sealing itself as the metal withdrew and Elisha taught his flesh once more to be whole. Strength flowed through him, cold as iron and malleable as tin.

Elisha smiled and cast aside the dagger as he rose from the floor.

"You are an unholy monster," said the archbishop.

"So are you." Elisha started forward.

The mancer stumbled back then pulled out a curved fleshing blade and grinned—from an image of Elisha's own face. Dark, familiar waves of hair curled over the imposter's shoulders but the grin froze upon his face and he hesitated as Elisha came on. A projection, nothing more, and Elisha dispelled it with the truth.

"Nothing you do can surprise me anymore." Power pulsed through him, and he flung out his awareness like a lash. The pendant the mancer wore was stained with Elisha's blood and strung upon a cord woven of Elisha's hair, allowing him to adopt Elisha's presence, to project it to others. Elisha felt the echo of his own touch. With one hand, he seized at the sensation, attacking through that contact.

The archbishop's face went pale. With quick fingers, the mancer tore away the talisman. In three long strides, he crossed the room and leapt at Elisha.

Elisha threw himself out of the way. He fetched up hard against the wall and would have cried out, if he could find the breath, as Rosalynn's blood wept upon his hands.

In answer, the channel of power at his skull opened, filling him with borrowed strength, the strength of the living, not of the dead. He surged back to his feet as the mancer caught up the dirty skin Elisha had cast away. Instead of succumbing to Rosie's panic, Elisha reached back through the blood, searching the memories and finding what he needed: rage. Rosie died in agony and fear but not without knowing anger, a boundless fury at the man she believed had done this to her. Elisha.

His fingers clenched the blood that stained him. It was hard to force the body against its natural tendencies, but toward them: simplicity itself. No one could be so foully murdered without wanting her revenge.

The mancer's will bent against Elisha's, tapping the horror of the queen's skin. They struggled for the same talisman. Contact: both men had that through the blood that spattered them. Affinity: the righteous anger of the dead sprang up through Elisha. Knowledge: Elisha understood injustice better than most. He twined these things together and finally cast, the power rippling through his hands, leaping the space between them, tossing Rosie's skin in a wicked dance. Her fury blasted back, as he woke the power of the death of a magus.

The release knocked him against the wall and pinned him there. His chest spasmed and his fingers dug into the grooves between the stones. He sensed that howling passage of Death through which the mancers moved and spirits fled. If he let go, surely the maelstrom would rip him away to Hell.

After a time, the tumult subsided, and the final moans faded away. Elisha cautiously opened his eyes.

In the far corner a figure lay, staring at the ceiling with eyes sharply veined, lips parted, utterly unmoving. His rigid arms held Rosie's skin to his chest like something precious. Elisha's living power had manifested Rosie's dying wish.

But any sense of success withered as he gazed upon the man, the archbishop overcome by his own talisman. The mancer died with his lips parted, but without ever saying what Elisha needed to know. What had the monsters done with Thomas?

The power that had come to him through Madoc's not-so-distant faith dwindled, like something irretrievable slipping away.

Elisha scrambled out the door into the growing light of day. Rain and wind struck from the south, pushing against his arm, fluttering his sleeve like a sail. He should not be so cold—he had broken contact with the dead man and his dreadful prize. "Madoc! Where are you?"

"Here," sighed a heavy voice. "I'm here, yer Majesty."

With his jerkin and tunic pulled off, Madoc sat leaning against the steps, one arm outstretched, dark blood oozing from a long slash. His chest rose and fell, but in ragged movements, as if losing the rhythm it had so long practiced. He cocked a shaggy eyebrow at Elisha. "Ye've won?" Then he gave a snort of laughter. "O'course ye did—ye lived."

Elisha dropped down beside him and clamped both hands about the wound. "Dear God, Madoc, what've you done?"

"Gave ye strength." He stared at Elisha's hands, and his own pale in the dawn's light. "Ye needed that, more than me."

"Damn it, not at the cost of your life." The force of Rosalynn's death still tremored through him, leaving him too weak for another casting.

Madoc's spit made the contact between them as he bled himself, and his faith bound the power of his bleeding to the urgency of Elisha's need. Now his life trickled between Elisha's fingers.

Madoc shook his shaggy head and rumbled, "At any cost—ye've got to find the king."

Sagging against the steps, Elisha, too, shook his head. "Ah, bloody Hell, Madoc, I don't even know where to look. Rosie only knew the ocean lay nearby, and we live on a bloody island!" She had hated him so thoroughly in those last moments that he feared to touch her again.

"They've slain the queen," Madoc breathed.

"And you," Elisha answered.

"Not dead yet, and the magic didn't get me," Madoc pointed out. "Got me Mum's blessing, haven't I?" His hand slid away and fumbled in the dark between them, rattling the little case that still hung at Elisha's belt. In a moment, his hand came up with a small bundle. "Bit of saint's bone, bit of the dirt where I come from, wrapped in the blanket that first wrapped me, and stitched up with a prick of Mum's blood to ward off curses."

Stitched up. Elisha lifted his head, then gave a short burst of laughter. "Curse me for a fool, Madoc—Even if I've not the strength to heal you, I'm still a barber." He snapped open the lid of the case he always carried, even as king, and he dug through for suture thread and the sharpest of his needles.

At the first prick, Madoc cracked open his eyes, and his teeth gleamed in a brief smile.

With every stitch, Elisha warmed, and the flow of power through him receded, until he set the knot and sealed away, at least for now, the possibility of Madoc's death, and with it, the power it had afforded. "You'll be weak. Drink a lot, eat red meat." He wrapped a bandage around the stitches as he spoke. "I have to leave you. I'm sorry. I hope they'll take care of you, even though you are a friend of mine." He swallowed. "When another witch touches the queen's skin, they'll believe that I killed her."

"Bring home the king, and they'll know better," Madoc mumbled.

Draping Madoc with the cloak he had discarded, Elisha rose. "Thanks. It's twice now I owe you my life."

"Yer life? I saved the bloody kingdom, right?"

"I'll see you knighted when we come home."

"Do that. The missus'd fair bust a gut to hear tell of it. Yer Majesty?"

Elisha glanced down.

"May the dawn find you joyful and the darkness hold no fear. Somm'at my people say. I don't guess it helps, but there we are, eh?" He took a deep breath.

"And I'll wish the same for you, Madoc."

"Look, there, yer Majesty." Madoc lifted his chin toward the ocean where the thin light of dawn began to spread.

On the horizon, a shadow rose, slowly revealed as a series of low mounds with tall shapes above: ships, the French fleet. Elisha's chest constricted, his mouth dry. On they came, with the expectation of a warm welcome from their allies. To the east, a spit of flame, then a soft rumbling. The line of ships rocked, and a sail went down. The rumbling grew, then the bombards roared.

At this distance, they could not smell the powder, not yet, but billows of dark smoke swirled along with lances of fire that struck red and gold into the sails of the enemy. Hulls cracked and masts fell. The ships pushed forward with the wind, and Elisha could imagine the terror on board, the desperate attempts to turn about or seek cover. With a groan of wood, one of the lead vessels pitched sideways, its masts falling, its hull broken. At the near end of the arc of vessels, one suddenly swept upward, smashing against the rocks at the cliff base. A few tiny figures tossed up into the sky and plunged into the sea beneath the onslaught of the waves and their own foundering vessels.

More ships ran afoul of the rocks as the commanders lost control and the line broke. At the center, they shattered, rocked, and sank. Those on the outside spread away, fleeing initially west, toward the Isle of Wight, away from the bombards' glare. A few ships would escape and circle round to France, to tell King Philip they found England not so weak as they believed.

Lord Robert and his men would be at the beach by now, ready to handle any survivors who might wash ashore, seizing them in the name of the king and exacting rich ransoms from the kin of any nobles. The breaking dawn lit a scene of struggle and fear: ships crashing on the rocks, cracking with the bombards' blast, sinking in the sea; men tumbling into the water, their prayers and screams inaudible at such a distance; the first wisps of smoke reaching Hythe from the thundering bombards. Above, the sky showed only a few clouds just edging with the sun's glow. A fair day in England. But her king had work to do.

With the shade of a smile, Elisha stepped once more through the door up the steps among the scattered bones. He had not the strength that Madoc had loaned him, but neither was he so weak as he might be — and he did have hope.

The air stank of decaying flesh, and he wondered how long Rosalynn had been dead. A couple of days, at least.

Elisha forced himself forward, walking mechanically toward the corpse on the floor, its arms around the remnants of the dead queen. First, he recovered the jeweled dagger, still icy with the potential of his own death, and his heart caught on the memory of the wound. Death could be a treacherous ally, so eager that even he was vulnerable when his defenses broke down. He called upon it cautiously, a master who can no longer trust the hound. Elisha shaped the cold of Death into a barricade just beneath his skin, using the affinity of its ever-present nature, which lurked even in himself. If he would face a lair of mancers, he could not walk alone. His emotions dulled, and he stared down dispassionately at the strange embrace of the victim and her killer.

Elisha circled the archbishop's body and crouched near the head, glancing down into the open eyes rimmed with darkness and shot through with blood. The force of a dead witch's fury was nothing to be taken lightly, especially for her murderer. He found the talisman of his own hair and blood that the mancer had used to such advantage, rolling the hair between his fingers. How had he gotten it at all, and how had he gotten so much? Elisha's hair had not been so long since he was hanged and the executioner cut off his queue, discarding it on the ground. Where someone took it for a talisman. Brigit.

She met Morag atop his own grave and caught their interest, the more so when they learned, through the archbishop, no doubt, that Elisha's mourner, Alaric's wife, was pregnant. Was she using them, or they her? She must have given them the hair around the time of the king's kidnapping. Then Elisha was crowned in Thomas's place, by the mancer archbishop. Brigit sought him out, offering him one last chance to ally himself with her. She would be queen. Not a threat, a promise. And his rejection had brought them to this. Like the blow to his heart, when the shock passed, he knew, this would be an agony.

Shifting his grip on the knife, Elisha hacked off a clump of the dead man's hair and wet it in the blood that trickled from the open mouth. The archbishop's deception gave him a slender plan, a thread he might cling to as he walked the dangerous path before him.

Elisha bound the archbishop's relic with the strands of his hair before stuffing it into his medical pouch. The dagger he stuck under his belt. To complete his guise, he worked the heavy ring from the archbishop's finger, then rolled the mancer and found his fleshing blade. Finally, Elisha stripped off the thick embroidered surcoat that marked his royal station and replaced it with the mancer's bloody cloak, layering the resonance, confusing his own presence with that of the dead man and the woman he had killed.

Mists of Rosie's shattered presence drifted along the floor, tracking the marks of her blood. He must put aside the dead and find the living. He centered his awareness again and searched not for Thomas, but for himself.

From the tendrils of awareness that spread through the early dawn and stretched across the land, the archbishop's body tugged at his attention, but he cast aside the lingering pain. His mind raced yet further out, ignoring the dark interior to trace the edge of the sea as if he followed the map Pernel made for him. Thomas coughing, marked with black streaks. Like a coal miner. Elisha ignored the churches, the castles and dungeons, and sank his awareness toward the earth, toward the mines.

There! A tenuous presence flared to life, a long way off yet steady. Focusing on it, Elisha felt a slicing pain and nearly fled the place. Catching his breath, his hands clasped, Elisha reached out again, gingerly, and found the source: the tempest of Rosie's death still swirling where she had been killed.

There were few deaths Elisha knew so intimately. Although his stomach rebelled, he could all too easily imagine himself there. Thomas himself would be guarded well. If Elisha extended his thoughts toward the echo, he caught the chill of the others there, hovering at the fringe of his awareness. He would face the mancers, in the place where they had killed so many, at the heart of their domain. He defeated the archbishop with the aid of Madoc's contact and Rosie's dying rage. Now, once again, Rosie provided the opening, the contact that he might use to carry this fight to their lair. That locked-away part of himself cried out—should he become like them, use the dead without regard? Elisha pressed his hands over his eyes: if he would defeat them and free the king, there was no other way.

Before he went, he focused on the archbishop, on all that he knew of the man; he remembered his mannerisms, the way he spoke, the way he smiled, the careful manipulation of his presence that allowed him to pass as *desolati* while projecting holiness, the subtle and terrible control that allowed him to claim Elisha's own presence when he slew Rosalynn. How long could Elisha maintain a similar deception? He had no way of knowing. Contact would make it stronger, but would the mancers allow him that close, even if they believed he was the archbishop? If not, he must be prepared to act quickly, to pray that surprise at his arrival could give him the opening he needed.

Elisha reached out along the terrible arc of Rosie's pain that connected her flesh and blood with the place where she had died. Death to death. Contact. He pulled himself through to a place he had never known but through her terror, and it was terror that drew him on.

Waves of dread assaulted him as he crashed through the space between living and dying. Fell voices wailed around him, resonating through his bones. His passage felt nothing like the golden glow the mancers summoned, but he recognized the shrieking. His eyes frosted over, slender ferns tingling across his vision, but he dared not shut them. His skull squeezed with the pressure building all around him and spirits streaked through his heart as if his wound gaped open to every demon who inhabited this special hell. The armor he forged so carefully quivered with the forces assailing him.

The talisman of Thomas's hair, so long dormant, trembled against his skin as if translating the other man's fear. In flashes he saw Thomas's face, the sudden brilliance of his infrequent smiles, and felt the swift strength in his long limbs. Their last moments in the garden before Thomas rode off to be king and Elisha to be buried: Thomas brought him scissors and a razor, though Elisha barely trusted himself not to kill another king. They spoke of what would come, and Thomas's words echoed back to him, *"If anyone can survive this, it will be you."* Thomas Rex had offered a weapon to a regicide in quiet, simple faith.

Elisha clung to that, driving away the cold with his determination. He who was struck through the heart and yet lived, he would be turned by fear no longer.

Light broke over him with a spectacular silence. His knees scraped rough stone—colder than any stone wrought by the hand of men—and Rosie's last moments shot through him once more. This time, Elisha did not fear them, remembering the sweetness of her smile.

Slowly, he lifted his chin and faced the growing day. The courtyard filled in around him, still shadowed, but he recalled it only too well through Rosie's memory as he knelt on the stone table that had ignored her tears. He rolled his shoulders, stood, and turned.

Over the walls and a broad swath of rough grass, the steely sea broke white upon rocks to the east. Inside, a low storehouse took up one wall, where a wood and metal brace stood over the black hole of the mine. Harnessed to the apparatus, a cob horse stood cropping up the meager grass. The gate opposite him hung open; indeed, one hinge tilted at the wrong angle, and none had bothered to repair it. Two men stood talking softly in the growing light, one keeping his face to the road while the other inspected the fingers of a flap of skin which had once been another man's hand. A third mancer, a tall woman, leaned over a well in the other corner, hauling on the rope and finally bringing up a bucket. She groaned beneath its weight, and half-turned. "William, lend me a—Christ upon the Cross!"

Both men jerked in the gateway and spun, their eyes flaring as they saw Elisha standing upon the table.

With a slight nod, and a smile, Elisha told them, "I've come for the king."

Chapter 21

❖

$\mathcal{T}$he mancers gaped back at him, startled by his arrival, but not leaping into action at the appearance of an enemy. Drawing up his knowledge of the archbishop, Elisha affected his manner. He sighed, glancing at the heavens. "Surely you must know better than to leave yourselves open like this, and now I am able to surprise you? Really." He affected the slightest drawl, and toyed with the heavy ring upon his finger.

The tall woman stepped lightly nearer, then planted her hands on her hips, gazing up at him. Elisha felt the casual stroke of her awareness, inquiring into his, and he smiled, projecting nothing, allowing nothing to pass his wall. Dark hair tumbled down to her waist, nearly concealing the skin that hung against her back—a small, slender child's skin that made Elisha's stomach churn. He prayed they would not notice the sweat that streaked his palms.

"You've been perfecting that guise," the woman said. "It's hard to feel you separate from him."

"When you've got a man's blood on your hands . . ." Elisha shrugged.

"You were not even sure he could be killed—is that not what the whole charade of his coronation was about, setting him up for disaster?" the bearded man demanded, his pronunciation foreign, his expression suspicious.

"It's high time we were rid of the barber, though the little game was fun while it lasted." The woman dangled something on a chain, a bit of skin that showed the weathering of premature age. She had slain the men Elisha marked after Martin's death. "And now we can be sure nothing he ever said will be believed." She cocked her head with that coy smile. "I was right then, Jonathan? It was her death that broke his defenses? Oh, he must have been a tasty one."

"Yes, what *did* happen back there?" The bearded man strode up, pushing the flapping arms of his talisman back over his shoulders.

The third, a stocky blond, wore the skin of his victim slung about his hips like a dancing belt. He hooked his fingers over it now as he slouched up to join them. "What about that, Your Grace? I lured off the guards like you said and left you to it, but I could sense there was trouble."

"Trouble indeed. You don't know half the night I have had," Elisha said, letting the edge of cold flow through his voice. "Even with her death in my hands, the barber put up a struggle. I hope today will run more smoothly, starting with one of you fetching me the king."

"Poor thing," said the woman brightly. "Have you suffered much? Will you share?" Her tongue darted out, pink and moist, to stroke her lips.

Elisha stifled his revulsion. He had made this nasty little show, and now he had to play his part. "Later, my love, don't you agree that anticipation is half the fun?"

She tossed back her head with laughter. "The invasion must be going well, then, if it's time to kill the king."

They knew about France, and the invasion triggered the next stages of their plan—whatever that might be. Every question asked might give him more information or reveal him as an imposter. Focusing on Thomas, Elisha grinned ferociously. "Let us say that many men will be surprised this morning. And many will be dead."

"I'm glad you didn't bring any of the damned French with you. But at least they're better than these dreadful Germans! Ugh!" She gave a mock-shudder, staring at the bearded man, then she spun a half-circle and beckoned to the blond. "C'mon, Wills, let's bring the guest of honor. I think the festival's beginning."

"We should wait," said the bearded man. "I assure you, the Germans will not be happy with any change of plan. Besides, we still believe it wise to work with her. There is no reason not to also adopt her plan."

Her. That, at least, Elisha knew. He leveled his gaze at his inquisitor. "She's not the queen."

The man gave a tilted grin, and a slight nod, like a gentleman acknowledging a challenge. "And you are not the king. That guise will not help you with the *desolati*, it only works on those of power. No matter what you think of her, it is not wise to alienate the other magi by rejecting one who might sway them."

Elisha gave a casual shrug. "I may well be regent by midday. With a few laws, a few words in the right ears, I might sway them myself."

"Ruling the church is not enough? No other of us can make himself a king, why should you?" The man took two steps nearer and leaned slightly forward, his nostrils flaring. "This does not feel right."

"Which part? Your not listening to me?" The flash of anger that escaped him needed no projection, and the other man straightened.

The winch squealed as the woman clucked the horse into motion, hauling up the platform meant for miners or coal. Elisha forced his attention to stay on the argument.

The bearded man thrust his finger at Elisha. "You are

not the king here, Jonathan, not even the bishop. We all
know how you won that appointment. Even should the
French grant you the papacy, among ourselves, we are an
electorate, and do not forget it."

Was that like a coven? Each new sign of his ignorance
made the pulse pound in his ears. "Then let's don't forget
that I am the one taking the risks."

"You ripped the queen. That does not confer the
right—" The man broke off, his gaze sliding to the side.

The tall woman led the way. Wills and two others followed, with a heavy burden slung between them. The
horse stamped and returned to its grass.

"Out of the way, Master," the woman purred, "we've
got work to do."

Two mancers carried out the king, and Elisha's stomach nearly betrayed him. An iron bar passed across
Thomas's back with his elbows hitched up over it, his
wrists chained across his chest and linked to the chains
at his ankles. A second bar behind his knees—padded
like the first—provided the anchor for a pair of leather
straps that circled both bars, binding the king into a brutal pose. As Rosalynn revealed, they had not hurt him;
they shed no blood that might lead a would-be rescuer,
even to padding the bars and lining the fetters with fur.
Elisha spied the point of an ermine's tail that poked out
by Thomas's chained ankle: the fur reserved to royalty.
Something in his chest burned.

Thomas's head dangled, his pale brown hair concealing his face as they carried him out like the main course
at a cannibals' feast.

Elisha's throat echoed with the name he dare not cry.
He checked the horror that reeled through him and
twisted it back into his fury. His teeth locked together so
hard that his jaw ached.

"Master? You've got to come down," the woman sang
out, holding up her hand.

Move. Somehow. Maintain the projection for as long as he needed it: he had to set Thomas free.

"Darling," she sighed through him with a stroke, *"We need not do this now. Have you already spoken across the water? The French will want to share this one. And Bardolph's friends will be angry."* She tipped her head toward the German.

"Bardolph," Elisha replied, letting the truth gleam through, *"is really starting to irritate me."*

"I know precisely what you mean." She squeezed his arm as she released him.

Elisha tossed away the dead man's cloak. If he could convince her, the dead man's lover, then surely he could convince the rest of these. He needed only enough time to establish contact. If he could get through to Thomas and get them both out of here—

They set the king down on the stone table, as gently as if they cared, and Thomas's head jerked up. Darkness rimmed his eyes, so bloodshot they looked more red than blue.

Elisha wanted to leap up to the table and take back the king. But two mancers leaned against the stone, a stout woman with her hand on Thomas as she loosened the gag, and a man with a broken nose, at her side, ready to aid her. Elisha's muscles tensed in the struggle between mind and spirit. He had to wait, he had to.

For a moment, Thomas stared at him through glazed eyes, then he sagged forward, as if all strength left him, and his forehead bumped the stone.

The stout woman chuckled and winked at Elisha. Wills, the blond man, slapped Thomas's exposed bottom. "What a king, eh?"

Fury blazed through Elisha, and he sought for death, the cold power flowing all around him in this God-forsaken place. Each mancer wore the skin of a brutalized victim, and the empty fingers swayed in a breeze that did not ruffle the grass. Five mancers. And him.

Bardolph lifted his head, his eyes flaring in Elisha's direction.

Snaring the cold, Elisha gathered it in his mind and smothered his fury. If before he had been armored, now he forged himself like a blade—molten in the fire and quenched in ice, waiting his time to strike.

Grateful that Thomas's head remained bowed, Elisha grinned. "Well?" He gestured to the table.

The stout woman produced a key, bending toward the king to find the locks.

"Let me," Elisha offered, but Bardolph's hand shot out, forestalling him with a palm set against his chest.

"Do not let him touch the king. He has too much power already." He forced Elisha back a step, wedging between him and the stone, blocking his view. The contact held the cool tingle of the mancer's awareness, probing him. Elisha projected arrogance and held murder in his heart, but Bardolph stared at him a little too hard. Tempted to guide his power across that touch, Elisha shifted back, breaking the contact, forcing himself to wait until Thomas could be freed.

"What if the French invasion is not enough to break the barons? We might still need her—we should still bring her in."

"What," said Elisha, "will she do the deed herself?" He had no idea—perhaps she would, perhaps this is what she would have been working toward.

But a few of the others laughed. "She still han't gone that far, Master," said Broken-nose. "She wanted to do the barber, but she han't got no stomach for the real stuff, eh?"

Elisha let himself relax just a little. He felt a tremor in his strength. He remained weak from his earlier battle, and he could not long maintain his projection. "Well then, she won't do it, and our friend here won't let me touch him. Who here is strong enough to kill the king?"

"I would," Wills offered, jumping up on the stone and sliding out one of the rods that held the king as the stout woman pulled free the second.

Thomas collapsed onto his side, his limbs still held close, dangling loose as if he were already dead. He coughed hard. The fall had knocked aside the shield of his hair, exposing his neck and the length of rope tied around it—not tightly, but it need not be, its only purpose was to ward off Elisha himself: It was braided with his hair. At least he saw now what he was up against.

"No," he said carefully, denying Wills' request, and searched for a reason. "Your skin is too fresh."

Wills lifted an edge of the sash he wore which still seeped blood from its raw side. "Damn."

The stout woman grabbed Thomas's ankles, and she and Broken-nose heaved him into position over the shallow outline in the stone.

Swinging away from the table, Elisha swept the tall woman into his arms and kissed her lightly. "How about you, love?"

"Me?" She beamed. "Don't worry, I'll share." For an instant, she melted against him, then pushed him away, her eagerness slapping against the stone he made of himself.

"No," said Bardolph. "Not now, like this."

"What has come over you?" she asked, tossing her hair and pulling out her fleshing knife, its curved edge catching the morning sun.

"Ask the arch-barber what's come over him," he snapped back with a jut of his chin toward Elisha. "Those across the water—"

"Don't be an ass." She brushed past him to the stone

where Thomas now lay, his lean body arranged for the kill, wrists and ankles chained through holes in the table's surface.

"He feels too strongly of the barber," Bardolph said. "She knows him, better than anyone. I can bring her —"

"What, are you a *desolati*, so insensitive you can't see but with your eyes?" said the tall woman. "She may know the barber, but I know him." She pointed at Elisha.

"Enough!" he shouted. "I've not come all this way to hear you moan, and I shall be missed if I am gone too long."

"Right you are, darling." The tall woman hiked up her skirts and held out her hand to Wills who helped her onto the stone. She towered over the king.

"Start with the throat," Elisha blurted. "Let him think you'll answer his prayers." He tilted up his chin and traced the line that Morag's blade once etched, from the point of his chin down to the V at the base of his throat.

"Oooh!" the tall woman smiled. "Yes, I like that." She set down her knife by Thomas's head and started to strip off her gown.

For a terrible instant, Elisha feared she had some plan of her own: one more humiliation would be too much for either of them.

Instead, she cast aside the heavy gown, revealing her lighter shift with its slim-fitting sleeves. She knelt straddling Thomas's chest, the child's skin she wore settling down over his thighs. She took up her blade once more, crooning over it gently, and the others moved nearer, leaning in, their breath caught behind their teeth. Wolves and vultures looked more kind.

With soft movements, she stroked the hair back from Thomas's forehead. Every time they touched Thomas, Elisha imagined he felt it, razor-sharp like the blade that slew his brother.

With one finger, she tipped up her prisoner's chin and smiled, her nose nearly brushing his. If she kissed him, Elisha would tear her face off.

She slipped the knife between them, placing one tip just above the rope. Thomas moaned as she drew the blade ever so slowly upward. He began to shake his head, and she lifted her other hand, pressing it up under his chin, holding him still. She cut so gently, Elisha thought of Mordecai the surgeon. In the wake of her knife, blood seeped through the parted skin, just a little as if she had barely scratched him. It oozed free and trickled down as she continued.

The blood caught against the rope. Elisha's scalp tingled as blood seeped into the strands of the rope woven through with his hair. With a searing bolt of panic, the lock of Thomas's hair surged to life as Thomas's blood cut the circle of warding that kept Elisha away. Elisha gasped, and Bardolph shouted, sweeping out his knife.

He leapt too late, for Elisha was already gone. He snatched himself through death, back to the table, ignoring the howls of despair that frosted his flesh and rimed his eyes. He caught hold of Thomas's presence and flung himself to the side of his king, staggering as he landed on the stone over the kneeling mancer.

The woman jerked back, gaping up at him.

He punched her jaw, the archbishop's ring breaking teeth, tumbling her to the side. With a quick gesture, he snapped away the skin of her last victim and sent it soaring on the frigid wind.

"What the hell are you doing!" she cried, dragging herself up, clutching her knife. Then she caught sight of the dagger he swept into his hand. "You're not Jonathan at all, you are the barber!"

She dodged the blade, but Elisha caught her leg with his foot and sent her the force of his fury. Death tore into her, his pack of hounds eager for the kill, and her scream broke into nothing as her throat withered with the blast, her knife clattering to his feet.

"I told you!" Bardolph thundered, leaping up to the stone. He jammed his foot down on Thomas's trapped hand, forcing contact and no longer caring if the king should bleed.

Elisha could send the waves of death through Thomas's body and into that contact, but he could not be sure of the king's safety, not with the manic pounding inside his own skull. He spun, setting his feet on either side of Thomas and threw the golden dagger. It sped toward his target.

Bardolph ducked to one side and put up his hand.

The dagger shot off at the brush of his finger down the hilt—the hilt still damp with Elisha's own blood.

Bardolph's eyes flew wide and he snapped his wrist to flick away the blood, then he was screaming as the contact flared to life, or rather to death. He clawed at his arm as his skin withered.

"Stop it!" someone shouted. "Let him go or the king dies!"

Elisha snapped back the power and turned on his heel, dropping to a crouch.

The stout woman held her fleshing knife against Thomas's heaving throat. The half-moon blade had only a shallow edge but it would serve.

Somewhere behind him, Bardolph gagged. The air rippled with cold and cracked with the awful power, then Bardolph was gone through that passageway of horrors to some lair of his own.

Elisha crept his hand downward, his fingers finding the handle of the stout woman's blade. Thomas's blood cried out his fear, but Elisha could not afford to hear it. He wrapped the handle, envisioned the leap of affinity— this blade to that one, both edged in the king's blood. He twisted the images, letting the bounding power of death consume the blade, its handle rotting, its blade dissolved in a cloud of rust.

"Bastard," the woman muttered as her own knife crumpled in her hand.

Iron to rust. Easy. Elisha lay his palm on Thomas's trembling chest and sent the gentlest power he could control streaming along the stretched limbs.

"Catch the king!" she shouted, flinging herself down across one arm even as the fetters puffed red mist and clattered away.

Wills rose up beside her, a long spear clutched in both hands.

"Thomas, do something!" Elisha shouted, springing back to his feet.

Thomas snapped onto his side as Broken-nose reached to snare his leg. Instead, the king curled into himself with a spasm as if he'd been struck by the bombards' blast. One arm lay outstretched buried beneath the woman's bulk — she who had been fed and rested these long weeks. She dug her fingers into his shoulder and clung.

Hands at the ready, Elisha faced the spearman.

Wills hesitated, knowing the strike would make contact, and feinted right.

Instinctively, Elisha dodged, but his heel jammed against Thomas's ribs. Elisha cried out as if he, too, felt the pain, and his own side burned with the blow.

A wail broke the air. Then Thomas kicked Elisha's knee, and he staggered forward, toppling onto his startled enemy. Wills gathered the horror of the skin at his waist, but it was only a single murder, a single small death, and the novice mancer made poor use of it. He sent the dread of the victim's last moments toward Elisha, but the wave passed through him, and he stood immovable.

Wills lifted his hand, blade in his grasp, and Elisha caught his wrist in a grip as cold and unshakeable as death itself. The mancer struggled as flesh peeled back from his fingers, flayed like an illustration from a medical master. His screaming battered Elisha's ears, and Elisha let all sound fall away into nothing. The hand he gripped broke apart layer by layer until the bones rattled to the ground.

Death cackled and danced in his soul. He was a man of flesh no longer, but a creature at one with eternity and nothing could move him now.

Even so, even as he knew it to be true, the tiny knot of humanity pinched at the pit of his stomach and a voice whispered through the ferns of ice embedded within.

"Ah," said Brigit, *"it seems I've gotten here just in time."*

Chapter 22

❖

What gave her that power? How dare she reach inside him and turn him from his need?

Elisha cast aside the ruined arm and turned, roaring. A pale face stared back, blue eyes flashing. Elisha pictured the layers of the skin, the naked skull beneath. The face receded as the man scrambled away, toward the mancers he must have fought hard to flee. Thomas!

Recognition flooded Elisha's senses. He vaulted back onto the table, the armor he had forged within him melting into rust as he stumbled on a hollow shaped to hold a leg. "Thomas!" he cried, his hope finding voice at last.

"Your Majesty!" Brigit called. "Thank God you're all right." She slid down from her horse and ran toward them.

"Whose side are you on?" Broken-nose shouted. The mancer lunged forward, catching hold of Thomas's arm and dragging him back. The king's wild eyes never left Elisha's face.

Thomas flailed against his captor, then his hand came up with a fleshing knife and slashed across the mancer's chest and arms.

"Goddamn it!" The mancer grappled with him, tossing him down and seizing the blade.

"No!" Elisha's and Brigit's voices joined in a harmony they had never before achieved, and he darted a look toward her.

She ran from the gate, her red-gold hair gleaming, something in her hand flashing in the light — a crucifix. "Back, you devils!" she howled. A crucifix meant nothing to a mancer, but she spoke as if it did. The mancers frowned and darted her glances, and the stout woman rolled her eyes: It was a signal in a script they no longer knew how to follow.

Thomas held back his attacker's arm, but it inched closer by the breath and the stout woman loomed up beside them.

"Give up, Elisha, either way, I win," she said, her words curling in his belly like a snake eating him from the inside out.

His power was scattered: he couldn't beat them all, and she knew it, but she must know, too, that he would try. He started moving again, putting out his hand, steeling his nerve as if he still held back death by his merest wish. The two mancers exchanged a tiny glance, then they pounced, lifting Thomas from the stone, and the woman swept out a long knife.

Thomas's despair swirled outward from the lock of hair that linked them, and Elisha fell to his knees, his sensitivity returning full-force as the last of his power dissipated, the black tide of Thomas's emotions and his own fear overwhelming him. The memories trapped in the stone below began to creep up through his knees, the pleading of the victims, their horrid cries as they finally died. Elisha tried to shake the cold that stole over him. Think! They'd done this to him before, using their evil talismans to bewilder him with other people's pain. This time, the victim lived, writhing in their grasp, and it was Elisha's own heart that stopped at the thought of his dying.

Broken-nose panted, trying to work his lips into a

sneer. As he twitched, blood and sweat dripped from his arms to splash against the table, splashes of life against the Death captured in the stone.

Contact. But how to use it without hurting Thomas? Too strong a casting could kill both the mancer and the king. Elisha steadied himself and met the mancer's gaze. "Release him, and I may yet be merciful."

The mancer giggled, a little too long, gulping his breaths. "You won't try—you'd hurt him same as me— I've got contact."

"So do I," Elisha murmured, through stone and Death and blood. The young fool thought his single murder would defend him. He knew nothing.

From the strands of horror woven through him, Elisha captured only the cold. He gathered the endless frigid night, the howling ice and the blast of wind.

The mancer's teeth chattered and his arm jerked with the chill as gooseflesh rose across his body. His blood froze into little crimson icicles dangling from their wounds and falling away as he shook, shattering on the stone. Dropping Thomas, the mancer staggered back, hitting the wall, falling away.

Thomas lay curled on the table a few feet from Elisha, the stout woman standing behind him, narrowing her eyes. Her glance shifted from him to Brigit and back. Elisha lifted his hands, palms open to the sky. "Go," he said softly, letting the last of the cold mist his breath. "Go now." The frozen droplets of moisture chimed against the stone as they fell.

She gave a single sharp nod, stepped back, and vanished with a sound like children dying.

Elisha shuddered, his bones threatening to give way within him. He'd been too weak for more than tricks— thank God that had been enough. On his hands and knees, he clambered across the table, over the human form carved into it, and caught Thomas, holding him to his chest.

The king tensed, then thrashed against him, shoving at him with weakened arms.

Elisha stroked his tattered hair. "Thomas," he sighed. "It's all right. You're safe now."

"Safe?" his voice cracked, and Elisha flinched to hear it. "Safe, with you?"

"Thomas, there's so much to explain." Elisha gathered his raw senses and sent his compassion, letting his hands warm against the chilled flesh.

"Will you tell him everything?" Brigit demanded. "You've only had lies for me. Don't worry, Your Majesty, I'm here for you—he threatened," she let a gasp interrupt her, not bothering to look distressed for Thomas's eyes were yet hidden. "He threatened the life of my child, your brother's child, or I should have helped you sooner."

Thomas stiffened in his arms.

"While you were gone, he usurped your throne. I'm sorry it took so long to find you. I wish," again, she broke off, and when she started, her voice rang with sorrow and quivered with reluctance. "It was Queen Rosalynn's death that led me here, Your Majesty. When I found out what had happened—"

"Brigit made a bargain with them, Your Majesty. She's part of their plan."

Thomas shifted against his chest, one thin arm snaking out around Elisha's waist.

The touch hurt, throbbing with the weakness and fear they both must master, and with Elisha's thrill of relief. Somehow, Thomas would be all right. He could make it so.

Something flared through Thomas, a quickening that Elisha, in his exhaustion, could not understand.

Thomas edged away to sit on his own, then slowly lifted his head. Elisha reached out to touch the king's face as once an angel had touched him, and sent the prayer for his recovery. A brief panic flickered across Thomas's face. "Elisha," Thomas breathed.

It hurt just to look at him, but Elisha refused to turn away. "I'm here."

Thomas's fist slammed into his face, knocking him against the stone with astonishing strength. Elisha's head rapped into the pit carved there for that very purpose.

The archbishop's dagger dove toward him in Thomas's hand, stopping short, tipping back his chin with the edge, carving a groove but no deeper. "You Goddamned son of a bitch," Thomas spat, flecking Elisha's face with droplets of blood that carried his rage. "She never hurt you! She never hurt anyone, Elisha, why?"

Elisha swallowed, the blade sinking a little deeper. His arms lay outstretched, his fingers trembling with the weakness of casting. Another day, it might have seemed laughable, the one man barely able to hold his knife, the other too weak to put him off. "I didn't kill her."

"Rosie was becoming a witch. She knew your touch. Anyone could lie to me, and I wouldn't know it, but how could they fool her?"

Elisha wet his lips, finding a way to breathe again, his awareness reaching through the hands that would kill him to look for trust. "With my hair, Thomas, and a little blood, and someone I trusted to tell them all about me."

Thomas's fingers tightened, his teeth gritting together. "No, Elisha, not when you murdered her, not when you raped her. She was screaming your name!"

Elisha stared into the face of his king, twisted by hatred and hurt, the blue eyes so clear now lost to the darkness that shadowed them. Gently, he searched for a way to heal, some means by which Thomas might be whole again. His hands trembled. He had defeated the mancers. He had carried Martin into the fire that killed him and quenched the fire that would have killed them all. His eyes stung with sudden tears.

Thomas's touch seethed with fury, but his lips trembled. "What the Hell do you have to cry about?"

Elisha shut his eyes, helpless to stop the tears, his heart thumping against the stone that drank death. "I can find no way to heal your pain," he whispered. "Not even with my death."

The fingers twitched against Elisha's throat, then something clattered away, and Thomas flung himself up, stumbling a few steps only to collapse again.

"Thomas." Elisha's throat caught against the bruises and the cut he had no strength to heal. He struggled and lifted himself enough to roll over, blinking at the bent architecture of bone that Thomas's back presented, the ribs heaving with sobs.

Elisha found his voice. "The archbishop, the necromancer, claimed me for king, and I used the post to search for you and Rosie. She was dear to me, Thomas. Almost as dear as you are."

The bony shoulders rose and fell, then the spine straightened, and Thomas lifted his head. "Is that what this has been about? My God." A tremor ran through Thomas's body before he spoke again. "The messenger, the one that got Rosie and I from the city, far from our guards, claimed that you needed us. Trust no one, said the messenger, not even Randall. Who else could have lured us there? We didn't want to believe you abducted us Your servants kept us like animals. You tortured and murdered my wife—" He drew a deep breath. "For what? For jealousy? Because you thought you could effect some daring rescue, and I would fall upon you as my savior."

Dumbstruck, Elisha's eyes widened.

"I'm not a damsel in some accursed story. I am done with stories." He pushed away and nearly fell onto the ground, but for Brigit's hands that caught him.

"Come away, Your Majesty. Don't listen to him. Please, come away. I'll find you some clothes." Her voice had a familiar lilt to it, a gentle quality Elisha had not known she possessed. "We'll get you back to the city, back to the throne."

Elisha's body went rigid as he placed the tone: it was his own. She imitated the manner he used to soothe his patients. "Thomas, she wants the throne, she doesn't care what she does to get it. She's made a truce with the mancers. What is she giving them in exchange for the throne?"

"But you're the one who stole it," said the king. "Can you deny it?"

Thomas sagged against Brigit, his long arm draped over her shoulder, but she glanced back, and a smile lit her face, and Elisha could feel her crowing move through him.

Meeting her pale green eyes, Elisha summoned what little strength remained. "If you ever hurt him, Brigit, nothing in Heaven or Hell will stand in my way."

At that, Thomas turned. He straightened to his full height, his chin dripping blood. "Nothing in Heaven cares a whit for you, and nothing in Hell would dare to oppose you. In that country, you are the king."

Elisha knelt on the table of sacrifice, watching them go, the woman leading her horse, leading the man just as surely, his desperate arm wrapped about her, her strong one tucked around his waist with unmistakable possession. Thomas stumbled as he walked, and she held him up and pushed him on until they turned the bend and disappeared.

Chapter 23

For a long time, Elisha lay still in the hollow carved to hold a man. The flickering shades of the dead moved through him, more distinct now than they had ever been before. Soldiers fought brief and silent battles against marauders from the north. They screamed and fell in anguish, only to rise up again and repeat the moment, an endless dance of dying captured by stone. Older shades walked among them, men cast up from the pounding sea, men in skirts of armor, women in deer hides or homespun woolens. One of these crossed from the broken gate to the well and cast herself in, over and over, an echo of her death. A steady stream of men and women struggled against invisible assailants to be flung upon the table where Elisha now lay. They sank through him with a slight chill, as if he had taken a deep breath of early spring, and each sacrifice long past imparted him a gasp of strength. Every twenty-five breaths or so, Rosalynn died again.

She plunged through him on the way to the stone and shivered him more closely than the others because he knew her. He knew the terror that strained her limbs and the awful betrayal that caught the pit of her stomach. He need not hear the words she cried, for he knew them already. She died screaming his name. Pleading for his mercy.

He could only pray that, as she sat among the angels in the Kingdom of Heaven, comforted at last, some one of them might tell her the truth and convince her of his innocence. As for himself, he had only to convince the king.

Thomas had lost another wife. Would he ever recover? The two women looked as different as spring and autumn, his first wife blonde and thin, the second round, dark, rosy. He had lost another child, too. Elisha squeezed his eyes shut. Thomas was strong, he had survived before—but then, he had not been made to hear the slaying, nor to believe his only friend was the killer.

The kingdom was more at risk than ever, the mancers had a new leader—one pregnant with a potential heir—and had orchestrated their efforts to ensure his friends would believe the worst of him. Elisha had no idea how he might counter the betrayal they believed of him. What could he say or do to show them the truth? The mancers were already winning, insinuating themselves into the kingdom and destroying it from the inside, like rats in a granary. They had set barons against barons, barons against peasants, and even, through the archbishop's role in proclaiming Elisha's anointed state, cast doubt upon the holy church itself. Defeating the French seemed the least possible victory. At every moment, his enemies grew stronger, his friends more endangered—he was damned if he knew how to prevent it, and damned all the more if he did not try.

Elisha had work to do. First up, learning as much as he could about his enemies. He jumped down from the table, scattering crows from the corpses. They protested in a racket, glaring at him, but he ran for the storehouse, the only building in the compound.

The regular stone of the walls showed a series of different shades, different lichens, suggesting it had been constructed and re-constructed over a period of years. A fragmentary arch stuck out from one long side, marking the ruin of a structure long-collapsed.

The cob horse snorted and stamped as he passed, giving a tug against its harness.

Inside the long, low structure, a few skips of coal stood by the door. The rest of the room held four beds with bedding, a few clothes, a table and benches, pots and pans, a chest containing ordinary flour, eggs, and some turnips. The lid thumped shut as Elisha dropped it and swung about. Nothing. A door at the back led to an open-air hearth with a huge pot on top, reeking of coal fire and old flesh. Elisha slammed the door and put his back to it, gagging. His brief glance had shown no hiding place for anything of worth. The chill awareness of death lingered there, but without any of the sting of dying—it was a rendering hearth for boiling flesh from bone, almost more terrible for its utter lack of secrecy. The dark hole of the mine still beckoned from the yard.

The shade of a miner looking the wrong way tumbled into the pit as Elisha came in for a closer inspection. The horse turned, prodding him with its nose and lipping his hair. He pushed it back, returning to the chest of supplies for the handful of turnips. One of these encouraged the animal to draw up the platform, and Elisha hurried over to climb aboard. When the horse finished chewing, it swung about, looking for more and gamely approached, the chain rattling and squealing, lowering Elisha into the darkness. Even before the pit swallowed him, the air chilled, and his skin tingled.

Black dust hovered in the air, stinging his eyes and making him cough. A circle of sunlight, cut by the brace of the lowering mechanism, illuminated the floor and part of the wall of Thomas's prison. Only Elisha's grave looked darker, and that had not reeked of rotting flesh.

A jug of water and a pile of straw filled one arc of the round chamber. The rest held a series of shelves and hooks around a thick wooden table grooved and stained with blood. A butcher's block.

As neatly laid out as the ossuary at St. Leonard's, but without the reverence of purpose, the unholy reliquary held bones, bottles, ragged bundles. Taking a last deep breath, smothering his cough, Elisha drew nearer. Each shelf carried a single skull, or none at all, and an organized set of bones. The leather flasks smelled of blood. Hair, fingers, and toes dangled from bundled skins. His muscles tensed to run, to flee the pit with all haste, but he forced himself to stay, to search among the dozen or more dead gathered there. A few echoed his approach, as if he had known them in life, and now they recognized him in death as well. When he concentrated on a single individual, touching a skull with trembling fingers, he caught the flash of death, the struggle as the victim was carried to the table. Some were strangers to him and must have died elsewhere. On the shelf behind the block, Elisha found what he was seeking: Anna, Thomas's first wife. No bones—they must have skinned her after burial and could not transport the body, but they divided the skin into a few pieces, including the face that Morag had carried.

Elisha lay his gentle palm over Anna's remains and opened himself to her death. As with Rosalynn, he entered late into the scene, this time at Thomas's familiar hunting lodge. Anna faced a pair of leering men, already bloody, and swung a dagger that caught one of them across the collarbone. They advanced, forcing her back, and she stumbled at the top of the stairs. She screamed, crying for her daughter, begging.

Then she caught her breath, Alfleda's wail filling her ears. The third man up the stairs carried the body of a girl, blonde as her daughter, mutilated.

"Take off yer gown, child," the man snarled.

"No! Leave her be!" Anna scrambled up, the dagger flashing, but the second man caught her, wrenching her arm so the dagger fell.

"Take off yer gown, or I'll kill yer mother." He held a knife at Anna's throat.

They'd kill her anyhow, Anna knew. They wore no masks, nor treated her with the respect of a royal hostage. But they might preserve her child. She nodded faintly, and Alfleda, her face tracked with tears, nodded back with similar reserve. Carefully, she stripped off the silken gown, her grandfather's gift. Anna smiled encouragement.

Outside, in the darkness behind the lodge, the chapel bell clanged. Biddy, the old woman who lived at the chapel, must be sounding the alarm. For a moment, they all froze.

"Shit!" spat the leader. "Hurry up!" One of them snatched up the gown, Alfleda trying to hide her nakedness as he wrestled the dead girl he had carried into the princess's gown.

Then he dropped the body and grabbed Alfleda, slinging her over his shoulder. She screamed all the way down the stairs, then shouted, "Biddy!" and "No, Biddy!" and "Mamma!" in a rising wail as the knife hacked into Anna's throat.

Jolted, Elisha flung himself back to the present and drew back his shaking hand. Alfleda might have survived that night. What then? He resumed his search. The shelves held only three children, two of them boys, the third, an older girl—too old to be the king's daughter, and too complete. If they had harvested the princess, some remnant of her would be here, laid aside for later use.

Elisha retreated from the shelves, coughing, eyes watering, but with a surge of hope. Five of the mancers were dead, never to kill again. And, somewhere, Alfleda lived.

He clambered onto the platform and pitched a turnip out the hole over his head. The horse gave a whinny and a burst of speed, spilling him over at the top, breathless and grateful for air.

Other mancers must come here, as Morag had done, storing their grisly trophies. And the one he had not killed, the stout woman, could return at any moment. He thought of taking one of the relics of Anna, to show the other magi what had happened there, if they could see it so long after her passing. But the risk of being caught with such a thing was too great.

He cast a few sparks and the acrid interior of the coal pit caught fire with a whoosh, sending the victims to their final rest and depriving the mancers of their arsenal. Elisha withdrew his awareness, unbuckling the horse to lead it away, out of the unholy yard. He took a few minutes to carry the bodies of the mancers—and the victims they wore—back to the flaming pit to cast them in. That done, Elisha scrubbed himself clean at the well and replaced his tunic.

Elisha could travel in the mancers' way, but the only death he knew here was Rosalynn's, and that would lead him back to St. Leonard's in Hythe where her horrified father must have found her by now, alongside the archbishop. Madoc's tale might convince him for a while, but Randall would bring his daughter to his magus-wife and they would see the story they were meant to believe. Elisha prayed they would be gentle with Madoc, and that his friend would not insist on Elisha's innocence too stubbornly. If he had thought more deeply before destroying the mancers' talismans below, he might at least have used Anna's remains to transport himself back to the lodge, the site of her murder, to search for anything that might bring him to her daughter. His shoulders sagged as he watched smoke furling up from the hole. Still, he could not be sure he knew her death well enough to make contact across that distance. Rosalynn's skin and the place of her dying were fresh, still raw, still so close to life.

He packed a sack with the remaining turnips, a few bags of oats, and whatever other food was unspoiled, along with a few things he found in a smaller chest: fancy buttons and buckles, knives and rings. The possessions of their victims, who he did not think would begrudge him these few things, easily traded, if it helped him find the rest of the mancers and put a stop to them.

The horse watched with interest as he tied on the sack. He found no saddle and hoped the animal would be steered by the simple headstall of its harness, even without a bit. If not, he'd have to walk. The mare Thomas had given him showed her breeding in the fine shape of her head and long legs, while the cob before him had a lump on its forehead, a ragged tail and a grubby dun coat. When he stroked its neck, little puffs of loose hair and coal dust rose up around his hands. He spoke to it softly, explaining the urgency of his goal, using the sound of his voice to settle the horse and the warmth of his hands to build trust, the spell of kindness. Where was Cerberus, Thomas's dog? Waiting in the royal kennel, forlorn—that was a reunion Elisha would like to have seen. His throat ached, and he shook off the thought. Brigit would be busy solidifying her power and her hold over Thomas, but that distraction would only last for so long. And she would never be so busy that she lost track of Elisha. Even if he dare not come to London, to his king, she would be waiting for him to reveal himself, to be drawn back in to her plans. She should have killed him when she had the chance. Thomas might well have helped her.

Could he stand against Brigit in the growing power of her pregnancy, never mind her insidious troop of mancers? If he ever reached her again, how could he defeat her without becoming the monster his friends already believed him to be? Elisha rested his forehead on the horse's withers, his long sigh echoing the horse's contented breathing.

At last, he swung up to the horse's back. The gelding stamped a little, tossing its head, but settled again in a way that suggested it had been ridden before. Thank God. He turned the animal's head and nudged it south, picturing again the map Pernel made him. Would Pernel reveal his part in the search? And if he did, would it help Elisha's cause, or simply turn Thomas against his servants as well?

Elisha's stomach rumbled a little, now that the reek of death and smoke was behind them, and he pulled out a dried sausage to chew while he rode, thankful for the desolate country. Brigit and Thomas would likely ride for the nearest royal port, reclaiming the kingship and making all haste for London. In days, the kingdom would be searching for the queen's killer. How quickly would his supporters believe they had been betrayed by a false messiah, one who killed the man who had anointed him?

He could not imagine, with what lay before him, that his life could do other than end badly, at Brigit's hands if not at Thomas's, or Randall's. He had no power against the past and the betrayals that haunted them all, but there was yet one chance to save the future. Thomas still had a child, one he believed was dead, preserved by the mancers for whatever else they might have planned. Find her, bring her home, and Thomas might begin to trust him. Find her before Brigit did.

He still had the problem of Brigit's awareness. She would be watchful, preparing for his next move, and the child they shared heightened their connection. How could he pass unseen from her knowledge? He shivered in the wind, and an answering chill rose up within him. For a moment, he resisted the near, familiar voice of death. What purpose remained in denying the truth? He opened himself to the cold.

The horse gave a whinny, bolting a few paces, then allowing itself to be gentled by his hand, the one part of him still warm. The shades of the dead sprang up around him—ancients, miners, soldiers, Scotsmen. His mount plodded steadily onward, through the mists of the dying. Each one gave Elisha that shiver of strength, and each one concealed him as he breathed it in, forging his affinity with death and denying his own life. The troubles of the flesh dwindled to nothing as the sense of purpose filled him. Moving ever southward, he stalked from death to death like a thief through shadows.

The ghosts shifted through him in brief passages of terror or gratitude. A woman prayed as disease took her, and her presence enveloped him briefly like a warm cloak. Tears pricked his eyes, and he longed to remain swathed in warmth, but he rode on. He entered another, a man who screamed his agony inside Elisha's veins, clawing at wounds that suddenly cut Elisha's own flesh. Elisha flinched, and the horse sprang away, leaving the pain behind. The next one felt young and small—a child parted from its mother.

He crossed an ancient battlefield where the dead cried out for help or hurled curses at those who struck them down. When he moved through, they fell briefly silent and still, then began again, like a eddy of leaves stirred up by winter wind. After a few days ride, he no longer sensed their dying moments. The barrage of memories and pain drifted away. He became a vessel of cold passing by day or night, shivering the evergreens. Dogs barked at his approach and howled as he departed. When he entered their presence, they made no sound.

During the day, villagers he passed would nod or look away. Once in a while, someone turned to watch as he passed, or gasped in his wake. Magi.

Somewhere outside Coventry, a man followed him, though not too near. Elisha stopped and turned, his horse pricking up its ears, so attuned were they now to each other. Elisha lifted his head and met the man's gaze. He sent a tendril of his awareness and felt an answering chill. The man straightened, blinking, and one hand tugged his bulky cloak a little tighter. A mancer, and one who wore his gruesome talisman.

Elisha glared. Death leapt up at his command, a clamoring that filled his ears.

The mancer's eyes widened, then he spun away and ran.

Almost, Elisha followed him, images of Thomas and Rosie darting across his memory, but his purpose lay elsewhere, and he turned once more to the south.

Not until he entered the deep trees of the New Forest did Elisha let his power ebb away. When the last wisps left him, he slid off his horse and collapsed to the ground, his lungs fighting for breath. The moon hung heavy overhead, veiled by clouds—must be three weeks since he'd begun his long ride. Off to the left, the ocean pounded. His frayed senses vibrated with every rustle in the leaves and mournful hoot of a distant owl. The scent of decaying leaves curled into his nostrils, then a sweeter fragrance followed. Now that he had let go of death, Brigit would once more be aware of him. She might guess where he was, but he hoped she would not guess at why he came. Let her imagine, in the smugness of her victory, that he came to the lodge to mourn his own loss. Wind creaked and groaned in the branches of the apple trees. A few crows broke the silence as well, and the scent of the earth and the orchard seeped up from the ground.

He turned the old cob loose by the riverside with an affectionate pat of its neck, but it simply stood and nuzzled him a moment before discovering the joy of early apples. Elisha faced the lodge, swallowing hard. Three weeks. What if Brigit already knew about Alfleda and had her quietly killed? He walked up to the door and found it unlocked as he had left it, as he had promised the king he would do, that his door should never again be barred against him.

Elisha braced himself to climb the narrow stairs. At their base, two men had died. At their head, a cold place marked where Anna herself was killed. A window at the end cast some light into the room, illuminating the low beds, their rope lattices bare of blankets. Chests along the wall held bedding and personal items, but Elisha moved toward the doorway at the end, opening into a narrow room piled with more chests, barrels, and sacks.

Elisha opened the first sack and peered inside. An item of Alfleda's clothing might do, but a toy would be better, something she had cared about which might still provide a connection. Without that, he had no way to search for her, never mind to be sure when he found her. After more than two years, would anything here carry enough of her presence to be of use?

Uncut fabric, along with needles and thread. Elisha closed the sack and put it aside, opening the chest underneath to reveal some musty leather, half-finished embroideries, a pair of books, a bundle of things to be mended, silver goblets, and a few carved plates. Sometimes, as he lifted an item into view, Elisha felt the strong, distinctive touch of Thomas's presence. A woolen hood still captured a few dark hairs in its hemline, and Elisha stroked them, sensing the warmth of the past, almost as if Thomas drew nearer as Elisha sat among his things.

"Hallo? Who's there?"

Elisha jerked, clutching the hood to his chest, his heart pounding beneath his scars. He was magic indeed if his touch could summon the man.

Light flared in the outside room and Elisha froze.

"Good God," Thomas breathed.

Chapter 24

❖

Slowly, Elisha put down the hood, but he dreaded the sight of Thomas's face, twisted as it must be with his fear and hatred. "Thomas," he said, "I did not know you were here."

"What are doing in my house, you filthy—Sweet Lord, if I had my bow!" Thomas advanced across the creaking floor.

Elisha flinched and faced him. "Thomas, please listen."

"To what, more lies?" He took a step back, lifting the candle. His eyes blazed from dark shadows, his face seemed more skull than flesh. "She said you were far away, that you couldn't touch me." Thomas's eyes narrowed. "How did you get here?"

"A long, terrible journey." Elisha put out his hands. "I am not your enemy, Thomas, far from it."

The king growled, and the candle flickered in his grasp. He reached toward his belt, slipping back his cloak from one shoulder to reveal the hilt of a sword.

Elisha scrambled to his feet in the doorway, his hands still low and empty. "What if I am innocent? You are the thinker, not me—think about this. What if I'm telling the truth, and the enemy is the woman who claimed your rescue? What if she and her friends discredited me and broke you to get her on the throne?"

"I am not broken," said Thomas evenly. He switched the candle to his left hand and drew the sword, its blade sending shards of candlelight bouncing around the rafters. "Far from it," he echoed.

The illness churned anew in Elisha's gut. "She's using you for your power, can't you see that?"

"So what?" Thomas set the candle into a stand by the stair rail. "In a week, I shall marry her, and at least have an heir of my brother's blood. If she wants power, why should I not give it to her? Why should I not give her whatever she asks?"

Elisha met Thomas's fevered stare. "If you don't know the answer to that, then you must betray me. If you believe in her, then I have to die."

The king stared back, the sword held between them, but he did not advance.

In spite of the pounding of his heart, Elisha smiled.

Thomas took a step forward, raising the sword. "What do you have to smile about?"

"Because every moment you doubt her means that there is hope for me."

"No," said Thomas. "I don't think so."

Elisha laughed, light and foolish, and Thomas, just for a moment, returned to himself, one corner of his mouth quirking up. "Once you trusted me to shave your chin—do you remember? I who had killed two kings, and you trusted me."

The suggestion of a smile vanished. "You had not yet killed a queen."

"I still have not." He prayed he never would, but Brigit's cold, triumphant stare burned in his memory.

"I was there. I heard everything."

"Even you admitted that you might be deceived. The archbishop borrowed my presence to betray Rosie. He used a talisman made of my hair and my blood. You were blindfolded, so you couldn't look too closely—you could only hear what Rosie was saying. Even she only believed it was me because of the contact he forced on her. And because she might have hoped for my coming." He swallowed. "I was miles away in the Tower."

"Save that you frequently sent out all of your attendants—I asked."

Hope flared again, but Elisha muted it. "You asked because you know I would not betray you, Thomas, not you, and not Rosalynn."

"Then why did you call for them to cut me?" Thomas studied him. "If it had not been for that . . ."

"The rope at your throat was bound with my hair. The circle prevented me from reaching you. God forgive me, Thomas, blood seemed the easiest way to break it." He kept his hands low, open, pleading. "They already doubted me. They wouldn't have simply cut the rope."

"Your Majesty," called a man's voice from below.

Elisha caught his breath, and Thomas stiffened, the sword wavering.

Elisha's hands came together, a gesture of prayer.

"Your Majesty? Where've you gone?"

"I'm here," Thomas answered. "Upstairs."

Elisha stepped back through the doorway into the storage area. He ducked to the side and stood trembling.

"The men're tending the horses and preparing to bed down in the barn. I've got a few here to stay with us." Someone mounted the stairs, a heavier tread that brought the voice nearer: Duke Randall, his one-time patron, Rosie's father.

Elisha swallowed, but his throat stayed dry. His heartbeat echoed through the brand that scarred his chest, and he could not imagine how they did not hear.

"Thanks, Randall. You don't know how much I've depended on you." Thomas sighed. "This has been an awful time for you, as well."

The tread stopped on the creaking floor at the head of the stairs. The haunted floor. "For both of us, Your Majesty. Why've you drawn your sword?"

"I still fear my own shadow."

"You have every reason to fear. He's a danger to you, and to Brigit. It behooves us all to be on edge if it means we are prepared to meet him."

"I am not sure I will be." Footsteps drew near and a shadow blocked the candlelight that fell through the door. Thomas's voice asked, "What if we are wrong?"

Elisha held his breath, his spine and palms pressed to the wall. He shut his eyes against the darkness and dared to pray.

"Wrong? Wrong about what?"

"You heard what that soldier said, about the archbishop—"

"Whom the barber also slew."

"What if the archbishop had a way to trick us both, with Brigit's help?" Thomas overrode the duke, his voice gaining strength. "If Elisha had been responsible for our abduction, why should he want me to witness Rosie's death? Even then, I did not see what happened, I only heard—"

"You don't believe that, Thomas! Please tell me you're not so far under his sway. The man's a fiend and a murderer. I rue the day I stayed his death, for all the grief he's caused us."

"I'm the king," Thomas shot back. "If it behooves me to be cautious, then, too, I must consider the chance that I've been misled."

"There is no chance." The duke pounded across the floor. "If you don't believe your own ears, for God's sake, Thomas, my wife can show you. Lay your hand on my daughter's skin—all that we have left of her—and you can feel every hideous thing he did to her, every way he tortured her before he tore her open."

Had Allyson really shared that horror with her husband? To lose a child must already have broken their hearts, but to know exactly how—Elisha recalled all too well his own encounter with Rosie's skin and how it nearly left him mad, willing to cut his own throat for the crimes she believed he had committed.

"Randall—" Thomas's voice shuddered, and Elisha clenched his fists. "God forgive me, if there's a chance. We are flying into danger if we're wrong. You cared for him, too, once. You even suggested they should marry."

"The more fool I." The duke stomped toward the stairs. "Allyson!" he bawled. "Bring up the casket. The king's no longer sure what manner of devil he faces."

Thomas's cloak swished, brushing against the doorway. "She's suffered enough, Randall. Don't ask it of her."

"Do you know what happened while you were gone? He sent my wife to be struck by lightning by one of his allies at Chelmsford. Only luck preserved her. I imagined, I hoped, he hadn't intended that, but after Rosie—" Randall's voice broke. "If you've already forgotten what he is capable of—what part of Hell gave birth to him, then you'll see it for yourself. You'll have no room for doubt alongside the need for vengeance! Allyson."

"I am here, Your Grace," said a weary voice that echoed up the stairs.

"Have you brought her?"

"Only to bury her, love."

"Thomas needs to see, to understand through his wife's own self, what was done to her. Can you show him?"

"If you feel I must, Your Grace, then I can." Slow steps began, a woman burdened.

Even without spreading his senses, Elisha felt chilled.

The hairs stood up along his arms and he drew breath but shallowly. The memory of Rosie's pain clamped hold of his stomach.

"If you must weigh the truth, Your Majesty, then at least you should have the full truth at hand. Allyson, let me." Randall crossed the room, and the ropes of one bed squeaked as something was set down upon it. "Come, Thomas. Touch her ruined hand and know the truth of what he's done."

The shadow passed from before the door.

"Here," said the duke, "help me with the lid."

Elisha's hands trembled. For a moment, he let his head back against the wall, then he heard Thomas's cloak settle to the floor and Elisha's breath stopped in his wounded lung. Elisha lurched around the door. "No, Thomas! Don't do it. As you value your soul, don't touch her."

Thomas knelt there, half-turned, his cloak pooled around him like a garment of shadows.

"Guards!" Randall staggered to his feet, the bed and casket separating him from Thomas. The duke snapped out his sword. His glance slid along its length, then back to the king. "Did you know this? Have you been hiding him?" He shook with rage.

Thomas remained where he was, hunched, fully clothed now, but the image of the last time they'd met face to face, when he crouched in despair, torn between the threat of the mancers, and his terror of Elisha himself.

If they forced him to touch the skin . . . "I hid myself, Your Grace. Let Thomas be. He needs no more grief, surely not from you."

"Who is it dares speak to me so, but the man who killed my daughter, the king's bride!" Randall swept his own wife behind him with one arm as he surged forward.

"I loved her, too," Elisha said, backing away, drawing

the man further from his king. "That's why it hurt her so much when they stole my touch to kill her."

"Of course it hurt when you betrayed her!" Randall howled.

"No, Your Grace. I would have saved her if—"

"What, give up the throne to look for those who should rightfully hold it?"

Elisha's fear collapsed beneath a fury that darkened his vision, and he stood his ground. "How did I even have time to do what you say? You were there for my reign, Your Grace. You supported the man who gave it to me. Ask Pernel who found the maps how often we searched for them, for Thomas and Rosie both. All I've ever wanted was to see Thomas crowned as he should be."

"Can't you hear his perversions, Your Majesty? How he uses you to excuse his atrocities?" Randall's teeth glinted. "Even had you not killed her, nor slaughtered a man of God, even then, Barber, you would deserve the worst."

"Randall, be careful," cried Allyson, her hands clasped together. "Don't touch him!"

Elisha met the eyes once so kind, and his anger subsided. Booted feet shook the stairs, and Lord Robert appeared, tall and well-armed, with a few more men at his back. "Here, Your Grace! By the Cross, you've found him!"

"I'll take him," said Randall softly, and he lunged.

Elisha leapt aside, but his head knocked loudly against the beam, and he nearly fell as he ducked. The sword bit into his thigh, but not too deep. As he slipped back from the blow, he scrambled to master his thoughts. The cloth talisman he carried inside his sleeve burst to sudden heat. His thigh, muscle, skin—he knitted them in place in his mind, sealing the wound as he searched for reason.

Elisha called, "Duchess Allyson, Your Grace, the

archbishop was a sensitive. He used a projection to make her believe—"

"A sensitive, you claim. Like you!" With a roar, the duke cut behind him.

Elisha turned left, only to feel the blade tear across his back. He fell forward, screaming, then got to his knees, deflecting the next blow though it smacked hard across his arm. Heal, heal, he urged the flesh. He saw an opening and dove low past the duke's legs. But the duke's men formed a wall before the stairs, blocking the other side of the room. They stood with swords to hand, but made no move to join the battle. Nor was there need.

Elisha reeled back from them and the sword caught his hip this time, deeper, harder. He staggered, losing his focus for a moment in this new pain. He gulped for breath, he must defend himself. But to harm the duke?

Blood pulsed from his wounds. Oh, God! Heal, heal. He gulped for breath and faced his attacker.

Randall waved his sword, blood flicking from the blade. "Come on, you devil! Where's your courage now? Or can you fight only unarmed women?"

"I don't want to hurt you." Elisha's breath burned. The duke's image parted into two, and he forced them back together.

"Me? No, it's the king you're after, since you murdered his wife. Barber, it's time you were trimmed." The duke danced forward again. Half mad after Rosie's disappearance, terrified at the thought he could have lost his wife as well when Sundrop aimed a lightning bolt at her, then to have his daughter returned to him in tatters and blood: it had utterly undone him. Randall was older than Elisha by half, his balding pate glinted with sweat, but he was trained for this and bolstered by his grief.

Elisha feinted left, then dropped and tumbled back to the right, the sword cutting over his head. He fetched up against something hard at the small of his back and caught a flash of fear that shot through his own pain. His head tipped back, and he glimpsed Thomas's face.

Then the duke's sword tore across his abdomen, and agony spun out from the wound. Elisha screamed, curling around it, rolling, his hand pressed to staunch the blood.

Randall's foot tipped under his ribs and shoved him over, Elisha's back arched, his throat burned. The healing spell shattered in his addled mind. His spasming fingers gripped a handful of fabric, twisting the wool as his scream rebounded to his ears. The cold power of death surged through him, leaping and cackling as the hounds turned on their fallen master. Death tightened his muscles, digging his fingers in, hunting still. Blood froze upon his trembling flesh.

Steel flashed through the darkness, and his enemy's breath came in pants of exertion and exaltation. If he died now, his death could shoot through every fleck of his blood that spattered the room, coated the swords, clung to the hands of those who hurt him. Death raced along his veins, and he struggled to force it back, to shape it to his will and bury the chance that, in his dying, he would kill all those he loved.

Elisha clung to the fabric; a snatch of reality against the madness that railed within. His awareness, unchained, sprang through his surroundings. Every drop of blood offered glimpses—the duke's fury and the grief that narrowed his vision and plugged up his ears, the righteous anger of his soldiers, the sorrow of Lord Robert to witness the death of a friend, the horror of the king re-living his nightmares. Thomas's cloak, warm and woolen, filled his grasp.

Elisha's hand convulsed, shaking away the cloth, the contact that meant Thomas's death if this mad power had its way. Feverish with the pain, Elisha heaved himself to his knees, one arm keeping his intestines where they belonged, blood coating his fingers.

He pushed himself away, farther from Thomas, as far as he could. Pray God he had not bled upon his king, if Death took hold of him, if he no longer controlled it. "The cloak, the cloak," he panted. Take it off, he wanted to say. The sword hacked into his back, and Elisha crumpled.

He gaped into the darkness, and death chilled the flames in his throat. Suddenly, Elisha realized that he could die. Despite everything, despite the power that coursed through him now, he could let it go, turning it inward, taking control. His power could tear through him until nothing else remained, scouring the moment and the pain, ripping him free of the flesh, tossing him from the world into oblivion. The thought comforted him as opium calms a fevered soul. Pain racked his stomach and back, death clamored for its due, and Elisha began to surrender.

"Stop," a voice thundered. "Stop in the name of the king."

It cut the darkness and shot lightning through the storm that lashed Elisha's mind. As if it obeyed mortal commands, the howling ebbed away. The pain remained, and Elisha ground his fist into his belly.

"Your Majesty, let me end it now! He's weak, it may be our only chance. You saw how he healed himself."

"I order you, as I am your lord, to sheath your weapon."

"You can't mean for him to live! Surely, Your Majesty, Thomas—"

"I can't know what I mean!" Thomas cried. His ragged breath shuddering through the darkness. "All I know is this, Your Grace, that I cannot watch him die. Not again, not if there is any chance he speaks the truth. If you will not hold for your king, then hold for my sake. As by marriage I am your son, I am asking you."

Elisha opened his eyes, turning his cheek to the floor, gazing sidelong up at his king. Tears blurred his vision, yet he saw Thomas standing tall and firm, one hand gripping Randall's sword arm. The smaller man faced him boldly, but his ribcage heaved with his exertions.

"You know what he's capable of, you more than any of us," the duke pleaded. "We may never have him so again, Thomas."

The king gave a slight nod. "At our mercy."

"Just so."

"Mercy," Thomas repeated. "It's a dangerous word." Thomas glanced down, his face impassive as he looked upon Elisha. He showed no flicker of compassion, yet, in that moment, Elisha remembered how to heal.

Chapter 25

❧andall made a guttural noise, as if he might spit, then he broke away, stepping back from the king as he rammed his sword back into its sheath. "Now what, Your Majesty? How do we hold him? What chain to bind Satan?" He shot a look at Elisha and his eyes flared. "Look at him, he's healing himself already!"

Elisha rested his head back on the floor, gritting his teeth against the pain. He sought the pathways of healing, guiding his flesh to merge together again. Thankfully, his intestines were not severed. He struggled to hold the image of wholeness in his mind while the duke raged over his head. Just as he thought he had it, a spasm of pain from the slash across his back jerked him once more into the world.

Elisha shut his eyes so tightly that red visions danced behind his eyelids. He started humming, low in his throat, the way he used to do when he faced a delicate operation. Quickly now, he brought the wounds together. He rushed to outpace the pain and whatever decisions the others might be making. When he finally unclenched his teeth and let go of his song, his stomach still burned but he no longer bled so profusely.

He lay near a bed, his head almost beneath it. He

breathed carefully, trying not to move, trying not to seem recovered enough to warrant another assault. The duke faced Thomas across a short patch of floor, both silent. Blood dripped from Randall's hand. Elisha's poorly-mended guts felt twisted at the sight, and he tipped his head back, averting his eyes. He should be angry, for the times he had saved the man's life. Instead, nausea crept up inside. This injustice paled beside the wrongs done to Rosalynn. The small casket that held her skin rested on the next bed, with her mother sitting beside it.

Allyson stared back at him, her eyes leaden. She rose heavily and paced over to her husband, taking his bloody hand in hers. "Randall, my love, you still fight like a tiger. He shall not soon forget that."

With a snort, the duke said, "It should be him we're burying."

"In time," she said, "all in good time," and her gaze shifted to Thomas.

The king folded his arms and made no reply.

"At the very least, he knows things that might be of use to us," Robert pointed out. "A more . . . reasoned investigation of her death might help us understand."

"Reasoned. What has reason to do with what he did?" Randall snapped, his sword hand trembling as if he might draw on Robert next.

They had him now, too weak to try another casting, too sickened to care what they did. Even the hope that shone so briefly when Thomas stopped his slaughter began to fade. Elisha looked away.

The rope lattice of the bed cut his view into squares, bounded on one side by the headboard carved with leaves. Elisha exhaled slowly, gulped a breath, and exhaled again. The breeze of his breath scattered the dust motes beneath the bed and something gleamed in a patch of candlelight, then retreated. He blew out again and watched the shimmer of gold. He inched his bloody hand under the bed and touched, with a shaky finger, the strands of hair trapped against the rope trusses. Fine, golden hair, not too long.

Resting his forehead against the floor, he indulged the silent laughter despite the twinges of pain from his belly. After all of this, all that they had done, why should he risk himself again? If they knew his plan, they would hack him to pieces where he lay, and even Thomas would not stop them, not if he believed Elisha was a danger to his daughter.

Except that she was already in danger, and Brigit would stop at nothing. Elisha stroked the hair with his fingertip, then gently plucked it free and brought it close. To his sensitive fingers, it gave off a faint warmth. It could not be the mother's, for her death would give answer. Here, then, was what he had been looking for, and he had the duke's vengeance to thank for it.

He curled the strands together and carefully reached back and winced at the stretching of new scars. With his fingernail, Elisha tucked the strands into his sleeve with her father's.

"Here, what's he doing?" Boots tramped the floor, and someone grabbed Elisha's leg, hauling him out into the light.

Elisha kicked away the hand and curled around his pain, much dulled, yet sharp enough.

"Don't touch him!" Allyson shouted, too late.

Rolling to his back, Elisha stared up at her, the edge of his anger returning with the pulsing of his wounds. "If I wanted you dead, any of you, it would be too late."

She glared back at him. "No, Devil, even you require contact."

Elisha focused on his blood and drew out a faint tendril of death, cold and bitter. With a flicker of his fingers, he sent it through every drop of blood he had shed in that place, from the filth on the hands of the duke, to the marks on Thomas's cloak, to the spatters that marked every man, to the shared guilt upon Allyson's fingers. *"Yes,"* he sent, *"I do. I fought to keep from killing you before I found the strength to heal myself."*

"Wipe off the blood, quickly—all of you, quickly!" Allyson shook her hands fiercely, then wiped them on her skirt. She sprang to her husband's side and seized a flask of wine.

"I did not do this thing, Your Grace. When you have passed your shock, you will find the truth," he insisted, then his contact with her fled as she splashed wine over them to wash him away.

"Curse it, woman, how are we to bind him if we can't touch him? How can we ever hope to keep him?" the duke muttered.

The duchess frowned, then cocked her head and said, "Your Majesty, she gave you a rope, didn't she?"

Once more the center of attention, Thomas lowered his hands from his eyes and swallowed hard. He ruffled a hand through his hair and finally met her gaze. "Yes," he sighed. "Yes, she did. In my saddlebag, on the left."

The rope. "She" would be Brigit. And the rope could only be the rope she had twined with Elisha's hair to prevent him from finding Thomas, a boundary against his reach. How much of the accursed stuff could there possibly be?

With a click of his heels, the returning guard held out a length of rope perhaps a yard long, with occasional dark fibers twisted through.

"Bind his hands," the duke ordered, stepping out of the way.

The man glanced down at Elisha, then back, stiffening. "Your Grace, where's his wounds?"

"He's healed them." The duke flapped his hand in Elisha's direction. "Get to it, man."

With a tip of his head toward the casket, waiting silently on the bed, the guard said, "Begging your pardon, Your Grace, but I'm not sure it's wise."

"You're not sure?" The duke raised his hand. "Give it here, I'll do it myself."

"No," cried Allyson at once, taking his arm. "I've lost a daughter, I'll not lose you as well."

"What choice do we have?"

Elisha watched them from the floor with a sort of detachment. They had nearly killed him and now fought over who would be bold enough to bind him. How indeed, do you chain the devil?

"Your Grace," said Robert from his post by the stairs, "I will—"

"No." Thomas slipped the rope from Randall's limp hand. "I'll do it."

"But Your Majesty—"

"Whatever he might have done, I do not think he wants me dead." He held the rope clenched in his fist and kicked aside his cloak as he started to kneel.

Elisha pushed himself up, and Thomas flinched, his knuckles white as he gripped that rope. For an instant, their eyes met, and Elisha felt the heat of Thomas's breath upon his face, then Elisha crossed his wrists before him.

At the first touch of those strong, trembling fingers, Elisha shut his eyes. All the hope, all the trust that he could gather, Elisha channeled to his own hands even as the rope looped around and clinched tight against the skin.

"Do you remember when we met?" Elisha murmured. "Not that moment at the ball, but in your stables?"

Thomas hesitated.

"You would have killed me then, and I bound you for my own safety. Before I knew who you were or what you had been through."

"Shut up," the duke snapped. "Your Majesty, just finish, don't listen to him."

A second loop slipped around the other wrist, more confident this time, though with a minimum of contact. The brush of Thomas's fingers echoed with a tension that ran all the way to his shoulder and down his spine, and a fatigue that went almost as deep.

"You have nothing to fear from me, Thomas," Elisha whispered, his scarred chest tight.

"Nothing to fear?" Randall snapped. "From a murderer? A scoundrel who would mutilate the very archbishop? A monster who tore the skin from our daughter? I watched you kill King Hugh with my own eyes—even then you wielded darkness."

"Your Grace." Elisha faced him, tilting up his chin and settling back on his heels. "I am no more a murderer than any man among you. I have killed to defend myself, my friends," he allowed himself a faint smile, "to defend you, Your Grace, and yes, my king. Every man of you has killed no more, nor less than I have done. Every one of you has fought your battles. I fight mine alone," he said, "and even victory gives me no peace."

The duke growled, but Robert piped up, "A pretty speech from one who once said he could not speak you fair."

A couple of the guards chuckled, and fell silent.

Elisha slowly rose to his feet, his audience clearing a space around him, just in case. He gave a nod to Lord Robert. "I have kept better company since then."

The lord blinked at him, dark eyes widening in his long face.

Elisha winced as his abdomen protested the change in position. "Let the monster be twice damned for daring to look so human," murmured one of the guards.

"If that trick with the French navy's any way to judge, sometimes it's not so bad to have the devil on our side," said Robert.

Randall growled. "Another trick to secure his place on the throne."

From outside came the sound of hoof beats and the jingling of harness. A man called out and horses snorted as they stamped to a halt.

"She's here, Your Majesty," the guard said.

In three strides, Thomas slipped past Elisha's shoulder and made for the stairs, his cloak rippling. He paused as he was about to duck beneath the floor and their eyes met. "Watch him close—there'll be no joy at this reunion." And he was gone to meet his betrothed.

"Get on, then, we'll be going down," said Robert.

Elisha, gazing after Thomas, gave a nod and started to move. A few of the guards preceded him, and he nearly swept them all down as the pain struck again upon the stairs. His hands jerked against the rope—the damned thing that kept his senses as tightly bound as the rest of him—but he had no way to stop himself. He would have fallen, but Robert grabbed his elbow and steadied him. No joy indeed. How could he look upon her, or she upon him?

"Must we?" asked Allyson, her voice drifting down from above.

"She'll be queen," answered her husband. "She did save his life."

"I know," she sighed.

Elisha took his place in the little procession. The guards walked with swords drawn, flanking him but keeping their distance. Elisha wanted to snarl and snap, just to watch them jump or to divert himself from what was to come.

A coach painted with royal lions stood before the manor, with a few outriders tending their steeds. Thomas brushed his cloak over one shoulder and stepped up to open the door. He offered his hand, assisting a frail, old priest down from the carriage, then waiting.

Most of the guards sank down on one knee. The rest hovered, swords pointing in Elisha's direction. "Down with you," managed the ruddy one, thrusting his sword at Elisha's chest.

Turning a sharp glare on the man Elisha said, "I will not kneel to her, and I think you will not make me."

"Who's the rascal who will not kneel?" Brigit ducked her head out of the darkness of the carriage and froze, her cream-white hand set upon Thomas's, her red-gold hair blazing in the sun. She stepped lightly down, clinging to the hand of the king. "This is indeed a betrothal gift, love." Her eyes traced Elisha's figure, focusing awhile on the gashes through his tunic. "Well done." She rose on her toes, tipping back her head in an obvious request.

Elisha's stomach lurched, but Thomas brushed his lips against her forehead. "I used the rope you gave me," he said, his back turned resolutely as he studied her.

"Don't tell me you touched him! Dear Lord, Thomas, you're lucky to be alive." She pressed her free hand to her chest.

"Not so lucky." He led her out of the way as one of the footmen handed down the last passenger, a plump young woman of about Brigit's age, whose limp, dark hair at first shielded her face, Brigit's companion, a magus Elisha knew as Briarrose.

Walking as near as the guards would let her, Brigit looked Elisha up and down. "Why are you here?"

Over her head, Elisha could see Thomas's back, his broad shoulders slumped, his head tipped up and to one side, as if he watched the birds drifting across the sunset over his orchard.

"Did you come for the king, to kill him as you did his wife?"

Elisha flicked his gaze over her. "How hard you must study to perfect your acting. You know I did not kill her.

What did you offer the mancers, Brigit, in exchange for your crown?"

"Come away, Brigit, there's no point to this," said Briarrose.

"Answer the question, if you dare. We should all like to know what you are doing here." The duke, with his wife's hand tucked over his elbow, stood by the house looking somehow stronger without his anger. Perhaps Allyson, magus that she was, channeled him some of her own quiet fortitude.

Elisha's toes curled a little into the dirt, but that availed him nothing against the chill of the oncoming evening. The tears in his tunic fluttered in the breeze like flags of surrender. Without his own full capacity, Elisha could not be sure how much of him Brigit was able to read, if the pregnancy increased her sensitivity enough to judge if he told her a lie. Elisha traced the shape of Thomas's too-distant form. "I was hoping to borrow a shirt; mine is rather the worse for wear."

Brigit snorted, but Thomas half-turned, his hands hanging loose, the trace of a smile returning to his face. With the rosy light that stroked his tired cheek, Thomas seemed younger. Gently, he shook his head, just once, then ruffled back his hair as the smile faded away.

"Hello, friend," Elisha whispered.

"What did you say?" Brigit thrust her chin forward.

"Truly, Highness, don't go any nearer," offered the guard.

Trapped as he was, bound and now cornered, Elisha found himself at a loss for a plan of escape. But if Thomas could smile, if he could soften even so much, might there not be reason to hope? Elisha suddenly thought that if he had to break his hands to get free of the rope and crawl all the way to wherever they kept the king's daughter, he would do it. If once more he could see Thomas's smile, not the slender trace that remained today, but that rare and brilliant grin of pure delight.

"Don't you look at him," Brigit hissed. "Don't you even raise your eyes to him or I swear I'll pluck them out and have them on toast. Even you cannot heal from that."

She snatched her cloak up and marched back to where Thomas dallied, still in profile. He stared down at her, and she stroked her hand along his arm. "I know you'd like to have the city be witness when you bring back the killer, but it might be best to execute him quickly. He's more devious than we know, if he could get all the way here without our notice."

"I've tried that already, my lady," the duke put in. "His Majesty would rather not watch."

Brigit arched a sharp eyebrow back at them, and pressed her cheek against Thomas's arm. "It must hurt you so, to face your betrayer," she murmured.

The king spoke into the sunset. "I cannot recall when I last had a day without pain."

The waiting horses misted the sky with their breath, and Thomas's words sank heavily upon Elisha's heart. When he had rescued his king, Elisha wept, for he could see no way to heal Thomas, even with his own death. He was tempted now, to offer it again, but if Elisha died, Brigit would be free to claim the crown she coveted, and to fulfill whatever dark bargain she had made. The pain gripped his belly, and Elisha bit down on the cry that stung his already hoarse throat.

A bark echoed from the stable, and Cerberus, Thomas's huge deerhound, clawed toward him, his leash clenched in Pernel's hands.

"Your Majesty," the servant began, then his eyes caught Elisha's. His hands slipped, the dog bounding through the midst of the guards to Elisha's side with a yip of joy and a fierce slapping of his tail. His tongue sought Elisha's hands, slurping.

Elisha knotted his fingers through the dog's collar, and said, "River!" He flung one leg over the dog's strong back as Cerberus bounded away down the slope, bouncing and dragging Elisha along with him.

The startled cob looked up, dripping water, and gave a snort as the dog plunged in.

Shouting echoed down the hill. Elisha let go, splashing, whistling for his ugly, trusty mount. He got hold of the harness and dragged himself up, wrapping his fingers around leather.

The horse sprang into motion, as much escaping the guards who thundered down after them as obeying the kick of Elisha's feet. They galloped down the river, Elisha slopping around the horse's back, clinging for all he was worth, and Cerberus barking and dashing alongside, thrilled to be back in the hunt. Fire flared in Elisha's belly and he gasped, bent upon the horse's neck.

At a whistle from behind, Cerberus stopped, whimpering, and let Elisha ride on, dodging trees. As long as he was bound, he could cast no magic, but Brigit could follow. Clinging to the horse's mane, Elisha turned his horse toward the barrows—the barrows where Alaric died, a death he knew, a place to which he was already attuned. He gnawed at the rope as he rode, nearly falling more than once, forced to take the road once they found it. Here, he allowed the horse to slow, sitting up and groping for the knife in his medical pouch. Bouncing along, he wriggled his hands a few times before he was free, stuffing the rope under his belt and replacing the knife. The king's men would pursue him, and he could ride faster with his hands free.

As for Brigit, she would pursue him by other means. Once he had the reins, Elisha reached for the dead. They were fewer here in the forest, but bandits and travelers still rose up, ancient shades shimmered from the barrows, and he cantered through them, cloaking himself once more from the living. He felt the king's riders as they galloped past on their search, but they did not find him. Instead of fleeing as they must expect, Elisha found a hiding place that suited his need. Among the stones where Alaric died, Elisha rested and sent his awareness creeping over the land. He sought the princess with the warmth of her golden hair and the chill of the mother who died to defend her.

Long before dawn, he rode again, guided by her presence as a sailor by a star.

Chapter 26

❖

$\mathfrak{M}$id-day found the horse walking slow, leaving the course of the river and riding through ever more sparse trees until they crested a hill and looked down onto a farming valley, the fields rich with summer wheat, a few pigs prodded away from the harvest by their keepers. A rambling convent of stone and plaster buildings dominated the opposite hill, sharing space with a field of crosses, and Elisha knew he had come to the right place: the dead here felt familiar.

He dismounted awkwardly, knees quivering, and leaned against the horse for a moment. His gut throbbed now that he had released his numbness. Leading the cob beneath the porcelain sky, Elisha approached the convent, exchanging nods with a few nuns working outside. One of these rose from her work bench, dusting off her hands from the carving she worked over, and came to greet him at the gate, though she looked him up and down, brow furrowed.

"Good day to you, traveler." The nun had dark, deep-set eyes and hands marked with layers of fine scars, as if she had taken a long time to learn her art or had been no stranger to knives.

"And to you, sister." He made a slight bow. "I would

ask the hospitality of your house for myself and my
mount, for a few hours only. We've ridden through the
night."

"This way." She waved her hand and a young woman
in the simple robes of a novice accepted the reins and
clucked up at the horse, her weary face brightening as
she gazed into the animal's eyes.

"Had a long night, have you?" she murmured as they
walked away.

Elisha smiled in her wake, and the nun beside him
sighed. "God makes a place for each of us, my lord, those
who work the fields and those who tend to all His creatures."

"Myself, I am a surgeon."

"Certes?" She set out into the gate, letting him follow
beneath its murky shadow, and then she turned under a
colonnade. "Trying to explain that wreck of a tunic, are
you? Next time you steal a horse, take yourself a new
shirt as well."

Elisha floundered for a reply, but she walked on and
brought him to an arched door, gesturing for him to enter. She walked briskly past him toward the broad fireplace at one end of the hall. Long tables and benches
formed three rows pointing in that direction, with a
handful of chairs at the end, and she brought him to one
of these. "You'll want to warm up after your ride. We've
already broken our fast, but some sustenance will be
found. Wait here. I shall tell the prioress of your arrival."
Her robes brushed the floor as she left him.

Elisha collapsed onto the chair, facing the crackling
fire. He dearly wished it made him feel warmer.

A series of shuttered windows marked the long wall
that bordered on the central yard, letting in the sound of
conversation and distant singing. Elisha shook off the
nun's suspicions. Whatever she thought, he couldn't very
well leave with his objective so near at hand. Someone

here, among the nuns or their lay-men assistants, spied for the mancers, keeping watch over their hidden treasure. He wondered if the very door-warden might not be the one, hurrying even now to send a message of his curious arrival. Or perhaps she merely went to rouse the laborers to hold him until the aggrieved party in his obvious robbery arrived in pursuit. Self-consciously, Elisha rubbed at his neck, and thanked God that it was still intact.

"Worried about your neck, are you?"

Elisha jumped from the chair and spun, heart pounding.

A taller woman stood beside the gatekeeper, her narrow nose giving her the look of a bird. "Sister." The prioress dropped the word like a stone into water.

The nun bowed her head and worked her fingers together into a semblance of propriety. "What is your will, Mother?"

"For whatever purpose he came, and from whatever he thinks to flee, I believe he asked the hospitality of a house of the Lord." She never turned her sharp face from Elisha, nor did her voice soften as she spoke, and the nun shrank inside her habit. "Our pantry is open to all."

"Yes, Mother." She hurried off to the kitchen behind the fireplace as the prioress studied Elisha's face and figure.

Fine wrinkles edged the woman's pale eyes. Elisha tried to relax, though he could not bring himself to sit again without invitation. He gently unfurled his awareness through the floor and into the air around them, beginning the process of attunement. From here out, he must open himself to magic, and Brigit would be able to find him. Time trickled through his hourglass.

"Are you a thief?"

"No, Mother," he answered automatically, then sighed. "Yes, Mother, in a manner of speaking."

"A manner of speaking." She unclasped her hands and tipped them outward. "This is the Lord's home as well as ours, sirrah, and He does not brook such dithering."

Elisha's scalp prickled, and he pushed back the tangle of his hair. "If you want to know did I steal the horse, then the answer is yes, plain and simple. Though its owner was dead."

For a time, they stared at one another. "Is anything about you plain or simple?"

Almost, Elisha wanted to smile. "Not anymore, Mother, but I was not always as you find me."

"You told Sister Sabetha that you are a surgeon. Truth?"

At that, Elisha gave a slight bow. "You will find me—whatever else you find—to be a good surgeon."

"Ah."

Elisha's intestines pinched, and he pressed a hand to his stomach, then dragged it away again. When he raised his head, the prioress met his gaze. "What would God find?"

"A sinner." The pain grew, and Elisha's knees trembled.

"Does He visit you now with pains, Sinner, that you recognize and repent of your sins?"

Elisha whispered hoarsely, "It was the hand of man, not God that dealt this blow."

"Are we not all hands of God, whether we so believe or no, enacting His great plan for us?"

Her words echoed those of the archbishop, proclaiming him king. Elisha winced. "I didn't come to debate God's means or motives, Mother, but dearly I would like to sit."

The eyebrows arched again, nearly invisible white bands of hair against her aged skin. "By all means, Sinner. Take what comfort the world has to offer. Still you shall find it wanting until you have allowed God both His means and His motives."

Pain fogged out her words. A sudden cold burst through him, moving swiftly, and Elisha jerked upright, gasping. A shadowy figure, translucent against the flames, whirled from the fireplace, slapping at her habit. The shade of one long-dead, she mouthed voiceless screams and fell through him. Elisha stumbled out of his chair and floundered a few feet away, out of the path of the restless spirit as invisible fire consumed her. She vanished, and he braced himself to see it all again.

"What have you come for, Sinner?" The prioress's voice boomed through the chamber. "You admit your thievery. What will you steal from us? From the Lord's own house?"

"Nothing!" he shouted, one arm pressed to his ear. "Nothing," he repeated as he sank to his knees. "Nothing that does not come of its own free will."

The prioress moved forward. "So, Sinner. You have come to take someone away from us." She stared down at him, hard and cold as the stone on which she stood. "Hospitality you may have, then you may go, and may God have mercy on your soul. No unrepentant thief shall lead anyone away from the house of God." She turned away and stalked from the room.

Elisha scrambled up, meaning to pursue her and find Alfleda.

A door clattered open to his left and someone shuffled through, accompanied by steam scented with oats and a touch of honey. The cook limped into view, her shoulders humped with age, her skin hanging loose in wrinkles around her mouth and down the thin arms revealed by her rolled-back sleeves. She carried a wooden tray, and her head swayed back and forth like a dog scenting the wind, revealing a long scar that parted her hair on one side and ran across her brow.

The gatekeeper, Sabetha, moved up beside her. "Here, Biddy." She put out her hands for the tray, but the old woman lurched past, one step, two, and slapped the tray down on the table with a triumphant grin, baring her few remaining teeth.

Biddy. A common enough name, but so near to the girl? Too much to be coincidence. Elisha turned from the door.

"Aha, aha!" Biddy bobbed her head and swiveled her wrinkled neck to face Elisha. A grayish-blue film covered both her eyes, but she sniffed. "So, barber, your meal. God bless."

Elisha blocked her path, allowing the shades to suffuse him with new strength. "What did you call me?"

"You smell too much of blood to be a regular surgeon, and Sabetha says you are no soldier. Barber it is, then." Her head bobbed, wisps of gray hair rising and falling with her like the flapping wings of lazy moths.

"Yes, Granny, I have been." The air around him hummed with an awareness like a web of sensing spread across the room. A magus, at least, but her presence felt warm, surprisingly sharp: not the mancer he expected.

"Aha," she said. "Mother is a strict ruler. She can be hard upon others. Especially when she finds weakness."

Her presence spread lightly in the room all around him, revealing how she cooked and served in this place — she must be attuned to it, and to its people.

"Came here for someone, did you? A wife, a sister?" Her wattled neck extended toward him. "A child?"

Elisha steeled himself. "I know where you were two years ago, Biddy, when they dunked you for a witch."

She gave a harsh sound at the back of her throat, and Sabetha said, "Have you come to finish the job then? Some sort of witch-hunter out to persecute a woman who's come to the Lord?"

"They found you bloody in the street, with a handful of her hair," Elisha said, focusing his awareness on her. "Did you lead the men who took her?" The tracery of her presence across the room intensified, a touch upon him from various directions. Biddy straightened as best she could, pushing back her sleeves, her sunken mouth working over something.

"Get up then and get out." Sabetha stomped closer to loom over him. "The Lord doesn't want such stories told of his own."

Biddy tapped the nun's arm and gave a shake of her head. "The Lord is my Shepherd," she intoned, then added, "As I am hers."

"Allie?" Sabetha demanded. "Is she what this is about?"

He breathed in the porridge steam, sweet and moist, mingled with the old woman's scents of ash and slight decay. She knew what he wanted, if not who he was. "I want to bring her back to her father."

Sister Sabetha let out a bark of disapproval. "Her father left her here. He wants no part of her, poor thing."

"What?" On Thomas's behalf, Elisha's anger rose. "No, Sister, she was taken from him, he still believes her dead."

"More likely, he wanted her dead," she snapped, setting her fists on her hips. "What, was she the mother's bastard, or his own? Or just too many mouths to feed, hmm?"

His stomach growled, and Biddy said, "Eat up, eat before it's cold and thick as stone. Like you are."

Elisha frowned at the blind old woman with her bobbing head. She was trying to tell him something, beyond the command. He carefully touched her arm. "Biddy, will you sit a while?"

Contact buzzed between them, and her deep chuckle resonated through his skin. "I will, Barber," she said. "I need my rest after a second round of breakfast, I do." She limped over to the chair he had abandoned and plopped down in it. "Take your rest, Sabetha."

"You don't command me, Biddy, and I'll not take comfort with the likes of him." She jerked her veil straight and poked at the wimple around her neck. "The father, indeed. You tell the father she's got a better family here, with us and with the Lord."

"That would break his heart, and he needs no more pain right now. I'm trying to be the one who brings him joy."

She snorted again, but she did not go, and Elisha sat across from Biddy as the old cook slid the tray over to him.

"Eat up, cold one. She's safe enough a little longer." Biddy's gapped grin looked oddly fierce. "Nobody goes near her without me knowing."

Elisha bent his head over the bowl and murmured, "Thank you, Lord, and thank these, your daughters, for this precious gift. Amen."

As he lifted the spoon, Sister Sabetha said, "There's no reverence in you, whatever you are."

He blew on the mouthful and ate it, drawing in warmth and comfort with the thick stuff. "Which was it for you, Sister? I'm wagering on the extra mouth to feed."

"The Lord provides for all of us here."

"You grew up around here?" he asked, between mouthfuls, then nodded to himself, catching Biddy's grin from across the table. "Perhaps your family had a place in the Forest before the Conqueror drove out those who'd lived there for centuries. That's a long time to bear a grudge."

"My folk never recovered," she said. "It was hard settling elsewhere and putting too many people in too few fields. My grandparents barely made it, my parents even less so." She plopped down on the end of a bench and set her hands upon her knees.

He took a swig from the mug of warm cider that shared the tray. "For us, it was the drought. We all up and went to the city, hoping for work. Same thing, only no trees."

"What about the girl, then? What's her story?" Sabetha leaned upon the table.

Elisha set down the spoon—the bowl was about empty anyhow. "You don't know?"

"Dropped here as an orphan, but it was pretty clear she wasn't, and the Mother taking such an interest, not to mention them soldiers checking in. I figured she's somebody's bastard, and the Mother getting good coin to keep her safe." She darted a glance toward Biddy. "This one came along a few months later, and we could see the girl was happy to have her."

Elisha considered whether these two were preparing to offer assistance, or simply gathering information for their prioress. "Her mother is dead, that much is true. Her father. . . he's a powerful man. Those people brought her here to keep her secret, to keep a hold over her father, if they needed it."

"I sent to the family, I did, when I found her." Biddy's hands curled as if she sought something to hold. "But her uncle says the danger's still too great, to keep an eye out,"—a snort of something like laughter—"and they'd send when it was safe. From her father, nothing." Her mouth snapped shut.

"And you're a queer sort of messenger," Sabetha said. "If he wants her now, why didn't he come himself?"

"Sister, nothing would give him more joy than to know she is alive and safe. He's suffered great losses in recent months, and this could well be his reason to go on living."

"You care a good deal for him," she observed.

"He is my dearest friend."

"How come your friends aren't here to support you?"

"They were—they are—deceived. Just as Alfleda was when someone said her father did not want her. He never had the chance."

Sabetha straightened and tipped her head toward the far door. "It's not us you need to convince any road. The prioress will never let you take her. If you'd've seen the little thing when they brought her here two years ago. It's a wonder she did not die of the grief."

Quietly, Elisha said, "Her father is dying of the same sickness. They may cure each other."

Sabetha pursed her lips, then pushed back and rose, making quickly for the colonnade with long, workman-like strides.

"There's a good girl," Biddy crooned. "I thought she'd come round." She reached out and pushed the tray to one side. "Give me your hand." When he hesitated, she waved her knobby fingers. "Give it here."

Elisha obeyed, laying his hand gently in hers, forcing his fingers to relax.

"Such cold! Why are you so cold?"

"Lady, I walk with death," he said through her skin.

"Tut, tut, Barber. A man who walks a cow pasture need not be covered in shit."

Elisha flinched, but her hand closed over his, her blind eyes rolling this way and that as she bobbed her head. The hot touch of her hand tingled all the way down his arm. Her presence loomed distant and impossibly grand, like a cliff seen from the ocean. *"You rang the bell that night, and you tried to take her back from them in the street, when they struck you down."*

The truth of it echoed within his flesh, with a stab of grief, then she flung his hand away and leaned back as the door opened again behind her.

Elisha massaged his hand, unsure if the interview had gone well. Sabetha entered, nudging before her a tall, thin girl whose golden hair blew around her face. She huddled in a plain shawl, her head down. Sabetha closed the door behind them, and the girl's hair settled softly over her shoulders. "Come, child." She took the girl's arm to lead her forward.

"Alfleda." Elisha rose, the hairs he carried were warm like a bird nestled against his flesh.

"We don't know that name, sir," the nun said, but the girl slowly raised her head.

The only portrait of her Elisha had seen must have been painted five years ago, when she was around three years old, and the only detail clear was the bright gleam of her blue eyes, so like her father's. Those eyes now met his, then slipped away again. She had round cheeks and full lips that brought to mind her mother, but the straight nose, the clear brow were all her father's. Elisha took a deep breath and came around the table.

Alfleda cringed, leaning against the nun who pressed an arm around her shoulders.

Stopping, Elisha lowered himself to his knees, his head now below hers by several inches. "Alfleda, I have come from your father's house to find you and bring you to him."

"He doesn't want me," she mumbled, turning her cheek against the nun's coarse robes. "He has a new wife and new babies."

"He had a wife, and he may have again." God forbid, Elisha added to himself. "But he has no other child, Alfleda, and he wants you more than anything."

She even frowned like Thomas, and Elisha's heart lurched. "Then why did he leave me here?"

"When your father came home, he thought you were dead." Elisha wet his lips. "Along with your mother."

The girl's eyes flared, and she clutched Sabetha's hand around herself. "When the bad men came."

"The people who came later told your father you were dead, too. He believes that they buried you."

"You should not speak of such things to a child," Sabetha said, stroking Alfleda's hair.

Elisha bit back the anger in his words and shook his head. "Sister, she was there. She needs to understand what happened to her that night, to her family."

"But Alaric wouldn't lie to Father, surely," Alfleda blurted. "He told me Father didn't want me, that I would remind him too much of Mother, and so I had to stay away."

Sister Sabetha startled, and Alfleda wriggled against her too-strong arm until the nun visibly relaxed. "Alaric?" she demanded. "Who's Alaric?"

"My father's brother," said Alfleda, annoyed.

Sabetha's eyelids fluttered, and the color vanished from her cheeks. "Your father's brother, Alaric. Dear Lord."

Elisha held up his hand. "Please, Sister, please say nothing more."

"But she's—but how?"

"Let the barber speak," Biddy said, pushing back her chair with a squeal across the stone floor. "I'd like to know the rest of this tale."

Rubbing his temples, Elisha considered how to make Alfleda understand that her uncle not only lied to his brother, but betrayed them to the bandits in the first place, and went on to accuse Thomas of trying to murder her grandfather. Which brought up the issue that it was Elisha himself who accomplished that task. Dear Lord, indeed.

"Who are you?" Alfleda asked. "Are you his barber? Is that what she meant?"

"It's more complicated than that. God knows I wish it were not so."

Her frown deepened, but she edged a little away from the nun's protective shadow. "Why do adults always say that it's complicated, when what you mean is that you're keeping secrets?"

With a faint smile, Elisha nodded. "Very well, then, Alfleda. Your father is very dear to me, and I am loyal to him, but we have not known each other long. I would have said he was my very best friend. Now, he thinks I have betrayed him, and, if he sees me, he might well kill me." He paused, his eyes stinging, but she blinked back at him.

"Did you betray him?"

"I did not."

Nodding, tucking her hair back behind her ear, she said, "Continue."

Elisha nearly laughed but caught himself, knowing laughter would only start the tears he could not afford. "When I learned you were alive, I thought, if I could bring you to him, he might believe me."

Gravely, she nodded once more. "You want him to be your friend again."

"Very much so." Elisha's chest constricted, and the air caught in his lungs.

Alfleda brought her thumb up to her mouth, and nibbled on the nail, though it was already as short as the rest. "It's a good story."

"Aye, it is, girl," said Biddy. "But do you believe it?"

"Do you?"

Biddy swayed her head this way, then that way. "More or less. I think it's true."

The bright blue eyes focused on Elisha, tracing over his face, down his figure, back up again to the face. She lowered the thumb from her teeth. "Right then. I'm going home."

"Halt!" someone shouted and a door banged open. Soldiers streamed through, swords drawn. "Halt in the name of the king!"

Chapter 27

❖

Inadvertently, Elisha obeyed. How could Thomas's men have found him so quickly? Unless they had searched through the darkness and knew which way to go. A dozen men pounded into the room, the prioress following on their heels, tall and foreboding as a storm-cloud. His glance flew from face to face, and he recognized no one from the lodge: these were not the king's men—not at all. "Sister, take the girl and run!"

"What?" she barked back.

"Is my father with you?" Alfleda ran a few steps nearer, but Elisha shot out his hand to stop her.

"These are not your father's men."

"How dare you, sir?" the captain shouted. "We come in the king's name and in his service! Give up the child and we shall not harm you."

Shaking his head, Elisha said, "No. If you are the king's men, you are disobeying the orders he gave this morning." Elisha had no gift of prophecy, but also had no doubt that neither the duke's men nor Thomas's would give him so much as a breath before they cut him down.

The captain started, one foot in the air. He cast a glance in the prioress's direction, his lips parted, but the surety slammed down again as they advanced. "We know our orders, sir, but there are ladies present."

"Do not shed blood in the halls of the Lord," the prioress intoned at his back. A few men split off, moving swiftly down the side aisle.

Beneath Elisha's hand, Alfleda's heart beat wildly. Her small, soft fingers gripped his arm.

He bent to her ear. "I have a horse in the stables. Tell Sabetha to take you. Go now. If I don't come soon, ride home. Look for your father and Countess Allyson Dunbury. Stop for no one—and don't go near your father's betrothed."

"Yes." She released him, backing away. In three steps, she darted for the door. The nun shrieked and sprang after her.

The soldiers ran, swords flashing. "Halt, I say!"

"Oh, my! Oh, Dear God!" wailed a disconsolate voice from behind. Biddy floundered out of her chair, arms waving, and blundered into the far table with such force that she knocked it askew, skidding the legs across the floor until its corner slammed the wall, blocking the exit. The lead soldier collided with it and slid beneath with a grunt.

"Heavens!" screeched the old cook. "What have I done? What's going on?"

Two men vaulted onto the table, only to have the old lady grab it again, as if trying to steady herself, and tip the lot of them onto the floor.

Elisha, too, ran for the door, but the fallen soldier tottered to his feet, one hand rubbing his bruises, the other still clenching his sword. Even winded, the man glared with a purpose and the sword gleamed steadily. Elisha drew his little knife and the man laughed.

Two soldiers fought their way past the table and burst out the door while the others advanced upon him.

"He's of no consequence!" roared the captain. "Get that girl!"

The others came up quick enough but only a few, and he realized the rest had gone back outside. They didn't care about him, only about Alfleda. Damn it!

"Please, sir, I'm blind," Biddy moaned, flinging herself upon the captain.

"Get off, Biddy, this is men's business," the prioress ordered, hiking up her habit in both hands as she hurried near. She caught hold of Biddy and dragged her away.

Elisha ducked a wild swing and staggered back a few paces flinging the tendrils of his awareness all around him. One more step, and he stood in the path of the shade. The spirit flared to life by the fire and ran, falling through him with a rush of cold. Elisha snatched at the power. He blasted the air with the wind of death.

The captain, nearly out the door now, stopped. On one heel, he pivoted and raised his head. His young face split into a grin, and he gave a slight nod of acknowledgement. "Have I the pleasure of meeting Elisha Barber? I heard what you did at the coal mine."

The other soldiers frowned from one to the other, and their captain held up his hand then pointed. "Let the others tend the child. And we shall handle him."

"We are to make sure she does not leave," one of them began.

"She won't get far." The captain gave a slight shake of his head. "I should have recognized him immediately. This is the man who killed the queen."

Elisha did not bother with denials as they came at him. By reflex, he gathered the howling wind of death and drew it near, letting it lie close to his skin like a coat of shadows.

Three of the men hesitated, one of them even staggering back a few steps, his eyes flashing white. The fourth snorted at his companions and plunged ahead.

Elisha raised his tiny knife and cried, "Halt, or die!" His voice echoed in the hall like the shattering of tree limbs in a storm.

The rearmost soldier turned to flee, but his captain eviscerated him with a stroke of his ready sword, his eyes never leaving Elisha's face.

The fourth soldier aimed a low swipe at Elisha's middle. Elisha twisted to one side and met steel with steel. He sent the blast of death from blade to blade through their slight contact. At the same time, he used that affinity to stretch his own blade into a sword worth the swinging.

The man's weapon shattered as the shock rang upon it and the hilt crumpled in his trembling hand. The hand still shook as the dark hair at his wrist turned gray. The soldier stumbled and whirled, his hand spotted with sudden age. He fled the room, stumbling over his dead companion, white hair falling from his scalp to drift upon the disturbed air.

The captain let him go and ceased his own advance. "Stay back, men, but stand your ground! See you now what evil opposes us!"

"Lord, have mercy!" beseeched the prioress. She fell to her knees, clutching her wooden crucifix in both hands. "Let this devil be shaken from the earth!"

Freed from her superior's grasp, Biddy gathered her skirts and swayed, mumbling, her milky eyes awash.

Across the room, the captain slid home his bloody blade into its scabbard. His expression remained blank and focused. One hand reached over his shoulder and emerged with a compact crossbow, the other hand drew a bolt from the quiver at his waist. He breathed once upon the silver tip, which blackened and sizzled in the air.

Elisha backed away, wrapping himself in cold, the other three soldiers approaching a step for each of his, though their swords wavered in their hands.

The captain lifted his crossbow and pulled.

Ducking the mantel, Elisha leapt into the heart of the fire, the light dazzling, the heat unable to reach him through the armor of Death. If the bolt struck the flames, he might turn it without harm.

He spun in the fire, struggled to maintain his footing, sent up a plume of sparks into the darkness of the chimney. Flames roared around him. A figure rose up before the fire: Biddy, cutting between him and the poisoned bolt.

With a thunk the bolt hit flesh. Elisha winced. The form before him slumped and tripped, laughing. The cold steel of death nearly left him as Biddy fell. He caught her with one arm, her wild gray hair already bursting to flames, her hands clawing at the shaft that stuck below her breast. Biddy's laughter sprayed blood that stung with cold. A second bolt thudded into her back.

A jolt of power flared between them. Soaring like the embers around them, Biddy and Elisha shot up the chimney. Elisha clung to her frail body, the stone channel scraping his shoulders and battering free his sword from numb fingers. Up they flew with the smoke and the outrage that crowded behind. The force of their flight, face-first through the blackness whipped tears from Elisha's eyes. Her blood seared him with a frigid certainty.

Elisha's nostrils burned with the gritty fumes, and he squeezed shut his eyes, expecting at any moment his already wounded lungs would burst. Biddy's presence, swelling with the desperate power of dying, enveloped him, overwhelming even death.

They struck the chill of open air and tumbled downward. Together, they slid down the roof and tumbled.

Biddy's presence sang in his ears and filled his aching throat. A brilliant light stunned his eyes, a radiance so strong, he forced them open to the wind rather than look upon it.

She turned him as they hit the air once more, and she broke his fall. Her fragile bones snapped as she struck the earth.

Elisha rolled and skidded, coming to a rest with his face in the dirt. He gulped for breath and heaved himself to his hands and knees, dragging himself up the slope to the woman who had saved him.

Biddy laughed no more, but her milky eyes stared skyward, and her lips yet smiled. Elisha lay a shaky hand upon her chest. The pain tried to devour him, each broken bone causing a twinge in his own flesh, his skull and spine flaring with the awful truth of injuries too great to heal.

Through the contact they shared, Biddy laughed again. The light reached up through him, blazing clear and banishing the shreds of darkness along with the pain. She felt it not.

"I could've stopped it, Biddy," he whispered.

"'Twas the devil's own dart—tipped with his poison," she said through his skin.

"I could—"

"The first," she sighed. *"But the second? The third?"*

"I don't know, Biddy, but why die for me?"

"Not for you, for her. And for her mother," she said. Her eyes blinked once and stared heavenward. That awesome spiral of power lifted away from her like a veil, leaving the old woman small, pale, and still. In the wake of that glow, something else settled in her limbs and in her touch. Not the cold and fear Elisha expected from Death, but something calm and endless as a sacred well, open to the sky, to the earth, to the souls parched and needy.

The cold wind of Death moaned so softly that its voice became an air of mourning and a hymn to peace. The last petals of Biddy's presence fell away, eddying around him with a tingling warmth that soothed his lungs like the first flowers of springtime. Elisha took a deep breath and drank in serenity.

Chapter 28

❖

Wiping the soot and tears from his face, Elisha stood. The wonder that cloaked him shimmered into the world as if he projected Biddy's dying radiance. Entranced, he smiled. He must hurry, he knew, but he felt, too, that there would be time. Three nuns stood with laundry baskets at their feet, and one slowly crossed herself, glancing at the rooftop, then back at him. The second, younger sister sprang forward, her cry of dismay breaking Elisha's silence as she flung herself down at Biddy's side.

Strength surged through Elisha's legs, driving him past a few other outbuildings on his way to the stables. The strength of Biddy's magic stayed with him, buoying him up. A witch could work miracles in that dying moment—like Rowena transforming to an angel, or Martin's quenching the fire that threatened London. The dirt and the pain scaled away with every step, leaving the moment of their flight an exhilarating journey, a daring leap through darkness and back to the light. Elisha vaulted a trough and skidded to a halt in the stable yard.

The sight that met him sapped his borrowed strength and froze the air in his lungs: Five soldiers crowded the stable, one of them clutching Alfleda to his chest as they watched the scene before them. Sister Sabetha faced off in the entrance against a sixth man, her face and fists already bloody, her nostrils flared with her fury. "Give over," she croaked. "Would you beat a nun, a bride of Christ?"

"I already am, woman, and you can't win back what we've taken." He chuckled and tipped his head toward the child. "She's a pretty one, though—mayhap I'll take some more, eh?"

The nun snorted and sprang forward to the brawl. Off to one side, holding Elisha's horse by its reins, stood the novice who had greeted him upon his arrival. His position behind the wall afforded a narrow view of his horse and the farthest soldiers. He rested his head against the wood and tried to gather his scattered wits. The soldiers might toy with Sabetha until their captain arrived—shortly, no doubt. Elisha had a few moments but no more. These men knew nothing about him save that he was their enemy. They did not know what he could do, but neither could he do it without contact, nor while one of them held Alfleda. Damnation. Then he thought of Biddy in the dining hall, knocking down soldiers with an old woman's guile.

Elisha sank to the ground, spreading his awareness through the soil, touching the feet of the men, finding the stamping hooves of the plow horses. He wriggled his left hand into the earth. Concentrating his awareness in his fingertips, he took a moment to understand the seeds hidden there, the richness of the manure mingled with rotting straw to warm the new growth. Sinking deep into this knowledge, Elisha listened to the catcalls of the soldiers and the scuffle beyond the wall.

"Lord be with me!" cried Sabetha, only to be caught by a fierce blow to her kidney. She tumbled, and Elisha felt her fall, the dirt cushioning her as she rolled.

Elisha reached to the secret locks of hair he carried.

Alfleda's hair tingled with hope and good tidings, while Thomas's sizzled with fear and anger. Elisha twined their strength with his own and sent the power gently rolling, a wave beneath the earth.

The stable shuddered, dust shifting down from the thatch. The horses snorted and stamped as the wave burst up in a ripple of soil. Men cursed and tripped. Elisha wriggled his fingers, and they fell, smashing into each other, lurching against the walls.

"Put that away, you'll hurt someone!"

"Bloody Hell, ye sodding churl, I told you—"

"Christ, what's happening?"

"Pray!" thundered the triumphant voice of Sister Sabetha. "Pray, you sorry souls, for the Lord despises the very earth you tread!"

Transferring the rumble to his own soles, Elisha slipped free his hand, letting the dirt cling, and walked. Every footfall sent a current through the groaning earth. He rounded the corner, the only man still standing, smiling at the novice who hung upon his horse's neck, wide-eyed.

The man holding Alfleda kept his grip despite the tossing earth that pitched him to and fro. Alfleda kicked at his legs and jabbed with her skinny elbows, howling.

Imagining that he might nudge aside the dirt that supported her captor, Elisha focused his power, channeling more, creating a hole.

With a muffled cry, the man slumped backward. His hands flailed in the air and Elisha sprang forward—his footing sure—and snatched Alfleda from the ground.

She shrieked at first, her golden hair flying as she kicked, then she tipped back her head and saw his face.

"Peace," Elisha murmured. He lifted her to his hip, holding her close as he balanced.

Reaching out his free hand, Elisha drew Sabetha back to her feet, his touch giving her the steady anchor she needed, although her mouth set into a hard line as she stared at him. Together, they crossed the pitching tide of soil.

"Sorry," Elisha told the novice.

She swung herself down from his horse, inching back from him until she stood against the shaking structure, rising and falling with the heaving earth. Elisha's stomach pitched uncomfortably just watching it. Turning his back, he slipped Alfleda up to the wide withers and started to mount behind her when a hand grabbed his elbow.

"You'll not be rid of me," Sabetha said, her fingers twitching to emphasize the point.

"I've no time, and only one horse."

"I'll run. I'll fall behind, but you'll not take her off without me, or, so help me whoever you are, I and all the Sisters of Mercy will beg torments upon your soul."

Scrambling onto the horse, Elisha called, "Then run!" He kicked the horse into motion, urging it down the slope among the graves, the girl clinging with both hands to the harness strap.

The ground gave a final tumult and lay still as scattered soldiers picked themselves up. To the left, by the convent wall, the captain strode toward them. Elisha cut low, aiming for the road and freedom. Alfleda's hair lashed at his face and the scrapes of his travel up the chimney, forgotten in the rush of battle, suddenly throbbed. His horse was sturdy and sound, but it was not swift. He caught a glimpse of the soldiers' mounts, tended by a few other nuns. "Run!" he shouted to the horses, plunging his own steed through their midst. The nuns sprang out of the way, their dark habits slapping the breeze.

The soldiers' horses kicked and whinnied, and were soon left behind. If he kept to the road, Elisha might outpace his pursuers, but the king's men would be searching along the road ahead. Some would be mounted, and they hunted to kill. The idea of turning off onto a forest track held little hope, for he did not know the landscape. Only Alfleda's hair had led him here. Which meant that Thomas's hair could lead him home. Elisha grinned into the breeze and broke to the left, through a copse of birches, then into a stream, chill droplets splashing to his knees.

Perched narrowly before him, Alfleda squealed. At first, he thought her injured, then recognized the thrill that sang through her. She clung to the horse's mane, her posture erect, staring ahead into what must seem a grand adventure. Despite the cold that gripped his chest, he felt lighter to share in her delight.

An arrow whistled by them, and he cut to the edge of the road, then heard a scream and a whinny. He glanced back to see a tumbled body at the wayside, and a nun galloping madly toward them, eyes wide.

"I ran down the archer, on his own bloody horse." Sister Sabetha blew out a cloud from her nostrils. "I saw you come bursting from the chimney." She glanced over at him as she came alongside. "Are ye the devil's spawn?"

"I was born a few miles from London," Elisha told her. "My parents were farmers."

"Means nothing," she sniffed, and he felt the pulse of Alfleda's anger rising to his defense.

Glancing up at him, her expression mingling concern and pity and strength, she looked so like Thomas that Elisha's eyes stung with tears. "You know that I am a witch."

She nodded gravely, golden hair sliding across her slim shoulders.

"Why trust me? Why come with me?"

"You wouldn't lie to me, and you will not hurt me."

"No," he said, "I would not."

"Trust a liar to give such an answer," Sabetha pointed out. "Biddy believed you, and she died for it."

Alfleda deserved the truth. "It's possible you will, too, Your Highness," Elisha said to her. "These men won't be the last who'll come for us. No place that you are with me will be safe."

Again, she nodded once. "Those men, they didn't know you, did they?"

"Not until I let them know," he said, frowning over the change in topic.

"So." She smiled, just a little. "Mother Superior summoned them for me. To kill me, I think." Elisha made no reply, but she filled the silence with her smile and went on, "If you had not been there, I would be dead, wouldn't I?"

Hoarsely, he answered, "I think they wanted to take you to see someone." Brigit. Who would kill her, and, if she'd given in to the mancers' ways, likely wear her skin for a trophy, revealing it to her father at the most opportune moment to shatter the king. The tide of hatred that stole over Elisha just then turned his stomach to bile. "If it remains in my power to save you, Alfleda, I swear I will not fail you, now or ever."

"I know. Come along, Sister." She slipped the reins from his numb fingers.

For now, at least, he was in good hands. He let himself drowse as they rode, absently drawing up the shades of the dead to cover their ride. He could not conceal Sabetha and her stolen mount, but neither would anyone be looking for her, certainly not with magic.

Over the next few days, they followed an arcing path around the New Forest, hoping to dodge the searchers there and still reach London in time to stop the wedding. But Elisha felt the persistent ache in his stomach, the pain of his ill-healed wound, overlaid with the sense of Brigit's seeking. He wrapped himself more tightly in death, pushing her away, refusing the connection with his own child that formed the link between them, and he groaned.

"Do you suffer the torments of the damned?" Alfleda whispered. "Because you are a witch?"

"It feels that way."

"Then I will pray for you. I know how to pray in Latin, so that Holy Mary will be sure to listen."

Alfleda murmured, her touch translating her hesitant words *". . . yea though I walk through the valley of the shadow of death, I shall fear no evil, for thou art with me."*

The valley of the shadow of death. He thought of that terrible void through which the mancers travelled, the one that carried him to their stronghold to rescue Thomas. Perhaps in that place, the dying left behind their fear and pain and sorrow. He did not know if he believed in Heaven, but Biddy's death had shown him another way of dying, and reminded him of Martin's final, floating laughter. Thomas strayed too long in that valley, living too deep among the shadows. It was high time that the king came home.

Chapter 29

─────────◆─────────

Tents and caravans spread out around London, colorful against a steely sky with their snapping banners and the liveried servants scurrying to and fro. Elisha sold the horses to a dealer on the outskirts of town and learned the wedding would be that afternoon, at Nones. It didn't leave them much time. The three went ahead on foot, picking their way among market stalls and crowds of visitors eager for a glimpse of the royal couple. Guardsmen, too, roamed the streets, craning their necks and peering down the makeshift alleyways. Elisha purchased a hat of nondescript wool and a cloak for Sabetha, who grudgingly concealed her nun's habit. He slouched into his rough cloak and kept hold of Alfleda's hand. He looked gaunt and ragged enough that his casual acquaintances would pass him by, but there were too many people who had seen him buried—or crowned. He unfurled his awareness like a net around them, reaching out three or four people beyond. All too often, he found the echoes of his own presence, as if the crowd anticipated his arrival. Certainly the guardsmen did, the way they stared at every man of his general height and build. Elisha projected poverty, stupidity. He buried deep his knowledge of death, and felt it cooling near his heart.

Alfleda gazed around herself in wonder, stumbling occasionally as she gawked at a juggler or a booth full of sweets.

"Watch your feet, girl, we can't afford an accident today," Sister Sabetha muttered.

"I'm sorry, I know," Alfleda whispered, instantly lowering her eyes, only to have them drift slowly back up again.

Elisha wished that he could share her excitement. He could still send Sabetha to bring the girl to the tower and introduce her. They might be safer without him, and he could quietly retire to some distant croft. After all, Brigit might be satisfied with being queen. Surely she would serve the magi better than they had been served before, and she might wreak no further vengeance on the king than to know she had snared him, along with his throne. But the mancers would not have bargained with her unless she offered something in exchange, and he did not yet know what that might be.

Then his out-spread senses caught the chill of a mancer walking by. He turned his trio at an angle, forcing himself to move slow. A few streets on, to the left, another well of cold emanated from a scribe's table, and there ahead were two women wreathed in that subtle stench he knew too well. Alfleda pulled nearer to him as they made a quick change of direction and stopped by the heat of a smithy as the mancers passed by.

With a gentle tug on his hand, she said, "What's wrong?"

"There are people searching for me. For you, too, if they know you're here."

"How d'ye know that, then? More sorcery?" Sabetha glowered into the street.

"I wish you'd not say such things aloud. These people are very sensitive. If they brush against you, they can feel your thoughts; if they just touch you, they can kill you."

"And you know who they are?" She raised an eyebrow at him.

"Some, I can feel. But if I'm hidden from them, chances are some of them are hidden from me." The smithy fire warmed his side but not enough to cover the new chill as another mancer passed by. How many were there? How many could there possibly be?

"Have ye got another plan, then?"

Elisha tipped back his hat to study her face. "I could send her on with you, straight to the Earl's. I'm not even sure if he'll help me, but a nun and a child—"

"I don't want to let you go," Alfleda said, pressing close to him.

Gathering Alfleda into his arms, her face now pressed against his shoulder, Elisha led them back into the streets until the great gate loomed up before them, nobles streaming through on horseback and in carriages, on their way to the cathedral. "Do you remember the turns I described?"

Sabetha nodded again. "I've got 'em. Trust me, eh?" Removing her cloak, she plunged through the crowd toward the gates, easily ducking the gazes of the dozen soldiers standing at the ready.

"Godspeed," Elisha wished her, then turned resolutely from the gate, heading for the public house where they would meet again. He dodged a wagon and stepped off the road.

"Daughter sick, is she?"

Elisha jerked and turned as one of the harmless presences around him advanced upon them. Alfleda whimpered as his arms tightened. "What do you want?" Elisha snapped, then cursed himself and forced a smile. "Sorry, yes."

"Mmm." The fellow nodded, and lifted something from a tray he carried by a strap over his shoulders. "Here, then, you'll be wanting one of these."

"I don't think so, thanks," Elisha said, but the girl lifted her head and shook back her hair.

"What's that?" she asked, her voice still small.

Holding aloft his offering, the vendor grinned his snaggle-teeth at her, then at her "father" and said, "These're the finest you'll get, sir, and no mistaking. Carved them myself, I did, not those flimsy castings that won't ward off a sniffle."

Alfleda held out her palm and the vendor dropped the charm into it. Crudely carved of bone, the thing was pointed at one end, jagged at the other, with a pair of small holes bored out in between and another at the jagged end, obviously a loop for hanging. Elisha realized he was seeing it upside down, and the shapes became suddenly familiar: a pair of shears surmounted by a crown.

"'Tis the badge of Saint Elisha," the vendor said proudly. "Proof against wounds and sickness, blessed by the earth of his martyrdom."

"Elisha's not a saint, he's a prophet," Alfleda said, pushing it back at him.

"Convent school." Elisha forced a smile. "We've got to go."

The vendor thrust out his charm. "No, sir, you must've heard the stories—Saint Barber, some call him. He was one of us, he was buried to fight the Devil at the crossroads, then risen again to take the throne. You've heard that much, at least."

Alfleda's hair swished against his face as she tipped her head back to look at him, blue eyes wide.

"I'm sorry. We have to go." Elisha gathered her closer and started to push past, his heart pounding. A familiar touch trembled along the edge of his awareness, and Elisha turned sharply away, but the vendor pounced once more in his path.

"Come on, then, sir! For your daughter! Here, wait,

I've got a witness right here." He waved his arm to the side. "Adam, come over here and tell your tale."

A young man clad in a penitent's brown robes emerged from the crowd, carrying a staff covered over with charms for the barber, some carved, some cast, some beaten of what might be gold. A shock of brown hair covered his face, and he impatiently shoved it aside. "You've not heard of Saint Barber, then?" His eyes met Elisha's and his mouth dropped open.

Elisha froze, the youth's familiar presence shocking him into immobility. Though he did not recognize the name, he knew that face. The last time he saw it, tears and blood and premature aging marked the cheeks before he healed the lad, before a mancer set Elisha on the throne.

"No, they don't know the miracles. Tell 'em yours, go on." The vendor prodded the young man, grinning and wiggling his eyebrows.

Adam crossed himself and started to sink to his knees. He brushed away the other man's beseeching hand. "Don't you know who this is? Did you not see him when we held the city, or the day that he was buried for our sake?"

Snatching at him too late, Elisha nearly overbalanced and Alfleda gripped tighter. "Get up, please—for my sake, Adam, get up."

"But we thought you were taken! Bodily! To heaven! When the archbishop died, weren't you—?"

"Shut up," Elisha hissed. He lurched away, crashing into a woman who'd stopped to gawk.

"No, wait, please, your holiness!" Adam's hands flailed in the air.

Over the heads of their little audience, Elisha saw three guardsmen moving fast. He clutched Alfleda against him and burst free, running like a madman. To the right, a blast of cold nearly knocked him down. Alfleda shrieked. Elisha cut through the crowd, death howling in his skull. He spied an opening in the booths across the road and made for it, plunging into the gloom.

At the same time, he threw off his projection and let death fill him up and spill over him, wrapping himself and the child he carried. As he had done on that long, terrible ride to the lodge, Elisha sucked down death and walked in the shadows. Ghosts rose up before him, enacting their awful, silent battles. Elisha burst through them, still running, praying the mancers could not see him.

"We're dead, we're dead, we're dead," he chanted as the fear in Alfleda's tears stung his throat.

The two women he'd noticed earlier stood before them, solid and smiling, spirits hovered at their backs, the strange doubling of the dead—their personal hauntings. One of them pointed.

Elisha spun away and ran down the back alley to a second row of booths more shaky than the first. Shouts rang out behind him, but the soldiers worried him less than the mancers, their murders touching him now on all sides as they converged.

Dodging a guard, turning again, Elisha ran along another alley, one that reeked of raw meat and slaughter. It should have sickened him, but the power of the place streamed through his open awareness.

Elisha stopped short and ducked under a row of sausages along the back of a stall. Holding his breath, he edged in among the swinging corpses of ducks and chickens, trying to shield Alfleda from the worst of the gore. She never raised her head, but trembled against him, and her prayers seeped through his skin.

Elisha slipped behind the outspread ribcage of a massive hog and pressed his back to the wall. Barely daring to breathe, he tucked his chin over Alfleda's head, staring down the narrow gap between the dangling animals and the rough wood.

Pale light filtered through on the street, cut by shadows as people walked by. In the street outside, a shady figure tumbled from a window only to vanish and tumble again a moment later. A pair of soldiers ran through the shade, spears waving. Four others followed more slowly, glancing into stalls and shouting questions.

The butcher emerged from someplace, wiping his hands, talking over his shoulder. "I've seen nobody, but I'm workin' at the back—they might'a gone by."

"Keep your eyes out."

"On butcher's row, m'lord? We've got plenty of eyes out!" he called after them, earning a groan from the guard, but a few chuckles from the other butchers.

The soldiers moved on, and the shopkeepers watched them go. A tall man stalked down from the other direction, his head swinging side to side, his nose wrinkled. Elisha felt the probing touch and repeated his silent chant, "We're dead, we're dead." His heart beat so loudly in his own ears, and Alfleda felt so hot against him, that he nearly collapsed in relief when the man stalked onward.

The two women came up from their way, one of them taking the tall man's arm then letting him go. The group of mancers exchanged the nod of strangers who suddenly recognize each other. Elisha dared not reach out his senses, even to know what they might say. Any change, he felt sure, would give him away.

One of the women, a fair, well-dressed lady, approached the shop, craning her neck this way and that, as if inspecting the wares.

"Help ye, m'lady?" the butcher offered.

"No, sorry." But she stared a moment longer into the darkness. Elisha shut his eyes and let his own prayers merge with Alfleda's. A hand of cold riffled through the meat. For a moment, the squealing of pigs and the honk of geese filled the air as if their spirits responded to the call.

"Here, what're ye doing?" The butcher sprang out into the street, then turned a slow circle, for the women and their compatriot had vanished.

After a long while, Elisha lowered some of his defenses, bit by bit. The shades around him faded into nothing, and he breathed deeply, despite the rancid air, until his lungs no longer burned and his heartbeat drew back from a gallop. He tipped his head this way and that, easing the ache in his neck, and realized how heavily the girl weighed in his arms.

"Am I dead?" Alfleda whispered.

"No, love, I don't think so."

Cautiously, she raised her head and blinked up at him, then her gaze shifted to the bulky hanging pig that concealed them. "I don't know that I shall ever eat pork again."

Elisha chuckled, very softly. "We owe much to that pig."

"Then I hope my father buys it and eats it and it's the finest roast he's ever had."

"Shh," he urged her, but he caught her tiny smile, and he did not silence her too sharply. Keeping his shoulders against the wall, he edged out again, glancing both ways and extending his creeping senses before they finally emerged into the street.

"Hello? Can I help you?" Disturbed by some stealthy noise, the butcher came up and frowned out at them.

Elisha grinned at him, feeling giddy, hoping the feeling would fade quickly and not consume him with idiocy. "You have some fine pork, there, sir."

"Only the best." He narrowed his eyes, looking Elisha up and down. "Ye look more like a vendor than a buyer."

Starting to chuckle, Elisha broke off gasping as the

pain throbbed at his middle, his poorly-healed wound reminding him he had taken no rest.

Alfleda wriggled down out of his arms. "Are you well?"

He leaned his shoulder against the wall and waited for the pain to pass, light-headed with pain.

The butcher stepped back quickly. "Take your sickness away and be gone with you!" He flapped his hands at them. "Be gone, or I'll call the guard."

Elisha breathed a prayer of thanks for the cleaner air beyond, as they left the butchers' row and made slow progress toward the inn where Sabetha would be expecting them. He had little notion how much time had passed since she left them, for time passed strangely in the kingdom of the dead. Then, in the church of St. Bartholomew, a bell began to ring. Others joined it, all across the city, tolling out the hour.

As the pain subsided, Elisha straightened and increased their pace. An hour more, and Thomas would be married. Regardless of the king's reasons, or the results of this madness, Elisha must be there. He stretched his senses, altering direction as soon as he felt the hint of death. Moving as quickly as caution allowed, they picked their way to the riverside and the battered inn frequented more often by sailors than by townsfolk.

Alfleda stopped abruptly, and Elisha stumbled with her as she blinked at the place. "Sister Sabetha won't like this at all."

"No," he said, "I don't guess that she will."

"She doesn't," the nun's voice announced as she came up from the opposite side. "I gave the message and came as quick as I could."

"Will the earl come, do you think?" Alfleda asked, still eyeing the sway-roofed structure before them.

"Not if he knows this place," Sabetha grumbled,

hitching her thumb in the direction of the inn. "Only the cross's kept me alive this long."

Elisha admitted that, even by daylight, the place looked desolate and angry. He learned of it himself only because a neighbor tended to fight over dice there, and Elisha and his brother had to fetch the man home to his angry wife. "Come on." Elisha led the way, Alfleda hanging back with the nun, and they ducked under the grimy leather flap into the main room.

"Women," sneered one of the patrons, and the others laughed as they walked inside. Elisha's head brushed the low beams of the sagging ceiling. A round fire pit lit the center of the room, revealing a half-dozen men slumped on benches, with their bowls or mugs, dropping the bones of their luncheon onto the dirt floor where a skinny dog snapped them up. A pair of dimly seen doors led out on the opposite wall, one tucked by a steep flight of stairs.

"The private room," Elisha demanded of a balding man toting a tray of mugs.

"'Aven't got one," the other spat. Aside from his nasty expression, the innkeeper looked somehow familiar.

Frowning, trying to place him, Elisha produced a silver coin and the sketchy eyebrows quivered, then the man transferred the mugs to his other hand and snatched the coin. "To the right." He glanced over the three of them. "Ale?"

"Wine," said Elisha. "And I'm expecting guests."

"Oh, aye, guests, is it?" The innkeeper grinned and slid the coin into his apron. "No more nuns, I hope—they give the place a bad name."

Elisha laughed and remembered that he had once treated the man's infected foot after he stepped on a broken mug. "How's the foot, Gervais?"

"No complaints." The innkeeper started to pass them, then frowned over his shoulder. "Who're—" He broke off and gave a grin that seemed a little warmer. "Wine," he said. "I'll fetch it."

"Yer daughter c'n stay wiv us, we'll entertain 'er!" someone called out, and the rest laughed as Alfleda cringed against the nun.

"Shut yer lip, or it's me you'll deal with," Sister Sabetha announced, balling her fist. "And God's on my side, I warrant."

They laughed again but let the three slip by into the low door on the right. A thin boy appeared behind them, carrying a candle to light the windowless room. Private indeed, Elisha thought, but no other way out. If the earl chose to turn against him, he was trapped here, the presence of Alfleda and Sabetha making him loath to apply his power again. A round table took up the center of the sloping room, with a few benches pushed against the wall. Wind off the river cut through the chinks in the walls, and the boy stooped to light a brazier. Beyond the interior wall, patrons murmured and someone rose from a creaky bench. "Sabetha, Sister," Elisha began, but the nun sighed and bobbed her head.

"Yes, I'll keep an eye out. I won't like it, though."

"I owe you an enormous debt already," Elisha told her.

She snorted. "Aye, well, don't die before ye repay me, right?"

"Right."

After patting Alfleda's shoulder, the nun bustled out through the door. "Right," she called out. "No teasing now, ye know I'm married."

As the flap slipped back in place, Alfleda ran the short distance between them and flung herself into Elisha's arms. He let the energy carry him to thump down onto a bench, resting his back against the wall as he held her. "Such a brave girl," he murmured over her golden head.

"No, I'm not," she sobbed against him, "I'm terrified."

"Courage isn't having no fear, it's what we can do in spite of it." Holding the princess, Elisha wished for a moment that he had someone to comfort him. She did her best, but she was only a child—and too grown-up already. Would anyone hold him so, and touch his hair, and make him believe things would be all right?

"My lord, I don't think we should—"

"Bosh and nonsense, this is the place," pronounced a loud voice from the main chamber. "And here's the nun herself. How fare you, Sister?"

"Well, m'lord. Better, once I'm free of these fools."

The Earl of Blackmere laughed, his voice still booming. "No fear, Sister, my man'll keep you company."

"I ought to come with you, my lord."

"Jeshua, the man I'm meeting is rather shy. I'd rather you stay here. If he kills me, I'll shout."

"My lord," the man answered, but said no more, his warning tone enough to carry the message.

A hand decked with rings swept aside the curtain and the earl admitted himself, a glittering presence of gold brocade under a capelet of satin and velvet, dyed crimson. In this setting, the earl gleamed like a diamond in a pig's trough. He stood about Elisha's height, ducking just a little to step inside. He let the curtain fall and folded his arms, the stiff fabric of his sleeves crinkling. False sleeves to match the capelet dangled from his elbows nearly to his knees, clad in parti-colored hose with light shoes unsuitable for anything but dancing. The outfit looked so preposterous that Elisha nearly laughed, but he recognized his fear for what it was.

Bowing his head over Alfleda's hunched form, Elisha said, "Forgive me not rising to offer a proper bow, my lord."

"It is you." The earl took a step nearer, the single candle revealing his astonishment. "I've thought you dead a hundred times, Elisha Barber, and that only since I was set to watch over you the night of your execution." He shook his head, curls of sandy hair brushing his shoulders.

"A thousand men have wished me dead, that many times and more. And I am still grateful for your care that night, my lord." His throat felt dry as he searched for words to ask for what he needed.

The earl gave a flicker of his fingers. "Never mind about the title. Either you and I are traitors together, or I'm about to make myself a hero to all your thousand enemies."

Elisha met his gaze. "I would not have you called traitor for my sake."

"Perhaps not for yours," the earl said, "but for hers?" He walked around the table and squatted down before Elisha, not quite placing his immaculate knee in the dirt of the floor though his capelet brushed against it. "Is this the king's daughter?"

Slowly, Alfleda turned from Elisha's chest and faced the earl. She sat straight, shifting the hair back behind her ears with a graceful gesture. "Yes, my lord. I am Alfleda, the daughter of Thomas."

He blinked at her, then smiled and bowed his head. "Your Highness, I believe that you are. I'm Phillip, Earl of Blackmere. You were at my house, the Yuletide before you . . . went away. Do you remember?"

Alfleda's face brightened, and she nodded eagerly. "I do, my lord! You have simply trunks and trunks of fabric. I made your lady furious by dressing up in them and playing at queen."

"That's right." He chuckled. "But you weren't to know she was furious. She was afraid to shout at the prince's daughter."

"I'm not stupid," Alfleda pointed out, then added, "my lord."

"On the contrary, Highness, I am your servant." The

earl met Elisha's gaze once more and put out his hand, clasping Elisha's in both of his own. "I've brought clothing, for both of you, but first thing you'll need is a haircut." Grinning almost ear to ear, he shouted, "Jeshua, I've a man here who needs a barber!" Leaning closer, gripping Elisha's shoulder, he whispered, "And a land as much in need of this one."

Elisha grinned like a fool. "But you didn't ask about Rosalynn, or the archbishop, or—"

The earl tapped his shoulder, his face turning serious. "You saved my life at Dunbury Ford, and I'll owe that debt to the end of my days; then you defended my foul shot on our hunting trip as well. As for the rest, I say, would the king's enemy bring up his daughter, risk his own life, and ask no ransom nor prize?"

"But you don't know—"

"What do I need to know, Elisha?" He shook his head. "What I know is this, that King Thomas should fall on his knees and thank the lord he has such a friend." He rose and turned away from Elisha's gratitude. "Hurry up, man," he bawled, "we're off to a wedding!"

Chapter 30

❖

Elisha stared down at the richly embroidered doublet Phillip's manservant was lacing up for him. Apparently Sister Sabetha had told the earl how thin Elisha was, for the earl had chosen his older clothes from leaner times. Despite his curiosity, Elisha was rather glad not to see how he looked, his hair trimmed, his nascent beard carved into a point; very stylish over the Channel, or so the earl assured him. He felt ridiculous.

Alfleda, on the other hand, clad in one of the earl's younger daughter's gowns, looked every inch the princess. She held herself taller, chin up, shoulders back. Elisha imagined a stern tutor instructing her on deportment. In a concession to disguise, a maid tucked Alfleda's long golden hair into a beaded hairnet, concealing its color and lending her a slightly older appearance. She stood solemn and expectant, re-adjusting to the idea of someone else's dressing her.

"What a vision you both are," the earl declared, taking a critical look. "Excellent, and let's be off." He clapped his hands, and the two servants drew back, bowing.

Slipping on a capelet of his own, Elisha nodded, then adjusted the wide cap that further disguised him. "Thank you, for all of this. I can't promise in what condition I'll return it."

"Just see that you're not buried in it."

Elisha managed a smile, and Alfleda snuck her hand into his as they followed the earl out. He flipped another coin to the innkeeper, who gaped at them as they passed by.

Sister Sabetha joined them, her eyebrows rising as she examined their new clothes. "Cor, such finery! Try not to look so ill about it, Barber."

"I'll try. See that you take care of yourself. We may not meet again after this."

"Oh, no, don't try that with me." She set her fists upon her ample hips. "You'll find me at Saint Bartholomew's, waiting to hear the word. And you—" She lifted Alfleda's chin with her finger. "You go with God, y'hear me?"

"I will, Sister," the child assured her, wrapping the nun in a one-armed embrace.

A large carriage waited outside, matched grey horses snorting into the light drizzle. Elisha stopped, but the earl put an arm about his shoulders and gestured toward the carriage.

"We're late already, Elisha. Late enough to attract the attention of the royal guard in any event." He shrugged. "And they will be expecting that you should sneak in by some other means, not march boldly up the front steps. No, this is the way. Further, I suggest that the princess stay with my wife until we are seated; try not to look as if you belong together."

They helped Alfleda into the carriage, reintroduced her to the earl's lovely wife, then followed her inside. A servant shut them in.

"You know, my lord, I've always thought of you as . . ." Elisha hesitated, unsure how to say it.

"You have expected less of me?" The earl nodded, smiling smugly. "Most do. They imagine, from the attention that I pay to my clothing, that I have little to spare for more pressing matters. My dear man, you have lived in this world, you know what the place is like—would you not rather immerse yourself in beauty and ignore the rest?"

"I would," Elisha agreed, his eyes coming to rest on the princess, self-possessed and watchful as her father. His own child grew in Brigit's womb, prisoner to its mother's ambition. "Perhaps, if I live so long, I will."

The earl pursed his lips, drumming his fingers on the seat for a moment, then leaned forward to Elisha on the opposite bench. "There's a Flemish vessel at anchor now, which leaves with the evening tide. You need not live here in fear, Elisha. I can arrange your passage."

As the carriage lumbered into motion, gathering speed for the short ride, Elisha leaned back against the cushions and blew out a breath. Alfleda watched him from the corner of her eye. She was brave, a child worthy of her father, and Thomas would look after her with the full strength of his love and his loyalty. "I wish I could sail away and act as if I have no more part in the affairs of kings."

The earl briefly bowed his head. "That's what I knew you'd say." He touched Elisha's knee, drawing back his gaze to the serious dark eyes. "After today, my place in the court will be as nothing; we're both of us wise enough to know that. I can hardly claim ignorance of your alleged crimes. I expect we'll retire back to Blackmere and hope to escape with our lives, if not our freedom. The king is not unjust, but he is despairing, and Randall's gone a bit mad. It's him I fear, more than the other."

Elisha's belly clenched, and he said, "I can only hope that what we do today will start Thomas on his way to healing. And may support my own cause with the duke. I'll do what I can to defend you."

With a quiet chuckle, the earl, too, leaned back, folding

his hands behind his head. "I am not sure that your defense will be of much use, but I thank you for it."

"God, and my father, will bless you, sir," Alfleda said.

The carriage rumbled to a halt, and its four occupants sat a long moment, not looking at each other, then a servant knocked, and the door opened wide, the man offering up his arm.

"God bless us all," the earl murmured, and his wife crossed herself. Then, with a tip of her head in Elisha's direction, she stepped from the carriage down to the carpet, holding out her hand.

"Come, child, we're late as it is."

"Yes'm." Alfleda gathered her skirts and crossed between the seats, her eyes round as she blinked up at Elisha. Saying nothing, she stepped out into the feeble light of day.

The earl followed, and Elisha took a deep breath, stilling his fears, spreading his senses, reaching for attunement. Dear God. The place pulsed with the malevolent cold of the mancers and their victims. Distant and warm, he sensed the spirit of hurt and strength that was Thomas, and the lock of hair he carried hummed against him. "Courage," he murmured and stepped down from the carriage.

The servant knocked again on the wooden panel, then swung up behind as the horses started off again to wait with the other carriages. At the earl's side, facing rows of royal guards who edged the carpet, Elisha gazed up at the arched façade of Westminster. Last time he came here, the false archbishop anointed him king and stole the blood that made his treachery possible.

The earl stretched out his hand in invitation and they started the long walk. A few paces ahead, Alfleda walked softly in her borrowed slippers, her skirts lifted just enough, her head held high. The guards shifted a bit as they passed, but stood erect, halberds at their sides, holding at bay the thousands who gawked for a glimpse of the lords. The earl swaggered as they went, waving to the audience, and doffing his hat to the occasional lady whose station was not quite sufficient to gain her admittance. For Elisha, it was all he could do not to bolt and run. Those familiar faces he spied in the crowd showed no sign of recognition, but he anticipated the shout and the shot that would inevitably follow once they spotted him.

"Halt!"

Elisha jerked to a stop, his heart thundering in his ears. He pressed a hand to his chest.

A pair of guards stood with their halberds to either side of the small door cut into the vast oaken gate which would gain them admittance. A third man faced them, bowing. "I'm afraid it's too late to announce you, my lords, the ceremony's begun."

"The fault is all mine, my good man. I could hardly decide what to wear." The earl smiled broadly as they were bowed to the door.

With a gracious curtsy, the earl's wife swept inside, closely shadowed by Alfleda. The earl offered Elisha first passage. Weak sunlight filtered through the great rose window, turning to bits of pale color on the floor and dappling the crowd inside. Once the door shut, blocking the breeze, the scent and the restless shifting of so many people made Elisha think rather more of a barn than a church. The earl touched his elbow and led him ahead down the aisle. A few heads turned, but most remained focused on the events at the distant altar. Already, a choir of monks began to sing and the bishop's golden miter bobbed slightly as he intoned Latin verses over the couple. Two figures knelt at his feet, with long cloaks that flowed over their shoulders and down the few steps. They bowed their heads, listening. Duke Randall stood near, with his wife beside him, and Lord Robert just behind. Brigit's father hovered by them, a new surcoat emphasizing his belly, his face ruddy with delight. Brigit glared at him.

"Not too close," Elisha whispered to the earl, who gave a slight nod, then tapped his wife on the shoulder.

She nudged her way into a row. "Pardon me, my lady deRoth," she murmured. The other woman gave an unfriendly grunt, then gave way, squeezing in nearer to her neighbor with a rustle of satin.

Darting a look to Elisha, the earl slipped in beside his wife, and Alfleda caught Elisha's hand in the gloom. She tipped her head this way and that, and lifted herself on tip-toe, until Elisha scooped her onto his hip, her arms wrapped around him. Together they watched as her father wed their enemy.

Elisha tried to follow the Latin at first, but his eyes drew back to rest upon Thomas, and he lost the will to understand the ritual. Ahead, and far away, Thomas raised his head, the crown glinting under flickering candles. His hair had the warm glow of a polished chestnut hull, and Elisha remembered the silk of it against his fingers that long ago day Thomas had trusted him to cut his hair. The bishop lifted something from a pillow at his side and offered it to the king: a delicate diadem that sparkled with jewels. Thomas turned to his wife. The word lodged in Elisha's throat, and his eyes stung.

"Can we not just run up and stop them? Can't we, please?" Alfleda's voice stroked with sadness across his cheek.

"I wish we could," he told her, eyeing the dozen men who clustered near the daïs—men who wore swords to a wedding. The presence of a few mancers, scattered through the audience, chilled him even in the heat of the crowd. If he let his guard down or broke his focus on the false projection he offered to the world, they would not hesitate. "I think it would be the death of me."

She stared hungrily toward the altar, and Elisha shut his eyes briefly. "You could go on your own, right now."

Yearning toward her father, she still glanced over at him, her eyebrows drawn up over glistening eyes. "No," she said. "He should have me back by your own hand."

"He may yet forgive me, just to have you back at all. I can be patient."

She gave a shake of her head. "My father needs you."

A tear streaked down her face, and he freed one hand to gently wipe it away. "Soon, you'll be together again." Elisha's jaw tightened, and it took a moment for him to recognize his envy. Alfleda would be with Thomas as he himself would not.

The lock shorn from Thomas's head translated a sudden wash of despair to Elisha's touch.

"Your Majesty," the bishop prompted, and Elisha heard the whisper through his skin as Thomas looked up, and finally put out his hand.

Brigit turned, her fine profile lit by her smile as she slid her hand into his.

"Whom the Almighty has brought together, let no man put asunder," the bishop intoned over their heads, wrapping a stole about their joined hands.

Brigit's smile flamed into the darkness, while a cry flew up in Thomas's breast, a cry Elisha nearly uttered, but which never passed the king's lips. Carefully, together, Brigit and Thomas rose. Brigit glowed, from the diadem atop her head to the rosy warmth of her hand resting in Thomas's. She wore a magnificent gown of purple edged with ermine. The royal shade might not serve her own coloring so well, but she beamed so widely that it dazzled the eyes, and Elisha's stomach churned.

Beside her, Thomas's solemn face, proud and empty, bore no trace of emotion. His eyes focused on some point beyond the rose window. He looked, indeed, so inanimate that Elisha imagined some spell worked upon his king. Perhaps Thomas wanted so badly to forget and to pretend all was well that he opened himself to Brigit's command. Then Thomas glanced toward her and smiled briefly, his eyes still bleak. He possessed a certain grandeur of despair, his eyes bluer than ever, and darker, too; the royal tunic and cape enhanced the lean grace of his figure. As the king looked forward again, emotionless, Elisha thought that he might look just that way on his bier, arrayed for a funeral of royal proportions, the center of attention in a world he had fled.

Elisha squeezed his eyes shut and took a shuddering breath. His arm ached from holding Alfleda, and he gently lowered her to the ground, both of her hands wrapping his as she leaned against him. As the cheering died down, the choir began again, something bright and joyous that he should have been able to name, if he cared anymore. The censers went back to work, swinging their globes of incense down the aisle, mingling the sweat and stale breath of the crowd with the smoky illusion of sanctity. Up ahead, the sound of marching feet echoed through the cathedral, drawing nearer, and Elisha forced himself to look up even as the great doors at his back groaned open, letting a spatter of raindrops fly through and settle upon the narrow carpet in the bitter light. Four pairs of royal guards marched by, stately and tall with their halberds held straight and swords at their sides. Every edge glowed with the possibility of his doom. His hand in Alfleda's felt clammy. As the last guard passed them to exit, she caught her breath, and Elisha steeled his resolve.

In two quick steps, before he could change his mind, Elisha stood before the king. He swept into a bow, averting his eyes until he straightened again and found himself face to face with Thomas.

"What—it's you!" the king breathed, frozen.

At his side, Brigit demanded, "Who are you?"

Elisha did not respond, grateful for the hat which dipped low over one cheek, obscuring his face but for the short, pointed beard. Instead, he smiled and said, "A wedding gift."

"Guards!" Brigit shouted.

"What's going on?" called the duke from his place behind another set of guards.

Keeping his eyes on the king, Elisha guided Alfleda before him. Thomas tensed, eyes narrowed as he glanced down—the merest flicker, assessing the danger as his hand reached for a sword he did not wear. Then, his eyes flew wide and his lips parted. He dropped to one knee, sweeping the hairnet from the girl's head. She gaped back at him, still holding Elisha's hand. With a soft cry, Thomas scooped her into his arms, his face pressed against her hair.

Over their heads, Duke Randall stared directly at Elisha. "That's him!" His finger thrust out and he, too, reached for a sword.

Elisha's belly clenched. "Long live the king," Elisha said, then he flashed a grin at Brigit. "And God save the queen."

"Did you hear that? He threatened me! Move, you idiots!"

The man behind drew his sword. With his daughter held tight, Thomas lurched to his feet. Tears streamed down his face, which broke into a grin that Elisha felt to his very soul.

"Out of the way, Your Majesty! Thomas, get out of the way," Randall roared, trying to push ahead with his two guards while Brigit floundered to the side in her heavy cape and gown.

The king stood thwarting the tide. One hand cradled his daughter's head against his chest as he blinked at Elisha, his smile lighting up his brilliant blue eyes. Elisha laughed aloud as he spun and ran.

The vanguard, returning double speed, broke apart in confusion as Elisha burst through their midst.

"Has nobody got a bow?" the duke shrieked as feet pounded back down the aisle.

"Shut the doors! For God's sake, shut them," Brigit urged.

Elisha ran as if he might launch into the sky and sprang out the huge double doors as the guards struggled to get them closed again.

Outside, rain shimmered in the air, and the crowd surged forward so it was all the soldiers could do to hold them back, expecting the king, not a madman who bounded down the stairs, whooping and laughing. Elisha's half-cape fluttered out in the breeze, his hat tumbling away to be seized up as evidence.

"Pull!" cried a new voice and bowstrings sang.

Giddy and light, Elisha flung himself into the air, spreading his awareness. Almost without thinking, he touched the rain, contact springing from drop to drop across the sky. An arrow buzzed toward him, and Elisha let his dreams run as wild as his heart. The arrows never struck home.

Around him, the crowd gasped. Some cheered and others cried out for the Virgin, and a few even shouted his name—not with the gathered fury of those behind him but with the veneration of people receiving a sign.

Heedless of faith or fury, Elisha ran through the rain, transforming it as he passed. Some part of him knew it was not over, that only his madness, only his sudden appearance and sudden flight defended him from his enemies. Elisha touched the rain and turned it bright with spring and promise. All around him fell a thousand tiny flowers, perfect in their beauty and blue as the sky, a carpet of petals, delicate as snowflakes to greet the king and his daughter as they started toward home together.

Chapter 31

———◈———

Elisha fled into the crowds. Turning this way, then that, he found a well-populated street between the market stalls and slowed to a walk, binding his presence once more to the dead. Alert and less tired than before, he strode onward, stopping at the nearest clothier's booth to buy a long woolen cloak with the last of his hoarded wealth. He flung up his hood and smiled his grim thanks. His own purpose might have been fulfilled, but he should do well to recall that others still searched for him. For a long time, he followed one little group of revelers then another, allowing his presence to mingle with theirs, acting the part of a drunk, dodging guards and mancers both, wishing he could find a place to curl up and rest. The guards dispersed quickly through the crowd, expecting him to bolt. The mancers, too, drifted slowly away, some of them simply winking out of existence. There was a moment when Elisha felt the murder clinging to one of them, that he was tempted to turn assassin. Instead, he watched for them, seeing the same ones who seemed to haunt the city: the pair of women, the tall man, others he began to recognize. Twenty-three mancers in all. Nearly four times as many as he'd fought before, and there still remained the stout woman from the coal mine. They would be carrying talismans that allowed them to use the Valley of the Shadow. If he tried to strike one of them, the others could converge upon him, or simply vanish. Pausing at a junction, Elisha considered what to do. Then he heard a bell strike nearby and thought of Sabetha.

Keeping well out from the city wall, where the guards would surely be given the new description of him, Elisha moved quickly out from the cluster of buildings and market stalls. He ought to shave his beard when he had the chance. He would more resemble himself, but the change might buy a little more time. Unfortunately, he could not risk seeing a barber. Any man of his former order might well recognize and report him, or simply cut his throat and claim whatever reward the duke offered.

Elisha's footsteps slowed as he stared ahead. The shape of the landscape looked familiar and his stomach clenched. With the gentle slope up, away from the city and the gray and white walls of Saint Bartholomew's behind, it looked like the place where Brigit's mother died upon the stake, but a large wooden building occupied the spot where the fire must have been. A few workmen moved up on the roof, binding on bundles of thatch. Tipping back his hood, Elisha watched them as he approached. The newly cut lumber still glowed pale in the subtle gleam of the setting sun, and stacks of tools and lumber surrounded the site. Something about it quickened his breathing and made his skin tingle with an unwelcome fear. The nun must wait a little longer. Frowning, Elisha stalked around the windowless place, then poked his head inside where a few masons worked by rushlight laying a stone floor. Two others leaned over a table to one side, studying a wax tablet diagram.

"Pardon me, Master," Elisha said, giving a short bow as the two stared back.

"If it's work you're after, we're nearly done," said the taller man, crossing his arms.

"No, I can see that. I've not been to the city for a couple of months, nor have I heard of any projects. Can you tell me what you're building?"

The two shared a look, and Elisha felt a slender shaft of cold too deep to be natural. He masked himself in confusion and country ways, borrowing from the owner of his second-hand cloak.

"It's a church."

Elisha glanced around the square room, surmounted by a peaked roof. Something the height of a dining table, but larger, hid beneath a cloth at its center. Elisha's uneasiness grew, the brand pricking upon his chest. With a smile, he faced the men—the master builder, and the mancer. "It's like no church I've ever seen. A central altar, is it?" He gestured toward the covered object.

"'Sright," said the builder. "A new design. She's right proud of it and won't have it changed."

"Ah, the queen's church." Elisha grinned even as the mancer, a hawk-nosed, gray-haired man, frowned back at him. "Come to think of it, I have heard tell. She chose this spot because her mother died here, am I right? It's a sort of memorial." Elisha rubbed his neck as he feigned admiration, his fingers returning to the scar where Morag would have had his hide. He scratched at his short beard, then lowered his hand, hoping it looked nonchalant.

"That's right," said the builder, smiling himself now. "See here, sir"—he pointed to the diagram—"there'll be four basins for holy water, at the corners of the altar, see?"

Elisha came nearer, keeping toward the builder's end of the table, and tucked his hands behind him as he studied the plan. Four basins. An altar just the size of a man, spread-eagled, built over a place of power for the queen herself. Bile crept up Elisha's throat.

"We've got no time for visitors," snapped the gray-haired man.

"Bosh," said the builder. "Should've given us more than two weeks before the dedication. Still, quick as we've worked, it'll be a right pretty church in honor of the queen's dam, 'f I do say so myself."

"No doubt," the mancer sniffed, his shaggy eyebrows furrowing as the cold finger of his attention prodded Elisha's defenses. Elisha stepped out the door just as a mounted party galloped by and turned down the well-trodden path toward Saint Bartholomew's. The wind of their passage cut through his cloak, and Elisha turned up his hood again, catching his breath. Mancers, at least half the ones he had counted, and a single servant in their midst borne upon the saddle of the lead rider. Most he recognized from the fair earlier. The others, no doubt, would recognize him. Dear God—and Sister Sabetha waited there for him.

Elisha set out after them, his knees feeling weak as he walked. He unfurled his senses before him, reaching toward the church and priory, skimming over the hospital where the fears of the dying crowded his attention. He strode forward, not running, not daring to waste his strength. They would find her quickly, or not, no matter how fast he ran. Besides, they wanted him: the nun was only a means to that end.

He came cautiously through the graveyard. Two men lounged against the low surrounding wall, their cloaks remarkably clean given the rake and hoe that leaned against the wall with them. His brother's grave lay a few rows up from the pair, but he kept walking, forcing his shoulders to relax. At least he felt sure he did not imagine their attention—soldiers of the duke or the king, set to guard any place where Elisha might appear. Rounding the corner, out of sight of the guards, he flattened himself against the wall. Two men stood with the horses, and they looked up. Elisha projected his absence, applying the Law of Polarity to create a deflection and hoping he'd done it soon enough that they had not already noticed him. If they did, they made no move. But would they? No, they would act as if nothing happened while alerting those inside to his presence, assuming the others did not know.

Elisha sent his awareness out through the earth, sorry now that it had stopped raining. Seeking attunement as he sought his hunters, Elisha reached up through stone and wood and into the sanctuary of Saint Bartholomew's. Eight more mancers waited inside, not grouped together but scattered singly and in pairs. He caught his breath. Brigit's presence glowed among them, bright as her hair. Only a handful of *desolati* occupied the church, and he had not known Sister Sabetha long enough to recognize her at such a distance. He squared his shoulders and walked to the door.

A slight chill caught Elisha's attention, and he glanced down to find a smear of blood on the threshold. He slid his booted foot over it, frowning. The blood belonged to no one he knew—a great relief—but it resonated inside the church on most of those cold forms lurking within. He smiled grimly and stepped over, carrying a bit of the blood with him in the stitching of his sole.

His footfalls echoed in the dark church, his shadow growing strong, then fading as he neared and passed each candelabra. As he walked, he let the projections fall away. Death gathered to him, seeping up from the graves outside and from the tombs of the rich patrons lining the walls. Heads turned. The mancers smiled, but let him pass. This one nodded a formal greeting, that one curtsied. Elisha ignored them all and moved steadily toward the bench at the side, where two women sat, their faces revealed in the glow of candlelight.

"But can it be that you didn't know?" Brigit asked. "It

must be hard for a man to conceal such evils, and you being a woman of God. No doubt you are more sensitive to such things."

"I came with him for the safety of the child, my lady. Seemed to me he wanted what's best for her, at any rate."

"Then you saw no reason to distrust him."

Sister Sabetha did not answer but looked away into the dim recesses beyond the altar. "You say he killed the last queen."

"Yes, and the prince, and our own archbishop—to attack a man of the cloth! Well, even those inclined to trust him before could hardly doubt after that." Her back to Elisha and the aisle, Brigit radiated concern as she leaned toward the nun. "Good Sister, I know, more than anyone, that he seems so worthy of trust. And more than any, I know how he betrays it. I don't blame you for believing."

Elisha cleared his throat, and Sabetha jumped, her hand flying to her cheek, but Brigit merely lifted her head. "Come and sit by me, Elisha Barber. We have so much to talk about."

Sister Sabetha lowered her hands and tried to master her expression. "Is it true, what she said?" She opened her clasped hands to reveal a medallion of Saint Elisha, and he sighed.

"I killed the archbishop, after a fashion, but he's the one who killed the queen. And the prince—Prince Alaric that was, this lady's betrothed—killed Alfleda's mother, had Alfleda brought to the convent, and would have killed King Thomas, given the chance. I took the chance away from him." Elisha softened nothing: if he offended the nun, she might up and go, taking herself out of harm's way.

Instead, Sabetha simmered with wrath of her own. "Have you lied to bring us here? And what've you done with the girl?"

"Exactly what I said I would—I brought her to her father."

"And ruined the royal wedding, one might add, though I did receive both crown and ring," Brigit remarked, slipping a strand of hair behind her ear, the gold ring flashing on her finger. She wore simple traveling clothes, warm and serviceable.

"Which makes me wonder why you're not there enjoying the feast."

Brigit leaned back. "The wedding was hours ago, Elisha. What crimes have you committed since then?"

"Let her go," Elisha said, softly.

"Nobody is holding her, Elisha, love." She bit off the word, her pretty face flushed with pink. "She has been waiting for you, for a long time. I simply came by to pray for my baby, and I offered to keep her company."

"You've been sitting here pouring acid into her ear, trying to find out what she knows about me."

"Now just you wait," Sabetha snapped, heaving herself to her feet. "Plain enough there's some history between you, no reason to make me a party to it."

"Between us? Oh, no, Sister." Brigit reached out and caught the nun's arm. "I once thought there was, you understand." She managed a teardrop that gleamed upon her cheek. "Only to find out later the truth about him." She shot Elisha a look that pierced his awareness, and he suddenly realized the mounting pressure of her presence, a force pushing against him. "But you're not a bugger, not really, are you, Elisha Barber?" She thrust a finger toward him. "You still want me, just like your precious Thomas wants me, like he's longing to come back up to our bed."

The revulsion overwhelmed any attraction he had for her, and Elisha shook his head. "You ground him down until he had no choice but to trust you. He'll never love you."

"He'll never love you, either, Elisha Barber." She flung her hands in the air as if it all meant nothing to her. "He cringes at the sound of your name." Taking up her skirt in two fists, Brigit came closer, lifting her face to look into his, so close that her breath burned across his lips as she hissed, "I come to him at night and whisper your name, just to hear him whimper."

Elisha backed away until his calves scraped against the next bench. Brigit came on, her chin forward, her eyes glittering by the light of dancing flames. "Oh, yes, Elisha, I lie there beside him, night after night," her voice sank away completely, yet still her words insinuated themselves in his mind. *"Sometimes I cry out, 'Stop, Elisha, please, no! Elisha, stop!' Every night he wakes up crying and crawls into my arms."*

Elisha surged forward, and Brigit fell to the side, snatching for Sabetha's support and wailing. "Stop him, please! My baby!"

Looming over her, Elisha froze. "You vicious bitch."

Two mancers leapt to defend her as she huddled in the nun's arms, and Sabetha glared back at him. "Holy Mother Mary, you are mad."

"Did you not hear what she's doing to him?" Elisha shouted, the fury howling through his skull.

But of course Sabetha had heard none of it, for Brigit struck through the air and the stone and whispered in places only Elisha knew. "You dare attack a pregnant woman, and in the house of the Lord? Because you envy her the bed of the king?" She wrapped her strong arms around Brigit. "Come away, Majesty. Let your men take care of this."

"Things will change, after today."

"Oh, yes, they will," said Brigit, resisting Sabetha's attempt to draw her away. "For we are married." She waved her hand before him, displaying the ring. "He's mine, Elisha, by all the laws of God and man. Your perversions can't touch him."

Reining in his anger, Elisha said, "He's got his daughter at his side right now, not you. It's she who'll tell him all she feels and all she knows."

Brigit's eyes narrowed and the mancers edged nearer but still did not touch him. "I wish he had killed you. I thought I might still have a place for you in the glory to come, but truly, I wish the duke had spilled your guts all over the floor. At the very least, I wish they'd had your head off that very night for all the trouble you've caused." She tipped her head, almost as if she sniffed the air. "You should never have gotten that close, not the first time. Certainly not today. How did you do it?"

"I know a few tricks."

"Did you see him arrive at the convent, Sister?"

"Yes, Majesty," said Sabetha, standing straighter under the queen's regard. "On a horse—a dun-colored cob, he was."

"But how did they get there? Did the sky open?"

Hesitantly, Sabetha answered, "No, Majesty, they came up the road, just as usual."

"He did not cross England on a bloody horse!" Brigit snarled. "He didn't travel three hundred miles beneath my notice on a bloody ordinary horse."

"Well, Your Majesty, how he got that far, I've no idea!" Sabetha's cheeks turned pink, then she started and shook herself. "Beneath your notice, Majesty? But how—?"

"She doesn't know anything, Brigit," Elisha said. "Nothing she tells you can help."

"What are you, Elisha Barber? What have you become?"

"And how can you become one, too, isn't that what you mean?"

She reached out swiftly and poked him. "How did you

change your own presence? How did you sever the contact of your own child?"

"Your child?" Sabetha gasped, but Elisha put up a hand to stave off her words.

Brigit ignored her completely. "Earlier today, you felt almost like yourself again. I was able to find you, but now, it's like you're not even there. Like a necromancer. What's your talisman? Is it another baby's head? Who have you killed to get this power?"

"Who would you have to kill to get your own? God only knows." But his eyes rested briefly on her stomach, and his heart hesitated in his breast.

"Who to kill? There are so many choices, I hardly know where to begin."

Himself? His baby? But it was her child, too, a child she conceived on purpose after marrying a prince. "They gave you the throne when I wouldn't. What are you giving them in return, Brigit?"

"What are you?" Sabetha's wide eyes encompassed both of them, the medallion swinging from her limp hands.

"She's a witch," Elisha replied, "like her mother before her."

With a sharp smile, Brigit answered, "He's a monster, like nothing ever seen upon this earth. He used to be a healer, but the day's long passed for that. I even offered him the chance to help me, to save our people, but he refused. Now he trades in insults, threats, and death."

A few candles blew out, then a few more, as if dark wings soared through the flames and plunged them into darkness.

"Is the king one, too?" Sabetha breathed. "A monster?"

"No," said Elisha, his eyes still fixed on Brigit's in the growing darkness. "He's a decent man who deserves better than a monster for his bride."

"You can't hurt me." Brigit's voice echoed through the chill, quiet space even as someone else cried out against the darkness. "I've already won."

"If that were true, you would not be here, talking to me. Your allies aren't telling you everything. They didn't even tell you about Alfleda until I'd nearly found her. Why would you ally with people like that?"

"I am giving them the past, Elisha, and they will give me the future."

Cold crackled in the air around them. Elisha said, "Sister, take my hand."

"Don't," cried Brigit's voice. "You know what he can do."

Darkness fell with a gust of wind that ruffled Elisha's hair and slapped his cloak against his legs. A stentorian voice called out, "Be still, my children, the lord will bring us light."

"Sabetha! Quickly!" he called out, sensing her as he felt the shapes that loomed out of the black to either side.

"Majesty, your hand, please!"

"Damn it all, Sister, don't do that!" Elisha cried.

"Too late—" Brigit's crow of triumph twisted into protest and a hand grabbed Elisha's.

"Work your spell, monster—the queen's angry," Sabetha's voice muttered.

With a snap of cold, Elisha sought the blood that stained his shoes. Together, he and the nun flashed from darkness into eternity accompanied by a howling wind of death and Brigit's cry of rage. Elisha snatched at Biddy's memory, the final gift of light she left him, and the horrors vanished as radiance filled his mind.

"Sweet Jesus, it's so beautiful," Sabetha sighed, her fingers entwined with his.

He heard her voice at a distance, a song from beyond a hill. Too soon, as he hit the threshold, Elisha stumbled and the pair of them tumbled out of the church and down the steps. His head thumped the ground. Sabetha sat up beside him, blinking into the last rays of crimson light, with the rising moon glowing silver on her hair.

"What was that?"

"The valley of the shadow of death." Elisha rolled and heaved himself to his feet, shaky but standing. They couldn't stay in a place marked by the mancers. If he could reach his brother's grave, they had a passage of their own, one no other could know so well.

"Come on." He put down his hand, and she took it without hesitation. Pulling her into motion, Elisha dashed past the pair of guards and the horses they tended just as a blast of wind struck them from behind as someone else opened the passage Elisha had followed. The horses whinnied and reared, stampeding in all directions to escape the fell voices howling on that wind. Elisha staggered and got his feet under him, gathering the dazed nun.

"How did they find you, Sister?" Elisha hissed as they ran.

"Sorry?"

"Do they have you marked, do they have anything from you?"

"No. 'T'was the earl's manservant. They bought him for a few coins. Cor, but I can't get over that valley."

"Get over it, Sister, we've got to run." He skidded to a halt by the wall, looking both ways in the strange light. It seemed as if the fires of Hell lit up the western sky while the silvery light of heaven drifted down on the opposite side.

"Can't we go back there? The valley, I mean, and get away?"

"Not so easy," he muttered. But the remark, delivered with such wistful appeal, gave him an idea, and he set off into the graveyard. His feet slammed down and stuck, dropping him to his knees with a force that nearly snapped bones. Elisha screamed.

"Get up, they're coming!" Sabetha urged, the glamour finally leaving her eyes.

Wrenching his feet free of the stained shoes, Elisha rose up again, barefoot.

Dirt erupted before them with a shriek. They fell to either side, and Elisha turned wild eyes upon the grave, expecting to see a corpse lurching toward him. Only earth, he realized, touched by the spattered blood from some unfortunate. Across the new hollow, Sabetha scrambled toward the low wall and freedom. Good—let her escape.

As Elisha picked himself up again, his arm numb from the second impact, Brigit stared down at him. "You see? They have been teaching me. And it was one of their German allies who came for me when you were slaughtering them at the mine."

"Halt in the name of the king!" Shouting and drawing their swords, the two watchmen bounded through the graveyard.

"Be careful!" Brigit screamed, in a bold imitation of terror. "It's Elisha Barber!"

Dirt erupted behind her off to the left. The guards cried out as the mancers struck, and Elisha did not know what they did, but the cries broke off abruptly. Mastering his alarm, he stepped back and breathed deep. He drew up death through his naked feet, up into his veins so that every pulse of his heart throbbed with power.

"Do you really think to challenge me in a graveyard, Your Majesty?"

Brigit patted her belly. "I know you too well, Elisha. I have no doubt you'd strike me down, but to kill your own child? I don't think so." The sinuous heat of her presence rose up, steaming from the earth at his feet and circled around his cold limbs.

Clamping his fingers into fists, Elisha managed to control his response. "Don't bother, Brigit, I don't care anymore."

"What, you care only for your king? But I should thank you for playing your part in helping me to win him over. If the French invasion failed, I was to ride in and save him. It worked perfectly for me to have you arrive in the flesh, urging his death. Even if he doubted that you slew Rosalynn, your own words shattered him, Elisha."

Death still lingered with him, but shivers of panic enflamed the wound in his belly.

"Poor barber," Brigit crooned, strolling nearer. She lifted her face to his, her breath stroking his lips. "You wanted so much to help and to heal and to make people whole. You wanted it so much that you destroyed yourself, and the man you desire."

Chapter 32

❖

Elisha turned his face from hers.

"Do you know the tragedy, Elisha? I only went to them to find you. When the priests exhumed the empty coffin, I searched for you."

"For love, Brigit, or because you wanted to make a talisman of my corpse?"

Her hand cradled the back of his neck. "They had the power you refused to share. Yes, I did make a bargain, to defend all the magi—for a little while, even you, in case you could be swayed by reason. The only thing I regret is my mother's prophecy that won't come true." Her breath carried more than regret, something like worry. "I would have liked for you to be there. You were to lead us home, my mother said, but it seems the task must fall to me, to show the *desolati* we are not to be abused. But then, prophecy is always such a tricky thing. Myself, I take inspiration from the past." She slid her arms around him.

"I've tried," she said through his skin. *"I've tried so hard to convince you. You have a talent that you squander on the ignorant—a talent you would never have had without my mother. And now all that remains is for me to kill you."* She pulled him nearer, one hand wrapped into his

hair, the other pressed to his back as she tried to kiss him.

Elisha wrenched away and fell, retching into the dirt.

"You might have died with my love upon your lips, Elisha Barber, but perhaps this is more appropriate."

As he stared up at her, the moon outlined her form, the growing shape of his child within. He sought desperately for some spell beyond death, but found none so well-practiced, none so easy to control. None that might not harm the baby.

The mancers hemmed him in, one of them drawing a fleshing blade, asking a question in French.

"Don't kill him yet," another one answered. "We're better served if he lives and half the kingdom still worships him."

"Your invasion failed," Brigit snapped, pointing at the Frenchman. "The archbishop's usurper here succeeded too well, and you can't create a civil war when your rebel figurehead is in love with the king! I'll bring the kingdom to heel, I told you. By tomorrow night, there'll be none left strong enough to hold—" Suddenly she shrieked, tumbling headlong over him to land in the dirt. Elisha scrambled out of the way and leapt to his feet, nearly colliding with Sister Sabetha.

"Run!" shouted the nun, still wielding the long-handled shovel she had used to strike the queen.

Scanning the nearby mounds, Elisha cut a ragged course, dodging this way and that to avoid the splashes of fresh blood from which mancers burst out like maggots from corpses. They stumbled to a halt and ran in another direction, at every turn showered with dirt, and once, something that clattered like bones. Sabetha began to scream, a long sustained wail of panic.

Brigit rose up to one side, a queer silhouette, long and jagged. The rake she held dripped blood, and Elisha whirled to meet her.

"Did I break her? I only meant to scratch her back."

Sister Sabetha sprawled at her feet, a series of puncture wounds dotting her back. She gurgled blood.

"Go on, heal the little nun. I'm curious, and I could use the time."

While he mustered his power, Elisha pulled the nun to his chest. He staggered with the weight of her, and Brigit swung the rake down, forcing him to stumble aside. She leaned on the handle, a callous farmwife with a vicious harvest. "You won't let her die, will you? That hardly seems like you."

Elisha sucked strength from the graves and the death that hovered all around them. Even Brigit hesitated, her face sharp and pale in the moonlight.

Quick as death, strong as eternity, Elisha made the final dash. Five strides, four, three, and he leapt to the grave. Half his concentration kept the woman alive, searching her wounds as her blood spilled over his arms. Pain stabbed his own back over and over as he showed her flesh how to heal. With the other half of his strength, he escaped.

Together, they spun through his brother's grave, into the maelstrom that was the Valley. The world ripped open like the gash across his brother's throat. Elisha tried to conjure Biddy's peace and found it mirrored around him here and there, but not enough to stop the tide of remembrance from his brother's death. Remorse flooded in.

Dead voices howled, although a few of them sang. The din built up inside his skull, and Elisha cried out, struggling to shield Sabetha even as he healed her. The Valley shocked him with its force, a raw surge like a thunderstorm. Elisha made for a patch of light and let himself reach out, drawing from that river, drinking it down and making of it what he needed.

Slipping free of the Valley, he sank to his knees before

a roaring fire. The chill of the floor, where his brother had died, ebbed away as he released the wonder and the power, and the woman stirred in his arms.

"So beautiful," she murmured, her eyes still shut. "Let me stay."

"No," he answered, "not this time."

"Well, hello," said a gruff voice behind him. "The very man I've been awaiting."

Elisha choked. So recently from the fight, his muscles beginning to tremble from his exertions, he doubted himself capable of more than weeping. To come so far, to escape an enemy bent upon his ruin only to fall into the lap of another — he should have known. If soldiers watched his brother's grave, they must guard this workshop as well, and keep a man outside his brother's house. The duke went to war for his daughter's virtue. What would he not do to avenge her death?

Nausea swirled in his guts, but Elisha forced it down as he lay Sabetha on the ground, and she slowly sat up. Elisha gathered the shards of his strength, his muscles twitching, and started to rise.

A firm hand planted itself on his shoulder. "Naw, don't get up on my behalf." A ruddy man came around and squatted down before him, grinning through his beard. "So there y'are, Elisha."

Elisha cupped a hand over his mouth as he blinked up at the welcome face of his one-time bodyguard, Madoc. "It's you. God, but you had me worried."

The stocky man patted his shoulder, and his grin widened. "Aye, and ye don't look as if ye'd stand much more worry tonight. Rest, rest, and keep you quiet. We've the duke's men sleeping on our doorstep." He raised shaggy eyebrows at the nun. "Who's this, then? Never known ye to be keeping with the women of God, though I know there's nunneries not so holy." But he broke off as Sabetha glared.

"I'll thank you, sir, to keep your jests to yourself," she whispered, dusting herself off as if she could wipe away all that she had seen. Her dark eyes met Elisha's for a moment, then glanced to the side as her hands kept dusting. Her eyes roved over the place and focused beyond Elisha's shoulder. "They can't . . . come that way, can they? Those witches, can they come up through the floor, through the Valley, I mean?"

The bloodstains on the floor had long been scraped away, covered over with fresh straw, but the place still held all that happened there. "I think not. They need fresh blood, slain by their own hand. This journey was more personal."

"It was your brother's grave that opened for us, eh?"

Jolted, Elisha gave a nod. "But how did you know?"

"You were holding me, like, and I could feel what happened in you, this powerful fear, then the strength—then a faith like no other I've known." She plucked at her skirt. "I could've stayed there a long time, even with the howling and all."

"I tried to shield you," he said.

"Aye, well. I'm sure there's things you felt that would've been the end of me, but that sense of," she stopped and screwed up her face. "A sense of being with you, joined, neither living nor dead but a part of it all. Is that what it's like for you, this power that you have?"

Elisha shook his head. "Mostly, it's terrifying."

"Well, then, I'm sorry for that. That union, I think that's what the priests get from God. They find their faith through solitude, by devoting themselves to the Lord. Maybe you've come at it the other direction, by devoting yourself to the flesh."

"I am the least holy person you'll ever meet. Twenty years ago, when I watched them burn an angel, I turned my back on God. I'm a sorcerer at best, a heretic by some accounts, and by others, the devil himself."

She stared straight at him until he fell silent. "I've met worse, and that just today."

"So then," Madoc put in, holding out steaming cups of cider to both of them, "you'll likely appreciate your surroundings."

Elisha sipped the sweet, spiced liquid, grateful for the way it cleared his throat if not his mind, still trying to place himself like a priest in relation to God. It was not until Sabetha burst into laughter that he looked around.

His brother's workshop had been transformed. The broad hearth remained from the tin smithy he used to run here, but otherwise Nathaniel would not have recognized it. Rugs and a few benches stood at one end, along with a pile of blankets where Madoc had evidently been sleeping. An altar faced these on the opposite wall, a simple stone, with a bit of carving—shears, a razor, curls that might have been hair, a variety of surgical tools. Atop this, candles of various heights, some still burning, reflected from a bronze basin brimming with water. For a moment, Elisha imagined it was his own basin and the breath froze in his lungs. He pictured it brimful of blood, his brother's life drained out by his own hand in this very room.

Above the altar with its basin and candles, offerings covered every inch of the wall. Some took the form of charms for "Saint Barber." Others, made of metal or crudely carved from wood, resembled hands, legs, even torsos and skulls, with a full-figure here or there, dangling like a doll among a carnage of its fellows.

"All healed by you, or by this place," Madoc supplied.

"It can't be. This whole thing is preposterous, as it has always been."

"Maybe so, but they believe it." Madoc nodded, gazing up at the wall. "I believe it, too."

Elisha rounded on his friend. "But you've known me since they hauled me off to war. You saw me nearly die."

"Aye, but ye didn't. And so I witnessed your very first miracles." He wagged a finger in Elisha's direction. "And don't say they're not. There's witches, sure I've seen some strange things before and after, but they can't do the things you can."

Elisha's head dropped to his scarred hands, his empty cup forgotten. "Oh, I am sick of this argument," he groaned toward the floor. He ached all over.

Madoc lifted the cup from the floor and re-filled it from his pot on the hearth, then set it back again, letting the spiced steam rise up to work its own magic. After a moment, a small loaf of bread lay beside the cup, topped by a chunk of meat.

Leather creaked as Madoc settled back on his haunches. "Someday, when you and I are old men sharing our houses with sheep and children, you'll tell me all, eh?"

Elisha murmured, "I don't know that I'll ever be an old man—or maybe I already am."

"Eat something." Sister Sabetha nudged the food a little nearer. "You look about ready to shake to pieces."

"Sister, here, let me show ye this," Madoc said, drawing the nun down toward the altar.

After a while, with their soft speech barely penetrating his growing exhaustion, Elisha raised his head. He sampled the meat, then the bread, and before he knew it, both had been devoured. It settled his stomach and allowed a beam of clarity into his mind. He huddled in his new cloak, watching the fire dance, and thought of Thomas, the light of his laughter as he came down the steps with his daughter in his arms. Brigit must already be making her way home, slipping in past the late mass, thinking of excuses in case Thomas caught her about— then exuding her glowing sexuality as she slid into bed beside the king, recalling the dreams her mother forced upon him so long ago.

He had never before hated anyone. He could not have hated her so much if he had not once believed he loved her. And she him. "God forgive me," he said to the fire.

"Sorry?" said Madoc, coming nearer.

"I never killed the last queen," he told his friend, "but I pray I might kill this one."

Sabetha held up her hands. "Nearly forgot." Plucking at her finger, she handed down a ring, a narrow band of old gold delicately inscribed with flowers, but Elisha could feel Brigit's foul touch upon it. Even that stain failed to hide Thomas's lingering presence, a sense that hummed against the lock of hair he carried.

"However did you manage it?"

Sabetha shrugged again, but her lips turned upward. "In the dark, when she offered her hand. Thought she'd taken me in, didn't she? Before they sent me t'convent, I was rather an ill-mannered girl."

Slipping it on his little finger, Elisha grinned up at her. "Thanks. I'm glad of it." Then his smile slid away. "Someone's coming."

Elisha lurched to his feet and turned as someone knocked once on the door before opening it.

"She's asked me to bring you some wood, though why—" The woman froze.

"Sister Lucretia, please, let me explain."

Arrested by the sight of him, his old friend stood framed by the doorway, an armload of firewood tucked against her hip, lips parted. "It's you."

"Aye," he whispered, acutely aware now of the guards who snored outside. "Come in, and let me explain."

"Explain?" Lucretia's voice rose. The load of wood tumbled from her grasp, save the one log she held in her hand. "I knew you were the devil's spawn, since that night in the dungeon—no matter what the archbishop said, God rest his soul. When he knew the truth about you, you killed him. A man of God! And him—" She pointed the log in Madoc's direction. "Helena should never have let him use this place, no matter what he pays. To have them come here, denying what you are, still pretending you're a king or even more."

Wincing, Elisha held out his hands, palms up. "I know what a trial this must be for you, for all of you, God help me, I—"

"You dare to think that God might help you? When you profane the wounds of his son to steal the throne from his anointed?" She jabbed the firewood toward. "And what of the queen? Did you flay her?"

"No, the archbishop did, that's why I had to kill him." He stepped forward. "He claimed me for king to send this nation into chaos. Lucretia, please."

"Guards!" she shouted. "Get up, you!"

Elisha stumbled another step. "No!"

She screamed and flailed.

The piece of wood slammed into the side of Elisha's head, knocking him against the wall and into nothingness.

Chapter 33

⸎

"Get to the king, Madoc," said a woman's voice from the beating blackness. "You've got to!"

"Oh, Sister, I mistook you for one who believed in his lies." Another woman's voice drifted over him.

"We've sent a runner already, sisters. The queen'll know soon enough, don't you worry." The owner of this voice—a man—tugged at Elisha's belt.

"The king!" the first woman shouted. "Not the queen, she's a monster!"

Elisha lost the voices, every sensation briefly silent. He woke again, feeling colder, his teeth chattering. Nausea oozed through his aching belly, and his head throbbed in pulses like bolts of lightning.

"Just to the bridge, that's the duke's order," a man was saying, a young, strong voice.

"Her majesty wants his things, and she's higher than your master, any road."

Images swam through Elisha's mind, but he could not find a face to match the fear that stabbed his belly when they mentioned the duke. Hands tugged him this way and that, stripping his clothes. Elisha groaned, trying to hold down his supper, but the taste of dirt suddenly filled his mouth. He struggled, and the hands dug in, sending a bolt of pain through his body. Elisha went limp. His jaw throbbed in rhythm with lights that pulsed behind his eyes.

"So long as justice is served upon him, I don't know that it matters whose master is higher," observed the younger man.

Elisha fell with a thunk back to the ground, ripples of pain rolling out from his skull. He raised his hand to try to find the source of the agony, or he thought he did, but his numb fingers were slow to respond.

"Here, now, he's moving."

"Well, stop him."

Hard hands wrapped his arm and gave it a twist. The soldier pried at Elisha's finger and tugged something off.

"Leave me alone," he whispered. He wanted the side of his face to melt away and take the horrible nausea along with it. Herbs flickered to mind. He used to be able to ease pain and stop the queasy feeling in his gut. Once, on a boat, someone gave him an herb that helped. Mordecai. What happened to him?

The hands stripped his hose, leaving him naked and shivering.

"Whyn't we just kill him now?" one of the soldiers complained.

"Because he has a power of healing," the duke's man explained. "A wound won't kill him. Drowning might work. It's why witches are dunked."

"Diabolical, I warrant," answered a soldier gruffly.

Elisha's wrists and ankles twitched against those who carried him, his head striking the ground. The throbbing entered his bones, and Elisha's stomach heaved. He tipped his head to the side and vomited.

"As if he needed to smell any worse."

"Bloody Hell," said one of the men at his feet.

Elisha's buttocks scraped against stone. They adjusted their grip, and he heard the guttering of water, a strong current. Waves shifted inside his skull, and he passed out again.

Water splashed over Elisha's face and ran down his shoulders. He sputtered and jerked, only to find his arms held taut, slightly twisted, to either side. Rough stone cobbles bit into his knees, so cold he remembered death and felt comforted. Another torrent of water struck him, and he cried out, trembling, his skull beating time to his heart.

"That's enough. He's awake."

"Thomas," Elisha gasped.

Someone slapped him. "You have no right to the king's name," Duke Randall's voice growled.

Fear lanced through the scar on his belly. "No, Your Grace."

"It doesn't matter," said Thomas.

"If you think that, Your Majesty, you're falling into his power. He'll do whatever he can to manipulate you."

Elisha's eyes crept open, but the feeble light of torches throbbed in his vision, and he shut them again. "Your daughter," Elisha stammered. "Your Majesty, how is she?"

"None of your concern," the duke answered.

"I wondered that myself, love," said Brigit's voice, growing nearer. "I never had the chance to bid her good-night."

Reflexively, Elisha mastered his senses, shaky as he was, and began the ordeal of attunement, reaching out to understand his surroundings.

"She's gone with Allyson," the king replied. "I can't say where."

Elisha lifted his head, opening only his left eye for blood still trickled into the right. Brigit stood to his left, too near the king, while the duke stood directly before him, feet planted, the sword hanging at his side. A handful of men in royal livery backed the king, with a good twenty more in the duke's colors arrayed all around them.

"I thought it best that she not be here." Thomas folded his arms. "I can't say where they went—I don't know." A phantom smile passed his lips.

"Well done, Your Majesty," Elisha sighed, drawing their eyes.

"The king needs praise from you like a man looks for compliments from Satan," said the duke.

"Found this on him." One of the guards offered the ring.

Brigit put out her hand, but Thomas took it between his fingers. "Interesting."

"You see the depths of his depravity, and his obsession, Your Majesty."

Thomas's gaze, sharp and blue, shifted back to Elisha's face.

"We had it from the queen's hand, T—Your Majesty—when she came to kill me," Elisha said. He searched in Thomas's direction, desperate to know what the king believed.

"Don't be absurd," Brigit said, "You can see for yourself I still have the ring." She flashed her hand at him, decked with a rather shiny copy. "Besides, I retired to my chamber and haven't left there since this afternoon. I get worn out so easily." She yawned, fluttering her beringed hand over her mouth.

Thomas slipped the ring onto his finger, though it reached only to the second knuckle. He made a fist around it.

Elisha's right eye would not open all the way, giving him a slanted view, stained with blood. These might be the last faces he saw, the last words he heard. Tension showed plain in Thomas's lean shoulders, and that fist still held. Each time he met Elisha's eyes, he shied away, and finally did not glance back in that direction.

"Is that all he had for a talisman? There must be others," Brigit said.

From his blind side, a man said, "A few locks of hair, some in his medical kit, and these from his sleeve."

"Give it here," commanded the queen.

"No," Thomas's voice overrode her. "That's mine." Then he paused. "And this . . . my daughter's hair, isn't it? This is why you went to the manor?"

"I had to keep her safe." With each throb of Elisha's skull, Thomas shifted in and out of focus.

"A ploy to earn your goodwill, Majesty. The only reason he brought her back is that Brigit's people already knew he'd taken her," the duke pointed out.

Elisha tried to focus on the king. "They would have killed her!" Each movement of his jaw sent shards of pain. "Alfleda must have said."

"She did," replied the king.

Madoc dropped a bow before the king. "Please, yer Majesty. He did not slay the queen. 'Twas the archbishop who came with that—"

"You did your duty in fetching us here, Madoc," the duke interrupted. "Don't make yourself a traitor for his sake."

The duke's men edged closer, swords at the ready, and Thomas caught Madoc's shoulder, easing him aside, but not letting go.

Elisha reached for strength and forced himself to speak. "It's not over with my death. There's two dozen mancers or more—"

The duke snapped, "Somebody shut him up."

"No, Your Majesty, go look at her church, it's a slaughterhouse—it's no altar they're carving. Thomas, don't trust her! Whatever you believe, do not trust her." He broke off as a soldier stood before him, cloth in hand.

The duke's man pried his jaw open and stuffed his mouth with a rag, then bound a length of rope tight about his head. At the man's touch, Elisha recognized the hum of power that underlay the other man's presence—another magus. *"You can feel that I'm telling the truth,"* he pleaded through the contact. *"You know I did not kill her."*

"You're a sensitive, God knows what lies you can project," the duke's magus answered.

A prim little smile settled on Brigit's lips. "Have you bound a witch before?"

At that, the magus had the grace to look a little uncomfortable. "No, Majesty."

She held out an imperious hand and took the rope—not, Elisha was glad to see, a rope made from his hair. He could not reach his senses very far without a talisman, but he retained some awareness. Then Brigit snapped the rope around his wrist and gave it a yank, searing the fibers into his skin and drawing blood. Elisha bit down on the cloth that gagged him.

"There's no need for cruelty."

"It's not cruelty, Thomas, it's good sense. A witch can't reach beyond a circle of his own blood. It reflects the power." She made a knot that squeezed Elisha's torn flesh, then handed off the rope to the duke's magus who tugged Elisha's arm behind his back and repeated the procedure on his right hand. As the knots pulled fast, Elisha's fading senses curled back into his skin. He felt suddenly very alone.

The magus wrapped a second length above Elisha's elbows, binding his arms tight against his chest.

Thomas pressed his fingers against his closed eyes.

"We can't afford to wait for execution," said the duke, more gently. "Look what happened last time."

"I know." Thomas squeezed the bridge of his nose and gave a short nod, then he opened his eyes. "You've got to at least give us time to get the queen away."

Brigit's chin rose. "You can't think I would miss this."

Setting his hands upon her shoulders, Thomas commanded her gaze. "Brigit, you know as well as I the power that a witch has upon dying. Think of your mother."

Her back went rigid, then she cupped her hands around Thomas's face and gave him a kiss. "Yes, love, I hear you." As she swished by Elisha, she glanced back over her shoulder. "I'll want to be certain we're safe, though. Do bring me his head."

Behind the pulsing of his blood, Elisha felt a trickle of sweat down his wet back as she walked away with two guards in her company. He imagined his own head in a jar, the betrayal of his death harnessed to Brigit's command. His eyes stung, and the right one slipped closed again as he watched. Already, he knelt half in darkness.

"You'd best go, too, Your Majesty. The drowning should sap his strength, on top of his injuries. I doubt he'll have the power for,"—the young magus glanced at the other soldiers—"for anything diabolical, but it's best you be far away. We'll give you half an hour."

With a grave nod, Thomas turned and stared down. Elisha lowered his eyes, trembling.

The touch came unexpectedly, sending a jolt through Elisha's aching frame. Hot and strong, Thomas's fingers traced the scar along his throat and tipped up his chin, bringing Elisha's eyes back to his own. From this angle, kneeling in the dirt, Elisha could trace the scar that marked Thomas's throat. "That night at the ball," the king murmured, "You did not mistake my feelings, Elisha, but it was not Rosalynn I was watching. For what it's worth."

Thomas let go, rose, and left. "Madoc! Pray attend me."

"God's blood, Elisha," Madoc muttered, his own head hanging.

"Y'heard the king—move it along."

Elisha stared after them as the king's soldiers closed rank around him, escorting the queen away, leaving the duke's men and their furious master. The ball seemed a lifetime ago. He shut his eyes. Elisha danced with the dishonored Rosalynn, watched by a ragged stranger whose attraction he had sensed. A stranger who turned out to be the elder prince, disguised and claimed for a traitor. In the darkness, he held Thomas's face, and Thomas's words, but their meaning eluded his addled mind.

"How's this?" one of the soldiers asked.

Something fell with a thud next to Elisha's legs, snapping his eye open. Scraping the rope over skin as Brigit had taught him, the young magus bound an iron hitching post to Elisha's ankle.

"Give it a long line. We'll want to haul him up in a while to be sure he's dead." Randall's voice sounded hollow, not victorious. With Elisha's drawing in the Earl of Blackmere and Lord Robert's earlier support, Randall must believe all his friends tainted. Elisha wished he could speak, that he could find the words to pierce Randall's fury and persuade him.

What was the alternative? To give up and surrender to the darkness. The air he sucked in through his nose stung with vomit and blood. Desperate for clean air, he fought the gag, trying to force it out or dislodge the binding rope against his shoulder.

Overhead, the broad bridge swept up to the near gate, crowned with a series of spikes. Mortimer's severed head stared down from bloody sockets, mouth gaping from its rotting flesh.

Elisha let his head drop and felt a wave of nausea. His right eye no longer responded. The area around it was hot and swollen. Lucretia had struck him well—a little harder, a different angle, and he would be dead.

"I mislike this," sighed the duke. "How will we know their majesties are safe?" He stared back at Elisha with no change of expression.

Slowly, Elisha shook his head.

Duke Randall scrubbed both hands over his face.

"Perhaps we should do it now, Your Grace," another soldier offered.

"Forgive me, Your Grace," said the young magus, stepping up with a quick bow. "We really ought to give them the full half-hour. This is the best plan we've made, but still, I'd not wish to risk the king's life on it."

"I've a candle, Your Grace. We could use it for time," one of the soldiers volunteered. He tugged something from his belt and placed it into the duke's hand. Randall tottered forward a few steps, turning the thing in his fingers as he came to the low wall of the bridge. With a blunt fingernail, he carved a line around the candle, not far from the top. Ceremoniously, he planted it on the wall. At a flick of his hand, a guard brought a torch and lit the candle's wick.

A curl of smoke drifted upward, sinuous and gray. The glow spread over the stone as it gained in strength. Light danced among the shadows lingering in the gaps between the stones.

Nobody spoke. Leather creaked and metal rattled from time to time, and the river rushed on below them. Nearby, a crow cawed.

The wax slowly gave way, the flame creeping closer to the duke's line. Elisha's mouth went dry. The bowl of the candle glistened as it melted. Drops beaded up and quivered, then slid down the candle's full height to the wall. Another followed, just as stately, gliding along the creamy surface to form a small mound below. Over and over, Elisha swallowed. If he had his breath and his lips to guide it, he could blow out the flame that burned so near.

"Good." The duke propped himself on the wall to the other side. For a moment, Elisha recalled a time they shared in Randall's own courtyard, the duke taking a bench beside Elisha and hoping to convince him to marry his daughter.

Oh, Rosalynn. If Elisha had wed her, would she yet live? In that other world, Elisha lived as a lord, his father-by-marriage a powerful man, second only to the king—a new, young king. Alaric. Prince Thomas, betrayed by his general on the northern border, came sneaking home, hoping for comfort and to convince his brother that he had been wronged. Not knowing that Alaric was the master of his betrayal, Thomas sought out his brother and died at his hand, quietly by the blade, or painfully by the mancers' command, his skin harvested to serve their ends. And Brigit would still be queen. The archbishop laughed, draped in the flesh of kings, then it was Brigit's laughter that echoed in his memory. A bargain to defend the magi, from both the mancers and the barons—what had been sacrificed to win it? The *desolati*, powerless as peasants beneath the power of others.

Elisha flinched, forcing back the vision. Who remained to oppose her? Blackmere and Lord Robert? Madoc and the other peasants who worshipped Saint Barber? But how could they defy the barons arrayed against them, never mind the mancers with their secret ways? When he died, she won. He squeezed shut his eyes. He knew what was coming, but could the knowledge save him? Not when his head throbbed so hard he almost wished for death.

"What makes it so hard," said the duke, and Elisha's eye snapped open, the right eye twitching in the attempt. Blinking back at him, Randall went on, "What makes it so hard is how much faith I placed in you, and how very wrong I have been. I have thought myself a fair judge of men, until you."

Elisha had to turn his head far to the right as the duke moved in close. In spite of his dazed vision, Elisha saw the depth of the man's wrinkles and the puffy flesh around his eyes. His cheeks sagged, his lips drawn down by their weight.

"That's why it wounds us so—first to suffer at your hands, then to cause you to suffer at ours. I was not sure Thomas had the stomach for it, even after what you did to his wife." Randall blinked a few times at that, his lips trembling. "There'll be no priest for you, just as there was none for her." His forehead furrowed over those watery eyes. "They would not take her at the church. After how the archbishop died, they feared the devil's touch upon her skin—all that we have of her. That's why we brought her west, because they denied my daughter the right to be buried in hallowed ground."

The man's breath heated Elisha's skin. If Elisha had his voice, he could tell them the king, and even the queen, had nothing to fear from him. He struggled to form a plan to survive, to find a way to fight back, but he had none; everything had been stripped from him, everything but the king's final words, and they gave him nothing. Randall should take him now and have done. To wait even a few minutes longer, for both of them, was simply torture.

The duke's eyes shifted toward the candle; then he dashed it aside. "Do it now! Now, I tell you!" He thrust a finger toward the waiting soldiers. "This devil knows them both too well for them to escape if he would have them. Kill him now!"

"Yes, Your Grace." They grabbed him, to wrest him to the top of the wall.

Elisha sobbed, twisting his head, catching a glimpse of the man who used to be his friend. He remembered Farus shrieking as the water closed over his head. He remembered the rush as he submerged and the struggle for breath. The post would drag him straight to the bottom for a death he could not heal.

"What, now you have remorse?" the duke thundered

over his head. "Now would you beg for the mercy you forbade my daughter? To Hell with you, Elisha Barber!"

Elisha pitched and struggled as the men hauled up his leg, the post wrenching his ankle.

At the back of his throat, Elisha screamed into the gag. For all that he had known of death, he should not fear it so. Except that now, bound with barriers of his own blood, he could not feel it coming. He could not feel the men's anger or the duke's grief. Blind and naked as his birth, Elisha faced his death.

The scream echoing in his throat and head almost hid the sound of the soldier's grunt. No one breathed. All sound died save the hoarse cry that Elisha could not voice.

A soft and distant something twanged.

Into the silence one of the soldiers fell, his hands sliding from Elisha's arm, almost pulling him back from the wall onto the bridge.

A second soldier wailed and blood spattered Elisha's back. Redness flooded his vision once more.

"Take cover!"

A feathered shaft protruded from the man's chest.

"Archers, Your Grace!" The young magus shouted. "Take cover!"

The hands shifted at Elisha's limbs. Rescue, by God! The answer he dared not hope from a prayer so hopeless he dare not frame it. Elisha seized the chance, in spite of his pain. In a burst of strength, he shoved to the side, trying to tumble back to the bridge. The iron post scraped and fell toward the river, tugging him in the wrong direction, the wall grinding into his stomach as he kicked.

"I'm fine, you damned fool," someone croaked. "The prisoner, give him a shove."

The remaining soldiers turned back and pushed.

Elisha screamed into the muffling gag as he fell, the post yanking him downward like the iron-mage's dying grasp. He slapped the surface of the water, then plunged into the river, sharp, cold, and dark, his nostrils stinging. The rope unreeled above him, the marker for his grave. What savior could reach him there? Which of his friends could even swim?

Overhead, the splashing continued as he sank, as someone entered the water with him. Then he could not discern between the thunder in his skull and the beating of the water outside of it. In moments, the two must become one.

Something brushed over his skin as he tossed and kicked, but the post dragged at him, his neck straining upward. When the post struck bottom, a jolt shivered through him from his bound ankle to his throbbing skull. Just deep enough.

He twisted against his captivity, his lungs laboring, burning despite the water that trapped him. The rope tugged from above, a hopeful fisherman checking on his catch.

Water filled him. The foul, polluted Thames clogged his ears and nose and crept around the edges of the gag. A warm touch slid down his back and the rope jerked again, this time from below as if someone took hold of it.

Blows buffeted his body, submerged objects assailing him. Something clung about his shoulders, and he thrashed, envisioning a shroud of weeds. Heat wrapped his body: a demon of Hell come to gather him home.

He thrashed, and his leg was suddenly free, the current shoving him as he rose, the demon still hanging on, fingers digging in, a blade pressed flat against his chest. They broke the surface, rushing downstream. Elisha snorted, shaking his head, shaking himself back into darkness for a moment. Dragging himself awake again, head and stomach churning, Elisha stared at the stars that wheeled over him as he spun below. Water overwhelmed him, shoving him back, the cold hand of Death trying to hold him down. Then his face emerged, some-one gasping at his ears, grappling with his shoulders.

Huge shadows rose up above him, cutting the stars, but he could not tell if they were real or merely the spikes of pain that cut his distorted vision. His side scraped wood, and the river pushed but could push him no further as he struck against a solid darkness that rocked beside him.

Bands of heat remained against the churning water. With a strong arm, a knife still clutched in his grasp, his captor cradled Elisha's head against his chest. No de-mon, but a savior true, warm and alive. The man's heart-beat thudded into Elisha's ear, joining the addled sounds within.

"Peace, Elisha," murmured Thomas's voice. "I'm with you."

Chapter 34

Elisha lay still, held tight against the side of the boat. Thomas's labored breathing filled his ears.

Blood oozed from his wounded skull. He began to tremble again, violently, the more so as he tried to control the shaking. Thomas's arm held him close. Thomas's other hand rose beside him, gripping a rope that looped down from the boat at their back.

"Dear God, I thought we were too late."

Elisha wanted to shake his head, to make some movement to reassure him, but he shivered. In moments, the shivering took hold so fiercely that Thomas tightened his arm, Elisha's head knocking against the king's breast. Thomas looked around, then hauled Elisha into motion. He shifted his hand under Elisha's arm, hanging on, as he reached for a dark shape that tipped and wallowed: a smaller boat.

"I won't lose you, Elisha. Take courage," the king said as he moved. "If you have nothing else, you do have courage." Then Elisha dangled while Thomas dragged himself into the boat one-handed. His other hand slipped and he cried out as the river tugged at Elisha's body once more, but he caught the rope at Elisha's chest and held him. For a moment, the king panted into the dark-

ness, Elisha's head pressed against the boat by the water's current, then the boat tipped dangerously as
Thomas reached to haul him in, his back and bound arms
scraping over the gunwale.

The floor rocked as Thomas settled him on his left
side. Elisha's guts rolled with the motion of the boat. The
world went black.

Light returned in shards and an oar scraped on wood
as Thomas pushed them along the ship then to the freedom of the river. Night already purpled toward dawn, or
did the pounding of his skull bring the colors?

Elisha moaned, or he would have, if the foul gag did
not stop his voice.

"Deo Gratias. I thought you had died after all of that.
Hold still."

As if Elisha were capable of moving. Something tugged
at the gag, then a cool bit of metal slid against his cheek,
the motion repeating until finally the rope let loose.
Thomas's hand cupped his head while he worked to free
the bloodied rope, then pluck out the wad of fabric. Elisha
gulped at the air. Water ran from his hair and his shivering
flesh. His stomach gave a heave, and Thomas slid an arm
around his chest as Elisha retched over the side of the
boat. It bucked under his knees, but Thomas held him
steady, and the retching subsided at last, leaving him gasping for air, his throat and nostrils scalded.

Thomas eased him back, his hand lingering on Elisha's cheek as he studied the blow to Elisha's head. He
glanced briefly over his shoulder, his face drawn.

Elisha concentrated on breathing. Every inhalation
caused streaks of pain from his head and arms, but it
cleared his vision, such as it was. The sky maintained its
violet hue.

"Will you be all right a little longer? I need to get you
warm and dry, but we're still too close." The king, too,
shivered, his tunic clinging to his skin.

Their eyes met, Thomas's looking brighter than they had for a long time. "Yes," Elisha breathed, grateful for even so feeble a voice.

Thomas resumed rowing, his arms reaching and pulling, each puff of his breath turning misty. The enemy would find them. Elisha had spilled too much blood in the workshop and on the bridge to remain hidden for long, not once Brigit knew how to look, and she might now have the sensitivity to seek him that way. But he could not speak to break the rhythm of Thomas's graceful movements, nor diminish the triumph of his rescue.

"I feared that Randall's patience would break." Thomas spoke softly. "I wish I could have brought you a blanket or clothing. Something," he broke off. "We had time for the arrows, but little else once I'd sent Brigit on her way. Madoc and Walter and some others came with me, to fight them off. We were supposed to have you before you hit the water. None of the others can swim." He gave a hard breath. "If not for that bloody rope, I'd never have found you at all."

Great shadows rose up from the deeper blackness of the river, waves lapping against the wooden hulls as the rigging groaned. Cautiously, Thomas guided their little boat among the larger vessels. Elisha shut his eye when he felt certain Thomas couldn't see him. Then he would hear Thomas's intake of breath and open it again, to assure his king he still lived. He drifted, unsure what he felt beyond the pain. Sometimes he shivered so badly that he thumped in the little boat and feared he'd tip them back into the river.

They left most of the ships behind, small houses and mills rose up along the banks of the wide river. Thomas slowed, each stroke long and weary. Night birds rose up crying from the riverside and other creatures rustled away at their approach, the steady splash of the oars driving them onward. Smoke clogged the air and Elisha's bruised lungs, stinging his eyes.

A thicket of docks at the river's left bank heralded a hamlet not yet astir. Thomas turned the bow inward and pulled up to one of the docks, their craft bumping against others. He tied off to a peg in the half-rotted wood, then stretched and moved carefully behind the seat at Elisha's back. His hands, two pools of warmth against the gooseflesh, encouraged Elisha to bend forward. He shifted his weight and began to cut the first rope, lifting it away from the scrapes.

Elisha's shoulders slumped painfully, and he stifled a cry. This task inflamed his broken skin, but he grit his teeth until it was done. Thomas eased his hands, first one, then the other, into his lap as Elisha tried to straighten. His shoulders jerked and twitched, but his hands lay like two dead things. Thomas slipped the golden ring from his smallest finger and slid it onto Elisha's. "You'll need a talisman. I sent Pernel to prepare a place not far off, where you'll be safe," Thomas told him. "Can you walk?"

Elisha managed a nod. A lie, mostly likely, but he must try.

Thomas helped Elisha out of the boat, as one might help a child, but Elisha stiffened as the king put an arm around him to lead him onward. Thomas faced him on the dock, the rising sun giving a faint glow to his profile. "Elisha, you have been more faithful to me than any man or woman ever has. But you have grown too used to stumbling on alone, regardless of your injuries. At least in part, it is my fault for abandoning you. Please let me help you."

Elisha tipped up his head, wobbling at the dizziness that followed. Thomas's hand rose, but hesitated, his brow furrowed. "Thomas," Elisha rasped, then swallowed, trying to find his voice. "If you go back now, they will let you in. Randall will be angry, but you are still king. The longer you stay—"

Shaking his head, Thomas parted his lips, but Elisha continued, "They will search for me, and whoever is with me, king or no, will not escape. This is what the mancers want, for the monarchy to shatter." The long speech wore him out, and it took all his effort to remain standing, to appear stronger than he was. He could not afford to plead with Thomas to make him go, but he would beg upon his knees if he had to, even as he wanted, with all of his heart, for him to stay.

"How long will you last if I leave you?" Thomas shouted, and Elisha flinched. "You can barely stand. Do you imagine you're fooling me? Good Lord, Elisha, the pain in you is killing me."

Swaying in the wake of Thomas's vehemence, Elisha did not know what to say, or even if he was capable of speech. Rarely had he seen Thomas so upset. In fact, the prior occasion had ended with Thomas trying to kill him. The scar that ran along Thomas's chin and down his throat looked pink and vulnerable in the new light.

Ruffling back his hair, Thomas gripped his skull and was silent. With his arms still raised, his fingers clenched in his hair, Thomas said, "You think that I don't know the danger, Elisha, but I do, and I know, too, that even you cannot protect me. Not without killing yourself. I will not watch you die."

"Then go now," Elisha whispered, "and you need not watch." The cold whistled in his right ear, louder by the moment. "When I walk the Valley, some of them will walk with me."

"Even you, even with your death, could you stop them all? Can you stop Brigit performing whatever sorcery she has in mind?"

Elisha hesitated, the dark town rocking in time with the throbbing of his skull. The clearing sky looked

bruised and beaten, on the verge of rain. Red blotches
drifted across the gray cloudbank, and Elisha failed to
blink them away.

Thomas touched him, a careful hand that stopped the
world from moving. "I told you it wasn't Rosie I watched
at the ball. What did you think I meant?"

The ball. Elisha tried to focus and remember. Thomas's desire as he watched Rosalynn dancing . . . with Elisha himself. Elisha tried to shake his head. Pain exploded
through his skull, radiating through his jaw, shooting
down his spine. He collapsed, his voice once more
snatched from him. Thomas swept him up and carried
him through the streets. Elisha's head rolled against him
as they ran, every step lashing through him. With each
pulse of pain came a moment of clarity, an image of a
drawn skull, fractured, lurking beneath his skin: his own
death's head. He imagined the irreparable shattered
mess of Martin's skull. Something banged outside of him,
a hollow pounding, then they passed through a brief
darkness into a warmer light.

"Clear the table!" Thomas shouted. "Pernel, more
light, and blankets."

Strong arms carried him and lay him down, gently, he
knew, but the impact jarred him so he gasped. Someone
cradled his head, pillowing it with his hands until something softer and colder could be brought. Piercing light
reached through his swollen right eye, his left getting a
close view of a pillow, a rough table, a fire across the
room, Thomas's anxious face.

Blankets settled over him from neck to toes, pressed
down, tucked against his legs. A warm hand settled at the
edge of his jaw, a different kind of strength seeping
through that touch. "A razor, please," said another voice,
soft and precise, just above his ear. The spread hand pinned
his chin. A sluice of liquid dripped then spilled over his
head; harmless across his forehead, it struck agony down

the right side, and he jerked against the hand, grabbing for its wrist, but the grip ghosted through his own flesh.

"*Yes*," the touch whispered, "*you know my hand as well as your own.*"

The hand that once he healed. Mordecai. Tears seeped from Elisha's eye into the pillow, and his grip trembled.

"We'll need to restrain him. There is no way to dull this pain," said Mordecai Surgeon, as calmly as if he sat in his library.

"I will hold him." Thomas's fingers gently pried away Elisha's hand, then he gripped Elisha's arms, drawing them out in front.

"Rose oil, more wine, and unroll that bundle here beside me," Mordecai instructed. "Do you know the tools by name?"

"Not all, Master, but I'll do it."

The noises of preparation echoed through the table, clattering tools, sloshing jars, the quiet, constant prayer of Thomas's grip upon him.

Through his left hand, Mordecai sent compassion. But his right carefully probed the wound, sending Elisha back into darkness. "*What is your diagnosis?*"

"*Compressed skull fracture,*" Elisha sent through the contact and sobbed without sound, Mordecai's hand and Thomas's grip were the only steady things in his world. Despite the blankets, Elisha's feet shivered, his left side already numb. "*I'm dying.*"

"*Once you told us you could not die,*" said Mordecai. Another sluice of liquid, scented now with wine, cleansed the wound.

"*Not the same as cannot feel pain,*" Elisha sent back, trying to jest, but Mordecai's thumb followed the edge of his jaw.

"*Do not waste your strength to protect me,*" Mordecai said. "*You know what I have to do.*"

Tiny tugs at his skin translated the snip of scissors

trimming his hair. *"Shave the scalp, make a cruciform incision, perforate, reginate, elevate."* His body shuddered, and Thomas's grip tightened. Briefly, Pernel's hands held his legs. Trephination. Mordecai would drill holes in his skull. Even a patient who lived might not be the same. *"I could have such a life that every day I'd wish that I were dead."*

"Pernel, place your hand here, good." Mordecai's hand lifted from his jaw and another took its place, strong, but not so steady, not so calm. "Firm grip, Your Majesty," the surgeon said, then touched his hand lightly to the back of Elisha's neck, radiating heat, urging him to listen, "Elisha, do not let go."

The cold edge of a razor touched Elisha's skin, scraping away the stubble of his hair, drawing down an edge of pain. *"I can't see."*

"The Lord is my shepherd, I shall not want," whispered the king.

"A common side effect. Usually passes." The razor withdrew, replaced by a new edge, sharper, slicing into his scalp, and Elisha cried out, struggling against the grip that held him.

Thomas's strength pushed him down, held him fast. "He leadeth me beside the still waters. He restoreth my soul." The king's voice cracked. "Elisha, be still."

A cruciform incision. Elisha sobbed into the pillow. Sabetha telling him he was like a priest who reached God not through the spirit but the flesh. His hands burned with pain as Morag spiked a dagger through to pin him down.

". . . yea, though I walk through the valley of the shadow of death . . ."

Mordecai lifted Elisha's head, pushing wads of wool into his ears. The chill of a metal brace set against his head, then it jiggled a little as Mordecai guided the bit into place. The grating of metal on bone resonated through his skull, echoing from ear to ear, the squeak of the bit drilling into him. Elisha could no longer hear Thomas's prayer, but he knew how it ended: I shall fear no evil.

The faces of mancers loomed up in the darkness, a dozen, two dozen, gathered around their new queen, splashed with blood, clad in skins, masters of pain. They reached out, the void of their awareness tingling against him. Mordecai's presence loomed up, a wash of equations, languages, diagrams, and images rolling through him, and the mancers faded.

Then a sharp, cold tool slipped inside his skull, prying upward. Elisha snapped free of the flesh and drifted away.

Chapter 35

❦

The small townhouse rose up around him, its loft open at one side with a ladder going up. Smoke curled from a handful of lanterns hung from the loft edge or placed on the benches. A fire glowed at the hearth, a tripod within held a bubbling pot. Nothing smelled, nor did the fire crack and pop. A man lay on the table in the center of the main room, on his side, most of his body concealed by blankets, his bloody head resting on a pillow, half shaved. The scalp peeled back in four triangles over the ear framing a crevice that marred the bone beneath.

A surgeon worked over him, a silver tool gripped in his hand. He moved the handle with precision, lifting a section of the shattered skull, easing it back into place. Elisha should have liked to study surgery with him.

Another man, a servant, stood close at the surgeon's back, a hand braced upon the patient's jaw, holding his head in place. His thumb rested at the pulse point, and so he might be fooled into thinking that the patient's pulse still leapt. As the surgeon's lips moved, his hand replacing one tool, the servant hesitated and chose another, then drooped, took it back, and gave a different one which the surgeon accepted, resuming his work.

A fourth man—assuming the patient could still be

counted in their number—knelt before the table, clinging to the dead man, his face hidden in the tangle of their
arms, his shoulders quaking. He already knew what the
others ignored.

The roof overhead opened up with sudden light, a
tempest of brilliance and wailing that struck down the
silence. Elisha gazed up into the tunnel that opened
there, a frightening place, now familiar. That was where
he belonged. He was already naked and light. Except his
left hand felt heavy, detached. He tried to shake the feeling away, then used the right hand to lift it up before his
face and figure out what the trouble was. Bloody scrapes
marked the wrist. Something small and gold encircled
the little finger. That wasn't right. He gave his hand a
shake, but the ring remained. It wasn't even his ring, it
was Brigit's. Oh, she would be angry about that, she
knew he had the real one. And she knew that Thomas
knew. He could never go back to her now. Damn, that
made things difficult.

The howling void overhead grew louder, but some
voices called more sweetly: an old witch, a repentant
traitor, a man who loved him, a young doctor he once
drew from a river. Elisha waved them away; he still had
this problem of the ring. He couldn't take it with him,
obviously, but he couldn't seem to shake it, and his good
hand couldn't grasp the thing to leave it behind, as if part
of him remained in some other place.

He stared down at the men around his body. Thomas
had put it here, and Thomas would just have to take it off
again and let him go. But Thomas looked too preoccu-
pied to disturb just now. Kneeling on the floor, he clung
to the corpse's hands. The corpse lay there, the surgeon
still close as he replaced the patches of skin, the servant
drawn back to his master, draping him with a blanket,
but reluctant to reach out with his blood-stained hands.

Elisha didn't want to go back, to sink into that flesh of

corruption and pain. Perhaps if he put his hand in the fire, the ring would melt, and he could go. He reached out his hand, the flames reaching back. No, not the flames, the angel.

Smiling, Elisha moved closer to her, his cheek warming with the memory of her touch. He could talk to her now. She didn't have to die alone, but she, too, refused the ring. Her daughter's ring. Wouldn't she be happy, now that Brigit was queen? Brigit built a church on the place where she had died. Brigit would commemorate her. Brigit would avenge her, and every witch ever wronged by *desolati*. Then Elisha wouldn't be alone, either, because all of his friends would be dead. His left hand responded, closing into a fist.

The howling passage sucked at his back, but he drew it down to him, into him, taking the cold, the light, the knowledge. As the surgeon anointed him with oil of roses, Elisha drew down his soul. He took a deep breath, armoring himself against the pain, and pulled himself home.

Red, streaking agony filled his vision, but Elisha held on, for a moment bridging the abyss between life and death. With a howl of fear and a bolt of light, the Valley slammed against him. Calling up the power of his brief passage, Elisha urged his skin to heal, and the surgeon let out a long breath, his hand lingering, his heat joining with Elisha's, lending him the strength of the living to match the power of the dead.

At last, Elisha opened his eyes, the right one flickering slowly, the lashes still thick with blood. But the left eye felt cold, a hollow in his skull, as if his eye had been replaced with a ball of ice. He wiped away the blood, and Pernel cried out.

Thomas's head jerked up, and he caught his breath. "Elisha. You're alive. Praise God!" His grin broke through his fading tears. Then his blue glance flickered over Elisha's face. "What's wrong with your eye?"

"I died." He gazed at the king, but the image seemed too deep, hovering shadows drifted at Thomas's shoulders.

"I don't understand."

He wiped his cold left eye. For a moment, the spirits were gone and then returned. Elisha gentled his voice. "I could have left this world, Thomas. I came back because I have to stop Brigit."

"We have to, you mean."

"I don't think that you can help me anymore."

The grin returned to Thomas's pale face and he shook his head. "You still wish me gone. Very well, your resistance is duly ignored. I'm fair with a blade, and an excellent archer."

An answering smile crept across Elisha's lips, and he pushed himself to sit up on the table, the blankets sliding down to pool across his lap. The rope burns at his hands and arms showed pink, barely healed, and a cautious hand found his scalp whole, though tender. Raised lines crossed the site of his incision, and hollows in the bone beneath, marked holes into his skull.

The floor creaked as Mordecai moved in front of him, wiping his hands on a cloth, his belt of books swaying at his hips. He examined his patient and inclined his head.

"Thank you," Elisha said, reaching to grasp the surgeon's hand, feeling the exhaustion that flowed back to him. Mordecai had performed delicate surgery, all the while using the strength of his knowledge to hide Elisha from the mancers. No wonder he was tired.

"Pleased to be of use," Mordecai told him through the contact, his damp eyes blinking a few times. *"Where did you go?"*

"The Valley of the Shadow. It's how the mancers travel, to a place they have marked with a victim's blood."

The surgeon shivered, drawing back his hand.

"Brigit has built a chapel over the place where her mother died. I think she'll use that to make contact with a crowd."

"She wanted the dedication ceremony to follow close upon the wedding, to ensure the nobility could attend. You'd called for a parliament, so all the great lords and the less are already in London." Thomas frowned. "Is she hoping for resurrection?"

Pernel filled a round of tankards, then climbed the ladder and returned with an armload of clothing that he piled on the table, beginning to ready each piece until Elisha waved him away.

"That's not possible." Elisha pulled on some of the new clothes while Pernel assisted Thomas in changing from his wet things. Elisha gulped at his drink, his body still shaky and seeking the comforts of the flesh. "In part, she wants revenge, but she also wants witches to rule. She'll find a way to demonstrate her power, and show the consequences of disobeying her. She promised the mancers she would break the kingdom."

"Come, Master," Pernel murmured, leading Mordecai to a chair as the surgeon gave a mighty yawn. Hours must have passed, with Mordecai working over his flesh and sending what comfort he could to his spirit as well. Hours . . . By tonight, it would be done. None left with the strength to resist her.

Elisha slid down from the table, unsteady on his feet, and Thomas reached out, his blue eyes sharp with concern. "I'm fine," Elisha told him. "Truly. I feel as if I'll live forever."

"Elisha—"

He braced himself on the table, then glanced away as a ghostly woman died in childbirth. Too much like Helena. "Have you stashed any horses in this rescue of yours?" A figure all of shadow moved as if opening the door, then plunged backward, falling from an unseen blade.

"Two," said Thomas. "How do we stop her?"

Elisha swung away toward the surgeon, but Mordecai's head already slumped to his chest, and Pernel was wrapping him with blankets. "Take good care of him."

The servant nodded, but his glance was for the king. "And his majesty?"

"I'll do my best."

Pernel gathered their empty mugs and nodded. "I believe you will, Your—" Then he gave a soft breath of laughter. "But I don't even know what to call you."

"Elisha," he said and put out his hand.

After a moment, Pernel grasped it, started to bow, and stopped himself. "Well met," he said at last, then he hurried to open the door and usher out his two kings.

Outside in the street, a pair of men struggled, one with a stick of wood in his hand, bludgeoning the other, both of them silent.

"How do we stop her?"

Elisha stared at the ghostly duel.

"Brigit," Thomas prompted. "How do we stop her?"

Both combatants fell to the earth, dissipating, only to rise again a moment later and resume fighting. "Right," said Elisha. He closed his left eye, and the figures vanished, though he could bring them back if he stretched out his awareness. "If I can get contact, I can probably kill her."

"The stable is this way." Thomas set off, Elisha trailing after as he edged past the spirits that rose up around him. "And the baby?"

"That's her defense against me," Elisha murmured. "She doesn't believe I would do it."

"Would you, even to stop her?"

Elisha weighed the lives around him. Thomas's eyes tracked a crow that soared overhead, his uplifted chin revealing the scar of the mancer's blade. Elisha imagined the baby, small and wrinkled, innocent, unscarred—his own unfamiliar flesh and blood. "I don't know," Elisha said at last, and the king touched his shoulder. Then the pair of them ducked inside a wretched stable where a lad leapt up to help with the horses.

As they rode, Elisha extended his senses all around them, trying to discern between the living and the dead. Thomas's presence glowed like a fire to his left, burning with renewed purpose. In the late afternoon, the sun finally broke through leaden clouds, giving the appearance of a heavy-lidded eye, displeased at being aroused from slumber. Elisha focused on what lay ahead and tried to work out what he might expect from Brigit and the mancers. He thought of using his own blood to mark Thomas's clothes, keeping the king close and safe, but the chance that Brigit could achieve contact as well posed too great a risk. Besides, Elisha reflected as his horse burst through a crew of spirits toiling by an ancient bridge, how safe could it be to keep close to a man so intimate with Death?

"She'll be expecting us," Elisha said at last. "She wants you to be there."

"Can she still . . . feel you?"

Elisha shook his head. "Something changed when I died. I hope that it will keep me invisible to her."

Looking off down the road, Thomas murmured, "I wish you would not say that so lightly."

"I don't know how else to say it. Each of my near-deaths changed me—the other magi observed that my presence felt different. After I travelled all the way to the lodge, even Brigit didn't recognize me until we stood face to face. A man can't be close to death for so long without changing. There's a young man who keeps bearing witness to his miracle and thinks it makes me some sort of hero. Some sort of—saint." Elisha took a deep breath and stopped babbling. Would it be harder to reassure Thomas, or himself? But Thomas did not know that they rode through the shades of the dead.

"You are a hero," the king said. "But not for that."

Their hoof beats filled the silence, and the horses snorted clouds into the long shadows.

As the city walls grew in the distance, tension built across Elisha's shoulders. London crouched on the horizon like a storm, ready to pound away the villages spread out before and thunder down upon them. To the left, by the river, the Tower glinted gold in its own palisade. Elisha thought of its dungeon and the bridge of traitors beyond, and turned his horse sharply away, across the moors and off among the smaller farms. Passing through the dead no longer thrilled him, but he missed that little burst of strength in these unsettled lands.

They rode a wide circle around the city, Elisha taking the lead. Few people walked the roads or tended the sheep and a knot of worry built in his gut. They passed a broken wagon laden with baked goods, small festival cakes spilling across the mud. The baker stood by cursing at his ox. "—sure to miss it now, ye bloody beast!"

Another festival. Dear God, what could Brigit mean by it? She summoned them all to witness—what? Something more dangerous and divisive than a French invasion. An event so devastating the mancers would accept her leadership to make it happen.

Something flickered in his vision, then more, and Elisha glanced up to find a flock of crows wheeling overhead. Thomas followed his gaze and crossed himself. They entered a cluster of houses and emerged again, reining in abruptly. Crows swirled before them, rank upon rank, a flurry surrounding the dark figure of a woman. Thomas swept his sword from its sheath, but Elisha stayed his hand.

"So, Barber, my brother Farus is dead." She stalked out, head lowered, eyes flicking from one rider to the other.

"He betrayed Chanterelle to the necromancers, lady," Elisha told her, his horse dancing as his fists tightened.

The crow-mistress bobbed her head, black garments ruffling. "We would've taken him ourselves." She gave a sharp cry and clicked her mouth shut, the crows settling around them. "Despite his bitter flesh." Her dark eyes focused on Thomas, and returned to Elisha. "They gather today, and we hope to be well-fed." A crow on her shoulder bounced up and down.

Elisha took a deep breath, dodging the shimmering eyes of the thousand birds. "Will you help me, lady, and help your king?"

"No king of mine! Last we helped him, it was we who fell." The crows screeched around her, and Elisha fought the urge to clamp his hands over his ears.

"She lent me the lives of her friends, to draw upon for healing you the night your brother died," he told the king. "I was careless, and some of them died."

Thomas nudged his mount a little nearer, inclining his head. "Mistress, please, thank your friends for their sacrifice. I would not wear the crown without your service."

She swiveled her head, staring at him, and a thousand crows stared with her, sharp, black beaks and shining black eyes. Then, she gave herself a ruffling shake and stalked to Elisha's horse. "The evil ones, you've seen them? Show me." She put out a hand knobbed with age and scarred by the grip of talons.

Elisha took her hand in his and remembered the mancers, each and every one that he had seen. Her eyes flicked this way and that, as if she looked upon a gallery of paintings, then she drew away, and gave that bob of her head. Another cry, and the crows took flight, spiraling up in the sky and flying in a black cloud toward London.

"What will they do?" Thomas asked softly as the crow-mistress let them pass.

"I've no idea—but I'll take any army at our back today."

They came from the shadow of a church, its cross cast

long and dark up the road before them. A party of soldiers blocked the way. Elisha nudged his horse into a gallop. "Stand aside, in the name of the king!"

"Halt!" one of them shouted, then fell back as they saw who followed.

"Be firm," cried someone else in the ranks. "The king's bewitched!"

"Bewitched?" Thomas sharply reined up his horse. "Who dares suggest it?"

A thickly bearded man pushed through and lifted his chin. "His Grace, the Duke of Dunbury gave us orders, Your Majesty. Said you'd be under the devil's influence." He tipped his head toward Elisha.

The man's presence felt at first, like nothing at all, an absence carved from the flow of life around him. But then the cold seeped through. A shade hung about him, echoing his movements, and Elisha stared, almost recognizing the ruined face.

"Your Majesty, this man is no ally," Elisha said.

Thomas's gaze sharpened, but he made no reply, instead facing down the man before him. "My wife has planned this festival, and you would bar my way?" Despite his borrowed clothing, he sat tall and regal, glaring down with all the arrogance of his throne. Elisha's blood warmed at the sight of him.

"And him?" The cold wind blew, and the edges of a dead soul rippled around the mancer, flickering terror barely tamped down. "You want me to allow in your last wife's killer? Your Majesty, 'tis plain you're not thinking clear."

The crowd of soldiers tightened, their eyes glinting white as their hands gripped spears and sword hilts. The mancer walked purposefully toward Elisha's horse, his hand already outstretched. He let the tattered edge of fear fly at his back, shaping the winds. The men stopped murmuring, their separate glows merged, carefully woven, their fear and anger directed at Elisha himself.

Elisha's horse danced a few paces back, eluding the hand set out to catch its head. "Do not touch the king," Elisha whispered, sending the words upon an icy breeze of his own.

The mancer's eyes crinkled, just a little, into a smile only Elisha could feel. "Come, sir, we don't want any bloodshed upon this sacred day."

"Well," Thomas cut in, "if it's Randall who would prevent us, then take us to him. Let him explain himself to his liege-lord."

"His Grace is on the way," called out a breathless man at the back, and Elisha straightened in his saddle. Beyond the bulk of Saint Bartholomew's, the squat shape of Brigit's chapel stood in a sea of people, soldiers, barons and peasants alike. A party of men hurried up the road, swords at the ready.

Cold crackled against Elisha's awareness, and he dodged his horse back again, narrowly avoiding the mancer's grasp. A hand caught his leg on the other side.

"Hold him! Keep him!"

A smaller group of soldiers in the duke's livery surged forward, separating the horses, surrounding Elisha.

"Release him, I say!" Thomas shouted. "He's an innocent man!"

They unhorsed him instead, Elisha gathering his power as he fell. Kicking away the hands that tried to snatch him, Elisha scrambled to his feet, projecting the awful menace of his fury. He spun a circle and spotted the mancer backing away into the crowd. Elisha lunged after him, reaching through the deathly power that suffused them both.

Pressing his hat to his head, the mancer whirled back, sword in hand, its edge dull with old blood.

Do you dare? Elisha spoke without words, sending the shock of his strength into the air and the earth.

A few of the soldiers drew back. "Captain—" one of them ventured, but the mancer ignored him.

"Have at me, then. Show them the truth about you!" the mancer urged him even as he backed away, fetching up against the twitching leg of Thomas's mount.

"Your Majesty, the hat!" Elisha called.

Thomas reached out and snatched it from the mancer's head, eliciting a cry, first from the man, then from those around him as scraps of flesh still bloody tumbled from the woolen cap. Growling, the mancer snatched at it as the bewildered soldiers withdrew. Elisha felt a grim satisfaction, until his left eye saw the cold shards of Death penetrate the heat of Thomas's presence, and he realized his mistake. Thomas flung the thing away, but the talisman had already marked him.

The mancer turned, hand atop his head, still streaked with blood.

Thomas stared at his own hand, his face pale, and moved as if to wipe off the stain.

"Make way for his Grace, the Duke of Dunbury!" someone shouted.

Elisha shot forward, leaping onto the mancer even as the wind howled into his ears, the mancer reaching for Thomas through the blood that marked him. He set his fingers against the man's skin and summoned death. The mancer screamed.

His hands grappled with Elisha, tearing his borrowed tunic. A black shadow wrapped Elisha's arm, like a ferret up a lady's sleeve, and he sucked it inside, his lungs swelling with borrowed strength. The screaming stopped, or perhaps Elisha could no longer hear it for the mad snapping in his skull, his faithful hounds baying for more. Elisha rose from the body, and none now lay a hand upon him.

From his horse, Thomas gave a slight bow and said, "Your Grace. We've been expecting you." He swallowed. His presence shivered with doubt and remembrance.

"How could you help him?" The duke's sword jutted

up toward the king, as steady as his voice was not. "You know, you were there," he gulped for breath. "How could you, after all of that?"

"Because Elisha is innocent of the crime you would kill him for."

"Rosalynn's murder! Can't you even say the words?"

Elisha stood calm, watching the pink-faced duke confront his latest betrayer. Thomas slid down from his horse at last, his travel-worn boots hitting the dirt not far from the dead man's open eyes, rimed with frost, the same color as the clouds which moved in to obscure the sun. Thomas proclaimed Elisha's innocence while overlooking the body at his feet. To all those around him, Thomas looked like a fool, like the very worst kind of hypocrite, or, after all, a man bewitched, for how else could he defend such a murderer?

"Randall," the king began softly, "you think that I've forgotten, but I have not. There is other evidence we have been blind to, evidence that it was the archbishop at the heart of this madness, and now Brigit has claimed his place. They've been trying to break our allegiances, to trap us each in our own grief and pain so that we did not see this day as it overtook us."

"She fears him so greatly, and yourself, Your Majesty"—another twist of the duke's lips—"that she set us here to guard against your arrival. Good God, man, what's he done to you?"

The stillness at Elisha's back, where a hundred soldiers shifted and stared, broke into muffled groans and curses. Before him, the duke's scowl wrenched briefly into a wince then returned again. His off-hand absently rested against his stomach and his sword-arm twitched.

"I do not wish to hurt you, Your Majesty," he said through clenched teeth. "After the ceremony is over, then Father Osbert can set about to exorcise this devil from you."

At another groan behind him, Elisha looked back. Several of the men held their stomachs, a few rubbed at their hands, blinking fiercely. "What's the matter, man?" demanded one of the few unaffected, a lad of perhaps seventeen years.

"I don't know. Too much drink. God, but it stings." The soldier's brow furrowed.

"Can't you smell it?" said another, an older man, rubbing at his eyes. "Wind must've shifted. Somebody's fire's blowing in my face." He coughed sharply. "Damn that smoke."

Through the clear air, Elisha stared. Many of the soldiers—most of the older ones—fidgeted with their hands, as the coughing spread, their eyes reddened, and their faces looked glossy.

His awareness flashed red-hot and Elisha whirled as the Duke slashed toward him. The blade arced toward his chest. Elisha's breath caught.

With a clang that shook his very teeth, a second sword struck away the first. Thomas's arm rigid, his blade stopped the point inches from Elisha's heart.

"If it's a fight you're after," said the king, "then I am for you."

The duke smothered a cough and gave his head a quick shake, tears glinting away from his face. "Don't make me kill you to see justice. I still believe you might be saved."

"Then let patience master your grief, Randall, and listen to reason." Thomas forced back the duke's blade, stepping between them, his body warming Elisha's. "You know all he's been through, all he's done in our behalf. If you can shake the horror of what happened to her, Randall, you'll know he would never have done it."

Elisha studied the afflicted men around him, the duke included. "Thomas, it's beginning."

His sharp blue eyes cut briefly to the side, meeting Elisha's gaze with the slightest nod.

Over Thomas's shoulder, beyond the duke, the low form of Brigit's temple glowed faintly gold in the sunshine. Yet a shadow loomed over it, a flickering, shifting thing, hard to make out. Even as Elisha watched, it grew stronger. It was a thing of memory, a projection—brought about by what? A contact forged across time in the place her mother had died. But a projection alone couldn't hurt, couldn't make a soldier imagine smoke where there was none. The *desolati* wouldn't even see it.

The duke retreated a step, scratching at his throat, then forcing his hand away. "Have at you, then, Your Majesty, I have God and justice on my side." His face crumpled with pain, and he shook his head, lurching another step back.

"Were you here, Your Grace?" Elisha asked, dodging Thomas's protective stance as the duke's young magus and Lord Robert emerged from among the duke's defenders. "Were you here? When they burned Rowena at the stake?"

"Of course I was—King Hugh was yet my friend! We were all here," the duke sputtered. He swayed and tugged at the straps of his breastplate.

Robert put out a hand to support him, despite the rising redness in his own face. Wiping his arm over his sweaty brow, he muttered, "God, but it burns."

A stab of inquiry flared out from the young magus, confusion darkening his face. Elisha pointed toward the temple and the staggering crowd that surrounded it, coughs and curses echoing among the church buildings. Towering over the little building, taller by far than ever it had been, loomed a vision of the stake, wreathed in dancing flames.

Chapter 36

❧lisha wrapped himself in the knowledge of death as a few of the soldiers began slapping at their clothes. The screaming began in earnest, spreading out in waves from the crowd around the temple. Priests thrust out their crosses, shouting prayers and exhortations only to be cramped by the phantom pains that swept the gathering.

"What's he doing to me?" Randall choked. Then he pushed away his supporters and staggered forward, his sword outstretched. Beads of sweat ran down his cheeks. He kept blinking, shaking his head to cast off whatever illusion possessed him.

The magus shot out his hand and caught hold of Elisha's arm, probing with his magical senses. "It isn't him," he reported, his touch bewildered. "There's a projection. It must be a strong one, to reach so many at such a distance, but I can barely feel it. How does the magus casting the spell have contact?"

"It's history," Elisha said, "turned wrong side out."

"Speak not in riddles!" the magus shouted. "What's happening to them?"

Soldiers dropped to the ground, rolling desperately and beating at themselves. Splashing from the riverbank told of other attempts to escape. But they could not flee the past, nor what they had seen, for Brigit reached into the heart of memory and conjured the flames.

"Brigit said she would give them the past, and they would give her the future. She said she would bring down the nobility of England," Elisha told him. "She's forged an affinity with her mother's death, and she's using it to make contact with everyone who was there, to reflect her mother's suffering onto them. I can't imagine how she's drawing the power to do it."

"Holy Christ," the magus breathed.

Stretching himself to the utmost, Elisha felt spasms of pain emanating from the hollow. Madness intensified around him. Men tore at their clothes. Their screams and curses rebounded from the churchyard walls. Elisha and Thomas stood forgotten by all but the duke's nearest intimates, and even these struggled to control the reactions of their own bodies. Thomas's presence echoed with fear, but he remained at Elisha's side, his face and figure revealing nothing.

A short, sharp draft touched Elisha's face, with the briefest howl of loss. The Valley of the Shadow tore open in the air and shrieked closed. A woman stood behind Robert where only soldiers stood before. The earth beneath their feet had been seeded with scraps of flesh, a net of blood to forge contact with any who touched it, and provide the means for the mancers to travel anywhere within the marked earth. Again and again, in dread staccato, the air tore open and mancers appeared: the stranger he'd seen on his long crossing of England, the two women, more of the people who hunted him in the marketplace. These unearthly wails pierced the agony of the crowd, a jagged cacophony. At the back of his throat, Elisha began to hum.

Trembling, the magus released Elisha's arm. Chaos howled from right, then left, then behind. Five, ten, fourteen mancers swathed in shreds of death and smiling.

"Stay back," the magus shouted, holding aloft his sword. "Duke's men to me! All who yet stand, to me!"

Drawing up the reins of death, Elisha invoked the power that gripped him and let it seep through the tainted ground and leap out through his awareness—threatening, but not yet deadly. The mancers stirred and shifted, the first two sharing a glance, but they did not approach. For a moment, they stood in balance, weighing the risks.

The duke screamed and dropped to his knees, tearing at his armor, his sword forgotten. Sweat drenched his face. "Oh, God, it burns! It burns!"

"Elisha," Thomas started, his voice low and beginning to tremble.

Pain and fear contorted the duke's face. For a moment, Elisha wondered if he himself had looked like that on the night that Randall's blade had cut him down. The scar on his belly pinched and his stomach constricted. Randall struck out the candle and called for his death on the bridge, the night before. Months before that, Randall slapped him, then offered him Rosie's hand, and knew he would not accept. Elisha's first and, until his daughter's death, most staunch of allies, Randall arched his back and clawed at his bracers as he cried out. His men, too, staggered, helpless in the throes of sorcery.

Kneeling beside the duke, Elisha called upon his skill, and the buckles slid free, the breastplate dropping away with a clang.

"Don't—you're scaring him," Robert managed, his sword waffling in the air. "He fears you." Then his face crumpled. He dropped the sword and sank to his knees.

Chuckling reverberated among the screams, nasty shivers of laughter that fell against Elisha's skin like freezing rain. The duke's body jerked and flailed. Elisha gathered him close, projecting what comfort he could from the cold that suffused him.

"Why don't they attack?" hissed Thomas at his ear.

"They will," Elisha muttered back, dividing his effort, maintaining the contact with all those too sensitive to death.

"You're holding them off," Thomas whispered.

"They fear me," Elisha answered. "Like everyone else. It won't last." He cupped the duke's fevered head in his hands and let his senses travel inward.

Heat seared along his skin. His flesh throbbed with the cutting ropes that bound him to the stake. Betrayed to his very core, he looked for hope, for help from anyone and found none. Thousands of faces all arrayed against him, church and king, lord, merchant, peasant; faces alive with hatred and excitement. Elisha shuddered, remembering his own trip to the grave, the humiliation of his shaved scalp, the taunting of the crowds, even those he once loved abandoning him to this fate. Rowena's bitterness, summoned to life, burned at his throat. His lungs filled with smoke and the bile turned to hate.

A hand touched his shoulder, and Elisha jerked back to himself, still cradling the duke. Pushing away the agony, Elisha stared up into Thomas's face, the keen blue eyes searching his. "Why not you?"

"I did not watch." Thomas's voice was as hoarse as if he, too, breathed the smoke of memory. "I couldn't. Another example of my cowardice." Then he nearly smiled. "And you. You were the only one among us who moved to help her."

Elisha reeled, the sharp clean air suddenly free of death as he recognized the truth. He gave a hollow laugh. "So that's why Rowena chose me. She even gave out a prophecy, a way for the magi to keep a watch and draw her daughter to me. The medical man with death in his hands. Brigit wanted me to be present today; another point of contact with the past." He kept his palm cool upon the duke's forehead, staring out through the

waiting mancers, over the writhing forms of those Brigit
held in thrall. Even if he chilled the flames of those
around him, those he cared for, thousands would die.
Even if Thomas survived this, he would be king of a
beaten people, terrified of the will of their queen. The
mancers had intended a war with France to divide the
nobility, forcing them to take sides against each other.
Brigit's plan would simply crush them.

He lowered his voice and Thomas leaned in close,
their breath mingling over the duke's vacant stare and
shuddering chest. "She cannot consummate this without
blood. She can't maintain contact with so many for so
long without that power. Right now she can't—" He
caught his breath and felt the mancers edge closer. "She
can't quite kill them."

"But what can you do? What can any man?"

"I am not any man," said Elisha. "Neither are you."

Thomas clutched his arm. "If you go there, she'll kill
you."

Drawing back his awareness, deliberately cutting off
his knowledge of Thomas, Elisha continued, "Some will
follow me, some will stay to pin you down. Be careful."

"Elisha, don't." His fingers dug in. "If you're what
she's after—"

"Watch over them," Elisha said. "You're their king."

"I can't do it without you."

"If I don't go, the kingdom will fall, and they will rise
over it." For a moment, their eyes locked. Elisha let himself grow cold, pushing Thomas away, even as nausea
swelled within him. Leave Thomas to face the mancers,
or bring him through death itself to face—what, God
only knew. Save Thomas's life and sacrifice a thousand
others. Elisha let the screaming fill his skull and remembered what it was to hate. Thomas's face softened, and
he took back his hand. Elisha lifted his palm from the
duke's hot skin, and the duke whimpered, rolling to the

side. Getting his feet under him, Elisha prepared to rise as Thomas readied his sword.

Randall heaved himself up, sword in hand, shrieking fit to deafen the angels. If there had been any angels.

The edge of the duke's madness stabbed Elisha's awareness. He held up his hand and caught the blade. His cold fist closed around it. Cutting his palm and fingers, the blade shattered. A piece nicked Thomas's cheek, and he winced.

Elisha clenched his jaw. He could not afford to weigh Thomas's life so highly that so many must die. That was what it meant to lead, to place the nation over all else.

"Elisha—" Thomas's voice broke.

"I know," Elisha answered, less a voice than a rumble of the earth and air.

The mancers stirred. One of them reached out to nudge a sobbing soldier with his toe. The soldier's scream curled on his lips, forever stilled. The mancer's silhouette shimmered with glee, a power Elisha knew all too well.

"What can we do?" moaned a pike man, clutching his weapon with whitened knuckles.

"Don't let them near you," the young magus warned. "Anyone who's not afflicted: Don't let them touch you."

Again, laughter blew around them, ruffling Elisha's hair. He reached out and set his hand on the young magus's shoulder. The young man jumped and swung, stopping his blade just short, his breath coming quick. Dark eyes met Elisha's.

"Courage," Elisha sent. *"Look to the king."*

Elisha dipped briefly to the grass, gathering a handful of blades, his palm still stinging from the duke's sword. Spinning, he flung out his hand, scattering a hundred tiny knives shot through with his own cold power.

The woman screamed and fell. A few others vanished. The first man raised his cloak and ducked behind it, the garment shredding as if it were woven from the wind.

Elisha feinted right.

The mancer lunged, and Elisha knocked him aside with a well-placed boot.

With a cry, the young magus sheathed his sword and snatched at the ground. The grassy blades he forged of magic were only blades without the power of Death, but they still carried a sting.

The remaining mancers drew swords or axes of their own, weapons that hummed through Elisha's presence with edges honed in murder. His throat and eyes burned as if he, too, felt the threat of Brigit's vengeance.

Somewhere to the side, steel rang and Thomas shouted, "Go!" and his cry echoed in the air as the crows plunged in. Hundreds of them dove upon the mancers, and Elisha's heart leapt to see them.

Elisha dodged a spear thrust. He sprang upon the blood-seeded earth, the ground these monsters marked with evil, and reached out. The air cracked around him, the way that ice shatters on a river as the tide pushes it onward. He stepped out of the light and breathed deep of the Valley, its dancing shades and flickering horrors so familiar now as to be ordinary. Spreading his awareness thin, Elisha felt the answering echoes of blood nearby, specks of it scattered on the roads, a perimeter of death where a skilled mancer could summon himself at will. Slivers of flesh, too, answered on every mancer, carried in hats or sleeves, carried close to the skin, a network as sure as Roman roads, with Brigit at its center, their combined strength set to defend any man of them against incursion.

Elisha gasped, his resolve shaken as he knew that touch: Walter, the king's man-servant, Pernel's lover, staying behind to fend off their enemies while the king took Elisha to safety. But Walter had not known how awful an enemy he faced, one who caught and shredded him, his riven flesh doled out as favors to the few, his tainted blood spattered to keep Elisha at a distance where they thought they could control him. Fury and protest swept through him. If he reached out now, through the blood that linked them—but the blood showed more than that. Not just the mancers touched upon the trail of gore, but a thousand soldiers, children, women. The web of contact carried Brigit's power out to every one of them. Contact was indeed a two-edged blade: how was he to separate the innocent from the damned?

The air around him shuddered, if air there was in such a place.

With a silence as of an indrawn breath, the howls around him stilled, and he was not alone.

When the sound began again, bursting against his ears, the howling wove into a concert wild as the song of wolves and just as full of purpose, even to those who did not understand. *Well met, Elisha Barber,* sang the dead, and those who passed among them.

Elisha's palm stung and the whirlwind filled his ears once more. He knew which way he had to go and whom he had to meet.

Chapter 37

Elisha stumbled out with a gasp into darkness. No—not quite. Candles lit each corner of the room and each corner of the broad, square altar at its center. Tendrils of smoke curled into the peaked ceiling above. It smelled of fresh wood and earth, dripping wax, and the tang of blood. An unearthly wailing filled the room, as if he had never left the Valley, but sobs broke the rhythm.

"Ecco il barbiere," said a voice nearby.

"English, please," intoned another.

"Here is the barber, as he said."

Seven figures stood just out of his reach, staring at him, barely visible in the gloom. Seven piercing, cold presences, but they were not alone. The magus Briarrose, Brigit's friend, stood by the altar, holding up a bowl to her mistress. Upon the altar of sobbing stone, Brigit stood wreathed in flame, tall and gleaming. Almost, Elisha lurched forward to save her, to once more beat out the flames as he had on the day they met, when he had known not who she was, only that she was burning. She wore only an ivory shift, just like any witch bound for the stake. One hand held the shallow half-moon of a skinning knife, dripping blood, the other hand held a flaming brand. The fire that rose up around her took shape, a second image flickering within as she invoked her mother. Rowena's face echoed and flickered around Brigit's, captured just as she had been twenty years ago when she died, exactly here, in exactly this way.

"What shall we do with him, mistress? Will you share him with us?" called a taunting voice.

Sobbing stone. Elisha took a step forward, his left eye caught by the rising shade of Rowena, doubling her daughter's form, but he forced himself to look down, where Brigit's bare legs braced to either side of her sacrifice. Wells for holy water, the builder had imagined, but Elisha knew better—they were wells to anchor chains and channel blood.

His arms and legs stretched with chains, her father lay upon the table, weeping, his round belly trembling and marked with blood, though Elisha could see no wounds. Here was the affinity she needed, the death of her father to mirror the death of her mother and bind the magic that would shatter her victims and leave the kingdom open to her command. Outside, the scattered remains of mancer victims on the broken earth formed her contact with them all, a web of power strengthened by the mancers. She nurtured those connections now, focused on her father, preparing the way and working toward that final moment when she slew him and sealed the fate of the present with the doom of the past.

At her father's head stood Briarrose, holding a brazier.

Elisha sucked death up from the earth. The place smelled of ashes, flooding his memory with fear and flames. He pushed them aside and reached for the cold, layering death against his skin until he steamed faintly in the light.

The two nearest mancers stepped up, one drawing his curved blade. The other laid a hand on Elisha's arm, hot fingers wrapping the skin. The hand trembled, violent shivers that crept up his arm and slowly consumed his shoulders and face. "Kill him," he urged the other who lashed out only to see his blade shatter as it touched Elisha's skin.

Smiling grimly, Elisha said, "I suggest you let go." The first mancer jerked back his hand, cursing in French.

"Don't be stupid," said Briarrose, her lips pinched. "Draw on the others."

Opening himself, Elisha sensed the network formed by Walter's flesh, radiating Brigit's pain as she concentrated on her mother's execution. Once, long ago, he had served as the focal point for energy sent to heal Mordecai's hand; this web worked in reverse, drawing off Brigit's power and sending it to the thousands outside, the shared talisman of death scattered within the earth reflecting the curse and transforming it from the memory of their shared guilt, to an overwhelming force with the strength to kill.

"Mother wanted him here, to witness my rise." Brigit's voice crackled with energy.

Her father's head wagged desperately side to side, and he managed another wail. She gazed down at him, a look almost loving. "This is the only way, Father—the way to make our vision come true." Her hands, too, looked dark. "At last, you'll give my mother her due." She brought the flame in her hand close to his face, fire lapping along his jaw as he screamed. Blood dripped down her wrist to sizzle against his skin, her blood forming the bond between the present victim and the past.

Outside the walls, the gale of human misery grew louder, and a priest urged all to repent their sins and escape this earthly torment. Brigit chuckled, very softly. Off to his left, three mancers reached out, each touching the shoulder of the one before, the last offering his hand to the one who still held his ruined knife. He did not take the hand, but spun and vanished into the Valley of the Shadow.

"Damned foreigners," muttered the leading mancer of the chain.

The howling power of death filled Elisha's skull, but he focused on Brigit and Briarrose, and the man they were torturing. Candles flickered in the gust of chill wind, and someone's teeth chattered. Elisha focused his awareness, but something stirred in his abdomen, and Brigit turned in his direction, her mother's flickering shade raised over her head.

"Or have you seen enough?" She swung her arm down, slashing with the fleshing blade, and her father screamed as she sliced down his stomach. The image of the stake sharpened, Rowena's mouth a black pit opening in Hell. Brigit's own blood oozed more slowly down her arms, mingling with her father's, linking the pain of his burning to Rowena's of the past, and sharing the echoes across the ruined Smithfield heath. The rakes and shovels, the mancers of the night before—they had not been there for Elisha, as he had assumed, but to seed the ground with blood and spread the net into which her victims must fly. How many dead lay scattered there, Walter's remains now mingled with them, to make an area broad enough to capture this great audience? Brigit would slay her father with fire and pain, and everyone who had borne witness to her mother's death would share in the death of her father. Elisha's left eye showed the three of them in a terrible balance, the living woman, the dying man, the burning witch, an unholy trinity of pain.

Outside, the priest fell silent.

The chain of mancers sprang to the attack, but Elisha reached for the Valley and snapped through it to Briarrose's side. "Aren't you worried about the baby?" he murmured as she hissed.

The air broke again with cold, and Elisha twisted away toward the table as the lead mancer in the chain shot out a hand and grabbed. Missing Elisha, the mancer seized Briarrose by the neck. She gave half a cry as her braid turned white and the flesh crumpled from her bones, the brazier with its stock of coals tumbling to the ground.

"Merde!" The chain of mancers stepped as one, their legs moving together, their minds joined to a single purpose. Elisha tensed, barely breathing. He could best any one of them but not all of them together.

"Idiots!" Brigit shrieked. "Take him!"

"He has contact," the leader snarled back at her.

Brigit's blood ran hot across his fingers, striking through him with the force of magic. Nine-year-old Elisha stood by the fire, appalled as the priests burned an angel. Could they not see the shadow she cast? Rowena burned, her features bright with flame and purpose, enraptured. Elisha ran toward her. He could save her— surely, something could be done, his painted banner forgotten in his hand, the last remnant of his childhood. Ranks upon ranks of the audience waited and cheered and shouted, drunk with excitement. It was they who deserved to die, they who wrought sorrow, death, and pain. The ignorant, the afraid, the *desolati*. The same crowd jeered twenty years later when Elisha was driven to his grave. The same priests gloated. The same nobles fanned their faces. The same prince shut his eyes. Why fight for those who would not fight for him?

His trembling hand clenched; the ring flashed gold upon his finger, already streaked with darkness. Atop the altar, Brigit faced him through a veil of flames.

"Barber," she crooned from her own dry throat, "the king bleeds."

"No!" Elisha cried. Surely he would feel if that were true. Then he glimpsed again the moment. Shattered bits of the duke's blade cut the air. One of them marked the face of his king. Where had it landed, the shard wet with Thomas's blood? Why had Elisha not seen?

"His life is mine, Elisha, it always has been."

The power of death trickled out slow, draining from his flesh to leave him weak, his senses already frayed. The mancers' presence enveloped him, sweeping over him to fill the hollows his strength had left.

"Take off the ring."

Another hand caught hold of his. Elisha clenched his fist but the fingers pried, the inexorable will of death arrayed against him this time. His hand gave way, aching as they slid Thomas's ring from his hand, and snapped his only link. Stupid not to have another talisman—

"We would have found it," rang the mancer's voice as a cold hand seized his arm. *"We find them all."*

Brigit slashed her fleshing knife, and her father screamed. The fire towered up through the roof, its crackling all but deafening, blocking the cries that rose outside. But she did not want to kill him quickly, not until his torture broke them all.

The room lurched, the ground unsteady beneath his feet. Elisha caught himself on the edge of the altar, the stone biting his hands. A palm cupped his temple, frigid fingers pressing in upon his shaven skull, finding the holes that Mordecai drilled. He shuddered as the cold strength of the mancers slipped inside.

The flame of her mother's death beat all around Brigit, bathing them both in a wild, orange glow. Hands outside struck against the walls and voices clamored to heaven to save them. "Hail Mary, full of grace," stammered a few, the words broken by pain and pleading. In moments, their prayers would be answered, and peace would rend them from the world.

Clasped by the hands of death, Elisha raised his face. His vision flickered, too, crimson streaks cutting his world. "I fought for your mother's life. Let me live to see her fly."

She smiled down at him, almost kindly. "Yes, Barber," she said as she reached her blade to her father's throat.

All around her, the flames leapt higher. Outside, the screams soared, even when Elisha thought they could be no worse. Then the shrouded figure rising over Brigit's head stirred against her bonds. Rowena gazed heavenward, her shoulders flexed. The memory surged with power and the flames rippled at her back. In Brigit's projection, the spreading wings spanned far beyond the temple she had built. Enormous, golden wings stretched outward and up, echoing the color of flames, trembling with glory and power, as if Rowena could snap her bonds and soar away into the heavens. It was just as awe-inspiring as Elisha remembered, the moment that had set him on his course. Rowena's final magic touching him as a boy, him swearing he would be ready; if ever again he saw an angel wounded, he would have the skill to save her. He had run toward her while all the others cowered in fear.

Elisha's bloody hand rose to his cheek, as a touch long forgotten flared again to life, and the soft feathers stroked his skin, gentle and strong as the breath of God. He dragged his fingers in the sign of the cross, painting his chest and arms with Brigit's blood. His cheek blazing with the angel's touch—blazing as it had not done since he first knew death—Elisha dared to hope.

Knocking away the hand that still squeezed his skull, Elisha surged to his feet. Mancers grappled with him, cold blasting him from all sides. If a man knew death, if it could take him far and near, could he not summon himself through life as well? Elisha reached out. He had no talisman, nothing but his need and the splashes of her blood. Elisha flung himself through the brilliant light to Brigit's side.

Brigit shrieked as he appeared, stumbling against her, knocked to his knees by the force of the journey. She slashed at him, catching him across the side as he half-turned to save himself. The pinned man moaned as she dropped alongside.

Pain slid along Elisha's ribs. The beating flames enveloped him. The angel screamed, and he was so near the past that he could hear her broken voice. Golden wings swept upward as if they all might fly away. Elisha remembered joy and found desire, he sent Brigit an image: the mirror of herself, as she wished them all to see her—vibrant, beautiful, powerful—then he wrapped his arms around her, all of his will bent upon this.

Her presence shivered with confusion, then Brigit's knife-hand slapped at his back. *"Let go of me, you fool. I don't believe you anymore."*

Elisha knotted together his fingers at her back. He made no reply, as he closed her in the circle of his arms.

"Get him off me!" she shrieked. Elisha lowered his head against her shoulder.

"Elisha." She jabbed him with the end of the blade, not long enough to stab him, though he could feel the wish that it were so. "I can still drag Thomas into this." Then she froze, as she felt the truth.

Sliding into Brigit's web, joining himself to every contact, Elisha insinuated his fingers a little tighter, making sure that blood met blood, completing the circle of her blood, beyond which she could spread no magic.

With a woof, the flames blew out. The angel's wings swept upward and vanished. The sudden silence hurt Elisha's ears as if his pounding skull exploded to fill the void.

The knife gouged into his back as she writhed, too shallow to kill but deep enough for pain. She struggled, careful not to injure her father and cause his death now while his dying could serve no end. Howling, Brigit bit

Elisha's neck, excited by the spray of his blood. Brigit's presence revealed her anticipation as the blood flowed down his chest. In moments, his own blood would break the circle and set her free.

Elisha drew down his remaining strength to heal the wound, praying it would not be too late.

"Take him!" Brigit struggled more wildly. Her power cracked against his, seeking an opening, a way to re-connect with the past and complete her conquest.

But if Brigit might bond with her mother across all time, then Elisha, too, could take hold—he had been there, and he had been neither afraid nor vengeful. Every twist of her sorcery, he met with one of his own, matching each attempt to re-gain her spell, forcing his presence to mingle with hers, he re-opened himself to the child she carried, forcing their connection ever deeper, feeling the shiver of each magical thrust. Memory streaked through the flesh—the angel's wings, the arrows shot. Brigit focused on injustice, channeling her mother's pain and fury, but Rowena's anger and betrayal wilted before the child he was, the one who would have saved her. For him alone, she was magnificent, gentle, perfect, and beautiful.

Fury swept through the contact, and the flames flared up again, trapped within the circle of Elisha's arms. A tiny wind tossed Brigit's hair, and she bared her teeth at him.

Icicles struck against his back, and Elisha jerked. His fingers twitched, suddenly ringed with cold. He fought the pain, but the images mounted behind his eyes, the layers of skin, muscle, tendon, bone. The mancers fought him, carving into him with blades they tempered in death. They would get her free by any means and leave his hands in bloody bits upon the stone.

Elisha reached again for death, and the hounds leapt howling to his call—the last hunt before they turned upon their master. Already his legs went numb as the ice crept up his spine. He had not the strength to heal himself as well as hold her at bay. He had to end this, to break her plans, no matter the cost.

A mancer wrapped Elisha's forehead in a frigid grip, trying to conjure his death from the holes that marred his skull.

Elisha roared, pulling away, burrowing his head closer to Brigit, her pulse leaping against his temple. The knife hacked at his neck. For a moment, Elisha relented and broke the circle.

Brigit's strength shot forth, the flames towering over her, the angel's shriek thundering through the room. She grappled with the reins of her power and the mancers, too, cried out, feeling the jerk of their renewed connection, like a yoke of oxen lashed again to their labor.

Where Brigit sent, Elisha followed, every pinpoint on her web glowing again as a star of death. He sought the tenuous contact, the glittering shard of Randall's blade, edged with Thomas's bright blood.

Desperate to outrace the ravenous power that consumed him, Elisha found contact, and love, the strength to keep himself alive.

"No!" Brigit kicked and spat and her skinning blade broke a point against his rib.

With a thought, he snapped the circle closed and wrested the power from her grasp, claiming her web as his own. He clung to her as the dying cling to breath. He ripped the strength of the mancers, the shock of their combined power lancing through his body, like ice flooding his veins. He arched his back, his throat already too hoarse to make a sound.

Brigit moaned. The fire wreathing her face turned white and singed Elisha's eyebrows to ash. But he did not let go.

Her mother's presence, ever re-creating the moment of her execution, blossomed again at Elisha's command.

Brigit crowed her victory, laughing as she gathered the memory. She called for fire, and Elisha let her have it. She forged again her affinity, the chain that linked present and past.

Gritting his teeth against a force that must tear him apart, Elisha channeled the powers she had joined. The fire danced and cackled as he reached to claim it.

Relaxing in his arms, Brigit chuckled. *"You cannot do that. What you're trying. You aren't strong enough to take what I have made, not to turn it to your own ends."*

"I can," he answered. *"And I am."* And Elisha threw down his walls. He opened himself completely to the rush of death and power that Brigit had channeled. Pain crashed over him. Knife wounds laced his back and arms, his blood raced and cooled too quickly in the icy wind. The ever-hungry hounds snapped their jaws about him, and he stiffened. Cold slammed into him like an ocean wave, splintering his awareness. His head throbbed with each gulp of air and his lacerated fingers pulsed, still digging into Brigit's back, mingling their blood.

With a whoosh, the fire exploded, and Brigit clawed at his face with her burning hand.

Under his knees, the altar, frozen by the power of death, cracked in the heat. It pitched sideways and broke, sliding them down, and her father groaned as he hung in his chains. Still, Elisha held her.

Brigit's own doom coiled within her, the power she forged to slay a thousand rebounding against herself. She lashed out, a searing blast of cold to douse the flames.

Elisha lay crushed against stone. The first time they met, then, too, he flung his arms about her. He wrapped her in his own cloak, to be sure she would not burn in a witch's fire. When the cold tempest of her desperation struck him full, Elisha drew his last breath. He sucked down the blackness and shadows and spun dozens of deaths into this one.

As the lives he reached for crumpled, one by one, terror burst against the roof of his mouth, like chilled grapes—succulent and brief. The mancers died, the chains they made to merge their power for their queen drawn back along all the wicked ways he now controlled.

Brigit's body went rigid in his arms. *"I loved you!"* She scratched the words across his chest and branded them into his bones. She fought to keep him out, sealing the channels of her mind, but Elisha pursued her even there, tearing any sign of her presence. She had to be open in order to share strength with the mancers: too open to shield herself now. He stripped from her the stuff of life, unraveling her presence into threads. He had crushed her power and destroyed her dreams. In moments, she would be dead.

A sharp, hot shock struck through his gut. They gasped as one. He had not the strength, she said? Oh, the power that now rose up through his hands with the death of her and of the child they shared. The power he could have, once he consummated his curse. For a moment he reeled at the edge of a new abyss. There remained but one connection, one last link in the chain of power he had seized in twisting himself into every strength she claimed and every contact she used: He had bound himself to the infant they shared. Elisha's gut burned, not from the wound, but from this knowledge, from the binding of fatherhood which he could shed only so long as he claimed no contact with the life they had created.

If he killed her, if the baby died now, while he was so thoroughly intertwined with them, he died, too, and she had known it. She dared him to try it, knowing that their magic mingled here too deeply. If he slew her now, sacrificing their child in the hopes of victory, he would be swept away along with their child. And if he died, all that he knew of the mancers, and the quest to stop them, died with him.

The abyss opened, the Valley calling, waiting to take them all: the innocent child, the shattered witch, and himself, the man who bound them together.

With a wrenching effort, Elisha reached out and sealed the breach that beckoned him. The Valley swirled shut. His circle of blood collapsed as he yanked away his ruined arms.

A wicked howl of wind flung up ashes that stung Elisha's eyes. He saw nothing. Chaos bloomed around him, but it sang with the voice of a distant angel.

Chapter 38

❖

Beneath the drift of burning thatch, Elisha's eyes fluttered open, and he groaned, rolling to his side. Brigit lay before him, her body tumbled, her skin too pale. He reached out to take her arm, covering the wounds she had inflicted to merge her blood with her father's and join the present to the past. With a gentle stroke, Elisha told her flesh to heal. In his doubled vision, he saw the golden shimmer of the Valley edging all around her, but she was not dead, not yet. Her chest rose convulsively and fell, her body still warm against his, as if they lay together in the exhaustion after love. Elisha slipped his hand lower, to her swelling abdomen, where the baby still lived, a little echo of life into the eddies of death that swirled around them, but any sense of Brigit had gone. She lay like a thing of straw, too warm to be a mancer, too blank to be alive.

Elisha slipped his arm from beneath her. Pain seared his back and arms. It seeped along his chest in a hundred wounds as he lifted his mangled hands before him. He must look the very corpse of Satan. The old man still hung in his chains, his throat and chest laid open in flaps that fluttered with a shuddering breath. Elisha reached up to brush the skin with the back of his hand, sealing the cuts with his trembling touch. With a murmur of rust, he struck down the chains, and Brigit's father fell into his arms. Elisha winced, rolling the man aside, curling into himself around his bloody hands.

Prayers and weeping rent the air around him, but there were no more screams, no curses, no pleas for death. The unfinished roof, shocked by the power he had drawn, shifted over his head, and a sharp beak thrust inside, then a few more, plucking aside the straw. With the last shreds of cold, Elisha urged his dangling fingers to heal, holding them carefully, eyes squeezed shut. At last, he pushed himself up, making the old man as comfortable as he might, and gathering the shell of Brigit in his aching arms. As he climbed outside, the crows gave welcome, hopping here and there among the fallen, finding the dead mancers and pecking at their eyes. Priests remained upon their knees, families held together, their children confused and crying, spared from the torturous touch of the past but witnessing their parents' suffering.

Blood dripped from his wounds, but Elisha no longer feared who might find him. If there were any mancers abroad in England, they could not reach him here. Abroad, he thought. They were in Naples and in France. They were in the court of the pope himself, and in the halls of the Holy Roman Emperor. For a moment, he caught his breath, holding Brigit against his chest, and gazed out across the ruin where the nobles of his land struggled to rise. Tendrils of fear drifted out and joined them, each to each. The travails of the dead overlaid them still. Closing his left eye, he saw the living, rising up, giving praise and thanks and love. Close the right eye and all was death—how London would look if Brigit succeeded. How the world would look, if the mancers won.

His head bowed, and Elisha sank to his knees, sobbing. Some of the foreign mancers—an Italian, a

Frenchman—had escaped back to their homes and their
wicked companions. As those distant mancers learned
what happened here, they would never join themselves
that way again. They would never make it so easy to
strike them down. He was still only one man. Not just
any man, but still. His wrist throbbed, then Mordecai was
there, leaning over him, kneeling down, his hands upon
Elisha's back.

Elisha's breath hitched into his lungs, and Madoc
came to receive Brigit's shell. "Food and water," Elisha
gulped. "Her child still lives."

"We will tend them," Mordecai said through his flesh.
"And you."

"I have to go," Elisha said. *"I have to hunt them down.
Among the Germans, French, Italians. They'll do this
again—they have made kings before, they said. And unmade them."* Then his head shot up. "Thomas!" he cried
and struggled up, the warmth of healing left behind.

Stumbling from the shadow of the walls, Elisha
searched the wasteland around him. Some of those re-
covering called out and pointed, crossing themselves at
the sight of him, but he moved on, turning. Where had he
left them?

"Elisha!" Lord Robert bellowed across the space between them, then he was running, laughing. "You're
alive!" They met in the middle, Robert's eyes flaring at
the sight of Elisha close-to, but he swallowed and gave a
quick nod, briefly clasping Elisha's shoulder. "This way."
Together, they dodged among the clumps of lords and
clusters of peasants, the groups intermixed in a way Elisha had never seen before. Father Michael and Father
Osbert walked among the citizens, murmuring softly,
though the inquisitor's book stayed closed.

Randall lay on the bloody ground, staring at the sky,
and Elisha thought for a moment it was too late. He
dropped to his knees, taking the duke's hand between

his: cold, but not icy, not yet. Closing his eyes, Elisha rallied the shreds of his awareness and felt the duke's exhaustion, his hand tremoring.

"No," sighed the duke, and Elisha looked into his face. The duke's chin trembled. His gaze roved away, then returned as he raised Elisha's hands before his face. Tears spilled down his cheeks, his strength collapsing, his head rolling to the side, blinking at the plain of ghosts as if he saw them, too.

The Valley of the Shadow glimmered into being, its wind growing, its glow near to hand, Randall's breath misting as he finally met Elisha's eyes. "Mea culpa, mea culpa, mea maxima culpa," he whispered. "I am so sorry. So very sorry."

"All is forgiven," Elisha told him, sending his goodwill through their grasp, into the hand that would have struck him down. He searched, and found no injury, no hurt but the duke's tremulous heart.

Randall drew breath, but his voice did not reach the air. *"Oh, my dear barber, you were a fine king."*

As the chill shadow rose, Elisha reached with him toward the void. He called up Biddy, and Martin, and Rosalynn, and softened the howls of the damned into a song of angels as he let him go.

With his scarred fingers, he closed Randall's eyelids, the duke's tears warm upon his fingertips, then cooling into his skin.

Robert fell, sobbing, to gather the duke into his arms, and Elisha had no comfort for him. He was not death's servant, nor, alas, its master, and some hurts would always be beyond his skill to heal.

Standing, Elisha left Robert to vent the grief they shared. He recognized Pernel stooping not far away, and would have to tell him about Walter. Then Pernel spotted him, blinking back tears, and Elisha saw that he already knew.

Another man rose up, then, from the gathering, a thin line of blood marking his cheek, his blue eyes keen as he stepped away from his retainers.

"Are we still meant to be enemies?" Elisha said. "I can't remember."

Thomas strode toward him. "I don't care." Someone had brought him a crown and a fresh cloak. Every inch the king.

Elisha started to bow, only to find his shoulders caught by strong hands as the king regarded him at arm's length. "Elisha Barber, I pardon you of all charges laid upon you, and I say before this company that you have always been my faithful servant." Then he shook his head sharply, his mouth twisting. "No . . . my loyal friend. From this day forth, you have the freedom of my lands and kingdom and the blessing of my crown."

Thomas leaned toward him, administering the kiss of peace, a chaste brush of one cheek, then the other.

"I'll have to go," Elisha whispered. "The mancers—"

"I know," said the king. "And you will carry my blessings and my faith, Elisha. Soon. But not today."

Thomas's grip radiated heat, and Elisha gave the slightest nod. Just for now, every spirit lay to rest.

Joshua Palmatier
Shattering the Ley

"Palmatier brilliantly shatters genre conventions. . . . An innovative fantasy novel with a very modern feel. . . . For readers who are willing to tackle a more challenging fantasy, without clear heroes and obvious conflicts, *Shattering the Ley* is an excellent read." —SFRevu

"*Shattering the Ley*, the terrific new fantasy from Joshua Palmatier, is built of equal parts innocence, politics, and treachery. It features a highly original magic system, and may well be the only fantasy ever written where some of the most exciting scenes take place in a power plant. I couldn't put it down." —S. C. Butler, author of *Reiffen's Choice*

ISBN: 978-0-7564-0991-3

And don't miss the *Throne of Amenkor* trilogy!

THE SKEWED THRONE   978-0-7564-0382-9
THE CRACKED THRONE   978-0-7564-0447-5
THE VACANT THRONE   978-0-7564-0531-1

To Order Call: 1-800-788-6262
www.dawbooks.com